非裔美国文学批评教程

王玉括——编著

上海交通大学出版社
SHANGHAI JIAO TONG UNIVERSITY PRESS

内容提要

本书选取了20世纪不同时期非裔美国文学批评代表性人物的主要批评文献,涵盖诗歌、戏剧、小说、自传等文类,旨在强调非裔美国文学批评的文学社会功能,关注其对文学的文本性、符号性与表意性等的阐释,尝试探讨非裔美国文学本身的特质及其与欧美主流文学乃至世界文学的联系。

图书在版编目(CIP)数据

非裔美国文学批评教程:英文 / 王玉括编著. —
上海:上海交通大学出版社,2022.6
ISBN 978 - 7 - 313 - 24305 - 8

Ⅰ.非… Ⅱ.①王… Ⅲ.①文学评论—美国—教材
—英文 Ⅳ.①I712.06

中国版本图书馆 CIP 数据核字(2022)第 134664 号

非裔美国文学批评教程
FEIYI MEIGUO WENXUE PIPING JIAOCHENG

编 著:王玉括
出版发行:上海交通大学出版社   地 址:上海市番禺路 951 号
邮政编码:200030   电 话:021 - 64071208
印 刷:常熟市文化印刷有限公司   经 销:全国新华书店
开 本:787mm×1092mm 1/16   印 张:24.5
字 数:544 千字
版 次:2022 年 6 月第 1 版   印 次:2022 年 6 月第 1 次印刷
书 号:ISBN 978 - 7 - 313 - 24305 - 8
定 价:78.00 元

前 言

　　进入 20 世纪,美国文学渐趋繁荣。20 世纪 30 年代以来,多位作家获得诺贝尔文学奖——目前共有十多位获奖者,间接说明美国文学在世界范围内的接受度。创作的繁荣催生研究的深入,第一次世界大战以来,威廉·传特(William Peterfield Trent)等主编的《剑桥美国文学史》(*The Cambridge History of American Literature*)于 1917—1921 年相继出版,预示着美国文学作为一门学科的创立。第二次世界大战以后,随着"美国研究"项目在世界很多国家的兴起,美国文学研究也随之繁荣。20 世纪 60 年代末以来,经过欧陆后结构主义与解构主义思潮洗礼的美国文学批评愈发学术化,成为世界文学研究领域的重要组成部分。

　　非裔美国文学的创作与批评经历了相似的发展历程。1773 年,菲利斯·惠特莉(Phillis Wheatley)出版诗集,标志着非裔美国文学的开始,但是直到 20 世纪 70 年代民权运动之后,才真正进入繁荣期。由于 20 世纪之前的非裔美国文学作品相对较少,相关的文学批评更少,因此,本教程重点选择 20 世纪以来的代表性批评文献,重点关注 20 世纪二三十年代的哈莱姆文艺复兴时期和六七十年代的黑人民权运动与黑人权力运动时期的非裔美国文学批评,以及 80 年代以来受后结构主义思潮、文化战争与经典反思等因素影响的非裔美国文学批评的发展、变化,尝试全面反映非裔美国文学发展的全貌以及非裔美国文学批评的发展与变化。

　　本教程尝试全方位地展示非裔美国文学对"种族"问题的思考,及其与"美国文学"传统的联系,紧紧围绕非裔美国文学批评具有什么样的特点,反映了什么样的文化思想与社会思潮,对促进美国社会与文化的多元与多样做出了哪些贡献等进行选材。

　　首先,本教程尝试涵盖 20 世纪不同时段非裔美国文学批评的代表人物及其批评论点,希望能够反映不同时段非裔美国文学批评的变化;其次,所选文章能够覆盖非裔美国诗歌、戏剧、小说、自传、奴隶叙事等文类,并有比较具体的分析;再次,直面非裔美国文学批评的主要问题,如非裔美国文学与美国文学的关系——是强调其作为美国文学的一部分,还是强调非裔美国文学自身的独特性;最后,尝试回答非裔美国文学中的种族特征及其变化——在争取自由、反对奴役、反对隔离、争取选举权、争取完整公民权的过程中产生的种族因素的文学,以及在"后民权"和所谓"后种族"时代,族裔特征减少而文化特征增加状态下非裔美国文学的发展及其论争。

鉴于早期美国社会与美国学术界对黑人学者研究成果比较漠视,出版者更看重非裔美国作家与社会活动家的社会知名度以及读者对他们的认可与接受程度,他们关于非裔美国文学的评价及相关论述成为我们了解、认识非裔美国文学的重要组成部分。因此,本教程收录了道格拉斯(Frederick Douglass)、杜波伊斯(W. E. B. Du Bois)、洛克(Alain Locke)、休斯(Langston Hughes)、布朗(Sterling A. Brown)、赖特(Richard Wright)、赫斯顿(Zora Neale Hurston)、鲍德温(James Baldwin)、艾里森(Ralph Ellison)、尼尔(Larry Neal)、巴拉卡(Amiri Baraka)、沃克(Alice Walker)、莫里森(Toni Morrison)、约翰逊(Charles Johnson)等人的批评成果。另外,随着文学批评的学术化倾向越来越明显,本教程收录了很多非裔美国学者的代表性批评成果,如布雷斯维特(William Stanley Braithwaite)、雷丁(J. Saunders Redding)、盖尔(Addison Gayle)、史密斯(Barbara Smith)、克里斯琴(Barbara Christian)、贝克(Houston A. Baker)、盖茨(Henry Louis Gates)等,特别是20世纪70年代以来,关于黑人女性主义主题,以及借鉴后结构主义批评思想对美国黑人文学传统的"考古"与"挖掘",及其所反映出的非裔美国文学批评与欧美主流批评思想的"共振"与"回应"。

由于美国奴隶制以及内战之后实施的种族隔离政策,非裔美国民族一直在努力争取自由、平等与公正,直到民权运动之后,他们才在法律层面真正获得美国公民的身份与权益,这些问题势必会反映在非裔美国文学创作中。正如杜波伊斯所预言的,美国20世纪的问题依然是种族分界线问题。因此,非裔美国文学批评也不可能忽略种族问题及其影响,因此引发的问题是,如果美国进入所谓"后种族"时代,种族与族裔因素淡化,非裔美国文学是否有必要继续存在? 如果继续存在,它与之前的文学形态有何差异? 对此问题的探讨早在哈莱姆文艺复兴时期就已经开始,经过20世纪50年代的融合时期,直到21世纪,特别是2011年沃伦(Kenneth Warren)教授出版《何谓非裔美国文学?》(*What Was African American Literature?*),把这场至今也不可能有最后答案的争论推向高潮。这不仅涉及非裔美国文学创作与批评,也对其他族裔的文学/批评有很大的借鉴意义,并引发对作为移民国家的美国文学的深入思考。

借鉴他人,是为了更好地发展自己。本教程借鉴《诺顿理论与批评文选》(*The Norton Anthology of Theory and Criticism*)、《诺顿美国文学选集》(*The Norton Anthology of American Literature*)、《诺顿非裔美国文学选集》(*The Norton Anthology of African American Literature*)、《威利·布莱克威尔非裔美国文学选集》(*The Wiley Blackwell Anthology of African American Literature*)等著作的编

写思路与视角,选取代表性文献,尝试探讨非裔美国文学具有哪些特征,是否具有自己的独到特征等核心问题。此外,本教程十分重视非裔美国文学批评早期强调文学的社会功能,近期关注文学的文本性、符号性与表意性特征等方面出现的变化,以及这种变化所反映的文学批评方面的新进展,及其对中国文学与文化研究的启示与意义。

王玉括

2021 年 10 月 18 日于仙林陋室

Contents

I. What to the Slave Is the Fourth of July
7月4日对奴隶意味着什么

Frederick Douglass

费雷德里克·道格拉斯

弗雷德里克·道格拉斯(1818—1895),演说家、记者、编辑和自传作者。1818年道格拉斯出生于马里兰州,母亲是黑人奴隶,父亲是白人。成功逃离美国南方来到北方之后,他加入加里森的废奴主义组织,成为著名的演讲者,后自立门户,创办报纸《北极星》,先后改名为《道格拉斯报》和《道格拉斯月刊》(1847—1864)。

他出版了三部自传作品,《弗雷德里克·道格拉斯:一个美国奴隶的自述》(*Narrative of the Life of Frederick Douglass，An American Slave：Written by Himself*，1845)、《我的奴役与我的自由》(*My Bondage and My Freedom*，1855)和《道格拉斯生平》(*Life and Times of Frederick Douglass*，1881),其中第一部自传《弗雷德里克·道格拉斯:一个美国奴隶的自述》揭示了黑人奴隶的悲惨遭遇,抨击了奴隶制的非人性,塑造了敢于抗争的奴隶形象,有效地推动了美国内战前废奴运动的深入。他所塑造的复杂的黑人形象,深化了后来黑人作者对自我的探寻。他的创作不仅让非裔美国人相信,肤色不可能永远阻挡他们实现自己梦想的脚步,而且也提醒美国白人有责任支持任何族裔的美国人追寻这个梦想。

1850年,《逃奴法案》的通过让美国关于废奴与蓄奴的争论更加激烈,奴役与自由的主题更加引人注目。道格拉斯在1852年美国独立日发表了题为《7月4日对奴隶意味着什么》(What to the Slave Is the Fourth of July)的演讲。他用诗一般的语言,告诉美国听众他们先辈争取独立、寻求自由的英勇事迹,这些先贤为了自由,甘冒失去生命与财产的危险,寻求殖民地的独立,并获得成功,他们的英勇事迹值得美国的民族文学大书特书,万古流芳。但是,道格拉斯也含蓄地强调,美国先辈们为了摆脱英国的奴役而战的行为,令人敬仰,现在的美国人仿佛忘记了他们先辈的英勇事迹与理想信念。如果说美国的民族文学应该歌颂独立、自由与公正,那么美国的黑人文学也面临同样的任务与目标——反对暴政,追求自由、平等与公正。

Mr . President，Friends and Fellow Citizens：

He who could address this audience without a quailing sensation，has stronger nerves than I have. I do not remember ever to have appeared as a speaker before any assembly more shrinkingly，nor with greater distrust of my ability，than I do this day. A feeling has crept over me，quite unfavorable to the exercise of my limited powers of speech. The task before me is one which requires much previous thought and study for its proper performance. I know that apologies of this sort are generally considered flat and unmeaning. I trust，however，that mine will not be so considered. Should I seem at ease，my appearance would much misrepresent me. The little experience I have had in addressing public meetings，in country school houses，avails me nothing on the present occasion.

The papers and placards say，that I am to deliver a 4th of July oration. This certainly sounds large，and out of the common way，for me. It is true that I have often had the privilege to speak in this beautiful Hall，and to address many who now honor me with their presence. But neither their familiar faces，nor the perfect gage I think I have of Corinthian Hall，seems to free me from embarrassment.

The fact is，ladies and gentlemen，the distance between this platform and the slave plantation，from which I escaped，is considerable—and the difficulties to be overcome in getting from the latter to the former，are by no means slight. That I am here to-day is，to me，a matter of astonishment as well as of gratitude. You will not，therefore，be surprised，if in what I have to say，I evince no elaborate preparation，nor grace my speech with any high sounding exordium. With little experience and with less learning，I have been able to throw my thoughts hastily and imperfectly together；and trusting to your patient and generous indulgence，I will proceed to lay them before you.

This，for the purpose of this celebration，is the 4th of July. It is the birthday of your National Independence，and of your political freedom. This，to you，is what the Passover was to the emancipated people of God. It carries your minds back to the day，and to the act of your great deliverance；and to the signs，and to the wonders，associated with that act，and that day. This celebration also marks the beginning of another year of your national life；and reminds you that the Republic of America is now 76 years old. I am glad，fellow-citizens，that your nation is so young. Seventy-six years，though a good old age for a man，is but a mere speck in the life of a nation. Three score years and ten is the allotted time for individual men；but nations number their years by thousands. According to this fact，you are，even now，only in the beginning of your national career, still lingering in the period of childhood. I repeat, I am glad this is so. There is hope in the thought, and hope is much needed, under the dark clouds which lower above the horizon. The eye of the reformer is met with angry flashes, portending disastrous times; but his heart may well beat lighter at the thought that America is young, and that she is still in the impressible stage of her existence. May he not hope that high lessons of wisdom, of justice and of truth, will yet give direction to her destiny? Were the nation older, the patriot's heart might be sadder, and the reformer's brow heavier. Its future might be shrouded in gloom, and the hope of its prophets go out in sorrow. There is consolation in the thought that America is young. Great streams are not easily turned from channels, worn deep in the course of ages. They may sometimes rise in quiet and stately majesty, and inundate the land, refreshing and fertilizing the earth with their mysterious properties. They may also rise in wrath and fury, and bear away, on their angry waves, the accumulated wealth of years of toil and hardship. They, however, gradually flow back to the same old channel, and flow on as serenely as ever. But, while the river may not be turned aside, it may dry up, and leave nothing behind but the withered branch, and the unsightly rock, to howl in the abyss-sweeping wind, the sad tale of departed glory. As with rivers so with nations.

Fellow-citizens, I shall not presume to dwell at length on the associations that cluster about this day. The simple story of it is that, 76 years ago, the people of this country were British subjects. The style and title of your "sovereign people" (in which you now glory) was not then born. You were under the British Crown. Your fathers esteemed the English Government as the home government; and England as the fatherland. This home government, you know, although a considerable distance from your home, did, in the exercise of its parental prerogatives, impose upon its colonial children, such restraints, burdens and limitations, as, in its mature judgement, it deemed wise, right and proper.

But, your fathers, who had not adopted the fashionable idea of this day, of the infallibility of government, and the absolute character of its acts, presumed to differ from the home government in respect to the wisdom and the justice of some of those burdens and restraints. They went so far in their excitement as to pronounce the measures of government unjust, unreasonable, and oppressive, and altogether such as ought not to be quietly submitted to. I scarcely need say, fellow-citizens, that my opinion of those measures fully accords with that of your fathers. Such a declaration of agreement on my part would not be worth much to anybody. It would, certainly, prove nothing, as to what part I might have taken, had I lived during the great controversy of 1776. To say *now* that America was right, and England wrong, is exceedingly easy. Everybody can say it; the dastard, not less than the noble brave, can flippantly discant on the tyranny of England towards the American Colonies. It is fashionable to do so; but there was a time when to pronounce against England, and in favor of the cause of the colonies, tried men's souls. They who did so were accounted in their day, plotters of mischief, agitators and rebels, dangerous men. To side with the right, against the wrong, with the weak against the strong, and with the oppressed against the oppressor! *here* lies the merit, and the one which, of all others, seems unfashionable in our day. The cause of liberty may be stabbed by the men who glory in the deeds of your fathers. But, to proceed.

Feeling themselves harshly and unjustly treated by the home government, your fathers, like men of honesty, and men of spirit, earnestly sought redress. They petitioned and remonstrated; they did so in a decorous, respectful, and loyal manner. Their conduct was wholly unexceptionable. This, however, did not answer the purpose. They saw themselves treated with sovereign indifference, coldness and scorn. Yet they persevered. They were not the men to look back.

As the sheet anchor takes a firmer hold, when the ship is tossed by the storm, so did the cause of your fathers grow stronger, as it breasted the chilling blasts of kingly displeasure. The greatest and best of British statesmen admitted its justice, and the loftiest eloquence of the British Senate came to its support. But, with that blindness which seems to be the unvarying characteristic of tyrants, since Pharoah and his hosts were drowned in the Red Sea, the British Government persisted in the exactions complained of.

The madness of this course, we believe, is admitted now, even by England; but we fear the lesson is wholly lost on our present rulers.

Oppression makes a wise man mad. Your fathers were wise men, and if they did not go mad, they became restive under this treatment. They felt themselves the victims of grievous wrongs, wholly incurable in their colonial capacity. With brave men there is always a remedy for oppression. Just here, the idea of a total separation of the colonies from the crown was born! It was a startling idea, much more so, than we, at this distance of time, regard it. The timid and the prudent (as has been intimated) of that day, were, of course, shocked and alarmed by it.

Such people lived then, had lived before, and will, probably, ever have a place on this planet; and their course, in respect to any great change, (no matter how great the good to be attained, or the wrong to be redressed by it), may be calculated with as much precision as can be the course of the stars. They hate all changes, but silver, gold and copper change! Of this sort of change they are always strongly in favor.

These people were called Tories in the days of your fathers; and the appellation, probably, conveyed the same idea that is meant by a more modern, though a somewhat less euphonious term, which we often find in our papers, applied to some of our old politicians.

Their opposition to the then dangerous thought was earnest and powerful; but, amid all their terror and affrighted vociferations against it, the alarming and revolutionary idea moved on, and the country with it.

On the 2nd of July, 1776, the old Continental Congress, to the dismay of the lovers of ease, and the worshippers of property, clothed that dreadful idea with all the authority of national sanction. They did so in the form of a resolution; and as we seldom hit upon resolutions, drawn up in our day, whose transparency is at all equal to this, it may refresh your minds and help my story if I read it.

> "Resolved, That these united colonies *are*, and of right, ought to be free and Independent States; that they are absolved from all allegiance to the British Crown; and that all political connection between them and the State of Great Britain *is*, and ought to be, dissolved."

Citizens, your fathers made good that resolution. They succeeded; and today you reap the fruits of their success. The freedom gained is yours; and you, therefore, may properly celebrate this anniversary. The 4th of July is the first great fact in your nation's history—the very ring-bolt in the chain of your yet undeveloped destiny.

Pride and patriotism, not less than gratitude, prompt you to celebrate and to hold it in perpetual remembrance. I have said that the Declaration of Independence is the ring-bolt to the chain of your nation's destiny; so, indeed, I regard it. The principles contained in that instrument are saving principles. Stand by those principles, be true to them on all occasions, in all places, against all foes, and at whatever cost.

From the round top of your ship of state, dark and threatening clouds may be seen. Heavy billows, like mountains in the distance, disclose to the leeward huge forms of flinty rocks! That *bolt* drawn, that *chain* broken, and all is lost. *Cling to this day—cling to it*, and to its principles, with the grasp of a storm-tossed mariner to a spar at midnight.

The coming into being of a nation, in any circumstances, is an interesting event. But, besides general considerations, there were peculiar circumstances which make the advent of this republic an event of special attractiveness.

The whole scene, as I look back to it, was simple, dignified and sublime. The population of the country, at the time, stood at the insignificant number of three millions. The country was poor in the munitions of war. The population was weak and scattered, and the country a wilderness unsubdued. There were then no means of concert and combination, such as exist now. Neither steam nor lightning had then been reduced to order and discipline. From the Potomac to the Delaware was a journey of many days. Under these, and innumerable other disadvantages, your fathers declared for liberty and independence and triumphed.

Fellow citizens, I am not wanting in respect for the fathers of this republic. The signers of the Declaration of Independence were brave men. They were great men too—great enough to give fame to a great age. It does not often happen to a nation to raise, at one time, such a number of truly great men. The point from which I am compelled to view them is not, certainly, the most favorable; and yet I cannot contemplate their great deeds with less than admiration. They were statesmen, patriots and heroes, and for the good they did, and the principles they contended for, I will unite with you to honor their memory.

They loved their country better than their own private interests; and, though this is not the highest form of human excellence, all will concede that it is a rare virtue, and that when it is exhibited, it ought to command respect. He who will, intelligently, lay down his life for his country, is a man whom it is not in human nature to despise. Your fathers staked their lives, their fortunes, and their sacred honor, on the cause of their country. In their admiration of liberty, they lost sight of all other interests.

They were peace men; but they preferred revolution to peaceful submission to bondage. They were quiet men; but they did not shrink from agitating against oppression. They showed forbearance; but that they knew its limits. They believed in order; but not in the order of tyranny. With them, nothing was "*settled*" that was not right. With them, justice, liberty and humanity were "*final*"; not slavery and oppression. You may well cherish the memory of such men. They were great in their day and generation. Their solid manhood stands out the more as we contrast it with these degenerate times.

How circumspect, exact and proportionate were all their movements! How unlike the politicians of an hour! Their statesmanship looked beyond the passing moment, and stretched away in strength into the distant future. They seized upon eternal principles, and set a glorious example in their defence. Mark them!

Fully appreciating the hardship to be encountered, firmly believing in the right of their cause, honorably inviting the scrutiny of an on-looking world, reverently appealing to heaven to attest their sincerity, soundly comprehending the solemn responsibility they were about to assume, wisely measuring the terrible odds against them, your fathers, the fathers of this republic, did, most deliberately, under the inspiration of a glorious patriotism, and with a sublime faith in the great principles of justice and freedom, lay deep the corner-stone of the national superstructure, which has risen and still rises in grandeur around you.

Of this fundamental work, this day is the anniversary. Our eyes are met with demonstrations of joyous enthusiasm. Banners and pennants wave exultingly on the breeze. The din of business, too, is hushed. Even Mammon seems to have quitted his grasp on this day. The ear-piercing fife and the stirring drum unite their accents with the ascending peal of a thousand church bells. Prayers are made, hymns are sung, and sermons are preached in honor of this day; while the quick martial tramp of a great and multitudinous nation, echoed back by all the hills, valleys and mountains of a vast continent, bespeak the occasion one of thrilling and universal interest—a nation's jubilee.

Friends and citizens, I need not enter further into the causes which led to this anniversary. Many of you understand them better than I do. You could instruct me in regard to them. That is a branch of knowledge in which you feel, perhaps, a much deeper interest than your speaker. The causes which led to the separation of the colonies from the British crown have never lacked for a tongue. They have all been taught in your common schools, narrated at your firesides, unfolded from your pulpits, and thundered from your legislative halls, and are as familiar to you as household words. They form the staple of your national poetry and eloquence.

I remember, also, that, as a people, Americans are remarkably familiar with all facts which make in their own favor. This is esteemed by some as a national trait—perhaps a national weakness. It is a fact, that whatever makes for the wealth or for the reputation of Americans, and can be had cheap! will be found by Americans. I shall not be charged with slandering Americans, if I say I think the American side of any question may be safely left in American hands.

I leave, therefore, the great deeds of your fathers to other gentlemen whose claim to have been regularly descended will be less likely to be disputed than mine!

(1852)

2. Introduction to My Bondage and My Freedom
《我的奴役与我的自由》引言

James McCune Smith
詹姆斯·麦丘恩·史密斯

詹姆斯·麦丘恩·史密斯(1813—1865),美国医生、药剂师、废奴主义者。1813 年史密斯出生于纽约市,其母亲是黑人奴隶,父亲是奴隶主。1827 年纽约州废除奴隶制,他获得自由。他在当地的非洲自由学校读书,之后先后申请位于纽约州的哥伦比亚大学与日内瓦医学院,均因种族原因被拒,后获得资助去苏格兰格拉斯哥大学求学。1835 年他以优异的成绩毕业,获得学士学位,1836 年获得硕士学位,1837 年获得医学博士学位。他是第一位获得大学训练的美国黑人医生,也是第一位在美国医学刊物发表文章的黑人,回国后在曼哈顿行医近 20 年。19 世纪 40 年代以来,他利用自己的医学知识,撰写了很多文章,发表系列演讲,揭露 19 世纪盛行的颅相学的非科学性,驳斥关于黑人能力低下的种族主义观念。早在 1859 年,他就提出种族并非生物性范畴,而是社会性范畴的观点。作为当时最著名的废奴主义领导人之一,他与道格拉斯一道,于 19 世纪 50 年代中期创立全国有色人种委员会(1853 年)。作为十三人委员会的成员之一,他反对 1850 年美国国会通过的逃奴追缉法案。

史密斯撰写了很多关于废奴主义及与种族议题相关的文章与评论。本文所选为他给道格拉斯的第二部自传《我的奴役与我的自由》所写的序言,他在这篇序言中自豪地向美国读者推荐这本为美国人而写的美国书,并介绍这位杰出的美国人。他明确指出,道格拉斯的毅力、文采、卓识与博大的同情心来自他的黑人血统,他的多才多艺是盎格鲁-撒克逊与黑人血统融合的结果。"只有拥有强大的自我才能对抗训奴师科维的残暴,才能挣脱加里森派的束缚,才能经受住作为有色人面临的很多侮辱。"他的演讲与写作不仅有力量,而且内容丰富、文风简洁,有力地推动了当时的废奴主义运动,成为美国文化史上一座高耸的丰碑。

When a man raises himself from the lowest condition in society to the highest, mankind pays him the tribute of their admiration; when he accomplishes this elevation by native energy, guided by prudence and wisdom, their admiration is increased; but when his course, onward and upward, excellent in itself, furthermore proves a possible, what had hitherto been regarded as an impossible, reform, then he becomes a burning and a shining light, on which the aged may look with gladness, the young with hope, and the downtrodden, as a representative of what they may themselves become. To such a man, dear reader, it is my privilege to introduce you.

The life of Frederick Douglass, recorded in the pages which follow, is not merely an example of self-elevation under the most adverse circumstances; it is, moreover, a noble vindication of the highest aims of the American anti-slavery movement. The real object of that movement is not only to disenthrall, it is, also, to bestow upon the Negro the exercise of all those rights, from the possession of which he has been so long debarred.

But this full recognition of the colored man to the right, and the entire admission of the same to the full privileges, political, religious and social, of manhood, requires powerful effort on the part of the enthralled, as well as on the part of those who would disenthrall them. The people at large must feel the conviction, as well as admit the abstract logic, of human equality; the Negro, for the first time in the world's history, brought in full contact with high civilization, must prove his title first to all that is demanded for him; in the teeth of unequal chances, he must prove himself equal to the mass of those who oppress him—therefore, absolutely superior to his apparent fate, and to their relative ability. And it is most cheering to the friends of freedom, today, that evidence of this equality is rapidly accumulating, not from the ranks of the half-freed colored people of the free states, but from the very depths of slavery itself; the indestructible equality of man to man is demonstrated by the ease with which black men, scarce one remove from barbarism—if slavery can be honored with such a distinction—vault into the high places of the most advanced and painfully acquired civilization. Ward and Garnett, Wells Brown and Pennington, Loguen and Douglass, are banners on the outer wall, under which abolition is fighting its most successful battles, because they are living exemplars of the practicability of the most radical abolitionism; for, they were all of them born to the doom of slavery, some of them remained slaves until adult age, yet they all have not only won equality to their white fellow citizens, in civil, religious, political and social rank, but they have also illustrated and adorned our common country by their genius, learning and eloquence.

The characteristics whereby Mr. Douglass has won first rank among these remarkable men, and is still rising toward highest rank among living Americans, are abundantly laid bare in the book before us. Like the autobiography of Hugh Miller, it carries us so far back into early childhood, as to throw light upon the question, "when positive and persistent memory begins in the human being." And, like Hugh Miller, he must have been a shy old-fashioned child, occasionally oppressed by what he could not well account for, peering and poking about among the layers of right and wrong, of tyrant and thrall, and the wonderfulness of that hopeless tide of things which brought power to one race, and unrequited toil to another, until, finally, he stumbled upon his "first-found Ammonite," hidden away down in the depths of his own nature, and which revealed to him the fact that liberty and right, for all men, were anterior to slavery and wrong. When his knowledge of the world was bounded by the visible horizon on Col. Lloyd's plantation, and while every thing around him bore a fixed, iron stamp, as if it had always been so, this was, for one so young, a notable discovery.

To his uncommon memory, then, we must add a keen and accurate insight into men and things; an original breadth of common sense which enabled him to see, and weigh, and compare whatever passed before him, and which kindled a desire to search out and define their relations to other things not so patent, but which never succumbed to the marvelous nor the supernatural; a sacred thirst for liberty and for learning, first as a means of attaining liberty, then as an end in itself most desirable; a will; an unfaltering energy and determination to obtain what his soul pronounced desirable; a majestic self-hood; determined courage; a deep and agonizing sympathy with his embruted, crushed and bleeding fellow slaves, and an extraordinary depth of passion, together with that rare alliance between passion and intellect, which enables the former, when deeply roused, to excite, develop and sustain the latter.

With these original gifts in view, let us look at his schooling; the fearful discipline through which it pleased God to prepare him for the high calling on which he has since entered—the advocacy of emancipation by the people who are not slaves. And for this special mission, his plantation education was better than any he could have acquired in any lettered school. What he needed, was facts and experiences, welded to acutely wrought up sympathies, and these he could not elsewhere have obtained, in a manner so peculiarly adapted to his nature. His physical being was well trained, also, running wild until advanced into boyhood; hard work and light diet, thereafter, and a skill in handicraft in youth.

For his special mission, then, this was, considered in connection with his natural gifts, a good schooling; and, for his special mission, he doubtless "left school" just at the proper moment. Had he remained longer in slavery—had he fretted under bonds until the ripening of manhood and its passions, until the drear agony of slave-wife and slave-children had been piled upon his already bitter experiences—then, not only would his own history have had another termination, but the drama of American slavery would have been essentially varied; for I cannot resist the belief, that the boy who learned to read and write as he did, who taught his fellow slaves these precious acquirements as he did, who plotted for their mutual escape as he did, would, when a man at bay, strike a blow which would make slavery reel and stagger. Furthermore, blows and insults he bore, at the moment, without resentment; deep but suppressed emotion rendered him insensible to their sting; but it was afterward, when the memory of them went seething through his brain, breeding a fiery indignation at his injured self-hood, that the resolve came to resist, and the time fixed when to resist, and the plot laid, how to resist; and he always kept his self-pledged word. In what he undertook, in this line, he looked fate in the face, and had a cool, keen look at the relation of means to ends. Henry Bibb, to avoid chastisement, strewed his master's bed with charmed leaves and *was whipped*. Frederick Douglass quietly pocketed a like *fetiche*, compared his muscles with those of Covey—and *whipped him*.

In the history of his life in bondage, we find, well developed, that inherent and continuous energy of character which will ever render him distinguished. What his hand found to do, he did with his might; even while conscious that he was wronged out of his daily earnings, he worked, and worked hard. At his daily labor he went with a will; with keen, well set eye, brawny chest, lithe figure, and fair sweep of arm, he would have been king among calkers, had that been his mission.

It must not be overlooked, in this glance at his education, that Mr. Douglass lacked one aid to which so many men of mark have been deeply indebted—he had neither a mother's care, nor a mother's culture, save that which slavery grudgingly meted out to him. Bitter nurse! may not even her features relax with human feeling, when she gazes at such offspring! How susceptible he was to the kindly influences of mother-culture, may be gathered from his own words, on page 57: "It has been a life-long standing grief to me, that I know so little of my mother, and that I was so early separated from her. The counsels of her love must have been beneficial to me. The side view of her face is imaged on my memory, and I take few steps in life, without feeling her presence; but the image is mute, and I have no striking words of hers treasured up."

From the depths of chattel slavery in Maryland, our author escaped into the caste-slavery of the north, in New Bedford, Massachusetts. Here he found oppression assuming another, and hardly less bitter, form; of that very handicraft which the greed of slavery had taught him, his half-freedom denied him the exercise for an honest living; he found himself one of a class—free colored men—whose position he has described in the following words:

Aliens are we in our native land. The fundamental principles of the republic, to which the humblest white man, whether born here or elsewhere, may appeal with confidence, in the hope of awakening a favorable response, are held to be inapplicable to us. The glorious doctrines of your revolutionary fathers, and the more glorious teachings of the Son of God, are construed and applied against us. We are literally scourged beyond the beneficent range of both authorities, human and divine. American humanity hates us, scorns us, disowns and denies, in a thousand ways, our very personality. The outspread wing of American christianity, apparently broad enough to give shelter to a perishing world, refuses to cover us. To us, its bones are brass, and its features iron. In running thither for shelter and succor, we have only fled from the hungry blood-hound to the devouring wolf—from a corrupt and selfish world, to a hollow and hypocritical church.

—"Speech before American and Foreign Anti-Slavery Society", May, 1854.

Four years or more, from 1837 to 1841, he struggled on, in New Bedford, sawing wood, rolling casks, or doing what labor he might, to support himself and young family; four years he brooded over the scars which slavery and semi-slavery had inflicted upon his body and soul; and then, with his wounds yet unhealed, he fell among the Garrisonians—a glorious waif to those most ardent reformers. It happened one day, at Nantucket, that he, diffidently and reluctantly, was led to address an anti-slavery meeting. He was about the age when the younger Pitt entered the House of Commons; like Pitt, too, he stood up a born orator.

William Lloyd Garrison, who was happily present, writes thus of Mr. Douglass' maiden effort: "I shall never forget his first speech at the convention—the extraordinary emotion it excited in my own mind—the powerful impression it created upon a crowded auditory, completely taken by surprise. I think I never hated slavery so intensely as at that moment; certainly, my perception of the enormous outrage which is inflicted by it on the godlike nature of its victims, was rendered far more clear than ever. There stood one in physical proportions and stature commanding and exact—in intellect richly endowed—in natural eloquence a prodigy."

It is of interest to compare Mr. Douglass's account of this meeting with Mr. Garrison's. Of the two, I think the latter the most correct. It must have been a grand burst of eloquence! The pent up agony, indignation and pathos of an abused and harrowed boyhood and youth, bursting out in all their freshness and overwhelming earnestness!

This unique introduction to its great leader, led immediately to the employment of Mr. Douglass as an agent by the American Anti-Slavery Society. So far as his self-relying and independent character would permit, he became, after the strictest sect, a Garrisonian. It is not too much to say, that he formed a complement which they needed, and they were a complement equally necessary to his "make-up." With his deep and keen sensitiveness to wrong, and his wonderful memory, he came from the land of bondage full of its woes and its evils, and painting them in characters of living light; and, on his part, he found, told out in sound Saxon phrase, all those principles of justice and right and liberty, which had dimly brooded over the dreams of his youth, seeking definite forms and verbal expression. It must have been an electric flashing of thought, and a knitting of soul, granted to but few in this life, and will be a life-long memory to those who participated in it. In the society, moreover, of Wendell Phillips, Edmund Quincy, William Lloyd Garrison, and other men of earnest faith and refined culture, Mr. Douglass enjoyed the high advantage of their assistance and counsel in the labor of self-culture, to which he now addressed himself with wonted energy. Yet, these gentlemen, although proud of Frederick Douglass, failed to fathom, and bring out to the light of day, the highest qualities of his mind; the force of their own education stood in their own way: they did not delve into the mind of a colored man for capacities which the pride of race led them to believe to be restricted to their own Saxon blood. Bitter and vindictive sarcasm, irresistible mimicry, and a pathetic narrative of his own experiences of slavery, were the intellectual manifestations which they encouraged him to exhibit on the platform or in the lecture desk.

A visit to England, in 1845, threw Mr. Douglass among men and women of earnest souls and high culture, and who, moreover, had never drank of the bitter waters of American caste. For the first time in his life, he breathed an atmosphere congenial to the longings of his spirit, and felt his manhood free and unrestricted. The cordial and manly greetings of the British and Irish audiences in public，and the refinement and elegance of the social circles in which he mingled，not only as an equal，but as a recognized man of genius，were，doubtless，genial and pleasant resting places in his hitherto thorny and troubled journey through life. There are joys on the earth，and，to the wayfaring fugitive from American slavery or American caste，this is one of them.

But his sojourn in England was more than a joy to Mr. Douglass. Like the platform at Nantucket，it awakened him to the consciousness of new powers that lay in him. From the pupilage of Garrisonism he rose to the dignity of a teacher and a thinker；his opinions on the broader aspects of the great American question were earnestly and incessantly sought，from various points of view，and he must，perforce，bestir himself to give suitable answer. With that prompt and truthful perception which has led their sisters in all ages of the world to gather at the feet and support the hands of reformers，the gentlewomen of England were foremost to encourage and strengthen him to carve out for himself a path fitted to his powers and energies，in the life-battle against slavery and caste to which he was pledged. And one stirring thought，inseparable from the British idea of the evangel of freedom，must have smote his ear from every side—

> *Hereditary bondmen！know ye not*
> *Who would be free，themselves mast strike the blow?*

The result of this visit was，that on his return to the United States，he established a newspaper. This proceeding was sorely against the wishes and the advice of the leaders of the American Anti-Slavery Society，but our author had fully grown up to the conviction of a truth which they had once promulged，but now forgotten，to wit: that in their own elevation—self-elevation—colored men have a blow to strike "on their own hook," against slavery and caste. Differing from his Boston friends in this matter，diffident in his own abilities，reluctant at their dissuadings，how beautiful is the loyalty with which he still clung to their principles in all things else，and even in this.

Now came the trial hour. Without cordial support from any large body of men or party on this side the Atlantic，and too far distant in space and immediate interest to expect much more，after the much already done，on the other side，he stood up，almost alone，to the arduous labor and heavy expenditure of editor and lecturer. The

Garrison party, to which he still adhered, did not want a *colored* newspaper—there was an odor of *caste* about it; the Liberty party could hardly be expected to give warm support to a man who smote their principles as with a hammer; and the wide gulf which separated the free colored people from the Garrisonians, also separated them from their brother, Frederick Douglass.

The arduous nature of his labors, from the date of the establishment of his paper, may be estimated by the fact, that anti-slavery papers in the United States, even while organs of, and when supported by, anti-slavery parties, have, with a single exception, failed to pay expenses. Mr. Douglass has maintained, and does maintain, his paper without the support of any party, and even in the teeth of the opposition of those from whom he had reason to expect counsel and encouragement. He has been compelled, at one and the same time, and almost constantly, during the past seven years, to contribute matter to its columns as editor, and to raise funds for its support as lecturer. It is within bounds to say, that he has expended twelve thousand dollars of his own hard earned money, in publishing this paper, a larger sum than has been contributed by any one individual for the general advancement of the colored people. There had been many other papers published and edited by colored men, beginning as far back as 1827, when the Rev. Samuel E. Cornish and John B. Russworm (a graduate of Bowdoin College, and afterward Governor of Cape Palmas) published the *Freedom's Journal*, in New York City; probably not less than one hundred newspaper enterprises have been started in the United States, by free colored men, born free, and some of them of liberal education and fair talents for this work; but, one after another, they have fallen through, although, in several instances, anti-slavery friends contributed to their support. It had almost been given up, as an impracticable thing, to maintain a colored newspaper, when Mr. Douglass, with fewest early advantages of all his competitors, essayed, and has proved the thing perfectly practicable, and, moreover, of great public benefit. This paper, in addition to its power in holding up the hands of those to whom it is especially devoted, also affords irrefutable evidence of the justice, safety and practicability of Immediate Emancipation; it further proves the immense loss which slavery inflicts on the land while it dooms such energies as his to the hereditary degradation of slavery.

It has been said in this Introduction, that Mr. Douglass had raised himself by his own efforts to the highest position in society. As a successful editor, in our land, he occupies this position. Our editors rule the land, and he is one of them. As an orator and thinker, his position is equally high, in the opinion of his countrymen. If a stranger in the United States would seek its most distinguished men—the movers of public opinion—he will find their names mentioned, and their movements chronicled, under the head of "BY MAGNETIC TELEGRAPH," in the daily papers. The keen caterers for the public attention, set down, in this column, such men only as have won high mark in the public esteem. During the past winter—1854-5—very frequent mention of Frederick Douglass was made under this head in the daily papers; his name glided as often—this week from Chicago, next week from Boston—over the lightning wires, as the name of any other man, of whatever note. To no man did the people more widely nor more earnestly say, "*Tell me thy thought*!" And, somehow or other, revolution seemed to follow in his wake. His were not the mere words of eloquence which Kossuth speaks of, that delight the ear and then pass away. No! They were *work*-able, *do*-able words, that brought forth fruits in the revolution in Illinois, and in the passage of the franchise resolutions by the Assembly of New York.

And the secret of his power, what is it? He is a Representative American man—a type of his countrymen. Naturalists tell us that a full grown man is a resultant or representative of all animated nature on this globe; beginning with the early embryo state, then representing the lowest forms of organic life, and passing through every subordinate grade or type, until he reaches the last and highest—manhood. In like manner, and to the fullest extent, has Frederick Douglass passed through every gradation of rank comprised in our national make-up, and bears upon his person and upon his soul every thing that is American. And he has not only full sympathy with every thing American; his proclivity or bent, to active toil and visible progress, are in the strictly national direction, delighting to outstrip "all creation."

Nor have the natural gifts, already named as his, lost anything by his severe training. When unexcited, his mental processes are probably slow, but singularly clear in perception, and wide in vision, the unfailing memory bringing up all the facts in their every aspect; incongruities he lays hold of incontinently, and holds up on the edge of his keen and telling wit. But this wit never descends to frivolity; it is rigidly in the keeping of his truthful common sense, and always used in illustration or proof of some point which could not so readily be reached any other way. "Beware of a Yankee when he is feeding," is a shaft that strikes home in a matter never so laid bare by satire before. "The Garrisonian views of disunion, if carried to a successful issue, would only place the people of the north in the same relation to American slavery which they now bear to the slavery of Cuba or the Brazils," is a statement, in a few words, which contains the result and the evidence of an argument which might cover pages, but could not carry stronger conviction, nor be stated in less pregnable form. In proof of this, I may say, that having been submitted to the attention of the Garrisonians in print, in March, it was repeated before them at their business meeting in May—the platform, *parexcellence*, on which they invite free fight, *a l'outrance*, to all comers. It was given out in the clear, ringing tones, wherewith the hall of shields was wont to resound of old, yet neither Garrison, nor Phillips, nor May, nor Remond, nor Foster, nor Burleigh, with his subtle steel of "the ice brook's temper," ventured to break a lance upon it! The doctrine of the dissolution of the Union, as a means for the abolition of American slavery, was silenced upon the lips that gave it birth, and in the presence of an array of defenders who compose the keenest intellects in the land.

"*The man who is right is a majority*" is an aphorism struck out by Mr. Douglass in that great gathering of the friends of freedom, at Pittsburgh, in 1852, where he towered among the highest, because, with abilities inferior to none, and moved more deeply than any, there was neither policy nor party to trammel the outpourings of his soul. Thus we find, opposed to all disadvantages which a black man in the United States labors and struggles under, is this one vantage ground—when the chance comes, and the audience where he may have a say, he stands forth the freest, most deeply moved and most earnest of all men.

It has been said of Mr. Douglass, that his descriptive and declamatory powers, admitted to be of the very highest order, take precedence of his logical force. Whilst the schools might have trained him to the exhibition of the formulas of deductive logic, nature and circumstances forced him into the exercise of the higher faculties required by induction. The first ninety pages of this "Life in Bondage," afford specimens of observing, comparing, and careful classifying, of such superior character, that it is difficult to believe them the results of a child's thinking; he questions the earth, and the children and the slaves around him again and again, and finally looks to "*God in the sky*" for the why and the wherefore of the unnatural thing, slavery. "*Yes, if indeed thou art, wherefore dost thou suffer us to be slain?*" is the only prayer and worship of the God-forsaken Dodos in the heart of Africa. Almost the same was his prayer. One of his earliest observations was that white children should know their ages, while the colored children were ignorant of theirs; and the songs of the slaves grated on his inmost soul, because a something told him that harmony in sound, and music of the spirit, could not consociate with miserable degradation.

To such a mind, the ordinary processes of logical deduction are like proving that two and two make four. Mastering the intermediate steps by an intuitive glance, or recurring to them as Ferguson resorted to geometry, it goes down to the deeper relation of things, and brings out what may seem, to some, mere statements, but which are new and brilliant generalizations, each resting on a broad and stable basis. Thus, Chief Justice Marshall gave his decisions, and then told Brother Story to look up the authorities—and they never differed from him. Thus, also, in his "Lecture on the Anti-Slavery Movement," delivered before the Rochester Ladies' Anti-Slavery Society, Mr. Douglass presents a mass of thought, which, without any showy display of logic on his part, requires an exercise of the reasoning faculties of the reader to keep pace with him. And his "Claims of the Negro Ethnologically Considered," is full of new and fresh thoughts on the dawning science of race-history.

If, as has been stated, his intellection is slow, when unexcited, it is most prompt and rapid when he is thoroughly aroused. Memory, logic, wit, sarcasm, invective pathos and bold imagery of rare structural beauty, well up as from a copious fountain, yet each in its proper place, and contributing to form a whole, grand in itself, yet complete in the minutest proportions. It is most difficult to hedge him in a corner, for his positions are taken so deliberately, that it is rare to find a point in them undefended aforethought. Professor Reason tells me the following: "On a recent visit of a public nature, to Philadelphia, and in a meeting composed mostly of his colored brethren, Mr. Douglass proposed a comparison of views in the matters of the relations and duties of 'our people;' he holding that prejudice was the result of condition, and could be conquered by the efforts of the degraded themselves. A gentleman present, distinguished for logical acumen and subtlety, and who had devoted no small portion of the last twenty-five years to the study and elucidation of this very question, held the opposite view, that prejudice is innate and unconquerable. He terminated a series of well dove-tailed, Socratic questions to Mr. Douglass, with the following: 'If the legislature at Harrisburgh should awaken, to-morrow morning, and find each man's skin turned black and his hair woolly, what could they do to remove prejudice?' 'Immediately pass laws entitling black men to all civil, political and social privileges,' was the instant reply—and the questioning ceased."

The most remarkable mental phenomenon in Mr. Douglass, is his style in writing and speaking. In March, 1855, he delivered an address in the assembly chamber before the members of the legislature of the state of New York. An eyewitness describes the crowded and most intelligent audience, and their rapt attention to the speaker, as the grandest scene he ever witnessed in the capitol. Among those whose eyes were riveted on the speaker full two hours and a half, were Thurlow Weed and Lieutenant Governor Raymond; the latter, at the conclusion of the address, exclaimed to a friend, "I would give twenty thousand dollars, if I could deliver that address in that manner." Mr. Raymond is a first class graduate of Dartmouth, a rising politician, ranking foremost in the legislature; of course, his ideal of oratory must be of the most polished and finished description.

The style of Mr. Douglass in writing, is to me an intellectual puzzle. The strength, affluence and terseness may easily be accounted for, because the style of a man is the man; but how are we to account for that rare polish in his style of writing, which, most critically examined, seems the result of careful early culture among the best classics of our language; it equals if it does not surpass the style of Hugh Miller, which was the wonder of the British literary public, until he unraveled the mystery in the most interesting of autobiographies. But Frederick Douglass was still calking the seams of Baltimore clippers, and had only written a "pass," at the age when Miller's style was already formed.

I asked William Whipper, of Pennsylvania, the gentleman alluded to above, whether he thought Mr. Douglass's power inherited from the Negroid, or from what is called the Caucasian side of his make-up? After some reflection, he frankly answered, "I must admit, although sorry to do so, that the Caucasian predominates." At that time, I almost agreed with him; but, facts narrated in the first part of this work, throw a different light on this interesting question. We are left in the dark as to who was the paternal ancestor of our author; a fact which generally holds good of the Romuluses and Remuses who are to inaugurate the new birth of our republic. In the absence of testimony from the Caucasian side, we must see what evidence is given on the other side of the house.

"My grandmother, though advanced in years, was yet a woman of power and spirit. She was marvelously straight in figure, elastic and muscular." (p. 46)[1]

After describing her skill in constructing nets, her perseverance in using them, and her wide-spread fame in the agricultural way he adds, "It happened to her—as it will happen to any careful and thrifty person residing in an ignorant and improvident neighborhood—to enjoy the reputation of being born to good luck." And his grandmother was a black woman.

---

[1] 此处系原文引用出处页码。本书为节选,保持与原文一致。全书体例统一,下文不再一一赘述。

"My mother was tall, and finely proportioned; of deep black, glossy complexion; had regular features; and among other slaves was remarkably sedate in her manners." "Being a field hand, she was obliged to walk twelve miles and return, between nightfall and daybreak, to see her children." (p. 54) "I shall never forget the indescribable expression of her countenance when I told her that I had had no food since morning. There was pity in her glance at me, and a fiery indignation at Aunt Katy at the same time; she read Aunt Katy a lecture which she never forgot." (p. 56) "I learned after my mother's death, that she could read, and that she was the only one of all the slaves and colored people in Tuckahoe who enjoyed that advantage. How she acquired this knowledge, I know not, for Tuckahoe is the last place in the world where she would be apt to find facilities for learning." (p. 57) "There is, in Prichard's Natural History of Man, the head of a figure—on page 157—the features of which so resemble those of my mother, that I often recur to it with something of the feeling which I suppose others experience when looking upon the pictures of dear departed ones." (p. 52)

The head alluded to is copied from the statue of Ramses the Great, an Egyptian king of the nineteenth dynasty. The authors of the *Types of Mankind* give a side view of the same on page 148, remarking that the profile, "like Napoleon's, is superbly European!" The nearness of its resemblance to Mr. Douglass' mother rests upon the evidence of his memory, and judging from his almost marvelous feats of recollection of forms and outlines recorded in this book, this testimony may be admitted.

These facts show that for his energy, perseverance, eloquence, invective, sagacity, and wide sympathy, he is indebted to his Negro blood. The very marvel of his style would seem to be a development of that other marvel—how his mother learned to read. The versatility of talent which he wields, in common with Dumas, Ira Aldridge, and Miss Greenfield, would seem to be the result of the grafting of the Anglo-Saxon on good, original, Negro stock. If the friends of "Caucasus" choose to claim, for that region, what remains after this analysis—to wit: combination—they are welcome to it. They will forgive me for reminding them that the term "Caucasian" is dropped by recent writers on Ethnology; for the people about Mount Caucasus, are, and have ever been, Mongols. The great "white race" now seek paternity, according to Dr. Pickering, in Arabia—"Arida Nutrix" of the best breed of horses & c. Keep on, gentlemen; you will find yourselves in Africa, by-and-by. The Egyptians, like the Americans, were a *mixed race*, with some Negro blood circling around the throne, as well as in the mud hovels.

This is the proper place to remark of our author, that the same strong self-hood, which led him to measure strength with Mr. Covey, and to wrench himself from the embrace of the Garrisonians, and which has borne him through many resistances to the personal indignities offered him as a colored man, sometimes becomes a hyper-sensitiveness to such assaults as men of his mark will meet with, on paper. Keen and unscrupulous opponents have sought, and not unsuccessfully, to pierce him in this direction; for well they know, that if assailed, he will smite back.

It is not without a feeling of pride, dear reader, that I present you with this book. The son of a self-emancipated bond-woman, I feel joy in introducing to you my brother, who has rent his own bonds, and who, in his every relation—as a public man, as a husband and as a father—is such as does honor to the land which gave him birth. I shall place this book in the hands of the only child spared me, bidding him to strive and emulate its noble example. You may do likewise. It is an American book, for Americans, in the fullest sense of the idea. It shows that the worst of our institutions, in its worst aspect, cannot keep down energy, truthfulness, and earnest struggle for the right. It proves the justice and practicability of Immediate Emancipation. It shows that any man in our land, "no matter in what battle his liberty may have been cloven down, no matter what complexion an Indian or an African sun may have burned upon him," not only may "stand forth redeemed and disenthralled," but may also stand up a candidate for the highest suffrage of a great people—the tribute of their honest, hearty admiration. Reader, *Vale*!

New York

JAMES MCCUNE SMITH

(1855)

3. Womanhood: A Vital Element in the Regeneration and Progress of a Race
女性:种族重生与进步的重要元素

Anna Julia Cooper

安娜·朱莉娅·库珀

安娜·朱莉娅·库珀(1858—1964),教育家,女性主义者。1858 年,库珀出生于北卡罗来纳州的罗利市,母亲是奴隶;她曾借助奖学金,就读于圣奥古斯丁中学。1881 年,库珀就读于奥伯林学院,1884 年从该校毕业,1888 年获得该校硕士学位,成为当时受教育程度最高的黑人女性。1887 年她成为 M 街高中老师,1902 年成为该校校长,致力于提升学校的学术声誉。由于与美国黑人教育家布克·华盛顿(Booker Washington, 1856—1915)所倡导的职业教育理念相悖,库珀一度被解聘,后被重新聘用,直至 1930 年退休。1914 年,她在哥伦比亚大学开始了博士阶段的课程学习,后转至巴黎大学,1925 年,她以 67 岁的高龄获得博士学位,用法语写的关于奴隶制的博士论文《奴隶制与法国革命者,1788—1805》后来以英语出版,她也成为美国历史上第一位获得博士学位的非裔美国女性。

19 世纪 90 年代,库珀参与黑人妇女俱乐部运动,追求种族与性别平等,成为受人欢迎的演说家。本文所选篇目《女性:种族重生与进步的重要元素》(Womanhood: A Vital Element in the Regeneration and Progress of a Race)是作者 1892 年所作的重要演讲。在这篇演讲中,她认为,如果说东方国家对女性有一些外在的限制与约束,那么法律、习俗等对女性的影响更大。她借用麦考利与爱默生等人的话说,衡量一个国家有多么文明,主要看他们对待女性的方式,以及善良女性能够产生多么大的影响。库珀特别关注黑人女性的状况,认为刚刚获得解放的黑人种族不仅需要时间回顾过去,汲取经验与智慧,更应展望未来,黑人种族重生与进步的基础是黑人女性,而现在已经到了行动起来的时候。

The two sources from which, perhaps, modern civilization has derived its noble and ennobling ideal of woman are Christianity and the Feudal System.

In Oriental countries woman has been uniformly devoted to a life of ignorance, infamy, and complete stagnation. The Chinese shoe of today does not more entirely dwarf, cramp, and destroy her physical powers, than have the customs, laws, and social instincts, which from remotest ages have governed our Sister of the East, enervated and blighted her mental and moral life.

Mahomet makes no account of woman whatever in his polity. The Koran, which, unlike our Bible, was a product and not a growth, tried to address itself to the needs of Arabian civilization as Mahomet with his circumscribed powers saw them. The Arab was a nomad. Home to him meant his present camping place. That deity who, according to our western ideals, makes and sanctifies the home, was to him a transient bauble to be toyed with so long as it gave pleasure and then to be thrown aside for a new one. Asa personality, an individual soul, capable of eternal growth and unlimited development, and destined to mould and shape the civilization of the future to an incalculable extent, Mahomet did not know woman. There was no hereafter, no paradise for her. The heaven of the Mussulman is peopled and made gladsome not by the departed wife, or sister, or mother, but by *houri*—a figment of Mahomet's brain, partaking of the ethereal qualities of angels, yet imbued with all the vices and inanity of Oriental women. The harem here, and dust to dust hereafter, this was the hope, the inspiration, the *summum bonum* of the Eastern woman's life! With what result on the life of the nation, the "Unspeakable Turk," the "sick man" of modern Europe, can today exemplify?

Says a certain writer: "The private life of the Turk is vilest of the vile, unprogressive, unambitious, and inconceivably low." And yet Turkey is not without her great men. She has produced most brilliant minds; men skilled in all the intricacies of diplomacy and statesmanship; men whose intellects could grapple with the deep problems of empire and manipulate the subtle agencies which check-mate kings. But these minds were not the normal outgrowth of a healthy trunk. They seemed rather ephemeral excrescencies which shoot far out with all the vigor and promise, apparently, of strong branches; but soon alas fall into decay and ugliness because there is no soundness in the root, no life-giving sap, permeating, strengthening, and perpetuating the whole. There is a worm at the core! The homelife is impure! and when we look for fruit, like apples of Sodom, it crumbles within our grasp into dust and ashes.

It is pleasing to turn from this effete and immobile civilization to a society still fresh and vigorous, whose seed is in itself, and whose very name is synonymous with all that is progressive, elevating, and inspiring, viz., the European bud and the American flower of modern civilization.

And here let me say parenthetically that our satisfaction in American institutions rests not on the fruition we now enjoy, but springs rather from the possibilities and promise that are inherent in the system, though as yet, perhaps, far in the future.

"Happiness," says Madame de Stael, "consists not in perfections attained, but in a sense of progress, the result of our own endeavor under conspiring circumstances *toward* a goal which continually advances and broadens and deepens till it is swallowed up in the Infinite." Such conditions in embryo are all that we claim for the land of the West. We have not yet reached our ideal in American civilization. The pessimists even declare that we are not marching in that direction. But there can be no doubt that here in America is the arena in which the next triumph of civilization is to be won; and here too we find promise abundant and possibilities infinite.

Now let us see on what basis this hope for our country primarily and fundamentally rests. Can anyone doubt that it is chiefly on the homelife and on the influence of good women in those homes? Says Macaulay: "You may judge a nation's rank in the scale of civilization from the way they treat their women." And Emerson, "I have thought that a sufficient measure of civilization is the influence of good women." Now this high regard for woman, this germ of a prolific idea which in our own day is bearing such rich and varied fruit, was ingrafted into European civilization, we have said, from two sources, the Christian Church and the Feudal System. For although the Feudal System can in no sense be said to have originated the idea, yet there can be no doubt that the habits of life and modes of thought to which Feudalism gave rise, materially fostered and developed it; for they gave us chivalry, than which no institution has more sensibly magnified and elevated woman's position in society.

Tacitus dwells on the tender regard for woman entertained by these rugged barbarians before they left their northern homes to overrun Europe. Old Norse legends too, and primitive poems, all breathe the same spirit of love of home and veneration for the pure and noble influence there presiding—the wife, the sister, the mother.

And when later on we see the settled life of the Middle Ages "oozing out," as M. Guizot expresses it, from the plundering and pillaging life of barbarism and crystallizing into the Feudal System, the tiger of the field is brought once more within the charmed circle of the goddesses of his castle, and his imagination weaves around them a halo whose reflection possibly has not yet altogether vanished.

It is true the spirit of Christianity had not yet put the seal of catholicity on this sentiment. Chivalry, according to Bascom, was but the toning down and softening of a rough and lawless period. It gave a roseate glow to a bitter winter's day. Those who looked out from castle windows revelled in its "amethyst tints." But God's poor, the weak, the unlovely, the commonplace were still freezing and starving none the less in unpitied, unrelieved loneliness.

Respect for woman, the much lauded chivalry of the Middle Ages, meant what I fear it still means to some men in our own day—respect for the elect few among whom they expect to consort.

The idea of the radical amelioration of womankind, reverence for woman as woman regardless of rank, wealth, or culture, was to come from that rich and bounteous fountain from which flow all our liberal and universal ideas—the Gospel of Jesus Christ.

And yet the Christian Church at the time of which we have been speaking would seem to have been doing even less to protect and elevate woman than the little done bysecular society. The Church as an organization committed a double offense against woman in the Middle Ages. Making of marriage a sacrament and at the same time insisting on the celibacy of the clergy and other religious orders, she gave an inferior if not an impure character to the marriage relation, especially fitted to reflect discredit on woman. Would this were all or the worst! but the Church by the licentiousness of its chosen servants invaded the household and established too often as vicious connections those relations which it forbade to assume openly and in good faith. "Thus," to use the words of our authority, "the religious corps became as numerous, as searching, and as unclean as the frogs of Egypt, which penetrated into all quarters, into the ovens and kneading troughs, leaving their filthy trail wherever they went." Says Chaucer with characteristic satire, speaking of the Friars:

> "Women may now go safely up and doun,
> In every bush, and under every tree,
> Ther is non other incubus but he,
> And he ne will don hem no dishonour."

Henry, Bishop of Liege, could unblushingly boast the birth of twenty-two children in fourteen years.

It may help us under some of the perplexities which beset our way in "the one Catholic and Apostolic Church" today, to recall some of the corruptions and incongruities against which the Bride of Christ has had to struggle in her past history and in spite of which she has kept, through many vicissitudes, the faith once delivered to the saints. Individuals, organizations, whole sections of the Church militant may outrage the Christ whom they profess, may ruthlessly trample under foot both the spirit and the letter of his precepts, yet not till we hear the voices audibly saying "Come let us depart hence," shall we cease to believe and cling to the promise, "*I am with you to the end of the world*."

"Yet saints their watch are keeping,
The cry goes up 'How long!'
And soon the night of weeping
Shall be the morn of song."

However much then the facts of any particular period of history may seem to deny it, I for one do not doubt that the source of the vitalizing principle of woman's development and amelioration is the Christian Church, so far as that church is coincident with Christianity.

Christ gave ideals not formulae. The Gospel is a germ requiring millennia for its growth and ripening. It needs, and at the same time helps, to form around itself a soil enriched in civilization, and perfected in culture and insight without which the embryo can be neither unfolded nor comprehended. With all the strides our civilization has made from the first to the nineteenth century, we can boast not an idea, not a principle of action, not a progressive social force but was already mutely foreshadowed, or directly enjoined in that simple tale of a meek and lowly life. The quiet face of the Nazarene is ever seen a little way ahead, never too far to come down to and touch the life of the lowest in days the darkest, yet ever leading onward, still onward, the tottering childish feet of our strangely boastful civilization.

By laying down for woman the same code of morality, the same standard of purity, as for man; by refusing to countenance the shameless and equally guilty monsters who were gloating over her fall—graciously stooping in all the majesty of his own spotlessness to wipe away the filth and grime of her guilty past and bid her go in peace and sin no more; and again in the moments of his own careworn and footsore dejection, turning trustfully and lovingly, away from the heartless snubbing and sneers, away from the cruel malignity of mobs and prelates in the dusty marts of Jerusalem to the ready sympathy, loving appreciation, and unfaltering friendship of that quiet home at Bethany; and even at the last, by his dying bequest to the disciple whom he loved, signifying the protection and tender regard to be extended to that sorrowing mother and ever afterward to the sex she represented—throughout his life and in his death he has given to men a rule and guide for the estimation of woman as an equal, as a helper, as a friend, and as a sacred charge to be sheltered and cared for with a brother's love and sympathy, lessons which nineteen centuries' gigantic strides in knowledge, arts, and sciences, in social and ethical principles have not been able to probe to their depth or to exhaust in practice.

It seems not too much to say then of the vitalizing, regenerating, and progressive influence of womanhood on the civilization of today, that, while it was foreshadowed among Germanic nations in the far away dawn of their history as a narrow, sickly, and stunted growth, it yet owes its catholicity and power, the deepening of its roots and broadening of its branches to Christianity.

The union of these two forces, the Barbaric and the Christian, was not long delayed after the Fall of the Empire. The Church, which fell with Rome, finding herself in danger of being swallowed up by barbarism, with characteristic vigor and fertility of resources, addressed herself immediately to the task of conquering her conquerors. The means chosen does credit to her power of penetration and adaptability, as well as to her profound, unerring, all-compassing diplomacy; and makes us even now wonder if aught human can successfully and ultimately withstand her far-seeing designs and brilliant policy, or gainsay her well-earned claim to the word *Catholic*.

She saw the barbarian, little more developed than a wild beast. She forbore to antagonize and mystify his warlike nature by a full blaze of the heartsearching and humanizing tenets of her great Head. She said little of the rule "If thy brother smite thee on one cheek, turn to him the other also"; but thought it sufficient for the needs of those times, to establish the so-called "Truce of God" under which men were bound to abstain from butchering one another for three days of each week and on Church festivals. In other words, she respected their individuality; non-resistance pure and simple being for them an utter impossibility, she contented herself with less radical measures calculated to lead up finally to the full measure of the benevolence of Christ.

Next she took advantage of the barbarian's sensuous love of gaudy display and put all her magnificent garments on. She could not capture him by physical force; she would dazzle him by gorgeous spectacles. It is said that Romanism gained more in pomp and ritual during this trying period of the Dark Ages than throughout all her former history.

The result was she carried her point. Once more Rome laid her ambitious hand on the temporal power, and allied with Charlemagne, aspired to rule the world through a civilization dominated by Christianity and permeated by the traditions and instincts of those sturdy barbarians.

Here was the confluence of the two streams we have been tracing, which, united now, stretch before us as a broad majestic river.

In regard to woman it was the meeting of two noble and ennobling forces, two kindred ideas the resultant of which, we doubt not, is destined to be a potent force in the betterment of the world.

Now, after our appeal to history comparing nations destitute of this force and so destitute also of the principle of progress, with other nations among whom the influence of woman is prominent coupled with a brisk, progressive, satisfying civilization, if in addition we find this strong presumptive evidence corroborated by reason and experience, we may conclude that these two equally varying concomitants are linked as cause and effect; in other words, that the position of woman in society determines the vital elements of its regeneration and progress.

Now, that this is so on *a priori* grounds all must admit. And this not because woman is better or stronger or wiser than man, but from the nature of the case, because it is she who must first form the man by directing the earliest impulses of his character.

Byron and Wordsworth were both geniuses and would have stamped themselves on the thought of their age under any circumstances; and yet we find the one a savor of life unto life, the other of death unto death. "Byron, like a rocket, shot his way upward with scorn and repulsion, flamed out in wild, explosive, brilliant excesses and disappeared in darkness made all the more palpable."

Wordsworth lent of his gifts to reinforce that "power in the Universe which makes for righteousness" by taking the harp handed him from Heaven and using it to swell the strains of angelic choirs. Two locomotives equally mighty stand facing opposite tracks; the one to rush headlong to destruction with all its precious freight, the other to toil grandly and gloriously up the steep embattlements to Heaven and to God. Who—who can say what a world of consequences hung on the first placing and starting of these enormous forces!

Woman, Mother, your responsibility is one that might make angels tremble and fear to take hold! To trifle with it, to ignore or misuse it, is to treat lightly the most sacred and solemn trust ever confided by God to human kind. The training of children is a task on which an infinity of weal or woe depends. Who does not covet it? Yet who does not stand awe-struck before its momentous issues! It is a matter of small moment, it seems to me, whether that lovely girl in whose accomplishments you take such pride and delight, can enter the gay and crowded salon with the ease and elegance of this or that French or English gentlewoman, compared with the decision as to whether her individuality is going to reinforce the good or the evil elements of the world. The lace and the diamonds, the dance and the theater, gain a new significance when scanned in their bearings on such issues. Their influence on the individual personality, and through her on the society and civilization which she vitalizes and inspires—all this and more must be weighed in the balance before the jury can return a just and intelligent verdict as to the innocence or banefulness of these apparently simple amusements.

Now the fact of woman's influence on society being granted, what are its practical bearings on the work which brought together this conference of colored clergy and laymen in Washington? "We come not here to talk." Life is too busy, too pregnant with meaning and far reaching consequences to allow you to come this far for mere intellectual entertainment.

The vital agency of womanhood in the regeneration and progress of a race, as a general question, is conceded almost before it is fairly stated. I confess one of the difficulties for me in the subject assigned lay in its obviousness. The plea is taken away by the opposite attorney's granting the whole question.

"Woman's influence on social progress"—who in Christendom doubts or questions it? One may as well be called on to prove that the sun is the source of light and heat and energy to this many-sided little world.

Nor, on the other hand, could it have been intended that I should apply the position when taken and proven, to the needs and responsibilities of the women of our race in the South. For is it not written, "Cursed is he that cometh after the king"? And has not the King already preceded me in "The Black Woman of the South"?

They have had both Moses and the Prophets in Dr. Crummell and if they hear not him, neither would they be persuaded though one came up from the South.

I would beg, however, with the Doctor's permission, to add my plea for the *Colored Girls* of the South—that large, bright, promising, fatally beautiful class that stand shivering like a delicate plantlet before the fury of tempestuous elements, so full of promise and possibilities, yet so sure of destruction; often without a father to whom they dare apply the loving term, often without a stronger brother to espouse their cause and defend their honor with his life's blood; in the midst of pitfalls and snares, waylaid by the lower classes of white men, with no shelter, no protection nearer than the great blue vault above, which half conceals and half reveals the one Care-Taker they know so little of. Oh, save them, help them, shield, train, develop, teach, inspire them! Snatch them, in God's name, as brands from the burning! There is material in them well worth your while, the hope in germ of a staunch, helpful, regenerating womanhood on which, primarily, rests the foundation stones of our future as a race.

It is absurd to quote statistics showing the Negro's bank account and rent rolls, to point to the hundreds of newspapers edited by colored men and lists of lawyers, doctors, professors, D.D's, LLD's, etc., etc., etc., while the source from which the life-blood of the race is to flow is subject to taint and corruption in the enemy's camp.

True progress is never made by spasms. Real progress is growth. It must begin in the seed. Then, "first the blade, then the ear, after that the full corn in the ear." There is something to encourage and inspire us in the advancement of individuals since their emancipation from slavery. It at least proves that there is nothing irretrievably wrong in the shape of the black man's skull, and that under given circumstances his development, downward or upward, will be similar to that of other average human beings.

But there is no time to be wasted in mere felicitation. That the Negro has his niche in the infinite purposes of the Eternal, no one who has studied the history of the last fifty years in America will deny. That much depends on his own right comprehension of his responsibility and rising to the demands of the hour, it will be good for him to see; and how best to use his present so that the structure of the future shall be stronger and higher and brighter and nobler and holier than that of the past, is a question to be decided each day by every one of us.

The race is just twenty-one years removed from the conception and experience of a chattel, just at the age of ruddy manhood. It is well enough to pause a moment for retrospection, introspection, and prospection. We look back, not to become inflated with conceit because of the depths from which we have arisen, but that we may learn wisdom from experience. We look within that we may gather together once more our forces, and, by improved and more practical methods, address ourselves to the tasks before us. We look forward with hope and trust that the same God whose guiding hand led our fathers through and out of the gall and bitterness of oppression, will still lead and direct their children, to the honor of His name, and for their ultimate salvation.

But this survey of the failures or achievements of the past, the difficulties and embarrassments of the present, and the mingled hopes and fears for the future, must not degenerate into mere dreaming nor consume the time which belongs to the practical and effective handling of the crucial questions of the hour; and there can be no issue more vital and momentous than this of the womanhood of the race.

Here is the vulnerable point, not in the heel, but at the heart of the young Achilles; and here must the defenses be strengthened and the watch redoubled.

We are the heirs of a past which was not of our fathers' moulding. "Every man the arbiter of his own destiny" was not true for the American Negro of the past: and it is no fault of his that he finds himself to-day the inheritor of a manhood and womanhood impoverished and debased by two centuries and more of compression and degradation.

But weaknesses and malformations, which to-day are attributable to a vicious schoolmaster and a pernicious system, will a century hence be rightly regarded as proofs of innate corruptness and radical incurability.

Now the fundamental agency under God in the regeneration, the re-training of the race, as well as the groundwork and starting point of its progress upward, must be the *black woman*.

With all the wrongs and neglects of her past, with all the weakness, the debasement, the moral thralldom of her present, the black woman of to-day stands mute and wondering at the Herculean task devolving upon her. But the cycles wait for her. No other hand can move the lever. She must be loosed from her bands and set to work.

Our meager and superficial results from past efforts prove their futility; and every attempt to elevate the Negro, whether undertaken by himself or through the philanthropy of others, cannot but prove abortive unless so directed as to utilize the indispensable agency of an elevated and trained womanhood.

A race cannot be purified from without. Preachers and teachers are helps, and stimulants and conditions as necessary as the gracious rain and sunshine are to plant growth. But what are rain and dew and sunshine and cloud if there be no life in the plant germ? We must go to the root and see that that is sound and healthy and vigorous; and not deceive ourselves with waxen flowers and painted leaves of mock chlorophyll.

We too often mistake individuals' honor for race development and so are ready to substitute pretty accomplishments for sound sense and earnest purpose.

A stream cannot rise higher than its source. The atmosphere of homes is no rarer and purer and sweeter than are the mothers in those homes. A race is but a total of families. The nation is the aggregate of its homes. As the whole is sum of all its parts, so the character of the parts will determine the characteristics of the whole. These are all axioms and so evident that it seems gratuitous to remark it; and yet, unless I am greatly mistaken, most of the unsatisfaction from our past results arises from just such a radical and palpable error, as much almost on our own part as on that of our benevolent white friends.

The Negro is constitutionally hopeful and proverbially irrepressible; and naturally stands in danger of being dazzled by the shimmer and tinsel of superficials. We often mistake foliage for fruit and overestimate or wrongly estimate brilliant results.

The late Martin R. Delany, who was an unadulterated black man, used to say when honors of state fell upon him, that when he entered the council of kings the black race entered with him; meaning, I suppose, that there was no discounting his race identity and attributing his achievements to some admixture of Saxon blood. But our present record of eminent men, when placed beside the actual status of the race in America to-day, proves that no man can represent the race. Whatever the attainments of the individual may be, unless his home has moved on *pari passu*, he can never be regarded as identical with or representative of the whole.

Not by pointing to sun-bathed mountain tops do we prove that Phoebus warms the valleys. We must point to homes, average homes, homes of the rank and file of horny-handed toiling men and women of the South (where the masses are) lighted and cheered by the good, the beautiful, and the true—then and not till then will the whole plateau be lifted into the sunlight.

Only the Black Woman can say "when and where I enter, in the quiet, undisputed dignity of my womanhood, without violence and without suing or special patronage, then and there the whole *Negro race enters with me*." Is it not evident then that as individual workers for this race we must address ourselves with no half-hearted zeal to this feature of our mission? The need is felt and must be recognized by all. There is a call for workers, for missionaries, for men and women with the double consecration of a fundamental love of humanity and a desire for its melioration through the Gospel; but superadded to this we demand an intelligent and sympathetic comprehension of the interests and special needs of the Negro.

I see not why there should not be an organized effort for the protection and elevation of our girls such as the White Cross League in England. English women are strengthened and protected by more than twelve centuries of Christian influences, freedom and civilization; English girls are dispirited and crushed down by no such all-levelling prejudice as that supercilious caste spirit in America which cynically assumes "A Negro woman cannot be a lady." English womanhood is beset by no such snares and traps as betray the unprotected, untrained colored girl of the South, whose only crime and dire destruction often is her unconscious and marvelous beauty. Surely then if English indignation is aroused and English manhood thrilled under the leadership of a Bishop of the English church to build up bulwarks around their wronged sisters, Negro sentiment cannot remain callous and Negro effort nerveless in view of the imminent peril of the mothers of the next generation. "*I am my Sister's keeper*!" should be the hearty response of every man and woman of the race, and this conviction should purify and exalt the narrow, selfish, and petty personal aims of life into a noble and sacred purpose.

We need men who can let their interest and gallantry extend outside the circle of their aesthetic appreciation; men who can be a father, a brother, a friend to every weak, struggling, unshielded girl. We need women who are so sure of their own social footing that they need not fear leaning to lend a hand to a fallen or falling sister. We need men and women who do not exhaust their genius splitting hairs on aristocratic distinctions and thanking God they are not as others; but earnest, unselfish souls, who can go into the highways and byways, lifting up and leading, advising and encouraging with the truly catholic benevolence of the Gospel of Christ.

As Church workers we must confess our path of duty is less obvious; or rather our ability to adapt our machinery to our conception of the peculiar exigencies of this work, as taught by experience and our own consciousness of the needs of the Negro, is as yet not demonstrable. Flexibility and aggressiveness are not such strong characteristics of the Church to-day as in the Dark Ages.

As a Mission field for the Church, the Southern Negro is in some aspects most promising; in others, perplexing. Aliens neither in language and customs, nor in associations and sympathies, naturally of deeply rooted religious instincts and taking most readily and kindly to the worship and teachings of the Church, surely the task of proselytizing the American Negro is infinitely less formidable than that which confronted the Church in the Barbarians of Europe. Besides, this people already look to the Church as the hope of their race. Thinking colored men almost uniformly admit that the Protestant Episcopal Church with its quiet, chaste dignity and decorous solemnity, its instructive and elevating ritual, its bright chanting and joyous hymning, is eminently fitted to correct the peculiar faults of worship—the rank exuberance and often ludicrous demonstrativeness of their people. Yet, strange to say, the Church, claiming to be missionary and Catholic, urging that schism is sin and denominationalism inexcusable, has made in all these years almost no inroads upon this semi-civilized religionism.

Harvests from this over ripe field of home missions have been gathered in by Methodists, Baptists, and not least by Congregationalists, who were unknown to the Freedmen before their emancipation.

Our clergy numbers less than two dozen priests of Negro blood and we have hardly more than one self-supporting colored congregation in the entire Southland. While the organization known as the A.M.E. Church has 14,063 ministers, itinerant and local, 4,069 self-supporting churches, 4,275 Sunday-schools, with property valued at $7,772,284, raising yearly for church purposes $1,427,000.

Stranger and more significant than all, the leading men of this race (I do not mean demagogues and politicians, but men of intellect, heart, and race devotion, men to whom the elevation of their people means more than personal ambition and sordid gain—and the men of that stamp have not all died yet), the Christian workers for the race, of younger and more cultured growth, are noticeably drifting into sectarian churches, many of them declaring all the time that they acknowledge the historic claims of the Church, believe her apostolicity, and would experience greater personal comfort, spiritual and intellectual, in her revered communion. It is a fact which any one may verify for himself, that representative colored men, professing that in their heart of hearts they are Episcopalians, are actually working in Methodist and Baptist pulpits; while the ranks of the Episcopal clergy are left to be filled largely by men who certainly suggest the propriety of a "*perpetual* Diaconate" if they cannot be said to have created the necessity for it.

Now where is the trouble? Something must be wrong. What is it?

A certain Southern Bishop of our Church reviewing the situation, whether in Godly anxiety or in "Gothic antipathy" I know not, deprecates the fact that the colored people do not seem *drawn* to the Episcopal Church, and comes to the sage conclusion that the Church is not adapted to the rude untutored minds of the Freedmen, and that they may be left to go to the Methodists and Baptists whither their racial proclivities undeniably tend. How the good Bishop can agree that all-foreseeing Wisdom, and Catholic Love would have framed his Church as typified in his seamless garment and unbroken body, and yet not leave it broad enough and deep enough and loving enough to seek and save and hold seven millions of God's poor, I cannot see.

But the doctors, while discussing their scientifically conclusive diagnosis of the disease, will perhaps not think it presumptuous in the patient if he dares to suggest where at least the pain is. If this be allowed a *Black woman of the South* would beg to point out two possible oversights in this southern work which may indicate in part both a cause and a remedy for some failure. The first is *not calculating for the Black man's personality*; not having respect, if I may so express it, to his manhood or deferring at all to his conceptions of the needs of his people. When colored persons have been employed it was too often as machines or as manikins. There has been no disposition, generally, to get the black man's ideal or to let his individuality work by its own gravity, as it were. A conference of earnest Christian men has met at regular intervals for some years past to discuss the best methods of promoting the welfare and development of colored people in this country. Yet, strange as it may seem, they have never invited a colored man or even intimated that one would be welcome to take part in their deliberations. Their remedial contrivances are purely theoretical or empirical, therefore, and the whole machinery devoid of soul.

The second important oversight in my judgment is closely allied to this and probably grows out of it, and that is not developing Negro womanhood as an essential fundamental for the elevation of the race, and utilizing this agency in extending the work of the Church.

Of the first I have possibly already presumed to say too much since it does not strictly come within the province of my subject. However, Macaulay somewhere criticizes the Church of England as not knowing how to use fanatics, and declares that had Ignatius Loyola been in the Anglican instead of the Roman communion, the Jesuits would have been schismatics instead of Catholics; and if the religious awakenings of the Wesleys had been in Rome, she would have shaven their heads, tied ropes around their waists, and sent them out under her own banner and blessing. Whether this be true or not, there is certainly a vast amount of force potential for Negro evangelization rendered latent, or worse, antagonistic by the halting, uncertain, I had almost said, *trimming* policy of the Church in the South. This may sound both presumptuous and ungrateful. It is mortifying, I know, to benevolent wisdom, after having spent itself in the execution of well conned theories for the ideal development of a particular work, to hear perhaps the weakest and humblest element of that work asking "what does't thou?"

Yet so it will be in life. The "thus far and no farther" pattern cannot be fitted to any growth in God's kingdom. The universal law of development is "onward and upward." It is God-given and inviolable. From the unfolding of the germ in the acorn to reach the sturdy oak, to the growth of a human soul into the full knowledge and likeness of its Creator, the breadth and scope of the movement in each and all are too grand, too mysterious, too like God himself, to be encompassed and locked down in human moulds.

After all, the Southern slave owners were right: either the very alphabet of intellectual growth must be forbidden and the Negro dealt with absolutely as a chattel having neither rights nor sensibilities; or else the clamps and irons of mental and moral, as well as civil, compression must be riven asunder and the truly enfranchised soul led to the entrance of that boundless vista through which it is to toil upwards to its beckoning God as the buried seed germ to meet the sun.

A perpetual colored diaconate, carefully and kindly superintended by the white clergy; congregations of shiny faced peasants with their clean white aprons and sunbonnets catechised at regular intervals and taught to recite the creed, the Lord's prayer, and the ten commandments—duty towards God and duty towards neighbor—surely such well-tended sheep ought to be grateful to their shepherds and content in that station of life to which it pleased God to call them. True, like the old professor lecturing to his solitary student, we make no provision here for irregularities. "Questions must be kept till after class," or dispensed with altogether. That some do ask questions and insist on answers, in class too, must be both impertinent and annoying. Let not our spiritual pastors and masters however be grieved at such self-assertion as merely signifies we have a destiny to fulfill and as men and women we must *be about our Father's business*.

It is a mistake to suppose that the Negro is prejudiced against a white ministry. Naturally there is not amore kindly and implicit follower of a white man's guidance than the average colored peasant. What would to others be an ordinary act of friendly or pastoral interest he would be more inclined to regard gratefully as a condescension. And he never forgets such kindness. Could the Negro be brought near to his white priest or bishop, he is not suspicious. He is not only willing but often longs to unburden his soul to this intelligent guide. There are no reservations when he is convinced that you are his friend. It is a saddening satire on American history and manners that it takes something to convince him.

That our people are not "drawn" to a church whose chief dignitaries they see only in the chancel, and whom they reverence as they would a painting or an angel, whose life never comes down to and touches theirs with the inspiration of an objective reality, may be "perplexing" truly (American caste and American Christianity both being facts) but it need not be surprising. There must be something of human nature in it, the same as that which brought about that "the Word was made flesh and dwelt among us" that He might "draw" us towards God.

Men are not "drawn" by abstractions. Only sympathy and love can draw, and until our Church in America realizes this and provides a clergy that can come in touch with our life and have a fellow feeling for our woes, without being imbedded and frozen up in their "Gothic antipathies," the good bishops are likely to continue "perplexed" by the sparsity of colored Episcopalians.

A colored priest of my acquaintance recently related to me, with tears in his eyes, how his reverend Father in God, the Bishop who had ordained him, had met him on the cars on his way to the diocesan convention and warned him, not unkindly, not to take a seat in the body of the convention with the white clergy. To avoid disturbance of their godly placidity he would of course please sit back and somewhat apart. I do not imagine that that clergyman had very much heart for the Christly (!) deliberations of that convention.

To return, however, it is not on this broader view of Church work, which I mentioned as a primary cause of its halting progress with the colored people, that I am to speak. My proper theme is the second oversight of which, in my judgment, our Christian propagandists have been guilty: or, the necessity of church training, protecting, and uplifting our colored womanhood as indispensable to the evangelization of the race.

Apelles did not disdain even that criticism of his lofty art which came from an uncouth cobbler; and may I not hope that the writer's oneness with her subject both in feeling and in being may palliate undue obtrusiveness of opinions here. That the race cannot be effectually lifted up till its women are truly elevated we take as proven. It is not for us to dwell on the needs, the neglects, and the ways of succor, pertaining to the black woman of the South. The ground has been ably discussed and an admirable and practical plan proposed by the oldest Negro priest in America, advising and urging that special organizations such as Church Sisterhoods and industrial schools be devised to meet her pressing needs in the Southland. That some such movements are vital to the life of this people, and the extension of the Church among them, is not hard to see. Yet the pamphlet fell still-born from the press. So far as I am informed the Church has made no motion towards carrying out Dr. Crummell's suggestion.

The denomination which comes next to our own in opposing the proverbial emotionalism of Negro worship in the South, and which in consequence, like ours, receives the cold shoulder from the old heads, resting as we do under the charge of not "having religion" and not believing in conversion—the Congregationalists—have quietly gone to work on the young, have established industrial and training schools, and now almost every community in the South is yearly enriched by a fresh infusion of vigorous young hearts, cultivated heads, and helpful hands that have been trained at Fisk, at Hampton, in Atlanta University, and in Tuskegee, Alabama.

These young people are missionaries actual or virtual both here and in Africa. They have learned to love the methods and doctrines of the Church which trained and educated them; and so Congregationalism surely and steadily progresses.

Need I compare these well-known facts with results shown by the Church in the same field and during the same or even a longer time?

The institution of the Church in the South to which she mainly looks for the training of her colored clergy and for the help of the "Black Woman" and "Colored Girl" of the South, has graduated since the year 1868, when the school was founded, *five young women*; and while yearly numerous young men have been kept and trained for the ministry by the charities of the Church, the number of indigent females who have here been supported, sheltered, and trained, is phenomenally small. Indeed, to my mind, the attitude of the Church toward this feature of her work is as if the solution of the problem of Negro missions depended solely on sending a quota of deacons and priests into the field, girls being a sort of *tertium quid* whose development may be promoted if they can pay their way and fall in with the plans mapped out for the training of the other sex.

Now I would ask in all earnestness, does not this force potential deserve by education and stimulus to be made dynamic? Is it not a solemn duty incumbent on all colored churchmen to make it so? Will not the aid of the Church be given to prepare our girls in head, heart, and hand for the duties and responsibilities that await the intelligent wife, the Christian mother, the earnest, virtuous, helpful woman, at once both the lever and the fulcrum for uplifting the race?

As Negroes and churchmen we cannot be indifferent to these questions. They touch us most vitally on both sides. We believe in the Holy Catholic Church. We believe that however gigantic and apparently remote the consummation, the Church will go on conquering and to conquer till the kingdoms of this world, not excepting the black man and the black woman of the South, shall have become the kingdoms of the

Lord and of his Christ.

That past work in this direction has been unsatisfactory we must admit. That without a change of policy results in the future will be as meagre, we greatly fear. Our life as a race is at stake. The dearest interests of our hearts are in the scales. We must either break away from dear old landmarks and plunge out in any line and every line that enables us to meet the pressing need of our people, or we must ask the Church to allow and help us, untrammelled by the prejudices and theories of individuals, to work aggressively under her direction as we alone can, with God's help, for the salvation of our people.

The time is ripe for action. Self-seeking and ambition must be laid on the altar. The battle is one of sacrifice and hardship, but our duty is plain. We have been recipients of missionary bounty in some sort for twenty-one years. Not even the senseless vegetable is content to be a mere reservoir. Receiving without giving is an anomaly in nature. Nature's cells are all little workshops for manufacturing sunbeams, the product to be *given out* to earth's inhabitants in warmth, energy, thought, action. Inanimate creation always pays back an equivalent.

Now, *How much owest thou my Lord*? Will his account be overdrawn if he call for singleness of purpose and self-sacrificing labor for your brethren? Having passed through your drill school, will you refuse a general's commission even if it entails responsibility, risk and anxiety, with possibly some adverse criticism? Is it too much to ask you to step forward and direct the work for your race along those lines which you know to be of first and vital importance?

Will you allow these words of Ralph Waldo Emerson? "In ordinary," says he, "we have a snappish criticism which watches and contradicts the opposite party. We want the will which advances and dictates [acts]. Nature has made up her mind that what cannot defend itself, shall not be defended. Complaining never so loud and with never so much reason, is of no use. What cannot stand must fall; *and the measure of our sincerity and therefore of the respect of men is the amount of health and wealth we will hazard in the defense of our right*."

(1892)

4. The New Negro

新黑人

Alain Locke

阿兰·洛克

阿兰·洛克(1885—1954)，美国著名教育家、哲学家和批评家，哈莱姆文艺复兴的精神导师，在20世纪非裔美国知识分子中具有举足轻重的地位。洛克出生于费城，父母都是教师。在哈佛大学读本科期间，他曾获得罗德奖学金，后去柏林大学读书，是第一位获此殊荣的美国黑人学者。1917年他毕业于哈佛大学，获得哲学博士学位。

作为当时最有学识的美国黑人之一，他编辑出版了影响深远的《新黑人》(1925)文集，成为后人了解非裔美国文学与文化、促进黑人文化意识觉醒的重要历史文献。在《新黑人》一文中，他分析了"新黑人"出现的历史语境与社会背景，提出了黑人的"自我决定"与"自我表达"主题，以及重新评价黑人过去的艺术成就与文化贡献的必要性。此外，1929—1953年，他每年都会对上一年度非裔美国文学与文化的状况进行回顾与总结，这在当时美国黑人文学地位不高，人们(包括黑人大众)更加倾向于阅读白人学者撰写的关于黑人文学的批评文章的年代，显得弥足珍贵。他在美国黑人文学传统的框架内，审视当时黑人的文学创作，而且始终关注同时代白人作家、社会学家与历史学家对种族问题的思考，并于1947年开始关注种族融合问题。在种族主义盛行、黑人本土文化卑微的年代，他高举文化多元主义的大旗，重视黑人音乐与黑人民俗文化，为后来的"黑人研究"与文化多元主义研究开启了航程。他关于文化多元主义、民族与价值理论的哲学思想影响了不同领域的读者，成为美国后来文化多元思想当之无愧的奠基人。

In the last decade something beyond the watch and guard of statistics has happened in the life of the American Negro and the three norns who have traditionally presided over the Negro problem have a changeling in their laps. The Sociologist，the Philanthropist，the Race-leader are not unaware of the New Negro，but they are at a loss to account for him. He simply cannot be swathed in their formulae. For the younger generation is vibrant with a new psychology; the new spirit is awake in the masses, and under the very eyes of the professional observers is transforming what has been a perennial problem into the progressive phases of contemporary Negro life.

Could such a metamorphosis have taken place as suddenly as it has appeared to? The answer is no; not because the New Negro is not here, but because the Old Negro had long become more of a myth than a man. The Old Negro, we must remember, was a creature of moral debate and historical controversy. His has been a stock figure perpetuated as an historical fiction partly in innocent sentimentalism, partly in deliberate reactionism. The Negro himself has contributed his share to this through a sort of protective social mimicry forced upon him by the adverse circumstances of dependence. So for generations in the mind of America, the Negro has been more of a formula than a human being—a something to be argued about, condemned or defended, to be "kept down," or "in his place," or "helped up," to be worried with or worried over, harassed or patronized, a social bogey or a social burden. The thinking Negro even has been induced to share this same general attitude, to focus his attention on controversial issues, to see himself in the distorted perspective of a social problem. His shadow, so to speak, has been more real to him than his personality. Through having had to appeal from the unjust stereotypes of his oppressors and traducers to those of his liberators, friends, and benefactors he has had to subscribe to the traditional positions from which his case has been viewed. Little true social or self-understanding has or could come from such a situation.

But while the minds of most of us, black and white, have thus burrowed in the trenches of the Civil War and Reconstruction, the actual march of development has simply flanked these positions, necessitating a sudden reorientation of view. We have not been watching in the right direction; set North and South on a sectional axis, we have not noticed the East till the sun has us blinking.

Recall how suddenly the Negro spirituals revealed themselves; suppressed for generations under the stereotypes of Wesleyan hymn harmony, secretive, half-ashamed, until the courage of being natural brought them out—and behold, there was folk-music. Similarly the mind of the Negro seems suddenly to have slipped from under the tyranny of social intimidation and to be shaking off the psychology of imitation and implied inferiority. By shedding the old chrysalis of the Negro problem we are achieving something like a spiritual emancipation. Until recently, lacking self-understanding, we have been almost as much of a problem to ourselves as we still are to others. But the decade that found us with a problem has left us with only a task. The multitude perhaps feels as yet only a strange relief and a new vague urge, but the thinking few know that in the reaction the vital inner grip of prejudice has been broken.

With this renewed self-respect and self-dependence, the life of the Negro community is bound to enter a new dynamic phase, the buoyancy from within compensating for whatever pressure there may be of conditions from without. The migrant masses, shifting from countryside to city, hurdle several generations of experience at a leap, but more important, the same thing happens spiritually in the life-attitudes and self-expression of the Young Negro, in his poetry, his art, his education, and his new outlook, with the additional advantage, of course, of the poise and greater certainty of knowing what it is all about. From this comes the promise and warrant of a new leadership. As one of them has discerningly put it:

> We have tomorrow
> Bright before us
> Like a flame.
> Yesterday, a night-gone thing
> A sun-down name.
>
> And dawn today
> Broad arch above the road we came.
> We march!

This is what, even more than any "most creditable record of fifty years of freedom," requires that the Negro of to-day be seen through other than the dusty spectacles of past controversy. The day of "aunties," "uncles," and "mammies" is equally gone. Uncle Tom and Sambo have passed on, and even the "Colonel" and "George" play barnstorm roles from which they escape with relief when the public spotlight is off. The popular melodrama has about played itself out, and it is time to scrap the fictions, garret the bogeys, and settle down to a realistic facing of facts.

First we must observe some of the changes which since the traditional lines of opinion were drawn have rendered these quite obsolete. A main change has been, of course, that shifting of the Negro population which has made the Negro problem no longer exclusively or even predominantly Southern. Why should our minds remain sectionalized, when the problem itself no longer is? Then the trend of migration has not only been toward the North and the Central Midwest, but city-ward and to the great centers of industry—the problems of adjustment are new, practical, local, and not peculiarly racial. Rather they are an integral part of the large industrial and social problems of our present-day democracy. And finally, with the Negro rapidly in process of class differentiation, if it ever was warrantable to regard and treat the Negro *en masse* it is becoming with every day less possible, more unjust, and more ridiculous.

In the very process of being transplanted, the Negro is becoming transformed.

The tide of Negro migration, northward and city-ward, is not to be fully explained as a blind flood started by the demands of war industry coupled with the shutting off of foreign migration, or by the pressure of poor crops coupled with increased social terrorism in certain sections of the South and Southwest. Neither labor demand, the boll-weevil, nor the Ku Klux Klan is a basic factor, however contributory any or all of them may have been. The wash and rush of this human tide on the beach line of the northern city centers is to be explained primarily in terms of a new vision of opportunity, of social and economic freedom, of a spirit to seize, even in the face of an extortionate and heavy toll, a chance for the improvement of conditions. With each successive wave of it, the movement of the Negro becomes more and more a mass movement toward the larger and the more democratic chance—in the Negro's case a deliberate flight not only from countryside to city, but from medieval America to modern.

Take Harlem as an instance of this. Here in Manhattan is not merely the largest Negro community in the world, but the first concentration in history of so many diverse elements of Negro life. It has attracted the African, the West Indian, the Negro American; has brought together the Negro of the North and the Negro of the South; the man from the city and the man from the town and village; the peasant, the student, the businessman, the professional man, artist, poet, musician, adventurer and worker, preacher and criminal, exploiter and social outcast. Each group has come with its own separate motives and for its own special ends, but their greatest experience has been the finding of one another. Proscription and prejudice have thrown these dissimilar elements into a common area of contact and interaction. Within this area, race sympathy and unity have determined a further fusing of sentiment and experience. So what began in terms of segregation becomes more and more, as its elements mix and react, the laboratory of a great race-welding. Hitherto, it must be admitted that American Negroes have been a race more in name than in fact, or to be exact, more in sentiment than in experience. The chief bond between them has been that of a common condition ratherthan a common consciousness; a problem in common rather than a life in common. In Harlem, Negro life is seizing upon its first chances for group expression and self-determination. It is—or promises at least to be—a race capital. That is why our comparison is taken with those nascent centers of folk-expression and self-determination which are playing a creative part in the world to-day. Without pretense to their political significance, Harlem has the same role to play for the New Negro as Dublin has had for the New Ireland or Prague for the New Czechoslovakia.

Harlem, I grant you, isn't typical—but it is significant, it is prophetic. No sane observer, however sympathetic to the new trend, would contend that the great masses are articulate as yet, but they stir, they move, they are more than physically restless. The challenge of the new intellectuals among them is clear enough—the "race radicals" and realists who have broken with the old epoch of philanthropic guidance, sentimental appeal, and protest. But are we after all only reading into the stirrings of a sleeping giant the dreams of an agitator? The answer is in the migrating peasant. It is the "man farthest down" who is most active in getting up. One of the most characteristic symptoms of this is the professional man himself migrating to recapture his constituency after a vain effort to maintain in some Southern corner what for years back seemed an established living and clientele. The clergyman following his errant flock, the physician or lawyer trailing his clients, supply the true clues. In a real sense it is the rank and file who are leading, and the leaders who are following. A transformed and transforming psychology permeates the masses.

When the racial leaders of twenty years ago spoke of developing race-pride and stimulating race-consciousness, and of the desirability of race solidarity, they could not in any accurate degree have anticipated the abrupt feeling that has surged up and now pervades the awakened centers. Some of the recognized Negro leaders and a powerful section of white opinion identified with "race work" of the older order have indeed attempted to discount this feeling as a "passing phase," an attack of "race nerves" so to speak, an "aftermath of the war," and the like. It has not abated, however, if we are to gauge by the present tone and temper of the Negro press, or by the shift in popular support from the officially recognized and orthodox spokesmen to those of the independent, popular, and often radical type who are unmistakable symptoms of a new order. It is a social disservice to blunt the fact that the Negro of the Northern centers has reached a stage where tutelage, even of the most interested and well-intentioned sort, must give place to new relationships, where positive self-direction must be reckoned with in ever increasing measure. The American mind must reckon with a fundamentally changed Negro.

The Negro too, for his part, has idols of the tribe to smash. If on the one hand the white man has erred in making the Negro appear to be that which would excuse or extenuate his treatment of him, the Negro, in turn, has too often unnecessarily excused himself because of the way he has been treated. The intelligent Negro of today is resolved not to make discrimination an extenuation for his shortcomings in performance, individual or collective; he is trying to hold himself at par, neither inflated by sentimental allowances nor depreciated by current social discounts. For this he must know himself and be known for precisely what he is, and for that reason he welcomes the new scientific rather than the old sentimental interest. Sentimental interest in the Negro has ebbed. We used to lament this as the falling off of our friends; now we rejoice and pray to be delivered both from self-pity and condescension. The mind of each racial group has had a bitter weaning, apathy or hatred on one side matching disillusionment or resentment on the other; but they face each other to-day with the possibility at least of entirely new mutual attitudes.

It does not follow that if the Negro were better known, he would be better liked or better treated. But mutual understanding is basic for any subsequent cooperation and adjustment. The effort toward this will at least have the effect of remedying in large part what has been the most unsatisfactory feature of our present stage of race relationships in America, namely the fact that the more intelligent and representative elements of the two race groups have at so many points got quite out of vital touch with one another.

The fiction is that the life of the races is separate, and increasingly so. The fact is that they have touched too closely at the unfavorable and too lightly at the favorable levels.

While inter-racial councils have sprung up in the South, drawing on forward elements of both races, in the Northern cities manual laborers may brush elbows in their everyday work, but the community and business leaders have experienced no such interplay or far too little of it. These segments must achieve contact or the race situation in America becomes desperate. Fortunately this is happening. There is a growing realization that in social effort the cooperative basis must supplant long-distance philanthropy, and that the only safeguard for mass relations in the future must be provided in the carefully maintained contacts of the enlightened minorities of both race groups. In the intellectual realm a renewed and keen curiosity is replacing the recent apathy; the Negro is being carefully studied, not just talked about and discussed. In art and letters, instead of being wholly caricatured, he is being seriously portrayed and painted.

To all of this the New Negro is keenly responsive as an augury of a new democracy in American culture. He is contributing his share to the new social understanding. But the desire to be understood would never in itself have been sufficient to have opened so completely the protectively closed portals of the thinking Negro's mind. There is still too much possibility of being snubbed or patronized for that. It was rather the necessity for fuller, truer self-expression, the realization of the unwisdom of allowing social discrimination to segregate him mentally, and a counter-attitude to cramp and fetter his own living—and so the "spite-wall" that the intellectuals built over the "colorline" has happily been taken down. Much of this reopening of intellectual contacts has centered in New York and has been richly fruitful not merely in the enlarging of personal experience, but in the definite enrichment of American art and letters and in the clarifying of our common vision of the social tasks ahead.

The particular significance in the re-establishment of contact between the more advanced and representative classes is that it promises to offset some of the unfavorable reactions of the past, or at least to re-surface race contacts somewhat for the future. Subtly the conditions that are molding a New Negro are molding a new American attitude.

However, this new phase of things is delicate; it will call for less charity but more justice; less help, but infinitely closer understanding. This is indeed a critical stage of race relationships because of the likelihood, if the new temper is not understood, of engendering sharp group antagonism and a second crop of more calculated prejudice. In some quarters, it has already done so. Having weaned the Negro, public opinion cannot continue to paternalize. The Negro to-day is inevitably moving forward under the control largely of his own objectives. What are these objectives? Those of his outer life are happily already well and finally formulated, for they are none other than the ideals of American institutions and democracy. Those of his inner life are yet in process of formation, for the new psychology at present is more of a consensus of feeling than of opinion, of attitude rather than of program. Still some points seem to have crystallized.

Up to the present one may adequately describe the Negro's "inner objectives" as an attempt to repair a damaged group psychology and reshape a warped social perspective. Their realization has required a new mentality for the American Negro. And as it matures we begin to see its effects; at first, negative, iconoclastic, and thenpositive and constructive. In this new group psychology we note the lapse of sentimental appeal, then the development of a more positive self-respect and self-reliance; the repudiation of social dependence, and then the gradual recovery from hyper-sensitiveness and "touchy" nerves, the repudiation of the double standard of judgment with its special philanthropic allowances and then the sturdier desire for objective and scientific appraisal; and finally the rise from social disillusionment to race pride, from the sense of social debt to the responsibilities of social contribution, and offsetting the necessary working and commonsense acceptance of restricted conditions, the belief in ultimate esteem and recognition. Therefore the Negro to-day wishes to be known for what he is, even in his faults and shortcomings, and scorns a craven and precarious survival at the price of seeming to be what he is not. He resents being spoken of as a social ward or minor, even by his own, and to being regarded a chronic patient for the sociological clinic, the sick man of American Democracy. For the same reasons, he himself is through with those social nostrums and panaceas, the so-called solutions of his "problem," with which he and the country have been so liberally dosed in the past. Religion, freedom, education, money—in turn, he has ardently hoped for and peculiarly trusted these things; he still believes in them, but not in blind trust that they alone will solve his life-problem.

Each generation, however, will have its creed, and that of the present is the belief in the efficacy of collective effort, in race cooperation. This deep feeling of race is at present the mainspring of Negro life. It seems to be the outcome of the reaction to proscription and prejudice; an attempt, fairly successful on the whole, to convert a defensive into an offensive position, a handicap into an incentive. It is radical in tone, but not in purpose and only the most stupid forms of opposition, misunderstanding or persecution could make it otherwise. Of course, the thinking Negro has shifted a little toward the Left with the world-trend, and there is an increasing group who affiliate with radical and liberal movements. But fundamentally for the present the Negro is radical on race matters, conservative on others, in other words, a "forced radical," a social protestant rather than a genuine radical. Yet under further pressure and injustice iconoclastic thought and motives will inevitably increase. Harlem's quixotic radicalisms call for their ounce of democracy today lest to-morrow they be beyond cure.

The Negro mind reaches out as yet to nothing but American wants, American ideas. But this forced attempt to build his Americanism on race values is a unique social experiment, and its ultimate success is impossible except through the fullest sharing of American culture and institutions. There should be no delusion about this. American nerves in sections unstrung with race hysteria are often fed the opiate that the trend of Negro advance is wholly separatist, and that the effect of its operation will be to encyst the Negro as a benign foreign body in the body politic. This cannot be—even if it were desirable. The racialism of the Negro is no limitation or reservation with respect to American life; it is only a constructive effort to build the obstructions in the stream of his progress into an efficient dam of social energy and power. Democracy itself is obstructed and stagnated to the extent that any of its channels are closed. Indeed they cannot be selectively closed. So the choice is not between one way for the Negro and another way for the rest, but between American institutions frustrated, on the one hand, and American ideals progressively fulfilled and realized, on the other.

There is, of course, a warrantably comfortable feeling in being on the right side of the country's professed ideals. We realize that we cannot be undone without America's undoing. It is within the gamut of this attitude that the thinking Negro faces America, but with variations of mood that are if anything more significant than the attitude itself. Sometimes we have it taken with the defiant ironic challenge of McKay:

> Mine is the future grinding down to-day
> Like a great landslip moving to the sea,
> Bearing its freight of debris far away
> Where the green hungry waters restlessly
> Heave mammoth pyramids, and break and roar
> Their eerie challenge to the crumbling shore.

Sometimes, perhaps more frequently as yet, it is taken in the fervent and almost filial appeal and counsel of Weldon Johnson's:

> O Southland, dear Southland!
> Then why do you still cling
> To an idle age and a musty page,
> To a dead and useless thing?

But between defiance and appeal, midway almost between cynicism and hope, the prevailing mind stands in the mood of the same author's *To America*, an attitude of sober query and stoical challenge:

How would you have us, as we are?
Or sinking 'neath the load we bear,
Our eyes fixed forward on a star,
Or gazing empty at despair?
Rising or falling? Men or things?
With dragging pace or footsteps fleet?
Strong, willing sinews in your wings,
Or tightening chains about your feet?

More and more, however, an intelligent realization of the great discrepancy between the American social creed and the American social practice forces upon the Negro the taking of the moral advantage that is his. Only the steadying and sobering effect of a truly characteristic gentleness of spirit prevents the rapid rise of a definite cynicism and counter-hate and a defiant superiority feeling. Human as this reaction would be, the majority still deprecate its advent, and would gladly see it forestalled by the speedy amelioration of its causes. We wish our race pride to be a healthier, more positive achievement than a feeling based upon a realization of the shortcomings of others. But all paths toward the attainment of a sound social attitude have been difficult; only a relatively few enlightened minds have been able as the phrase puts it "to rise above" prejudice. The ordinary man has had until recently only a hard choice between the alternatives of supine and humiliating submission and stimulating but hurtful counter-prejudice. Fortunately from some inner, desperate resourcefulness has recently sprung up the simple expedient of fighting prejudice by mental passive resistance, in other words by trying to ignore it. For the few, this manna may perhaps be effective, but the masses cannot thrive upon it.

Fortunately there are constructive channels opening out into which the balked social feelings of the American Negro can flow freely.

Without them there would be much more pressure and danger than there is. These compensating interests are racial but in a new and enlarged way. One is the consciousness of acting as the advance-guard of the African peoples in their contact with twentieth-century civilization; the other, the sense of a mission of rehabilitating the race in world esteem from that loss of prestige for which the fate and conditions of slavery have so largely been responsible. Harlem, as we shall see, is the center of both these movements; she is the home of the Negro's "Zionism." The pulse of the Negro world has begun to beat in Harlem. A Negro newspaper carrying news material in English, French, and Spanish, gathered from all quarters of America, the West Indies, and Africa has maintained itself in Harlem for over five years. Two important magazines, both edited from New York, maintain their news and circulation consistently on a cosmopolitan scale. Under American auspices and backing, three pan-African congresses have been held abroad for the discussion of common interests, colonial questions, and the future cooperative development of Africa. In terms of the race question as a world problem, the Negro mind has leapt, so to speak, upon the parapets of prejudice and extended its cramped horizons. In so doing it has linked up with the growing group consciousness of the dark-peoples and is gradually learning their common interests. As one of our writers has recently put it: "It is imperative that we understand the white world in its relations to the non-white world." As with the Jew, persecution is making the Negro international.

As a world phenomenon this wider race consciousness is a different thing from the much asserted rising tide of color. Its inevitable causes are not of our making. The consequences are not necessarily damaging to the best interests of civilization. Whether it actually brings into being new armadas of conflict or argosies of cultural exchange and enlightenment can only be decided by the attitude of the dominant races in an era of critical change. With the American Negro, his new internationalism is primarily an effort to recapture contact with the scattered peoples of African derivation. Garveyism may be a transient, if spectacular, phenomenon, but the possible role of the American Negro in the future development of Africa is one of the most constructive and universally helpful missions that any modern people can lay claim to.

Constructive participation in such causes cannot help giving the Negro valuable group incentives, as well as increased prestige at home and abroad. Our greatest rehabilitation may possibly come through such channels, but for the present, more immediate hope rests in the revaluation by white and black alike of the Negro in terms of his artistic endowments and cultural contributions, past and prospective. It must be increasingly recognized that the Negro has already made very substantial contributions, not only in his folk-art, music especially, which has always found appreciation, but in larger, though humbler and less acknowledged ways. For generations the Negro has been the peasant matrix of that section of America which has most undervalued him, and here he has contributed not only materially in labor and in social patience, but spiritually as well. The South has unconsciously absorbed the gift of his folk-temperament. In less than half a generation it will be easier to recognize this, but the fact remains that a leaven of humor, sentiment, imagination, and tropic nonchalance has gone into the making of the South from a humble, unacknowledged source. A second crop of the Negro's gifts promises still more largely. He now becomes a conscious contributor and lays aside the status of a beneficiary and ward for that of a collaborator and participant in American civilization. The great social gain in this is the releasing of our talented group from the arid fields of controversy and debate to the productive fields of creative expression. The especially cultural recognition they win should in turn prove the key to that revaluation of the Negro which must precede or accompany any considerable further betterment of race relationships. But whatever the general effect, the present generation will have added the motives of self-expression and spiritual development to the old and still unfinished task of making material headway and progress. No one who understandingly faces the situation with its substantial accomplishment or views the new scene with its still more abundant promise can be entirely without hope. And certainly, if in our lifetime the Negro should not be able to celebrate his full initiation into American democracy, he can at least, on the warrant of these things, celebrate the attainment of a significant and satisfying new phase of group development, and with it a spiritual Coming of Age.

(1925)

5. The Negro in American Literature
美国文学中的黑人

William Stanley Braithwaite
威廉·斯坦利·布雷斯维特

　　威廉·斯坦利·布雷斯维特（1878—1962），诗人、批评家。1878年他出生于马萨诸塞州的波士顿，父亲来自西印度群岛，外祖母是北卡罗来纳州的奴隶，母亲很可能是奴隶主的女儿。布雷斯维特小时候在家跟父亲学习，12岁起开始干活贴补家用。他热爱诗歌，崇拜英国浪漫主义诗人济慈、雪莱和华兹华斯等，并深受其诗歌风格的影响。此后，他编撰诗歌选集，成立出版公司，担任亚特兰大大学创意写作教授，1945年退休后，在哈莱姆定居。

　　布雷斯维特的这篇文章较早关注"美国文学中的黑人"这个主题。他首先梳理了比较有代表性且对后来影响较大的美国白人作家笔下的黑人，如斯托夫人《汤姆叔叔的小屋》中的汤姆叔叔，美国内战结束之后的白人作家，如佩奇（Thomas Nelson Page）、凯布尔（George W. Cable）与狄克逊（Thomas Dixon）等人笔下的刻板黑人，以及克莱恩（Stephen Crane）、奥尼尔（Eugene O'Neill）等人作品中的具有点缀性的黑人。更为重要的是，布雷斯维特简要分析了美国黑人文学的发展及其对黑人的艺术处理。首先，美国黑人文学的主要成就在诗歌，小说、随笔与戏剧方面的成就乏善可陈；其次，在惠特莉与邓巴之间（18世纪下半叶到19世纪末），美国几乎没有什么堪称重要的黑人作家，道格拉斯与华盛顿等人的自传作品文献性较强而文学性较弱；最后，他对黑人小说的发展寄予厚望，不仅盛赞杜波伊斯（W. E. B. Du Bois）的写作，而且非常欣赏年轻作家图默（Jean Toomer）的小说《甘蔗》所体现出的艺术激情以及对黑人生活的真实处理，比较准确地反映了他对黑人文学发展的远见卓识，成为研究"美国文学中的黑人形象"的先驱。1937年，布朗有专门介绍"美国文学中的黑人形象"主题的书出版，比较详细地梳理了黑人形象的变迁；20世纪60年代的美国黑人争取民权运动，特别是之后的"黑人研究"项目更加重视黑人形象问题，进一步深化了此类研究。

　　True to his origin on this continent, the Negro was projected into literature by an overmastering and exploiting hand. In the generations that he has been so voluminously written and talked about he has been accorded as little artistic justice as social justice. Antebellum literature imposed the distortions of moralistic controversy and made the Negro a wax-figure of the market place: postbellum literature retaliated with the condescending reactions of sentiment and caricature, and made the Negro a *genre* stereotype. Sustained, serious or deep study of Negro life and character has thus been entirely below the horizons of our national art. Only gradually through the dull purgatory of the Age of Discussion, has Negro life eventually issued forth to an Age of Expression.

Perhaps I ought to qualify this last statement that the Negro was *in* American literature generations before he was part of it as a creator. From his very beginning in this country the Negro has been, without the formal recognition of literature and art, creative. During more than two centuries of an enslaved peasantry, the race has been giving evidence, in song and story lore, of an artistic temperament and psychology precious for itself as well as for its potential use and promise in the sophisticated forms of cultural expression. Expressing itself with poignancy and a symbolic imagery unsurpassed, indeed, often unmatched, by any folk-group, the race in servitude was at the same time the finest national expression of emotion and imagination and the most precious mass of raw material for literature America was producing. Quoting these stanzas of James Weldon Johnson's *O Black and Unknown Bards*, I want you to catch the real point of its assertion of the Negro's way into domain of art:

> O black and unknown bards of long ago,
>   How came your lips to touch the sacred fire?
> How, in your darkness, did you come to know
>   The power and beauty of the minstrel's lyre?
> Who first from midst his bonds lifted his eyes?
>   Who first from out the still watch, lone and long,
> Feeling the ancient faith of prophets rise
>   Within his dark-kept soul, burst into song?
>
> There is a wide, wide wonder in it all,
>   That from degraded rest and servile toil
> The fiery spirit of the seer should call
>   These simple children of the sun and soil.
> O black slave singers, gone, forgot, unfamed,
>   You—you, alone, of all the long, long line

Of those who've sung untaught, unknown, unnamed,

Have stretched out upward, seeking the divine.

.

How misdirected was the American imagination, how blinded by the dust of controversy and the pall of social hatred and oppression, not to have found it irresistibly urgent to make literary use of the imagination and emotion it possessed in such abundance.

Controversy and moral appeal gave us *Uncle* Tom's *Cabin*—the first conspicuous example of the Negro as a subject for literary treatment. Published in 1852, it dominated in mood and attitude the American literature of a whole generation; until the body of Reconstruction literature with its quite different attitude came into vogue. Here was sentimentalized sympathy for a downtrodden race, but one in which was projected a character, in Uncle Tom himself, which has been unequalled in its hold upon the popular imagination to this day. But the moral gain and historical effect of Uncle Tom have been an artistic loss and setback. The treatment of Negro life and character, overlaid with these forceful stereotypes, could not develop into artistically satisfactory portraiture.

Just as in the antislavery period, it had been impaled upon the dilemmas of controversy, Negro life with the Reconstruction became involved in the paradoxes of social prejudice. Between the Civil War and the end of the century the subject of the Negro in literature is one that will some day inspire the literary historian with a magnificent theme. It will be magnificent not because there is any sharp emergence of character or incidents, but because of the immense paradox of racial life which came up thunderingly against the principles and doctrines of democracy, and put them to the severest test that they had known. But in literature, it was a period when Negro life was a shuttlecock between the two extremes of humor and pathos. The Negro was free, and was not free. The writers who dealt with him for the most part refused to see more than skin-deep—the grin, the grimaces and the picturesque externalities. Occasionally there was some penetration into the heart and flesh of Negro characters, but to see more than the humble happy peasant would have been to flout the fixed ideas and conventions of an entire generation. For more than artistic reasons, indeed against them, these writers refused to see the tragedy of the Negro and capitalized his comedy. The social conscience had as much need for this comic mask as the Negro. However, if any of the writers of the period had possessed gifts of genius of the first caliber, they would have penetrated this deceptive exterior of Negro life, sounded the depths of tragedy in it, and produced a masterpiece.

American literature still feels the hold of this tradition and its indulgent sentimentalities. Irwin Russell was the first to discover the happy, carefree, humorous Negro. He became a fad. It must be sharply called to attention that the tradition of the antebellum Negro is a postbellum product, stranger in truth than in fiction. Contemporary realism in American fiction has not only recorded his passing, but has thrown serious doubts upon his ever having been a very genuine and representative view of Negro life and character. At best this school of Reconstruction fiction represents the romanticized highlights of a regime that as a whole was a dark, tragic canvas. At most, it presents a Negro true to type for less than two generations. Thomas Nelson Page, kindly perhaps, but with a distant view and a purely local imagination did little more than paint the conditions and attitudes of the period contemporary with his own manhood, the restitution of the overlordship of the defeated slave owners in the Eighties. George W. Cable did little more than idealize the aristocratic tradition of the Old South with the Negro as a literary foil. The effects, though not the motives of their work, have been sinister. The "Uncle" and the "Mammy" traditions, unobjectionable as they are in the setting of their day and generation, and in the atmosphere of sentimental humor, can never stand as the great fiction of their theme and subject: the great period novel of the South has yet to be written. Moreover, these type pictures have degenerated into reactionary social fetishes, and from that descended into libelous artistic caricature of the Negro, which has hampered art quite as much as it has embarrassed the Negro.

Of all of the American writers of this period, Joel Chandler Harris has made the most permanent contribution in dealing with the Negro. There is in his work both a deepening of interest and technique. Here at least we have something approaching true portraiture. But much as we admire this lovable personality, we are forced to say that in the Uncle Remus stories the race was its own artist, lacking only in its illiteracy the power to record its speech. In the perspective of time and fair judgment the credit will be divided, and Joel Chandler Harris regarded as a sort of providentially provided amanuensis for preserving the folk tales and legends of a race. The three writers I have mentioned do not by any means exhaust the list of writers who put the Negro into literature during the last half of the nineteenth century. Mr. Howells added a shadowy note to his social record of American life with *An Imperative Duty* and prophesied the Fiction of the Color Line. But his moral scruples—the persistent artistic vice in all his novels—prevented him from consummating a just union between his heroine with a touch of Negro blood and his hero. It is useless to consider any others, because there were none who succeeded in creating either a great story or a great character out of Negro life. Two writers of importance I am reserving for discussion in the group of Negro writers I shall consider presently. One ought perhaps to say in justice to the writers I have mentioned that their nonsuccess was more largely due to the limitations of their social view than of their technical resources. As white Americans of their day, it was incompatible with their conception of the inequalities between the races to glorify the Negro into the serious and leading position of hero or heroine in fiction. Only one man that I recall, had the moral and artistic courage to do this, and he was Stephen Crane in a short story called *The Monster*. But Stephen Crane was a genius, and therefore could not besmirch the integrity of an artist.

With Thomas Dixon, of *The Leopard's Spots*, we reach a distinct stage in the treatment of the Negro in fiction. The portraiture here descends from caricature to libel. A little later with the vogue of the "darkey-story," and its devotees from Kemble and McAllister to Octavus Roy Cohen, sentimental comedy in the portrayal of the Negro Similarly degenerated to blatant but diverting farce. Before the rise of a new attitude, these represented the bottom reaction, both in artistic and social attitude. Reconstruction fiction was passing out in a flood of propagandist melodrama and ridicule. One hesitates to lift this material up to the plane of literature even for the purposes of comparison. But the gradual climb of the new literature of the Negro must be traced and measured from these two nadir points. Following *The Leopard's Spots*, it was only occasionally during the next twenty years that the Negro was sincerely treated in fiction by white authors. There were two or three tentative efforts to dramatize him. Sheldon's *The Nigger*, was the one notable early effort. And in fiction Paul Kester's *His Own Country* is, from a purely literary point of view, its outstanding performance. This type of novel failed, however, to awaken any general interest. This failure was due to the illogical treatment of the human situations presented. However indifferent and negative it may seem, there is the latent desire in most readers to have honesty of purpose and a full vision in the artist: and especially in fiction, a situation handled with gloves can never be effectively handled.

The first hint that the American artist was looking at this subject with full vision was in Torrence's *Granny Maumee*. It was drama, conceived and executed for performance on the stage, and therefore had a restricted appeal. But even here the artist was concerned with the primitive instincts of the Race, and, though faithful and honest in his portrayal, the note was still low in the scale of racial life. It was only a short time, however, before a distinctly new development took place in the treatment of Negro life by white authors. This new class of work honestly strove to endow the Negro life with purely aesthetic vision and values, but with one or two exceptions, still stuck to the peasant level of race experience, and gave, unwittingly; greater currency to the popular notion of the Negro as an inferior, superstitious, half-ignorant and servile class of folk. Where they did in a few isolated instances recognize an ambitious impulse, it was generally defeated in the course of the story.

Perhaps this is inevitable with an alien approach, however well-intentioned. The folklore attitude discovers only the lowly and the naive: the sociological attitude finds the problem first and the human beings after, if at all. But American art in a reawakened seriousness, and using the technique of the new realism, is gradually penetrating Negro life to the core. George Madden Martin, with her pretentious foreword to a group of short stories, *The Children in the Mist*—and this is an extraordinary volume in many ways—quite seriously tried, as a Southern woman, to elevate the Negro to a higher plane of fictional treatment and interest. In succession, followed Mary White Ovington's *The Shadow*, in which Miss Ovington daringly created the kinship of brother and sister between a black boy and white girl, had it brought to disaster by prejudice, out of which the white girl rose to a sacrifice no white girl in a novel had hitherto accepted and endured; then Shands's *White and Black*, as honest a piece of fiction with the Negro as a subject as was ever produced by a Southern pen—and in this story, also, the hero, Robinson, making an equally glorious sacrifice for truth and justice as Miss Ovington's heroine; Clement Wood's *Nigger*, with defects of treatment, but admirable in purpose, wasted though, I think, in the effort to prove its thesis on wholly illogical material; and lastly, T. S. Stribling's *Birthright*, more significant than any of these other books, in fact, the most significant novel on the Negro written by a white American, and this in spite of its totally false conception of the character of Peter Siner.

Mr. Stribling's book broke ground for a white author in giving us a Negro hero and heroine. There is an obvious attempt to see objectively. But the formula of the Nineties—atavistic race-heredity, still survives and protrudes through the flesh and blood of the characters. Using Peter as a symbol of the man tragically linked by blood to one world and by training and thought to another, Stribling portrays a tragic struggle against the pull of lowly origins and sordid environment. We do not deny this element of tragedy in Negro life—and Mr. Stribling, it must also be remembered, presents, too, a severe indictment in his painting of the Southern conditions which brought about the disintegration of his hero's dreams and ideals. But the preoccupation, almost obsession of otherwise strong and artistic work like O'Neill's *Emperor Jones*, *All Gods Chillun Got Wings*, and Culbertson's *Goat Alley* with this same theme and doubtful formula of hereditary cultural reversion suggests that, in spite of all good intentions, the true presental of the real tragedy of Negro life is a task still left for Negro writers to perform. This is especially true for those phases of culturally representative race life that as yet have scarcely at all found treatment by white American authors. In corroborating this, let me quote a passage from a recent number of the *Independent*, on the Negro novelist which reads:

During the past few years stories about Negroes have been extremely popular. A magazine without a Negro story is hardly living up to its opportunities. But almost every one of these stories is written in a tone of condescension. The artists have caught the contagion from the writers, and the illustrations are ninety-nine times out of a hundred purely slapstick stuff. Stories and pictures make a Roman holiday for the millions who are convinced that the most important fact about the Negro is that his skin is black. Many of these writers live in the South or are from the South. Presumably they are well acquainted with the Negro, but it is a remarkable fact that they almost never tell us anything vital about him, about the real human being in the black man's skin. Their most frequent method is to laugh at the colored man and woman, to catalogue their idiosyncrasies, their departure from the norm, that is, from the ways of the whites. There seems to be no suspicion in the minds of the writers that there may be a fascinating thought life in the minds of the Negroes, whether of the cultivated or of the most ignorant type. Always the Negro is interpreted in the terms of the white man. Whiteman psychology is applied and it is no wonder that the result often shows the Negro in a ludicrous light.

I shall have to run back over the years to where I began to survey the achievement of Negro authorship. The Negro as a creator in American literature is of comparatively recent importance. All that was accomplished between Phyllis [sic] Wheatley and Paul Laurence Dunbar, considered by critical standards, is negligible, and of historical interest only. Historically it is a great tribute to the race to have produced in Phyllis Wheatley not only the slave poetess in eighteenth century Colonial America, but to know she was as good, if not a better, poetess than Ann [sic] Bradstreet whom literary historians give the honor of being the first person of her sex to win fame as a poet in America.

Negro authorship may, for clearer statement, be classified into three main activities: Poetry, Fiction, and the Essay, with an occasional excursion into other branches. In the drama, until very recently, practically nothing worth while has been achieved, with the exception of Angelina Grimke's *Rachel*, notable for its somber craftsmanship. Biography has given us a notable life story, told by himself, of Booker T. Washington. Frederirk Douglass's story of his life is eloquent as a human document, but not in the graces of narration and psychologic portraiture, which has definitely put this form of literature in the domain of the fine arts. Indeed, we may well believe that the efforts of controversy, of the huge amount of discursive and polemical articles dealing chiefly with the race problem, that have been necessary in breaking and clearing the impeded pathway of racial progress, have absorbed and in a way dissipated the literary energy of many able Negro writers.

Let us survey briefly the advance of the Negro in poetry. Behind Dunbar, there is nothing that can stand the critical test. We shall always have a sentimental and historical interest in those forlorn and pathetic figures who cried in the wilderness of their ignorance and oppression. With Dunbar we have our first authentic lyric utterance, an utterance more authentic, I should say, for its faithful rendition of Negro life and character than for any rare or subtle artistry of expression. When Mr. Howells, in his famous introduction to the *Lyrics of Lowly Life*, remarked that Dunbar was the first black man to express the life of his people lyrically, he summed up Dunbar's achievement and transported him to a place beside the peasant poet of Scotland, not for his art, but precisely because he made a people articulate in verse.

The two chief qualities in Dunbar's work are, however, pathos and humor, and in these he expresses that dilemma of soul that characterized the race between the Civil War and the end of the nineteenth century. The poetry of Dunbar is true to the life of the Negro and expresses characteristically what he felt and knew to be the temper and condition of his people. But its moods reflect chiefly those of the era of Reconstruction and just a little beyond—the limited experience of a transitional period, the rather helpless and subservient era of testing freedom and reaching out through the difficulties of life to the emotional compensations of laughter and tears. It is the poetry of the happy peasant and the plaintive minstrel. Occasionally, as in the sonnet to *Robert Gould Shaw* and the *Ode to Ethiopia* there broke through Dunbar, as through the crevices of his spirit, a burning and brooding aspiration, an awakening and virile consciousness of race. But for the most part, his dreams were anchored to the minor whimsies; his deepest poetic inspiration was sentiment. He expressed a folk temperament, but not a race soul. Dunbar was the end of a regime, and not the beginning of a tradition, as so many careless critics, both white and colored, seem to think.

After Dunbar many versifiers appeared—all largely dominated by his successful dialect work. I cannot parade them here for tag or comment, except to say that few have equalled Dunbar in this vein of expression, and none have deepened it as an expression of Negro life. Dunbar himself had clear notions of its limitations;—to a friend in a letter from London, March 15,1897, he says: "I see now very clearly that Mr. Howells has done me irrevocable harm in the dictum he laid down regarding my dialect verse." Not until James W Johnson published his *Fiftieth Anniversary Ode* on the emancipation in 1913, did a poet of the race disengage himself from the background of mediocrity into which the imitation of Dunbar snared Negro poetry. Mr. Johnson's work is based upon a broader contemplation of life, life that is not wholly confined within any racial experience, but through the racial he made articulate that universality of the emotions felt by all mankind. His verse possesses a vigor which definitely breaks away from the brooding minor undercurrents of feeling which have previously characterized the verse of Negro poets. Mr. Johnson brought, indeed, the first intellectual substance to the content of our poetry, and a craftsmanship which, less spontaneous than that of Dunbar's, was more balanced and precise.

Here a new literary generation begins; poetry that is racial in substance, but with the universal note, with the conscious background of the full heritage of English poetry. With each new figure somehow the gamut broadens and the technical control improves. The brilliant succession and maturing powers of Fenton Johnson, Leslie Pinckney Hill, Everett Hawkins, Lucien Watkins, Charles Bertram Johnson, Joseph Cotter, Georgia Douglas Johnson, Roscoe Jameson and Anne Spencer bring us at last to Claude McKay and the poets of the younger generation and a poetry of the masterful accent and high distinction. Too significantly for mere coincidence, it was the stirring year of 1917 that heard the first real masterful accent in Negro poetry. In the September *Crisis* of that year, Roscoe Jameson's *Negro Soldiers* appeared:

> These truly are the Brave,
> These men who cast aside

Old memories to walk the blood-stained pave

Of Sacrifice, joining the solemn tide

That moves away, to suffer and to die

For Freedom—when their own is yet denied!

O Pride! A Prejudice! When they pass by

Hail them, the Brave, for you now crucified.

The very next month, under the pen name of Eli Edwards, Claude McKay printed in *The Seven Arts*,

The Harlem Dancer

Applauding youths laughed with young prostitutes

And watched her perfect, half-clothed body sway;

Her voice was like the sound of blended flutes

Blown by black players upon a picnic day.

She sang and danced on gracefully and calm,

The light gauze hanging loose about her form;

To me she seemed a proudly-swaying palm

Grown lovelier for passing through a storm.

Upon her swarthy neck black, shiny curls

Profusely fell; and, tossing coins in praise

The wine-flushed, bold-eyed boys, and even the girls

Devoured her with their eager, passionate gaze;

But, looking at her falsely-smiling face

I knew her self was not in that strange place.

With Georgia Johnson, Anne Spencer and Angelina Grimke, the Negro woman poet significantly appears. Mrs. Johnson especially has voiced in true poetic spirit the lyric cry of Negro womanhood. In spite of lapses into the sentimental and the platitudinous, she has an authentic gift. Anne Spencer, more sophisticated, more cryptic but also more universal, reveals quite another aspect of poetic genius. Indeed, it is interesting to notice how today Negro poets waver between the racial and the universal notes.

Claude McKay, the poet who leads his generation, is a genius meshed in this dilemma. His work is caught between the currents of the poetry of protest and the poetry of expression; he is in turn the violent and strident propagandist, using his poetic gifts to clothe arrogant and defiant thoughts, and then the pure lyric dreamer, contemplating life and nature with a wistful sympathetic passion. When the mood of *Spring in New Hampshire* or the sonnet *The Harlem Dancer* possesses him, he is full of that spirit and power of beauty that flowers above any and all men's harming. How different in spite of the admirable spirit of courage and defiance, are his poems of which the sonnet *If We Must Die* is a typical example. Negro poetic expression hovers for the moment, pardonably perhaps, over the race problem, but its highest allegiance is to Poetry—it must soar.

Let me refer briefly to a type of literature in which there have been many pens, but a single mind. Dr. Du Bois is the most variously gifted writer which the race has produced. Poet, novelist, sociologist, historian and essayist, he has produced books in all these fields with the exception, I believe, of a formal book of poems, and has given to each the distinction of his clear and exact thinking, and of his sensitive imagination and passionate vision. *The Souls of Black Folk* was the book of an era; it was a painful book, a book of tortured dreams woven into the fabric of the sociologist's document. This book has more profoundly influenced the spiritual temper of the race than any other written in its generation. It is only through the intense, passionate idealism of such substance as makes *The Souls of Black Folk* such a quivering rhapsody of wrongs endured and hopes to be fulfilled that the poets of the race with compelling artistry can lift the Negro into the only full and complete nationalism he knows-that of the American democracy. No other book has more clearly revealed to the nation at large the true idealism and high aspiration of the American Negro.

In this book, as well as in many of Dr. Du Bois's essays, it is often my personal feeling that I am witnessing the birth of a poet, phoenix-like, out of a scholar. Between *The Souls of Black Folk* and *Darkwater*, published four years ago, Dr. Du Bois has written a number of books, none more notable, in my opinion, than his novel *The Quest of the Silver Fleece*, in which he made Cotton the great protagonist of fate in the lives of the Southern people, both white and black. I only know of one other such attempt and accomplishment in American fiction—that of Frank Norris—and I am somehow of the opinion that when the great epic novel of the South is written this book will prove to have been its forerunner. Indeed, the Negro novel is one of the great potentialities of American literature. Must it be written by a Negro? To recur to the article from which I have already quoted:

The white writer seems to stand baffled before the enigma and so he expends all his energies on dialect and in general on the Negro's minstrel characteristics .... We shall have to look to the Negro himself to go all the way. It is quite likely that no white man can do it. It is reasonable to suppose that his white psychology will always be in his way. I am not thinking at all about a Negro novelist who shall arouse the world to the horror of the deliberate killings by white mobs, to the wrongs that condemn a free people to political serfdom. I am not thinking at all of the propaganda novel, although there is enough horror and enough drama in the bald statistics of each one of the annual Moton letters to keep the whole army of writers busy. But the Negro novelist, if he ever comes, must reveal to us much more than what a Negro thinks about when he is being tied to a stake and the torch is being applied to his living flesh; much more than what he feels when he is being crowded off the sidewalk by a drunken rowdy who may be his intellectual inferior by a thousand leagues. Such a writer, to succeed in a big sense, would have to forget that there are white readers; he would have to lose self-consciousness and forget that his work would be placed before a white jury. He would have to be careless as to what the white critic might think of it; he would need the self-assurance to be his own critic. He would have to forget for the time being, at least, that any white man ever attempted to dissect the soul of a Negro.

What I here quoteis both an inquiry and a challenge! Well informed as the writer is, he does not seem to detect the forces which are surely gathering to produce what he longs for.

The development of fiction among Negro authors has been, I might almost say, one of the repressed activities of our literary life. A fair start was made the last decade of the nineteenth century when Chestnutt [sic] and Dunbar were turning out both short stories and novels. In Dunbar's case, had he lived, I think his literary growth would have been in the evolution of the Race novel as indicated in *The Uncalled* and the *Sport of the Gods*. The former was, I think, the most ambitious literary effort of Dunbar; the latter was his most significant; significant because, thrown against the background of New York City, it displayed the life of the race as a unit, swayed by currents of existence, of which it was and was not a part. The story was touched with that shadow of destiny which gave to it a purpose more important than the mere racial machinery of its plot. But Dunbar in his fiction dealt only successfully with the same world that gave him the inspiration for his dialect poems; though his ambition was to "write a novel that will deal with the educated class of my own people." Later he writes of *The Fanatics*: "You do not know how my hopes were planted in that book, but it has utterly disappointed me." His contemporary, Charles W. Chestnutt [sic], was concerned more primarily with the fiction of the Color Line and the contacts and conflicts of its two worlds. He was in a way more successful. In the five volumes to his credit, he has revealed himself as a fiction writer of a very high order. But after all Mr. Chestnutt is a storyteller of genius transformed by racial earnestness into the novelist of talent. His natural gift would have found freer vent in a flow of short stories like Bret Harte's, to judge from the facility and power of his two volumes of short stories, *The Wife of His Youth and Other Stories* and *The Conjure Woman*. But Mr. Chestnutt's serious effort was in the field of the novel, where he made a brave and partially successful effort to correct the distortions of Reconstruction fiction and offset the school of Page and Cable. Two of these novels, *The Marrow of Tradition* and *The House Behind the Cedars*, must be reckoned among the representative period novels of their time. But the situation was not ripe for the great Negro novelist. The American public preferred spurious values to the genuine; the coinage of the Confederacy was at literary par. Where Dunbar, the sentimentalist, was welcome, Chestnutt, the realist, was barred. In 1905 Mr. Chestnutt wrote *The Colonel's Dream*, and thereafter silence fell upon him.

From this date until the past year, with the exception of *The Quest of the Silver Fleece*, which was published in 1911, there has been no fiction of importance by Negro authors. But then suddenly there comes a series of books, which seems to promise at least a new phase of race fiction, and possibly the era of the major novelists. Mr. Walter White's novel *The Fire in the Flint* is a swift moving straightforward story of the contemporary conflicts of black manhood in the South. Coming from the experienced observation of the author, himself an investigator of many lynchings and riots, it is a social document story of firsthand significance and importance; too vital to be labelled and dismissed as propaganda, yet for the same reason too unvarnished and realistic a story to be great art. Nearer to the requirements of art comes Miss Jessie Fauset's novel *There Is Confusion*. Its distinction is to have created an entirely new milieu in the treatment of the race in fiction. She has taken a class within the race of established social standing, tradition and culture, and given in the rather complex family story of *The Marshalls* a social document of unique and refreshing value. In such a story, race fiction, detaching itself from the limitations of propaganda on the one hand and genre fiction on the other, emerges from the color line and is incorporated into the body of general and universal art.

Finally in Jean Toomer, the author of *Cane*, we come upon the very first artist of the race, who with all an artist's passion and sympathy for life, its hurts, its sympathies, its desires, its joys, its defeats and strange yearnings, can write about the Negro without the surrender or compromise of the artist's vision. So objective is it, that we feel that it is a mere accident that birth or association has thrown him into contact with the life he has written about. He would write just as well, just as poignantly, just as transmutingly, about the peasants of Russia, or the peasants of Ireland, had experience brought him in touch with their existence. *Cane* is a book of gold and bronze, of dusk and flame, of ecstasy and pain, and Jean Toomer is a bright morning star of a new day of the race in literature.

(1925)

6. Criteria of Negro Art
黑人艺术的标准

W. E. B. Du Bois

杜波伊斯

W. E. B. 杜波伊斯(1868—1963),美国著名社会学家、历史学家、社会活动家和自传作者。1868 年 2 月 23 日,他出生于马萨诸塞州的大巴林顿(Great Barrington);1888 年,毕业于费斯克大学,获得第一个学士学位;1890 年,以优等生的成绩毕业于哈佛大学,获得第二个学士学位。1895 年,杜波伊斯完成博士学业,成为第一位获得哈佛大学博士学位的非裔美国人,在非裔美国社区享有很高的声望与知名度。他一生笔耕不辍,出版了 22 本书,发表了数以千计的论文与书评,主要关注美国黑人历史,特别关注美国的种族问题。1903 年杜波伊斯出版的《黑人的灵魂》预言般地提出"20 世纪美国的问题是种族问题,是种族分界线问题",体现出他非凡的远见卓识。

他特别关注文学的社会功能,强调文艺为提升黑人种族服务的重要性。1926 年,他发表"黑人艺术的标准"的演讲,矫枉过正地提出"所有艺术都是宣传,……我一点也不关心那些不是用于宣传的艺术"的主张,这篇演讲被收入多部批评文集,俨然成为他文艺思想的全部,以至于很多人都忽略了他文艺思想的丰富性。只有了解 20 世纪初美国文学几乎一边倒地反对黑人,才能更好地理解他所提倡的艺术为提升黑人种族服务思想中的积极意义,为读者更好地了解美国特定时期的文学批评,还原批评的具体历史语境,提供了极好的范例。1939 年,他在《美国社会秩序中黑人的态度:我们将走向何方?》一文中所提出的"为何不从黑人观众的角度来看待黑人文学"的思想有助于纠正白人的宰治,启发了 20 世纪 60 年代和 70 年代的黑人艺术运动与黑人美学运动,推动了非裔美国文学批评的深入开展。

I do not doubt but there are some in this audience who are a little disturbed at the subject of this meeting, and particularly at the subject I have chosen. Such people are thinking something like this: "How is it that an organization like this, a group of radicals trying to bring new things into the world, a fighting organization which has come up out of the blood and dust of battle, struggling for the right of black men to be ordinary human beings how is it that an organization of this kind can turn aside to talk about Art? After all, what have we who are slaves and black to do with Art?"

Or perhaps there are others who feel a certain relief and are saying, "After all it is rather satisfactory after all this talk about rights and fighting to sit and dream of something which leaves a nice taste in the mouth."

Let me tell you that neither of these groups is right. The thing we are talking about tonight is part of the great fight we are carrying on and it represents a forward and an upward look—a pushing onward. You and I have been breasting hills; we have been climbing upward; there has been progress and we can see it day by day looking back along blood-filled paths. But as you go through the valleys and over the foothills, so long as you are climbing, the direction—north, south, east or west—is of less importance. But when gradually the vista widens and you begin to see the world at your feet and the far horizon, then it is time to know more precisely whither you are going and what you really want.

What do we want? What is the thing we are after? As it was phrased last night it had a certain truth: We want to be Americans, full-fledged Americans, with all the rights of other American citizens. But is that all? Do we want simply to be Americans? Once in a while through all of us there flashes some clairvoyance, some clear idea, of what America really is. We who are dark can see America in a way that white Americans can not. And seeing our country thus, are we satisfied with its present goals and ideals?

In the high school where I studied we learned most of Scott's "Lady of the Lake" by heart. In after life once it was my privilege to see the lake. It was Sunday. It was quiet. You could glimpse the deer wandering in unbroken forests; you could hear the soft ripple of romance on the waters. Around me fell the cadence of that poetry of my youth. I fell asleep full of the enchantment of the Scottish border. A new day broke and with it came a sudden rush of excursionists. They were mostly Americans and they were loud and strident. They poured upon the little pleasure boat—men with their hats a little on one side and drooping cigars in the wet corners of their mouths; women who shared their conversation with the world. They all tried to get everywhere first. They pushed other people out of the way. They made all sorts of incoherent noises and gestures so that the quiet home folk and the visitors from other lands silently and half-wonderingly gave way before them. They struck a note not evil but wrong. They carried, perhaps, a sense of strength and accomplishment, but their hearts had no conception of the beauty which pervaded this holy place.

If you tonight suddenly should become full-fledged Americans; if your color faded, or the color line here in Chicago was miraculously forgotten; suppose, too, you became at the same time rich and powerful; —what is it that you would want? What would you immediately seek? Would you buy the most powerful of motor cars and outrace Cook County? Would you buy the most elaborate estate on the North Shore? Would you be a Rotarian or a Lion or a What—not of the very last degree? Would you wear the most striking clothes, give the richest dinners and buy the longest press notices?

Even as you visualize such ideals you know in your hearts that these are not the things you really want. You realize this sooner than the average white American because, pushed aside as we have been in America, there has come to us not only a certain distaste for the tawdry and flamboyant but a vision of what the world could be if it were really a beautiful world; if we had the true spirit; if we had the Seeing Eye, the Cunning Hand, the Feeling Heart; if we had, to be sure, not perfect happiness, but plenty of good hard work, the inevitable suffering that always comes with life; sacrifice and waiting, all that—but, nevertheless, lived in a world where men know, where men create, where they realize themselves and where they enjoy life. It is that sort of a world we want to create for ourselves and for all America.

After all, who shall describe Beauty? What is it? I remember tonight four beautiful things: The Cathedral at Cologne, a forest in stone, set in light and changing shadow, echoing with sunlight and solemn song; a village of the Veys in West Africa, a little thing of mauve and purple, quiet, lying content and shining in the sun; a black and velvet room where on a throne rests, in old and yellowing marble, the broken curves of the Venus of Milo; a single phrase of music in the Southern South—utter melody, haunting and appealing, suddenly arising out of night and eternity, beneath the moon.

Such is Beauty. Its variety is infinite, its possibility is endless. In normal life all may have it and have it yet again. The world is full of it; and yet today the mass of human beings are choked away from it, and their lives distorted and made ugly. This is not only wrong, it is silly. Who shall right this well-nigh universal failing? Who shall let this world be beautiful? Who shall restore to men the glory of sunsets and the peace of quiet sleep?

We black folk may help for we have within us as a race new stirrings; stirrings of the beginning of a new appreciation of joy, of a new desire to create, of a new will tobe; as though in this morning of group life we had awakened from some sleep that at once dimly mourns the past and dreams a splendid future; and there has come the conviction that the Youth that is here today, the Negro Youth, is a different kind of Youth, because in some new way it bears this mighty prophecy on its breast, with a new realization of itself, with new determination for all mankind.

What has this Beauty to do with the world? What has Beauty to do with Truth and Goodness—with the facts of the world and the right actions of men? "Nothing," the artists rush to answer. They may be right. I am but an humble disciple of art and cannot presume to say. I am one who tells the truth and exposes evil and seeks with Beauty and for Beauty to set the world right. That somehow, somewhere eternal and perfect Beauty sits above Truth and Right I can conceive, but here and now and in the world in which I work they are for me unseparated and inseparable.

This is brought to us peculiarly when as artists we face our own past as a people. There has come to us—and it has come especially through the man we are going to honor tonight—a realization of that past, of which for long years we have been ashamed, for which we have apologized. We thought nothing could come out of that past which we wanted to remember; which we wanted to hand down to our children. Suddenly, this same past is taking on form, color and reality, and in a half shamefaced way we are beginning to be proud of it. We are remembering that the romance of the world did not die and lie forgotten in the Middle Age; that if you want romance to deal with you must have it here and now and in your own hands.

I once knew a man and woman. They had two children, a daughter who was white and a daughter who was brown; the daughter who was white married a white man; and when her wedding was preparing the daughter who was brown prepared to go and celebrate. But the mother said, "No!" and the brown daughter went into her room and turned on the gas and died. Do you want Greek tragedy swifter than that?

Or again, here is a little Southern town and you are in the public square. On one side of the square is the office of a colored lawyer and on all the others sides are men who do not like colored lawyers. A white woman goes into the black man's office and points to the white-filled square and says, "I want five hundred dollars now and if I do not get it I am going to scream."

Have you heard the story of the conquest of German East Africa? Listen to the untold tale: There were 40,000 black men and 4,000 white men who talked German.

There were 20,000 black men and 12,000 white men who talked English. There were 10,000 black men and 400 white men who talked French. In Africa then where the Mountains of the Moon raised their white and snowcapped heads into the mouth of the tropic sun, where Nile and Congo rise and the Great Lakes swim, these men fought; they struggled on mountain, hill and valley, in river, lake and swamp, until in masses they sickened, crawled and died; until the 4,000 white Germans had become mostly bleached bones; until nearly all the 12,000 white Englishmen had returned to South Africa, and the 400 Frenchmen to Belgium and Heaven; all except a mere handful of the white men died; but thousands of black men from East, West and South Africa, from Nigeria and the Valley of the Nile, and from the West Indies still struggled, fought and died. For four years they fought and won and lost German East Africa; and all you hear about it is that England and Belgium conquered German Africa for the allies!

Such is the true and stirring stuff of which Romance is born and from this stuff come the stirrings of men who are beginning to remember that this kind of material is theirs; and this vital life of their own kind is beckoning them on.

The question comes next as to the interpretation of these new stirrings, of this new spirit: Of what is the colored artist capable? We have had on the part of both colored and white people singular unanimity of judgment in the past. Colored people have said: "This work must be inferior because it comes from colored people." White people have said: "It is inferior because it is done by colored people." But today there is coming to both the realization that the work of the black man is not always inferior. Interesting stories come to us. A professor in the University of Chicago read to a class that had studied literature a passage of poetry and asked them to guess the author. They guessed a goodly company from Shelley and Robert Browning down to Tennyson and Masefield. The author was Countee Cullen. Or again the English critic John Drinkwater went down to a Southern seminary, one of the sort which "finishes" young white women of the South. The students sat with their wooden faces while he tried to get some response out of them. Finally he said, "Name me some of your Southern poets." They hesitated. He said finally, "I'll start out with your best: Paul Laurence Dunbar!"

With the growing recognition of Negro artists in spite of the severe handicaps, one comforting thing is occurring to both white and black. They are whispering, "Here is a way out. Here is the real solution of the color problem. The recognition accorded Cullen, Hughes, Fauset, White and others shows there is no real color line.

Keep quiet! Don't complain! Work! All will be well!"

I will not say that already this chorus amounts to a conspiracy. Perhaps I am naturally too suspicious. But I will say that there are today a surprising number of white people who are getting great satisfaction out of these younger Negro writers because they think it is going to stop agitation of the Negro question. They say, "What is the use of your fighting and complaining; do the great thing and the reward is there." And many colored people are all too eager to follow this advice; especially those who are weary of the eternal struggle along the color line, who are afraid to fight and to whom the money of philanthropists and the alluring publicity are subtle and deadly bribes. They say, "What is the use of fighting? Why not show simply what we deserve and let the reward come to us?"

And it is right here that the National Association for the Advancement of Colored People comes upon the field, comes with its great call to a new battle, a new fight and new things to fight before the old things are wholly won; and to say that the Beauty of Truth and Freedom which shall some day be our heritage and the heritage of all civilized men is not in our hands yet and that we ourselves must not fail to realize.

There is in New York tonight a black woman molding clay by herself in a little bare room, because there is not a single school of sculpture in New York where she is welcome. Surely there are doors she might burst through, but when God makes a sculptor He does not always make the pushing sort of person who beats his way through doors thrust in his face. This girl is working her hands off to get out of this country so that she can get some sort of training.

There was Richard Brown. If he had been white he would have been alive today instead of dead of neglect. Many helped him when he asked but he was not the kind of boy that always asks. He was simply one who made colors sing.

There is a colored woman in Chicago who is a great musician. She thought she would like to study at Fontainebleau this summer where Walter Damrosch and a score of leaders of Art have an American school of music. But the application blank of this school says: "I am a white American and I apply for admission to the school."

We can go on the stage; we can be just as funny as white Americans wish us to be; we can play all the sordid parts that America likes to assign to Negroes; but for any thing else there is still small place for us.

And so I might go on. But let me sum up with this: Suppose the only Negro who survived some centuries hence was the Negro painted by white Americans in the novels and essays they have written. What would people in a hundred years say of black

Americans? Now turn it around. Suppose you were to write a story and put in it the kind of people you know and like and imagine. You might get it published and you might not. And the "might not" is still far bigger than the "might." The white publishers catering to white folk would say, "It is not interesting" — to white folk, naturally not. They want Uncle Toms, Topsies, good "darkies" and clowns. I have in my office a story with all the earmarks of truth. A young man says that he started out to write and had his stories accepted. Then he began to write about the things he knew best about, that is, about his own people. He submitted a story to a magazine which said, "We are sorry, but we cannot take it." "I sat down and revised my story, changing the color of the characters and the locale and sent it under an assumed name with a change of address and it was accepted by the same magazine that had refused it, the editor promising to take anything else I might send in providing it was good enough."

We have, to be sure, a few recognized and successful Negro artists; but they are not all those fit to survive or even a good minority. They are but the remnants of that ability and genius among us whom the accidents of education and opportunity have raised on the tidal waves of chance. We black folk are not altogether peculiar in this. After all, in the world at large, it is only the accident, the remnant, that gets the chance to make the most of itself; but if this is true of the white world it is infinitely more true of the colored world. It is not simply the great clear tenor of Roland Hayes that opened the ears of America. We have had many voices of all kinds as fine as his and America was and is as deaf as she was for years to him. Then a foreign land heard Hayes and put its imprint on him and immediately America with all its imitative snobbery woke up. We approved Hayes because London, Paris and Berlin approved him and not simply because he was a great singer.

Thus it is the bounden duty of black America to begin this great work of the creation of Beauty, of the preservation of Beauty, of the realization of Beauty, and we must use in this work all the methods that men have used before. And what have been the tools of the artist in times gone by? First of all, he has used the Truth—not for the sake of truth, not as a scientist seeking truth, but as one upon whom Truth eternally thrusts itself as the highest handmaid of imagination, as the one great vehicle of universal understanding. Again artists have used Goodness—goodness in all its aspects of justice, honor and right—not for sake of an ethical sanction but as the one true method of gaining sympathy and human interest.

The apostle of Beauty thus becomes the apostle of Truth and Right not by choice but by inner and outer compulsion. Free he is but his freedom is ever bounded by Truth and Justice; and slavery only dogs him when he is denied the right to tell the Truth or recognize an ideal of Justice.

Thus all Art is propaganda and ever must be, despite the wailing of the purists. I stand in utter shamelessness and say that whatever art I have for writing has been used always for propaganda for gaining the right of black folk to love and enjoy I do not care a damn for any art that is not used for propaganda. But I do care when propaganda is confined to one side while the other is stripped and silent.

In New York we have two plays: "White Cargo" and "Congo." In "White Cargo" there is a fallen woman. She is black. In "Congo" the fallen woman is white. In "White Cargo" the black woman goes down further and further and in "Congo" the white woman begins with degradation but in the end is one of the angels of the Lord. You know the current magazine story: A young white man goes down to Central America and the most beautiful colored woman there falls in love with him. She crawls across the whole isthmus to get to him. The white man says nobly, "No." He goes back to his white sweetheart in New York.

In such cases, it is not the positive propaganda of people who believe white blood divine, infallible and holy to which I object. It is the denial of a similar right of propaganda to those who believe black blood human, lovable and inspired with new ideals for the world. White artists themselves suffer from this narrowing of their field. They cry for freedom in dealing with Negroes because they have so little freedom in dealing with whites. Du Bose Heywood writes "Porgy" and writes beautifully of the black Charleston underworld. But why does he do this? Because he cannot do a similar thing for the white people of Charleston, or they would drum him out of town. The only chance he had to tell the truth of pitiful human degradation was to tell it of colored people. I should not be surprised if Octavius Roy Cohen had approached the *Saturday Evening Post* and asked permission to write about a different kind of colored folk than the monstrosities he has created; but if he has, the *Post* has implied, "No. You are getting paid to write about the kind of colored people you are writing about."

In other words, the white public today demands from its artists, literary and pictorial, racial prejudgment which deliberately distorts Truth and Justice, as far as colored races are concerned, and it will pay for no other.

On the other hand, the young and slowly growing black public still wants its prophets almost equally unfree. We are bound by all sorts of customs that have come down as secondhand soul clothes of white patrons. We are ashamed of sex and we lower our eyes when people will talk of it. Our religion holds us in superstition. Our worst side has been so shamelessly emphasized that we are denying we have or ever had a worst side. In all sorts of ways we are hemmed in and our new young artists have got to fight their way to freedom.

The ultimate judge has got to be you and you have got to build yourselves up into that wide judgment, that catholicity of temper which is going to enable the artist to have his widest chance for freedom. We can afford the Truth. White folk today cannot. As it is now we are handing everything over to a white jury. If a colored man wants to publish a book, he has got to get a white publisher and a white newspaper to say it is great; and then you and I say so. We must come to the place where the work of art when it appears is reviewed and acclaimed by our own free and unfettered judgment. And we are going to have a real and valuable and eternal judgment only as we make ourselves free of mind, proud of body and just of soul to all men.

And then do you know what will be said? It is already saying. Just as soon as true Art emerges; just as soon as the black artist appears, someone touches the race on the shoulder and says, "He did that because he was an American, not because he was a Negro; he was born here; he was trained here; he is not a Negro—what is a Negro anyhow? He is just human; it is the kind of thing you ought to expect."

I do not doubt that the ultimate art coming from black folk is going to be just as beautiful, and beautiful largely in the same ways, as the art that comes from white folk, or yellow, or red; but the point today is that until the art of the black folk compells recognition they will not be rated as human. And when through art they compell [sic] recognition then let the world discover if it will that their art is as new as it is old and as old as new.

I had a classmate once who did three beautiful things and died. One of them was a story of a folk who found fire and then went wandering in the gloom of night seeking again the stars they had once known and lost; suddenly out of blackness they looked up and there loomed the heavens; and what was it that they said? They raised a mighty cry: "It is the stars, it is the ancient stars, it is the young and everlasting stars!"

(1926)

7. The Negro Artist and the Racial Mountain
黑人艺术家与种族山

Langston Hughes
兰斯敦·休斯

兰斯敦·休斯(1902—1967),美国诗人、小说家、剧作家、随笔与自传作者。1902年他出生于密苏里州的乔普林,1921年发表诗歌"黑人说河";1922年来到纽约,在哥伦比亚大学读书,后虽因经济原因辍学,但是他进入哈莱姆文化圈,结识了当时的黑人才俊杜波伊斯、福赛特(Jessie Fauset)、卡伦、赫斯顿(Zora Neale Hurston)与洛克等人。这些人影响了休斯的非裔美国身份意识。休斯热爱诗歌,想在自己的诗歌中表达黑人的语言、经历与音乐形式。他出版了50多部作品,如诗集《疲惫的布鲁斯》(*The Weary Blues*,1926)、小说《不是没有笑声》(*Not Without Laughter*,1930)、戏剧《混血儿》(1935)、自传《大海》(*The Big Sea*:*An Autobiography*,1940)和《我徘徊我彷徨》(*I Wonder as I Wander*,1956)等。

休斯主要以诗歌作品为人熟知,但是他1926年发表的批评文章《黑人艺术家与种族山》体现了美国黑人的文化自觉(与自决)意识,成为非裔美国文学批评史上的代表性文献。虽然在20世纪二三十年代哈莱姆文艺复兴运动期间,涌现了许多才华横溢的年轻黑人作家,但是面对白人赞助人以及白人读者群,很多黑人作家选择了放弃自己的黑人文化身份而采取妥协姿态,当时最有前途的一位黑人年轻诗人曾表示自己"想做诗人"而非"黑人诗人"的想法极具代表性。休斯认为,这位诗人希望像白人诗人那样进行创作,其潜意识就是要做"白人诗人",而更深层次的真实的想法就是"想成为白人"。休斯认为,这种青睐白人性,渴望把自己的黑人个性置于美国标准的模子里,远离黑人性的想法,像一座大山,横亘于真正的美国黑人艺术家面前。黑人艺术家只有不管白人高兴与否,都能真正无惧无畏地表达自己黑皮肤的自我,只有不管黑人满意与否,都能自由地站在高山之巅,才能真实地表达自己,实现艺术自由的目标。

One of the most promising of the young Negro poets said to me once, "I want to be a poet—not a Negro poet," meaning, I believe, "I want to write like a white poet"; meaning, subconsciously, "I would like to be a white poet"; meaning behind that, "I would like to be white." And I was sorry the young man said that, for no great poet has ever been afraid of being himself. And I doubted then that, with his desire to run away spiritually from his race, this boy would ever be a great poet. But this is the mountain standing in the way of any true Negro art in America—this urge within the race toward whiteness, the desire to pour racial individuality into the mold of American standardization, and to be as little Negro and as much American as possible.

But let us look at the immediate background of this young poet. His family is of what I suppose one would call the Negro middle class: people who are by no means rich, yet never uncomfortable nor hungry—smug, contented, respectable folk, members of the Baptist church. The father goes to work every morning. He is a chief steward at a large white club. The mother sometimes does fancy sewing or supervises parties for the rich families of the town. The children go to a mixed school. In the home they read white papers and magazines. And the mother often says, "Don't be like niggers" when the children are bad. A frequent phrase from the father is, "Look how well a white man does things." And so the word white comes to be unconsciously a symbol of all the virtues. It holds for the children beauty, morality and money. The whisper of "I want to be white" runs silently through their minds. This young poet's home is, I believe, a fairly typical home of the colored middle class. One sees immediately how difficult it would be for an artist born in such a home to interest himself in interpreting the beauty of his own people. He is never taught to see that beauty. He is taught rather not to see it, or if he does, to be ashamed of it when it is not according to Caucasian patterns.

For racial culture the home of a self-styled "high-class" Negro has nothing better to offer. Instead there will perhaps be more aping of things white than in a less cultured or less wealthy home. The father is perhaps a doctor, lawyer, landowner, or politician. The mother may be a social worker, or a teacher, or she may do nothing and have a maid. Father is often dark but he has usually married the lightest woman he could find. The family attends a fashionable church where few really colored faces are to be found. And they themselves draw a color line. In the North they go to white theaters and white movies. And in the South they have at least two cars and a house "like white folks." Nordic manners, Nordic faces, Nordic hair, Nordic art (if any), and an Episcopal heaven. A very high mountain indeed for the would-be racial artist to climb in order to discover himself and his people.

But then there are the low-down folks, the so-called common element, and they are the majority—may the Lord be praised! The people who have their nip of gin on Saturday nights and are not too important to themselves or the community, or too well fed, or too learned to watch the lazy world go round. They live on Seventh Street in Washington or State Street in Chicago and they do not particularly care whether they are like white folks or anybody else. Their joy runs, bang! into ecstasy. Their religion soars to a shout. Work maybe a little today, rest a little tomorrow. Play awhile. Sing awhile. O, let's dance! These common people are not afraid of spirituals, as for a long time their more intellectual brethren were, and jazz is their child. They furnish a wealth of colorful, distinctive material for any artist because they still hold their own individuality in the face of American standardizations. And perhaps these common people will give to the world its truly great Negro artist, the one who is not afraid to be himself. Whereas the better-class Negro would tell the artist what to do, the people at least let him alone when he does appear. And they are not ashamed of him—if they know he exists at all. And they accept what beauty is their own without question.

Certainly there is, for the American Negro artist who can escape the restrictions the more advanced among his own group would put upon him, a great field of unused material ready for his art. Without going outside his race, and even among the better classes with their "white" culture and conscious American manners, but still Negro enough to be different, there is sufficient matter to furnish a black artist with a lifetime of creative work. And when he chooses to touch on the relations between Negroes and whites in this country, with their innumerable overtones and undertones, surely, and especially for literature and the drama, there is an inexhaustible supply of themes at hand. To these the Negro artist can give his racial individuality, his heritage of rhythm and warmth, and his incongruous humor that so often, as in the Blues, becomes ironic laughter mixed with tears. But let us look again at the mountain.

A prominent Negro clubwoman in Philadelphia paid eleven dollars to hear Raquel Meller sing Andalusian popular songs. But she told me a few weeks before she would not think of going to hear "that woman," Clara Smith, a great black artist, sing Negro folksongs. And many an upper-class Negro church, even now, would not dream of employing a spiritual in its services. The drab melodies in white folks' hymn books are much to be preferred. "We want to worship the Lord correctly and quietly. We don't believe in 'shouting.' Let's be dull like the Nordics," they say, in effect.

The road for the serious black artist, then, who would produce a racial art is most certainly rocky and the mountain is high. Until recently he received almost no encouragement for his work from either white or colored people. The fine novels of Chesnutt go out of print with neither race noticing their passing. The quaint charm and humor of Dunbar's dialect verse brought to him, in his day, largely the same kind of encouragement one would give a sideshow freak (A colored man writing poetry! How odd!) or a clown (How amusing!).

The present vogue in things Negro, although it may do as much harm as good for the budding colored artist, has at least done this: it has brought him forcibly to the attention of his own people among whom for so long, unless the other race had noticed him beforehand, he was a prophet with little honor. I understand that Charles Gilpin acted for years in Negro theaters without any special acclaim from his own, but when Broadway gave him eight curtain calls, Negroes, too, began to beat a tin pan in his honor. I know a young colored writer, a manual worker by day, who had been writing well for the colored magazines for some years, but it was not until he recently broke into the white publications and his first book was accepted by a prominent New York publisher that the "best" Negroes in his city took the trouble to discover that he lived there. Then almost immediately they decided to give a grand dinner for him. But the society ladies were careful to whisper to his mother that perhaps she'd better not come. They were not sure she would have an evening gown.

The Negro artist works against an undertow of sharp criticism and misunderstanding from his own group and unintentional bribes from the whites. "O, be respectable, write about nice people, show how good we are," say the Negroes. "Be stereotyped, don't go too far, don't shatter our illusions about you, don't amuse us too seriously. We will pay you," say the whites. Both would have told Jean Toomer not to write *Cane*. The colored people did not praise it. The white people did not buy it. Most of the colored people who did read *Cane* hate it. They are afraid of it. Although the critics gave it good reviews the public remained indifferent. Yet (excepting the work of Du Bois) *Cane* contains the finest prose written by a Negro in America. And like the singing of Robeson it is truly racial.

But in spite of the Nordicized Negro intelligentsia and the desires of some white editors we have an honest American Negro literature already with us. Now I await the rise of the Negro theater. Our folk music, having achieved world-wide fame, offers itself to the genius of the great individual American Negro composer who is to come. And within the next decade I expect to see the work of a growing school of colored artists who paint and model the beauty of dark faces and create with new technique the expressions of their own soul-world. And the Negro dancers who will dance like flame and the singers who will continue to carry our songs to all who listen—they will be with us in even greater numbers tomorrow.

Most of my own poems are racial in theme and treatment, derived from the life I know. In many of them I try to grasp and hold some of the meanings and rhythms of jazz. I am sincere as I know how to be in these poems and yet after every reading I answer questions like these from my own people: "Do you think Negroes should always write about Negroes? I wish you wouldn't read some of your poems to white folks. How do you find anything interesting in a place like a cabaret? Why do you write about black peoople? You aren't black. What makes you do so many jazz poems?"

But jazz to me is one of the inherent expressions of Negro life in America: the eternal tom-tom beating in the Negro soul—the tom-tom of revolt against weariness in a white world, a world of subway trains and work, work, work; the tom-tom of joy and laughter, and pain swallowed in a smile. Yet the Philadelphia clubwoman is ashamed to say that her race created it and she does not like me to write about it. The old subconscious "white is best" runs through her mind. Years of study under white teachers, a lifetime of white books, pictures, and papers, and white manners, morals, and Puritan standards made her dislike the spirituals. And now she turns up her nose at jazz and all its manifestations—likewise almost everything else distinctly racial. She doesn't care for the Winold Reiss portraits of Negroes because they are "too Negro." She does not want a true picture of herself from anybody. She wants the artist to flatter her, to make the white world believe that all Negroes are as smug and as near white in soul as she wants to be. But, to my mind, it is the duty of the younger Negro artist, if he accepts any duties at all from outsiders, to change through the force of his art that old whispering, "I want to be white," hidden in the aspirations of his people, to "Why should I want to be white? I am a Negro—and beautiful!"

So I am ashamed for the black poet who says, "I want to be a poet, not a Negro poet," as though his own racial world were not as interesting as any other world. I am ashamed, too, for the colored artist who runs from the painting of Negro faces to the painting of sunsets after the manner of the academicians because he fears the strange un-whiteness of his own features. An artist must be free to choose what he does, certainly, but he must also never be afraid to do what he might choose.

Let the blare of Negro jazz bands and the bellowing voice of Bessie Smith singing

Blues penetrate the closed ears of the colored near-intellectuals until they listen and perhaps understand. Let Paul Robeson singing "Water Boy," and Rudolph Fisher writing about the streets of Harlem, and Jean Toomer holding the heart of Georgia in his hands, and Aaron Douglas drawing strange black fantasies cause the smug Negro middle class to tum from their white, respectable, ordinary books and papers to catch a glimmer of their own beauty. We younger Negro artists who create now intend to express our individual dark-skinned selves without fear or shame. If white people are pleased we are glad. If they are not, it doesn't matter. We know we are beautiful. And ugly too. The tom-tom cries and the tom-tom laughs. If colored people are pleased we are glad. If they are not, their displeasure doesn't matter either. We build our temples for tomorrow, strong as we know how, and we stand on top of the mountain, free within ourselves.

（1926）

8. The Negro-Art Hokum
黑人艺术的废话

George S. Schuyler

乔治·斯凯勒

乔治·斯凯勒(1895—1977),批评家、记者与讽刺作家。1895 年出生于纽约罗德岛的普罗维登斯,很早就非常自信,自诩祖先早在美国独立革命战争时期就是自由民。1912—1919 年,他曾服过 7 年兵役;1923—1928 年担任《信使》的助理编辑。1927—1933年,在门肯主编的《美国水星》(*American Mercury*)上发表了 10 篇文章,是 20 世纪初最杰出的记者和随笔作者之一。1933—1939 年,他以笔名发表了 54 篇短篇小说、20 部长篇和中篇小说,1966 年出版自传《黑人与保守分子》(*Black and Conservative*)。但是真正为他赢得讽刺作家声誉的是 1931 年出版的长篇小说《不再黑》(*Black No More*)。这部具有科幻元素的小说攻击白人至上与种族纯洁的迷思,指出种族主义坚如磐石背后的经济原因。

虽然斯凯勒一直攻击白人种族主义,致力于暴露美国种族社会的欺伪,但还是让一些美国黑人怀疑他的种族忠诚。1926 年,他发表《黑人艺术的废话》一文,引发很大的争议。在哈莱姆文艺复兴运动蓬勃发展的过程中,他在文章第一段就提出美国几乎不存在“黑人艺术”,黑人艺术是非洲的黑人国家的艺术,这种论调显然有点“不合时宜”;另外,他认为源自美国南方的灵歌、劳动号子、布鲁斯、爵士乐等艺术表现方式,恐怕也难以代表整个黑人种族。更为重要的是,他认为非裔美国人的文学、绘画与雕塑和美国白人的没有什么大的区别,都或多或少地受欧洲的影响。他认为,既然所有黑人的作品都体现美国的民族特性而非种族特性,那么区分“黑人艺术”的意义何在? 这一论点直到今天依然十分重要,成为探讨非裔美国文学“普通”还是“独特”的重要参考。

Negro art "made in America" is as nonexistent as the widely advertised profundity of Cal Coolidge, the "seven years of progress" of Mayor Hylan, or the reported sophistication of New Yorkers. Negro art there has been, is; and will be among the numerous black nations of Africa; but to suggest the possibility of any such development among the ten million colored people in this republic is self-evident foolishness. Eager apostles from Greenwich Village, Harlem, and environs proclaimed a great renaissance of Negro art just around the corner waiting to be ushered on the scene by those whose hobby is taking races, nations, peoples, and movements under their wing. New art forms expressing the "peculiar" psychology of the Negro were about to flood the market. In short, the art of Homo Africanus was about to electrify the waiting world. Skeptics patiently waited. They still wait.

True, from dark-skinned sources have come those slave songs based on Protestant hymns and Biblical texts known as the spirituals, work songs and secular songs of sorrow and tough luck known as the blues, that outgrowth of ragtime known as jazz (in the development of which whites have assisted), and the Charleston, an eccentric dance invented by the gamins around the public marketplace in Charleston, S.C. No one can or does deny this. But these are contributions of a caste in a certain section of the country. They are foreign to Northern Negroes, West Indian Negroes, and African Negroes. They are no more expressive or characteristic of the Negro race than the music and dancing of the Appalachian highlanders or the Dalmation peasantry are expressive or characteristic of the Caucasian race. If one wishes to speak of the musical contributions of the peasantry of the South, very well. Any group under similar circumstances would have produced something similar. It is merely a coincidence that this peasant class happens to be of a darker hue than the other inhabitants of the land. One recalls the remarkable likeness of the minor strains of the Russian mujiks to those of the Southern Negro.

As for the literature, painting, and sculpture of Aframericans—such as there is— it is identical in kind with the literature, painting, and sculpture of white Americans: that is, it shows more or less evidence of European influence. In the field of drama little of any merit has been written by and about Negroes that could not have been written by whites. The dean of the Aframerican literati is W. E. B. Du Bois, a product of Harvard and German universities; the foremost Aframerican sculptor is Meta Warwick Fuller, a graduate of leading American art schools and former student of Rodin; while the most noted Aframerican painter, Henry Ossawa Tanner, is dean of American painters in Paris and has been decorated by the French Government. Now the work of these artists is no more "expressive of the Negro soul"—as the gushers put it—than are the scribblings of Octavus Cohen or Hugh Wiley.

This, of course, is easily understood if one stops to realize that the Aframerican is merely a lampblacked Anglo-Saxon. If the European immigrant after two or three generations of exposure to our schools, politics, advertising, moral crusades, and restaurants becomes indistinguishable from the mass of Americans of the older stock (despite the influence of the foreign language press), how much truer must it be of the sons of Ham who have been subjected to what the uplifters call Americanism for the last three hundred years. Aside from his color, which ranges from very dark brown to pink, your American Negro is just plain American. Negroes and whites from the same localities in this country talk, think, and act about the same. Because a few writers with a paucity of themes have seized upon imbecilities of the Negro rustics and clowns and palmed them off as authentic and characteristic Aframerican behavior, the common notion that the black American is so "different" from his white neighbor has gained wide currency. The mere mention of the word "Negro" conjures up in the average white American's mind a composite stereotype of Bert Williams, Aunt Jemima, Uncle Tom, Jack Johnson, Florian Slappey, and the various monstrosities scrawled by the cartoonists. Your average Aframerican no more resembles this stereotype than the average American resembles a composite of Andy Gump, Jim Jeffries, and a cartoon by Rube Goldberg.

Again, the Africamerican is subject to the same economic and social forces that mold the actions and thoughts of the white Americans. He is not living in a different world as some whites and a few Negroes would have us believe. When the jangling of his Connecticut alarm clock gets him out of his Grand Rapids bed to a breakfast similar to that eaten by his white brother across the street; when he toils at the same or similar work in mills, mines, factories, and commerce alongside the descendants of Spartacus, Robin Hood, and Eric the Red; when he wears similar clothing and speaks the same language with the same degree of perfection; when he reads the same Bible and belongs to the Baptist, Methodist, Episcopal, or Catholic church; when his fraternal affiliations also include the Elks, Masons, and Knights of Pythias; when he gets the same or similar schooling, lives in the same kind of houses, owns the same makes of cars (or rides in them), and nightly sees the same Hollywood version of life on the screen; when he smokes the same brands of tobacco, and avidly peruses the same puerile periodicals; in short, when he responds to the same political, social, moral; and economic stimuli in precisely the same manner as his white neighbor, it is sheer nonsense to talk about "racial differences" as between the American black man and the American white man. Glance over a Negro newspaper (it is printed in good Americanese) and you will find the usual quota of crime news, scandal, personals, and uplift to be found in the average white newspaper—which, by the way, is more widely read by the Negroes than is the Negro press. In order to satisfy the cravings of an inferiority complex engendered by the colorphobia of the mob, the readers of the

Negro newspapers are given a slight dash of racialistic seasoning. In the homes of the black and white Americans of the same cultural and economic level one finds similar furniture, literature, and conversation. How, then, can the black American be expected to produce art and literature dissimilar to that of the white American?

Consider Coleridge-Taylor, Edward Wilmot Blyden, and Claude McKay, the Englishmen; Pushkin, the Russian; Bridgewater, the Pole; Antar, the Arabian; Latino, the Spaniard; Dumas, *pere* and *fils*, the Frenchmen; and Paul Laurence Dunbar, Charles W. Chestnutt [sic] , and James Weldon Johnson, the Americans. All Negroes; yet their work shows the impress of nationality rather than race. They all reveal the psychology and culture of their environment—their color is incidental. Why should Negro artists of America vary from the national artistic norm when Negro artists in other countries have not done so? If we can foresee what kind of white citizens will inhabit this neck of the woods in the next generation by studying the sort of education and environment the children are exposed to now, it should not be difficult to reason that the adults of today are what they are because of the education and environment they were exposed to a generation ago. And that education and environment were about the same for blacks and whites. One contemplates the popularity of the Negro-art hokum and murmurs, "How come?"

This nonsense is probably the last stand of the old myth palmed off by Negrophobists for all these many years, and recently rehashed by the sainted Harding, that there are "fundamental, eternal, and inescapable differences" between white and black Americans. That there are Negroes who will lend this myth a helping hand need occasion no surprise. It has been broadcast all over the world by the vociferous scions of slaveholders, "scientists" like Madison Grant and Lothrop Stoddard, and the patriots who flood the treasury of the Ku Klux Klan; and is believed, even today, by the majority of free, white citizens. On this baseless premise, so flattering to the white mob, that the blackamoor is inferior and fundamentally different, is erected the postulate that he must needs be peculiar; and when he attempts to portray life through the medium of art, it must of necessity be a peculiar art. While such reasoning may seem conclusive to the majority of Americans, it must be rejected with a loud guffaw by intelligent people.

(1926)

9. Our Literary Audience
我们的文学读者

Sterling A. Brown

斯特林·布朗

斯特林·布朗(1901—1989),诗人、批评家和文选编撰家。1901年,布朗出生于华盛顿的黑人中产阶级家庭;1918年,毕业于著名的邓巴高中;1922年,以优异成绩毕业于威廉姆斯学院;1923年,获得哈佛大学英语硕士学位。在不同学校教书期间,他敏锐地感受到非裔美国民间生活和民俗语言的诗意与哲理,广泛吸收,奠定其注重民俗的艺术特征。他的诗集《南方之路》(*Southern Road*,1931)广受好评,体现了他尝试利用黑人民俗语言,更好地理解黑人民族,更加准确地描绘他们生活的目标。

布朗的批评文章《我们的文学读者》可以视为杜波伊斯提出的文学为黑人种族服务,以及阿兰·洛克比较侧重文学的审美功能与文化意义等观点的延续与深入。他指出20世纪20年代中期以来批评中的某些谬误,如不管作者意图,把黑人的书作为所有黑人的代表;为了种族宣传,黑人的书一定要理想化、乐观化;害怕真实、讽刺;从美国资产阶级、种族辩护士的角度进行批评,等等。布朗认为,即便教导黑人青年我们有引以为豪的种族遗产,也要基于事实,而且一定要比较富有艺术性。他认为,黑人族群中确实存在个体差异,确实有阴暗面,我们无须否认,也同样予以真实地呈现,因为无论宣传怎样显得合理,都不可能比真实更有力。但是针对当时美国社会把文学作品中出现的某些反面黑人形象作为整个黑人族群的代表,黑人社会也想避免这类指责,提倡创作没有缺陷的黑人形象的做法,布朗坚持文学作品的真实性与个性化表达。他举例说,虽然并非所有的法国女人都像包法利,但是《包法利夫人》是部伟大的作品。虽然不是所有俄国人都像渥伦斯基,但是《安娜·卡列尼娜》是部伟大的作品。因此,虽然关于黑人的书可能无法真实反映所有黑人,但是仍有其价值,我们不能只塑造那些理想化的上层社会黑人,如果我们只描写那些成功的黑人,那将是文学的噩梦。另外,布朗非常重视读者的作用,明确提出"没有伟大的读者,我们就不可能有伟大的文学"的主张,把传统文学批评中对作者的重视引向读者。

We have heard in recent years a great deal about the Negro artist. We have heard excoriations from the one side, and flattery from the other. In some instances we have

85

heard valuable honest criticism. One vital determinant of the Negro artist's achievement or mediocrity has not been so much discussed. I refer to the Negro artist's audience, within his own group. About this audience a great deal might be said.

I submit for consideration this statement, probably no startling discovery: that those who might be, who should be a fit audience for the Negro artist are, taken by and large, fundamentally out of sympathy with his aims and his genuine development.

I am holding no brief for any writer, or any coterie of writers, or any racial credo. I have as yet, no logs to roll, and no brickbats to heave. I have however a deep concern with the development of a literature worthy of our past, and of our destiny; without which literature certainly, we can never come to much. I have a deep concern with the development of an audience worthy of such a literature.

"Without great audiences we cannot have great poets." Whitman's trenchant commentary needs stressing today, universally. But particularly do we as a racial group need it? There is a great harm that we can do our incipient literature. With a few noteworthy exceptions, we are doing that harm, most effectually. It is hardly because of malice; it has its natural causes; but it is nonetheless destructive.

We are not a reading folk (present company of course forever excepted). There are reasons, of course, but even with those considered, it remains true that we do not read nearly so much as we should. I imagine our magazine editors and our authors if they chose, could bear this out. A young friend, on a book-selling project, filling in questionnaires on the reason why people did not buy books, wrote down often, with a touch of malice—"Too much bridge." Her questionnaires are scientific with a vengeance.

When we do condescend to read books about Negroes, we seem to read in order to confute. These are sample ejaculations: "*But we're not* all *like that*." "*Why does he show such* a level *of society? We have better Negroes than that to write about*." "*What effect* will *this have on the opinions of white people*." (Alas, for the ofay, forever ensconced in the lumber yard!) ... "*More dialect. Negroes don't use dialect anymore*." Or if that sin is too patent against the Holy Ghost of Truth—"*Negroes of my class don't use dialect anyway*." (Which *mought* be so, and then again, which *moughtn't*.)

Our criticism is vitiated therefore in many ways. Certain fallacies I have detected within at least the last six years are these:

We look upon Negro books regardless of the author's intention, as representative of all Negroes, i.e. as sociological documents.

We insist that Negro books must be idealistic, optimistic tracts for race advertisement.

We are afraid of truth telling, of satire.

We criticize from the point of view of bourgeois America, of racial apologists.

In this division there are, of course, overlappings. Moreover all of these fallacies might be attributed to a single cause, such as an apologistic chip on the shoulder attitude, imposed by circumstance; an arising snobbishness; a delayed Victorianism; or a following of the wrong lead. Whatever may be the primary impulse, the fact remains that if these standards of criticism are perpetuated, and our authors are forced to heed them, we thereby dwarf their stature as interpreters.

One of the most chronic complaints concerns this matter of Representativeness. An author, to these sufferers, never intends to show a man who happens to be a Negro, but rather to make a blanket charge against the race. The syllogism follows: Mr. A. shows a Negro who steals; he means by this that all Negroes steal; all Negroes do not steal; Q. E. D. Mr. A. is a liar, and his book is another libel on the race.

For instance, *Emperor Jones* is considered as sociology rather than drama; as a study of the superstition, and bestiality, and charlatanry of the group, rather than as a brilliant study of a hard-boiled pragmatist, far more "American" and "African," and a better man in courage, and resourcefulness than those ranged in opposition to him. To the charge that I have misunderstood the symbolism of Brutus Jones' visions, let me submit that superstition is a human heritage, not peculiar to the Negro, and that the beat of the tom-tom, as heard even in a metropolitan theatre, can be a terrifying experience to many regardless of race, if we are to believe testimonies. But no, O'Neill is "showing us the Negro race," not a shrewd Pullman Porter, who had for a space, a run of luck. By the same token, is Smithers a picture of the white race? If so, O'Neill is definitely propagandizing against the Caucasian. O'Neill must be an East Indian.

All *Gods Chillun Got Wings* is a tract, say critics of this stamp, against intermarriage; a proof of the inferiority of the Negro (why he even uses the word Nigger!!! when he could have said Nubian or Ethiopian!); a libel stating that Negro law students all wish to marry white prostitutes. (The word prostitute by the way, is cast around rather loosely, with a careless respect for the Dictionary, as will be seen later.) This for as humane an observation of the wreck that prejudice can bring to two poor children, who whatever their frailties, certainly deserve no such disaster!.

This is not intended for any defense of O'Neill, who stands in no need of any weak defense I might urge. It is to show to what absurdity we may sink in our determination to consider anything said of Negroes as a wholesale indictment or exaltation of all Negroes. We are as bad as Schuyler says many of "our white folks" are; we can't admit that there are individuals in the group, or at least we can't believe that men of genius whether white or colored can see those individuals.

Of course, one knows the reason for much of this. Books galore have been written, still are written with a definite inclusive thesis, purposing generally to discredit us. We have seen so much of the razor toting, gin guzzling, chicken stealing Negro; or the pompous walking dictionary spouting malapropisms; we have heard so much of "learned" tomes, establishing our characteristics, "appropriativeness," short memory for joys and griefs, imitativeness, and general inferiority. We are certainly fed up.

This has been so much our experience that by now it seems we should be able to distinguish between individual and race portraiture, i.e., between literature on the one hand and pseudoscience and propaganda on the other. These last we have with us always. From Dixon's melodramas down to Roark Bradford's funny stories, from Thomas Nelson Page's "Ole Virginny retainers" to Bowyer Campbell's *Black Sadie* the list is long and notorious. One doesn't wish to underestimate this prejudice. It is ubiquitous and dangerous. When it raises its head it is up to us to strike, and strike hard. But when it doesn't exist, there is no need of tilting at windmills.

In some cases the author's design to deal with the entire race is explicit, as in Vachel Lindsay's *The Congo*, subtitled "A Study of the Negro Race"; in other cases, implicit. But an effort at understanding the work should enable us to detect whether his aim is to show one of ours, or all of us (in the latter case, whatever his freedom from bias, doomed to failure). We have had such practice that we should be rather able at this detection.

We have had so much practice that we are thin-skinned. Anybody would be. And it is natural that when pictures of us were almost entirely concerned with making us out to be either brutes or docile housedogs, i.e., infrahuman, we should have replied by making ourselves out superhuman. It is natural that we should insist that the pendulum be swung back to its other extreme. Life and letters follow the law of the pendulum. Yet, for the lover of the truth, neither extreme is desirable. And now, if we are coming of age, the truth should be our major concern.

This is not a disagreement with the apologistic belief in propaganda. Propaganda must be counterchecked by propaganda. But let it be found where it should be found, in books explicitly propagandistic, in our newspapers, which perhaps must balance white playing up of crime with our own playing up of achievement; in the teaching of our youth that there is a great deal in our racial heritage of which we may be justly proud. Even so, it must be artistic, based on truth, not on exaggeration.

Propaganda, however legitimate, can speak no louder than the truth. Such a cause as ours needs no dressing up. The honest, unvarnished truth, presented as it is, is plea enough for us, in the unbiased courts of mankind. But such courts do not exist? Then what avails thumping the tub? Will that call them into being? Let the truth speak. There has never been a better persuader.

Since we need truthful delineation, let us not add every artist whose picture of us may not be flattering to our long list of traducers. We stand in no need today of such a defense mechanism. If a white audience today needs assurance that we are not all thievish or cowardly or vicious, it is composed of half wits, and can never be convinced anyway. Certainly we can never expect to justify ourselves by heated denials of charges which perhaps have not even been suggested in the work we are denouncing.

To take a comparison at random. Ellen Glasgow has two recent novels on the Virginia gentry. In one she shows an aging aristocrat, a self-appointed lady killer, egocentric, slightly ridiculous. In another she shows three lovely ladies who stooped to "folly." It would be a rash commentator who would say that Ellen Glasgow, unflinching observer though she is, means these pictures to be understood as ensemble pictures of all white Virginians. But the same kind of logic that some of us use on our books would go farther; it would make these books discussions of all white Americans.

Such reasoning would be certainly more ingenious than intelligent.

The best rejoinder to the fuming criticism "But all Negroes aren't like that" should be "Well, what of it. Who said so?" or better, "Why bring that up?" ... But if alas we must go out of our group for authority, let this be said, "All Frenchwomen aren't like Emma Bovary but *Madame Bovary* is a great book; all Russians aren't like Vronsky, but *Anna Karenina* is a great book; all Norwegians aren't like Oswald but *Ghosts* is a great play." Books about us may not be true of all of us; but that has nothing to do with their worth.

As a corollary to the charge that certain books "aiming at representativeness" have missed their mark, comes the demand that our books must show our "best." Those who criticize thus, want literature to be "idealistic"; to show them what we should be like, or more probably, what we should like to be. There's a great difference. It is sadly significant also, that by "best" Negroes, these idealists mean generally the upper reaches of society; i.e. those with money.

Porgy, because it deals with Catfish Row is a poor book for this audience; *Green Thursday*, dealing with cornfield rustics, is a poor book; The *Walls of Jericho* where it deals with a piano mover, is a poor book. In proportion as a book deals with our "better" class it is a better book.

According to this scale of values, a book about a Negro and a mule would be, because of the mule, a better book than one about a muleless Negro; about a Negro and a horse and buggy a better book than about the mule owner; about a Negro and a Ford, better than about the buggy rider; and a book about a Negro and a Rolls Royce better than one about a Negro and a Ford. All that it seems our writers need to do, to guarantee a perfect book and deathless reputation is to write about a Negro and an aeroplane. Unfortunately, this economic hierarchy does not hold in literature. It would rule out most of the Noble prize winners.

Now Porgy in his goat cart, Kildee at his ploughing, Shine in a Harlem poolroom may not be as valuable members of the body economic and politic as "more financial" brethren. (Of course, the point is debatable.) But that books about them are less interesting, less truthful, and less meritorious as works of art, is an unwarranted assumption.

Some of us look upon this prevailing treatment of the lowly Negro as a concerted attack upon us. But an even cursory examination of modern literature would reveal that the major authors everywhere have dealt and are dealing with the lowly. A random ten, coming to mind, are Masefield, Hardy, Galsworthy in England; Synge and Joyce in Ireland; Hamsun in Norway; O'Neill, Willa Cather, Sherwood Anderson, Ernest Hemingway in America. Not to go back to Burns, Crabbe, Wordsworth. The dominance of the lowly as subject matter is a natural concomitant to the progress of democracy.

This does not mean that our books must deal with the plantation or lowly Negro. Each artist to his taste. Assuredly let a writer deal with that to which he can best give convincing embodiment and significant interpretation. To insist otherwise is to hamper the artist, and to add to the stereotyping which has unfortunately, been too apparent in books about us. To demand on the other hand that our books exclude treatment of any character other than the "successful" Negro is a death warrant to literature.

Linked with this is the distaste for dialect. This was manifested in our much earlier thrice told denial of the spirituals. James Weldon Johnson aptly calls this "Second Generation Respectability."

Mr. Johnson is likewise responsible for a very acute criticism of dialect, from a literary point of view, rather than from that of "respectability." Now much of what he said was deserved. From Lowell's *Bigelow Papers* through the local colorists, dialect, for all of its rather eminent practitioners, has been a bit too consciously "*quaint*," too *condescending*. Even in Maristan Chapman's studies in Tennessee mountaineers there is a hint of "outlandishness" being shown for its novelty, not for its universality.

Negro dialect, however, as recorded by the most talented of our observers today, such as Julia Peterkin, Howard Odum, and Langston Hughes, has shown itself capable of much more than the "limited two stops, pathos and humor." Of course, Akers and Octavus Roy Cohen still clown, and show us Negroes who never were, on land or sea, and unreconstructed Southrons show us the pathetic old mammy weeping over vanished antebellum glories. But when we attack these, we do not attack the medium of expression. The fault is not with the material. If Daniel Webster Davis can see in the Negro "peasant" only a comic feeder on hog meat and greens, the fault is in Davis' vision, not in his subject.

Lines like these transcend humor and pathos:

"I told dem people if you was to come home cold an 'stiff in a box, I could look at you same as a stranger an' not a water wouldn' drean out my eye."

Or this:

"Death, ain't yuh got no shame?"

Or this:

"Life for me ain't been no crystal stair."

Or:

"She walked down the track, an' she never looked back.

I'm goin' whah John Henry fell dead."

Julia Peterkin, Heyward, the many other honest artists have shown us what is to be seen, if we have eyes and can use them.

There is nothing "degraded" about dialect. Dialectical peculiarities are universal. There is something about Negro dialect, in the idiom, the tum of the phrase, the music of the vowels and consonants that is worth treasuring.

Are we to descend to the level of the lady who wanted Swing Low, Sweet Chariot metamorphosed into "Descend, welcome vehicle, approaching for the purpose of conveying me to my residence?"

Those who are used only to the evasions and reticences of Victorian books, or of Hollywood (!) (i.e. the products of Hollywood, not the city as it actually is) are or pretend to be shocked by the frankness of modern books on the Negro. That the "low" rather than the "lowly" may often be shown; that there is pornography I do not doubt. But that every book showing frankly aspects of life is thereby salacious, I do stoutly deny. More than this, the notions that white authors show only the worst in Negro life and the best in theirs; that Negro authors show the worst to sell out to whites, are silly, and reveal woeful ignorance about modern literature.

Mamba and Hagar are libellous portraits say some; *Scarlet Sister Mary* is a showing up of a "prostitute" say others. "Our womanhood is defamed." Nay, rather, our intelligence is defamed, by urging such nonsense. For these who must have glittering falsifications of life, the movie houses exist in great plenty.

The moving picture, with its enforced happy ending, may account for our distaste for tragedy; with its idylls of the leisure class, may account for our distaste for Negro portraiture in the theatre. Maybe a shrinking optimism causes this. Whatever the reason, we do not want to see Negro plays. Our youngsters, with some Little Theatre Movements the honorable exceptions, want to be English dukes and duchesses, and wear tuxedoes and evening gowns. Our "best" society leaders want to be mannequins.

Especially taboo is tragedy. Into these tragedies, such as *In Abraham's Bosom* we read all kinds of fantastic lessons. "Intended to show that the Negro never wins out, but always loses." "Intended to impress upon us the futility of effort on our part." Some dramatic "critics" say in substance that the only value of plays like *Porgy*, or *In Abraham's Bosom* is that they give our actors parts. "Worthwhile," "elevating" shows do not get a chance. They are pleading, one has reason to suspect, for musical comedy which may have scenes in cabarets, and wouldn't be confined to Catfish Row. With beautiful girls in gorgeous "costumes," rather than Negroes in more but tattered clothing.

"These plays are depressing," say some. Alas, the most depressing thing is such criticism. Should one insist that *In Abraham's Bosom* is invigorating, inspiring; showing a man's heroic struggle against great odds, showing the finest virtue a man can show in the face of harsh realities—enduring courage; should one insist upon that, he would belong to a very small minority, condemned as treasonous. We seem to forget that for the Negro to be conceived as a tragic figure is a great advance in American Literature. The aristocratic concept of the lowly as clowns is not so far back. That the tragedy of this "clown" meets sympathetic reception is a step forward in race relations.

I sincerely hope that I have not been crashing in open doors. I realize that there are many readers who do not fit into the audience I have attempted to depict. But these exceptions seem to me to fortify the rule. There are wise leaders who are attempting to combat supersensitive criticism. The remarks I have seen so much danger in are not generally written. But they are prevalent and powerful.

One hopes that they come more from a misunderstanding of what literature should be, than from a more harmful source. But from many indications it seems that one very dangerous state of mind produces them. It may be named—lack of mental bravery. It may be considered as a cowardly denial of our own.

It seems to acute observers that many of us, who have leisure for reading are ashamed of being Negroes. This shame make us harsher to the shortcomings of some perhaps not so fortunate economically. There seems to be among us a more fundamental lack of sympathy with the Negro farthest down, than there is in other groups with the same Negro.

To recapitulate. It is admitted that some books about us are definite propaganda; that in the books about us, the great diversity of our life has not been shown (which should not be surprising when we consider how recent is this movement toward realistic portraiture), that dramas about the Negro character are even yet few and far between. It is insisted that these books should be judged as works of literature; i.e., by their fidelity to the truth of their particular characters, not as representative pictures of all Negroes; that they should not be judged at all by the level of society shown, not at all as good or bad according to the "morality" of the characters; should not be judged as propaganda when there is no evidence, explicit or implicit, that propaganda was intended. Furthermore those who go to literature as an entertaining building up of dream worlds, purely for idle amusement, should not pass judgment at all on books which aim at fidelity to truth.

One doesn't wish to be pontifical about this matter of truth. "What is truth, asked Pontius Pilate, and would not stay for an answer." The answer would have been difficult. But it surely is not presumptuous for a Negro, in Twentieth Century America, to say that showing the world in idealistic rose colors is not fidelity to truth. We have got to look at our times and at ourselves searchingly and honestly; surely there is nothing of the farfetched in that injunction.

But we are reluctant about heeding this injunction. We resent what doesn't flatter us. One young man, Allison Davis, who spoke courageously and capably his honest observation about our life has been the target of second rate attacks ever since. George Schuyler's letter bag seems to fill up whenever he states that even the slightest something may be rotten on Beale Street or Seventh Avenue. Because of their candor, Langston Hughes and Jean Toomer, humane, fine grained artists both of them, have been received in a manner that should shame us. This is natural, perhaps, but unfortunate. Says J. S. Collis in a book about Bernard Shaw, the Irish cannot bear criticism; for like all races who have been oppressed they are still *without mental bravery*. They are afraid to see themselves exposed to what they imagine to be adverse criticism... But the future of Ireland largely depends upon *how much she* is *prepared* to *listen* to *criticism* and how far she is capable of preserving peace between able men." These last words are worthy of our deepest attention.

We are cowed. We have become typically bourgeois. Natural though such an evolution is, if we are *all* content with evasion of life, with personal complacency, we as a group are doomed. If we pass by on the other side, despising our brothers, we have no right to call ourselves men.

Crime, squalor, ugliness there are in abundance in our Catfish Rows, in our Memphis dives, in our Southwest Washington. But rushing away from them surely isn't the way to change them. And if we refuse to pay them any attention, through unwillingness to be depressed, we shall eventually, be dragged down to their level. We, or our children. And that is true "depression."

But there is more to lowliness than "lowness." If we have eyes to see, and willingness to see, we might be able to find in Mamba, an astute heroism, in Hagar a heartbreaking courage, in Porgy, a nobility, and in E. C. L. Adams' Scrip and Tad, a shrewd, philosophical irony. And all of these qualities we need, just now, to see in our group.

Because perhaps we are not so far from these characters, being identified racially with them, at least, we are revolted by Porgy's crapshooting, by Hagar's drinking, by Scarlet Sister Mary's scarletness. We want to get as far away as the end of the world. We do not see that Porgy's crapshooting is of the same fabric, fundamentally, psychologically, as a society lady's bridge playing. And upon honest investigation it conceivably might be found that it is not moral lapses that offend, so much as the showing of them, and most of all, the fact that the characters belong to a low stratum of society. Economically low, that is. No stratum has monopoly on other "lowness."

If one is concerned only with the matter of morality he could possibly remember that there is no literature which is not proud of books that treat of characters no better "morally" than Crown's Bess and Scarlet Sister Mary. But what mature audience would judge a book by the morality of its protagonist? Is *Rollo* a greater book than *Tom Jones* or even than *Tom Sawyer*?

Negro artists have enough to contend with in getting a hearing, in isolation, in the peculiar problems that beset all artists, in the mastery of form and in the understanding of life. It would be no less disastrous to demand of them that they shall evade truth, that they shall present us a Pollyanna philosophy of life, that, to suit our prejudices, they shall lie. It would mean that as self-respecting artists they could no longer exist.

The question might be asked, why should they exist? Such a question deserves no reply. It merely serves to bring us, alas, to the point at which I started.

Without great audiences we cannot have great literature.

(1930)

IO. Blueprint for Negro Writing
黑人文学的蓝图

Richard Wright
理查德·赖特

　　理查德·赖特（1908—1960），美国小说家，1908 年 9 月 24 日出生于密西西比州靠近纳齐兹的农场，母亲是教师，父亲是租种土地的农民。在他的童年与少年时期，饥饿是他的玩伴，贫穷与疾病是他们家庭的常客。在密西西比长大的赖特了解黑人生活的狭隘，以及美国种族主义的可怕，生怕自己因为说错做错（或没说没做）什么而违背了当时盛行的吉姆·克劳伦理，从而招致杀身之祸。因此，他早年与白人直接接触的生活经历让他非常紧张，认识到黑人之间的亲密关系也深受种族因素的强烈影响。他的所有作品几乎都在揭示美国黑人与白人的社会关系，无论是南方还是北方，种族的影响无处不在。

　　在 20 世纪 30 年代的大萧条时期，美国的左翼思潮比较盛行，很多黑人文学青年受其影响，赖特是其中比较有代表性的一位。他在《黑人文学的蓝图》中开宗明义地指出，过去的黑人文学非常谦卑，像循规蹈矩、端庄得体的大使，试图向美国白人证明，黑人并非低人一等，但是美国白人从来没有正眼看过这些黑人作家，更不会真的关心黑人文学在美国文化中的作用。在此情况下，黑人文学仿佛成为某种点缀，并没有针对黑人的需要，再现他们的苦难与渴望，而是祈求白人的公正。赖特认为，在黑人教堂的道德威信逐渐下降，黑人中产阶级越来越优柔寡断的情况下，黑人作家需要承担新的角色，黑人文学必须回答这个问题：黑人文学是为黑人大众写作，引导他们走向新的目标，还是继续祈求白人认可黑人的人性？赖特的回答非常明确，黑人作家必须为黑人种族创造能够为之奋斗、实践、牺牲的价值观。

The Role of Negro Writing: Two Definitions

Generally speaking, Negro writing in the past has been confined to humble novels, poems, and plays, prim and decorous ambassadors who went a-begging to white America. They entered the Court of American Public Opinion dressed in the knee-pants of servility, curtsying to show that the Negro was not inferior, that he was human, and that he had a life comparable to that of other people. For the most part these artistic ambassadors were received as though they were French poodles who do clever tricks.

White America never offered these Negro writers any serious criticism. The mere fact that a Negro could write was astonishing. Nor was there any deep concern on the part of white America with the role Negro writing should play in American culture; and the role it did play grew out of accident rather than intent or design. Either it crept in through the kitchen in the form of jokes; or it was the fruits of that foul soil which was the result of a liaison between inferiority-complexed Negro "geniuses" and burnt-out white Bohemians with money.

On the other hand, these often technically brilliant performances by Negro writers were looked upon by the majority of literate Negroes as something to be proud of. At best, Negro writing has been something external to the lives of educated Negroes themselves. That the productions of their writers should have been something of a guide in their daily living is a matter which seems never to have been raised seriously.

Under these conditions Negro writing assumed two general aspects: (1) It became a sort of conspicuous ornamentation, the hallmark of "achievement." (2) It became the voice of the educated Negro pleading with white America for justice.

Rarely was the best of this writing addressed to the Negro himself, his needs, his sufferings, his aspirations. Through misdirection, Negro writers have been far better to others than they have been to themselves. And the mere recognition of this places the whole question of Negro writing in a new light and raises a doubt as to the validity of its present direction.

The Minority Outlook

Somewhere in his writings Lenin makes the observation that oppressed minorities often reflect the techniques of the bourgeoisie more brilliantly than some sections of the bourgeoisie themselves. The psychological importance of this becomes meaningful when it is recalled that oppressed minorities, and especially the petty bourgeois sections of oppressed minorities, strive to assimilate the virtues of the bourgeoisie in the assumption that by doing so they can lift themselves into a higher social sphere. But not only among the oppressed petty bourgeoisie does this occur. The workers of a minority people, chafing under exploitation, forge organizational forms of struggle to better their lot. Lacking the handicaps of false ambition and property, they have access to a wide social vision and a deep social consciousness. They display a greater freedom and initiative in pushing their claims upon civilization than even do the petty bourgeoisie. Their organizations show greater strength, adaptability, and efficiency than any other group or class in society.

That Negro workers, propelled by the harsh conditions of their lives, have demonstrated this consciousness and mobility for economic and political action there can be no doubt. But has this consciousness been reflected in the work of Negro writers to the same degree as it has in the Negro workers' struggle to free Herndon and the Scottsboro Boys, in the drive toward unionism, in the fight against lynching? Have they as creative writers taken advantage of their unique minority position?

The answer decidedly is *no*. Negro writers have lagged sadly, and as time passes the gap widens between them and their people.

How can this hiatus be bridged? How can the enervating effects of this longstanding split be eliminated?

In presenting questions of this sort an attitude of self-consciousness and self-criticism is far more likely to be a fruitful point of departure than a mere recounting of past achievements. An emphasis upon tendency and experiment, a view of society as something becoming rather than as something fixed and admired is the one which points the way for Negro writers to stand shoulder to shoulder with Negro workers in mood and outlook.

A Whole Culture

There is, however, a culture of the Negro which is his and has been addressed to him; a culture which has, for good or ill, helped to clarify his consciousness and create emotional attitudes which are conducive to action. This culture has stemmed mainly from two sources: (1) the Negro church; and (2) the folklore of the Negro people.

It was through the portals of the church that the American Negro first entered the shrine of western culture. Living under slave conditions of life, bereft of his African heritage, the Negroes' struggle for religion on the plantations between 1820-60 assumed the form of a struggle for human rights. It remained a relatively revolutionary struggle until religion began to serve as an antidote for suffering and denial. But even today there are millions of American Negroes whose only sense of a whole universe, whose only relation to society and man, and whose only guide to personal dignity comes through the archaic morphology of Christian salvation.

It was, however, in a folklore molded out of rigorous and inhuman conditions of life that the Negro achieved his most indigenous and complete expression. Blues, spirituals, and folk tales recounted from mouth to mouth; the whispered words of a black mother to her black daughter on the ways of men, to confidential wisdom of a black father to his black son; the swapping of sex experiences on street corners from boy to boy in the deepest vernacular; work songs sung under blazing suns—all these formed the channels through which the racial wisdom flowed.

One would have thought that Negro writers in the last century of striving at expression would have continued and deepened this folk tradition, would have tried to create a more intimate and yet a more profoundly social system of artistic communication between them and their people. But the illusion that they could escape through individual achievement the harsh lot of their race swung Negro writers away from any such path. Two separate cultures sprang up: one for the Negro masses, unwritten and unrecognized; and the other for the sons and daughters of a rising Negro bourgeoisie, parasitic and mannered.

Today the question is: Shall Negro writing be for the Negro masses, molding the lives and consciousness of those masses toward new goals, or shall it continue begging the question of the Negroes' humanity?

The Problem of Nationalism in Negro Writing

In stressing the difference between the role Negro writing failed to play in the lives of the Negro people, and the role it should play in the future if it is to serve its historic function; in pointing out the fact that Negro writing has been addressed in the main to a small white audience rather than to a Negro one, it should be stated that no attempt is being made here to propagate a specious and blatant nationalism. Yet the nationalist character of the Negro people is unmistakable. Psychologically this nationalism is reflected in the whole of Negro culture, and especially in folklore.

In the absence of fixed and nourishing forms of culture, the Negro has a folklore which embodies the memories and hopes of his struggle for freedom. Not yet caught in paint or stone, and as yet but feebly depicted in the poem and novel, the Negroes' most powerful images of hope and despair still remains in the fluid state of daily speech. How many John Henrys have lived and died on the lips of these black people? How many mythical heroes in embryo have been allowed to perish for lack of husbanding by alert intelligence?

Negro folklore contains, in a measure that puts to shame more deliberate forms of Negro expression, the collective sense of Negro life in America. Let those who shy at the nationalist implications of Negro life look at this body of folklore, living and powerful, which rose out of a unified sense of a common life and a common fate. Here are those vital beginnings of a recognition of value in life as it is *lived*, a recognition that marks the emergence of a new culture in the shell of the old. And at the moment this process starts, at the moment when a people begin to realize a *meaning* in their suffering, the civilization that engenders that suffering is doomed.

The nationalist aspects of Negro life are as sharply manifest in the social institutions of Negro people as in folklore. There is a Negro church, a Negro press, a Negro social world, a Negro sporting world, a Negro business world, a Negro school system, Negro professions; in short, a Negro way of life in America. The Negro people did not ask for this, and deep down, though they express themselves through their institutions and adhere to this special way of life, they do not want it now. This special existence was forced upon them from without by lynch rope, bayonet and mob rule. They accepted these negative conditions with the inevitability of a tree which must live or perish in whatever soil it finds itself.

The few crumbs of American civilization which the Negro has got from the tables of capitalism have been through these segregated channels. Many Negro institutions are cowardly and incompetent; but they are all that the Negro has. And, in the main, any move, whether for progress or reaction, must come through these institutions for the simple reason that all other channels are closed. Negro writers who seek to mold or influence the consciousness of the Negro people must address their messages to them through the ideologies and attitudes fostered in this warping way of life.

The Basis and Meaning of Nationalism in Negro Writing

The social institutions of the Negro are imprisoned in the Jim Crow political system of the South, and this Jim Crow political system is in turn built upon a plantation-feudal economy. Hence, it can be seen that the emotional expression of group-feeling which puzzles so many whites and leads them to deplore what they call "black chauvinism" is not a morbidly inherent trait of the Negro, but rather the reflex expression of a life whose roots are imbedded deeply in Southern soil.

Negro writers must accept the nationalist implications of their lives, not in order to encourage them, but in order to change and transcend them. They must accept the concept of nationalism because, in order to transcend it, they must *possess* and *understand* it. And a nationalist spirit in Negro writing means a nationalism carrying the highest possible pitch of social consciousness. It means a nationalism that knows its origins, its limitations; that is aware of the dangers of its position; that knows its ultimate aims are unrealizable within the framework of capitalist America; a nationalism whose reason for being lies in the simple fact of self-possession and in the consciousness of the interdependence of people in modern society.

For purposes of creative expression it means that the Negro writer must realize within the area of his own personal experience those impulses which, when prefigured in terms of broad social movements, constitute the stuff of nationalism.

For Negro writers even more so than for Negro politicians, nationalism is a bewildering and vexing question, the full ramifications of which cannot be dealt with here. But among Negro workers and the Negro middle class the spirit of nationalism is rife in a hundred devious forms; and a simple literary realism which seeks to depict the lives of these people devoid of wider social connotations, devoid of the revolutionary significance of these nationalist tendencies, must of necessity do a rank injustice to the Negro people and alienate their possible allies in the struggle for freedom.

Social Consciousness and Responsibility

The Negro writer who seeks to function within his race as a purposeful agent has a serious responsibility. In order to do justice to his subject matter, in order to depict Negro life in all of its manifold and intricate relationships, a deep, informed, and complex consciousness is necessary; a consciousness which draws for its strength upon the fluid lore of a great people, and molds this lore with the concepts that move and direct the forces of history today.

With the gradual decline of the moral authority of the Negro church, and with the increasing irresolution which is paralyzing Negro middle-class leadership, a new role is devolving upon the Negro writer. He is being called upon to do no less than create values by which his race is to struggle, live and die.

By his ability to fuse and make articulate the experiences of men, because his writing possesses the potential cunning to steal into the inmost recesses of the human heart, because he can create the myths and symbols that inspire a faith in life, he may expect either to be consigned to oblivion, or to be recognized for the valued agent he is.

This raises the question of the personality of the writer. It means that in the lives of Negro writers must be found those materials and experiences which will create a meaningful picture of the world today. Many young writers have grown to believe that a Marxist analysis of society presents such a picture. It creates a picture which, when placed before the eyes of the writer, should unify his personality, organize his emotions, buttress him with a tense and obdurate will to change the world.

And, in turn, this changed world will dialectically change the writer. Hence, it is through a Marxist conception of reality and society that the maximum degree of freedom in thought and feeling can be gained for the Negro writer. Further, this dramatic Marxist vision, when consciously grasped, endows the writer with a sense of dignity which no other vision can give. Ultimately, it restores to the writer his lost heritage, that is, his role as a creator of the world in which he lives, and as a creator of himself.

Yet, for the Negro writer, Marxism is but the starting point. No theory of life can take the place of life. After Marxism has laid bare the skeleton of society, there remains the task of the writer to plant flesh upon those bones out of his will to live. He may, with disgust and revulsion, say *no* and depict the horrors of capitalism encroaching upon the human being. Or he may, with hope and passion, say *yes* and depict the faint stirrings of a new and emerging life. But in whatever social voice he chooses to speak, whether positive or negative, there should always be heard or *over-heard* his faith, his necessity, his judgement.

His vision need not be simple or rendered in primer-like terms; for the life of the Negro people is not simple. The presentation of their lives should be simple, yes; but all the complexity, the strangeness, the magic wonder of life that plays like a bright sheen over the most sordid existence, should be there. To borrow a phrase from the Russians, it should have a *complex simplicity*. Eliot, Stein, Joyce, Proust, Hemingway, and Anderson; Gorky, Barbusse, Nexo, and Jack London no less than the folklore of the Negro himself should form the heritage of the Negro writer. Every iota of gain in human thought and sensibility should be ready grist for his mill, no matter how farfetched they may seem in their immediate implications.

The Problem of Perspective

What vision must Negro writers have before their eyes in order to feel the impelling necessity for an about-face? What angle of vision can show them all the forces of modern society in process, all the lines of economic development converging toward a distant point of hope? Must they believe in some "ism"?

They may feel that only dupes believe in "isms"; they feel with some measure of justification that another commitment means only another disillusionment. But anyone destitute of a theory about the meaning, structure and direction of modern society is a lost victim in a world he cannot understand or control.

But even if Negro writers found themselves through some "ism," how would that influence their writing? Are they being called upon to "preach"? To be "salesmen"? To "prostitute" their writing? Must they "sully" themselves? Must they write "propaganda"?

No; it is a question of awareness, of consciousness; it is, above all, a question of perspective.

Perspective is that part of a poem, novel, or play which a writer never puts directly upon paper. It is that fixed point in intellectual space where a writer stands to view the struggles, hopes, and sufferings of his people. There are times when he may stand too close and the result is a blurred vision. Or he may stand too far away and the result is a neglect of important things.

Of all the problems faced by writers who as a whole have never allied themselves with world movements, perspective is the most difficult of achievements. At its best, perspective is a preconscious assumption, something which a writer takes for granted, something which he wins through his living.

A Spanish writer recently spoke of living in the heights of one's time. Surely, perspective means just *that*.

It means that a Negro writer must learn to view the life of a Negro living in New York's Harlem or Chicago's South Side with the consciousness that one-sixth of the earth surface belongs to the working class. It means that a Negro writer must create in his readers' minds a relationship between a Negro woman hoeing cotton in the South and the men who loll in swivel chairs in Wall Street and take the fruits of her toil.

Perspective for Negro writers will come when they have looked and brooded so hard and long upon the harsh lot of their race and compared it with the hopes and struggles of minority peoples everywhere that the cold facts have begun to tell them something.

The Problem of Theme

This does not mean that a Negro writer's sole concern must be with rendering the social scene; but if his conception of the life of his people is broad and deep enough, if the sense of the *whole* life he is seeking is vivid and strong in him, then his writing will embrace all those social, political, and economic forms under which the life of his people is manifest.

In speaking of theme one must necessarily be general and abstract; the temperament of each writer molds and colors the world he sees. Negro life may be approached from a thousand angles, with no limit to technical and stylistic freedom.

Negro writers spring from a family, a clan, a class, and a nation; and the social units in which they are bound have a story, a record. Sense of theme will emerge in Negro writing when Negro writers try to fix this story about some pole of meaning, remembering as they do so that in the creative process meaning proceeds *equally* as much from the contemplation of the subject matter as from the hopes and apprehensions that rage in the heart of the writer.

Reduced to its simplest and most general terms, theme for Negro writers will rise from understanding the meaning of their being transplanted from a "savage" to a "civilized" culture in all of its social, political, economic, and emotional implications. It means that Negro writers must have in their consciousness the foreshortened picture of the *whole*, nourishing culture from which they were torn in Africa, and of the long, complex (and for the most part, unconscious) struggle to regain in some form and under alien conditions of life a *whole* culture again.

It is not only this picture they must have, but also a knowledge of the social and emotional milieu that gives it tone and solidity of detail. Theme for Negro writers will emerge when they have begun to feel the meaning of the history of their race as though they in one life time had lived it themselves throughout all the long centuries.

Autonomy of Craft

For the Negro writer to depict this new reality requires a greater discipline and consciousness than was necessary for the so-called Harlem school of expression. Not only is the subject matter dealt with far more meaningful and complex, but the new role of the writer is qualitatively different. The Negro writers' new position demands a sharper definition of the status of his craft, and a sharper emphasis upon its functional autonomy.

Negro writers should seek through the medium of their craft to play as meaningful a role in the affairs of men as do other professionals. But if their writing is demanded to perform the social office of other professions, then the autonomy of craft is lost and writing detrimentally fused with other interests. The limitations of the craft constitute some of its greatest virtues. If the sensory vehicle of imaginative writing is required to carry too great a load of didactic material, the artistic sense is submerged.

The relationship between reality and the artistic image is not always direct and simple. The imaginative conception of a historical period will not be a carbon copy of reality. Image and emotion possess a logic of their own. A vulgarized simplicity constitutes the greatest danger in tracing the reciprocal interplay between the writer and his environment.

Writing has its professional autonomy; it should complement other professions, but it should not supplant them or be swamped by them.

The Necessity for Collective Work

It goes without saying that these things cannot be gained by Negro writers if their present mode of isolated writing and living continues. This isolation exists *among* Negro writers as well as *between* Negro and white writers. The Negro writers' lack of thorough integration with the American scene, their lack of a clear realization among themselves of their possible role, have bred generation after generation of embittered and defeated literati.

Barred for decades from the theater and publishing houses, Negro writers have been *made* to feel a sense of difference. So deep has this white-hot iron of exclusion been burnt into their hearts that thousands have all but lost the desire to become identified with American civilization. The Negro writers' acceptance of this enforced isolation and their attempt to justify it is but a defense-reflex of the whole special way of life which has been rammed down their throats.

This problem, by its very nature, is one which must be approached contemporaneously from *two* points of view. The ideological unity of Negro writers and the alliance of that unity with all the progressive ideas of our day is the primary prerequisite for collective work. On the shoulders of white writers and Negro writers alike rests the responsibility of ending this mistrust and isolation.

By placing cultural health above narrow sectional prejudices, liberal writers of all races can help to break the stony soil of aggrandizement out of which the stunted plants of Negro nationalism grow. And, simultaneously, Negro writers can help to weed out these choking growths of reactionary nationalism and replace them with hardier and sturdier types.

These tasks are imperative in light of the fact that we live in a time when the majority of the most basic assumptions of life can no longer be taken for granted. Tradition is no longer a guide. The world has grown huge and cold. Surely this is the moment to ask questions, to theorize, to speculate, to wonder out of what materials can a human world be built.

Each step along this unknown path should be taken with thought, care, self-consciousness, and deliberation. When Negro writers think they have arrived at something which smacks of truth, humanity, they should want to test it with others, feel it with a degree of passion and strength that will enable them to communicate it to millions who are groping like themselves.

Writers faced with such tasks can have no possible time for malice or jealousy. The conditions for the growth of each writer depend too much upon the good work of other writers. Every first-rate novel, poem, or play lifts the level of consciousness higher.

(1937)

II. American Negro Literature

美国的黑人文学

J. Saunders Redding

桑德斯·雷丁

桑德斯·雷丁(1906—1988),教育家、批评家,1906 年 10 月 13 日出生于特拉华州的威尔明顿,1928 年获得布朗大学的学士学位,1932 年获得艺术硕士学位。雷丁在多所黑人与白人的学院任教,如莫尔豪斯学院、南方大学、汉普顿学院、乔治·华盛顿大学和康奈尔大学等。他对非裔美国思想的最大贡献体现在批评黑人民族主义,重新审视杜波伊斯提出的双重意识的概念,认为杜波伊斯的双重意识对黑人的心理健康有负面影响。

雷丁的《美国的黑人文学》简要梳理了 20 世纪上半叶美国黑人文学的发展,并重点分析了几个重要阶段美国黑人文学的主要特征,是我们了解 20 世纪上半叶美国黑人文学发展的重要批评文献。他简要分析了 1907 年前以邓巴和切斯纳特为代表的诗人与小说家面对种族歧视的严峻形势所做的妥协,以及在新黑人的发展过程中,黑人作家抗争意识的觉醒,特别是自 20 世纪 30 年代末 40 年代初以来,黑人作家可以逐步摆脱要么为黑人读者创作要么为白人读者创作的困境,能够愈发真诚地描绘黑人生活的进步。此外,雷丁选取不同时段的代表性作家进行分析,比如说,诗人邓巴当时不得不根据白人读者可能的接受程度,创作为白人读者所认可的方言诗歌;布克·华盛顿的文化妥协姿态及其影响;以杜波伊斯为代表的黑人知识分子对华盛顿的反批评;新黑人文艺复兴的自我意识与实验性特征,特别是赖特 30 年代末 40 年代初对种族隔离时代黑人的"临床研究"等。雷丁认为,美国黑人文学目前已经进入健康发展的阶段,也会迎来更加光明的未来。

There is this about literature by American Negroes—it has uncommon resilience. Three times within this century it has been done nearly to death: once by indifference, once by opposition, and once by the unbounded enthusiasm of its well-meaning friends.

By 1906, Charles W. Chesnutt, the best writer of prose fiction the race had produced, was silent; Paul Laurence Dunbar, the most popular poet, was dead. After these two, at least in the general opinion, there were no other Negro writers. Booker Washington had published *Up from Slavery*, but Washington was no writer—he was the orator and the organizer of the march to a questionable new Canaan. The poetic prose of Du Bois, throbbing in *The Souls of Black Folk*, had not yet found its audience. Polemicists like Monroe Trotter, Kelly, Miller and George Forbes were faint whispers in a lonesome wood. Indifference had stopped the ears of all but the most enlightened who, as often as not, were derisively labeled "nigger lovers."

But this indifference had threatened even before the turn of the century. Dunbar felt it, and the purest stream of his lyricism was made bitter and all but choked by it. Yearning for the recognition of his talent as it expressed itself in the pure English medium, he had to content himself with a kindly, but condescending praise of his dialect pieces. Time and again he voiced the sense of frustration brought on by the neglect of what he undoubtedly considered his best work. Writing dialect, he told James Weldon Johnson, was "the only way he could get them to listen to him." His literary friend and sponsor, William D. Howells, at that time probably the most influential critic in America, passing over Dunbar's verse in pure English with only a glance, urged him to write "of his own race in its own accents of our English."

During Dunbar's lifetime, his pieces in pure English appeared more or less on sufferance. The very format of the 1901 edition of *Lyrics of the Hearthside*, the book in which most of his nondialect poetry was published, suggests this. No fancy binding on this book, no handsome paper, no charming, illustrative photographs. *Lyrics of the Hearthside* was the least publicized of all his books of poetry, and four lines from his "The Poet" may tell why.

> He sang of love when earth was young,
>
> And love itself was in his lays,
>
> But, ah, the world it turned to praise
>
> A jingle in a broken tongue.

Enough has been said about the false concepts, the stereotypes which were effective—and to some extent are still effective—in white America's thinking about the Negro for the point not to be labored here. History first, and then years of insidious labor to perpetuate what history had wrought, created these stereotypes. According to them, the Negro was a buffoon, a harmless child of nature, a dangerous despoiler (the concepts were contradictory), an irresponsible beast of devilish cunning—soulless, ambitionless and depraved. The Negro, in short, was a higher species of some creature that was not quite man.

What this has done to writing by American Negroes could easily be imagined, even without the documentation, which is abundant. No important critic of writing by American Negroes has failed to note the influence of the concept upon it. Sterling Brown, one of the more searching scholars in the field, gives it scathing comment in "The Negro Author and His Publisher." James Weldon Johnson touches upon it in his preface to the 1931 edition of his anthology, but he does so even more cogently in "The Negro Author's Dilemma." The introduction to Countee Cullen's *Caroling Dusk* is a wry lament over it. In *The New Negro*, Alain Locke expresses the well-founded opinion that the Negro "has been a stock figure perpetuated as an historical fiction partly in innocent sentimentalism, partly in deliberate reactionism."

There can be no question as to the power of the traditional concepts. The Negro writer reacted to them in one of two ways. Either he bowed down to them, writing such stories as would do them no violence; or he went to the opposite extreme and wrote for the purpose of invalidating, or at least denying, the tradition. Dunbar did the former. Excepting only a few, his short stories depict Negro characters as whimsical, simple, folksy, not-too-bright souls, all of whose social problems are little ones, and all of whose emotional cares can be solved by the intellectual or spiritual equivalent of a stick of red peppermint candy. It is of course significant that three of his four novels are not about Negroes at all; and the irony of depicting himself as a white youth in his spiritual autobiography, *The Uncalled*, needs no comment.

Charles Chesnutt's experience is also to the point. When his stories began appearing in the *Atlantic Monthly* in 1887, it was not generally known that their author was a Negro. Stories like "The Gray Wolf's Ha'nt" and "The Goophered Grapevine" were so detached and objective that the author's race could not have been detected from a reading of them. The editor of the *Atlantic Monthly*, Walter H. Page, fearing that public acknowledgment of it would do the author's work harm, was reluctant to admit that Chesnutt was a Negro, and the fact of his race was kept a closely guarded secret for a decade. It was this same fear that led to the rejection of Chesnutt's first novel, *The House Behind the Cedars*, for "a literary work by an American of acknowledged color was a doubtful experiment... entirely apart from its intrinsic merit." The reception of Chesnutt's later books—those that came after 1900—was to prove that literary works by an "American of color" were more than doubtful experiments. *The Colonels Dream* and *The Marrow of Tradition* did not pay the cost of the paper and the printing. They were honest probings at the heart of a devilish problem; they were, quite frankly, propaganda. But the thing that made the audience of the day indifferent to them was their attempt to override the concepts that were the props of the dialect tradition. Had Chesnutt not had a reputation as a writer of short stories (which are, anyway, his best work), it is likely that his novels would not have been published at all.

The poetry of Dunbar and the prose of Chesnutt proved that even with the arbitrary limitations imposed upon them by historical convention, Negro writers could rise to heights of artistic expression. They could even circumvent the convention, albeit self-consciously; and create credible white characters in a credible white milieu.

II

After about 1902, indifference began to crystallize into opposition to the culture-conscious, race-conscious Negro seeking honest answers to honest questions. It was opposition to the Negro's democratic ambitions which were just then beginning to burgeon. It was opposition to the Negro who was weary of his role of clown, scapegoat, doormat. And it was, of course, opposition to the Negro writer who was honest and sincere and anxious beyond the bounds of superimposed racial polity.

There is danger here of oversimplifying a long and complex story. Even with the advantage of hindsight, it is hard to tell what is cause and what is effect. But let us have a look at some of the more revealing circumstances. In 1902 came Thomas Dixon's *The Leopard's Spots*, and three years later *The Clansman*. They were both tremendously popular. In 1906 there were race riots in Georgia and Texas, in 1908 in Illinois. ... By this later year, too, practically all of the Southern states had disfranchised the Negro and made color caste legal. ... The Negro's talent for monkeyshines had been exploited on the stage, and coon songs (some by James Weldon Johnson and his brother!) had attained wide popularity. Meantime, in 1904, Thomas Nelson Page had published the bible of reactionism, *The Negro, the Southerner's Problem*. And, probably most cogent fact of all, Booker Washington had reached the position of undisputed leader of American Negroes by advocating a racial policy strictly in line with the traditional concept.

There had been a time when the old concept of the Negro had served to ease his burden. He had been laughed at, tolerated, and genially despaired of as hopeless in a modern, dynamic society. White Americans had become used to a myth—had, indeed, convinced themselves that myth was reality. All the instruments of social betterment—

schools, churches, lodges—adopted by colored people were the subjects of ribald jokes and derisive laughter. Even the fact that the speeches which Booker Washington was making up and down the country could have been made only by a really intelligent and educated man did not strike them as a contradiction of the concept. And anyway, there was this about Washington: he was at least half-white, and white blood in that proportion excused and accounted for many a thing, including being intelligent, lunching with President Theodore Roosevelt, and getting an honorary degree from Harvard.

Today any objective judgment of Booker Washington's basic notion must be that it was an extension of the old tradition framed in new terms. He preached a message of compromise, of humility, of patience. Under the impact of social change the concept was modified to include the stereotype of the Negro as satisfied peasant, a docile servitor under the stern but kindly eye of the white boss; a creature who had a place, knew it, and would keep it unless he got *bad* notions from somewhere. The merely laughable coon had become also the cheap laborer who could be righteously exploited for his own good and to the greater glory of God. By this addition to the concept, the Negro-white status quo—the condition of inferior-superior caste—could be maintained in the face of profound changes in the general society.

What this meant to the Negro artist and writer was that he must, if he wished an audience, adhere to the old forms and the acceptable patterns. It meant that he must work within the limitations of the concept, or ignore his racial kinship altogether and leave unsounded the profoundest depths of the peculiar experiences which were his by reason of his race. But fewer and fewer Negro writers were content with the limitations. The number of dialect pieces (the term includes the whole tradition) written after 1907 is very small indeed. Among Negro writers the tradition had lost its force and its validity. White writers like Julia Peterkin and Gilmore Millen, and, in a different way, Carl Van Vechten and Du Bose Heyward, were to lend it a spurious strength down through the 1920's.

Negro writers of unmistakable talent chose the second course, and some of them won high critical praise for their work in nonracial themes. Their leader was William Stanley Braithwaite. Save only a few essays written at the behest of his friend, W. E. B. Du Bois, nothing that came from his pen had anything about it to mark it as Negro. His leading essays in the Boston *Transcript*, his anthologies of magazine verse, and his own poetry, might just as well have been written by someone with no background in the provocative experience of being colored in America.

Though the other Negro poets of this genre (which was not entirely a genre) developed a kind of dilettantist virtuosity, none carried it to Braithwaite's amazing lengths of self-conscious contrivance. They were simpler and more conventional in their apostasy. Alice Dunbar, the widow of Paul, wrote sonnets of uncommon skill and beauty. Georgia Johnson and Anne Spenser were at home in the formal lyric, and James Weldon Johnson in "The White Witch" and "My City" set a very high standard for his fellow contributors to the *Century Magazine*.

But given the whole web of circumstance—empirical, historic, racial, psychological—these poets must have realized that they could not go on in this fashion. With a full tide of race-consciousness bearing in upon them individually and as a group, they could not go on forever denying their racehood. To try to do this at all was symptomatic of neurotic strain. They could not go on, and they did not. The hardiest of them turned to expression of another kind the moment the pressure was off.

The pressure was not off for another decade and a half. As a matter of fact, it mounted steadily. For all of Booker Washington's popularity and ideological appeal among whites, who had set him up as *the* leader of the Negro race, and for all of his power, there was rebellion against him in the forward ranks of Negroes. Rebellion against Washington meant dissatisfaction with the social and economic goals which he had persuaded white Americans were the proper goals for the Negro race. The whites had not counted on this disaffection, and their reaction to it was willful, blind opposition.

What had happened was that Booker Washington, with the help of the historic situation and the old concept, had so thoroughly captured the minds of most of those white people who were kindly disposed to Negroes that not another Negro had a chance to be heard. Negro schools needing help could get it from rich and powerful whites only through Booker Washington. Negro social thought wanting a sounding board could have it only with the sanction of the Principal of Tuskegee. Negro politicians were helpless without his endorsement. Negro seekers after jobs of any consequence in either public or private capacities begged recommendations from Booker Washington.

This despotic power—and there is scarcely another term for it—was stultifying to many intelligent Negroes, especially in the North. White editors, who would have published anything under the signature of Booker Washington, consistently rejected all but the most innocuous work of other Negroes. Publishers were not interested in the ideas of Negroes unless those ideas conformed to Washington's, or in creative work by and about Negroes unless they fell into the old pattern.

So intelligent, articulate Negroes grew insurgent, and the leader of this insurgence was W. E. B. Du Bois. Nor wash is the only voice raised in protest. Charles Chesnutt spoke out, and so did John Hope and Kelly Miller. In 1900 the *Chicago Defender* had been founded, and in 1901 Monroe Trotter's *Boston Guardian*. Courageous as these polemical organs were, they had not yet grown into full effectiveness. Neither had Du Bois, but he was growing fast. By 1903 the Atlanta University Studies of the Negro were coming out regularly under his editorship. In that year he published *The Souls of Black Folk*, which contained the essay "Of Mr. Booker T. Washington and Others," sharply critical of the Tuskegee leader. Du Bois was in on the founding of the National Association for the Advancement of Colored People, and in 1910 he became editor of the new monthly, the *Crisis*.

From the very first the *Crisis* was much more than the official organ of the NAACP. It was a platform for the expression of all sorts of ideas that ran counter to the notion of Negro inferiority. Excepting such liberal and non-popular journals as the *Atlantic Monthly* and *World's Work* and the two or three Negro newspapers that had not been bought or throttled by the "Tuskegee Machine," the *Crisis* was the only voice the Negro had. The opposition to that voice was organized around the person and the philosophy of Booker Washington, and there were times when this opposition all but drowned out the voice.

Nevertheless protestation and revolt were becoming bit by bit more powerful reagents in the social chemistry that produced the New Negro. Year by year more Negroes were transformed—and a lot of them needed transforming. Once James Weldon Johnson himself had written "coon songs" and been content to carol with sweet humility "Lift Every Voice and Sing." When Johnson wrote it in 1900, it had the approval of Booker Washington and became the "Negro National Anthem." Then followed Johnson's period of apostasy and such jejune pieces as "The Glory of the Day Was in Her Face," among others. But in 1912, when he was already forty-one, he wrote the novel *The Autobiography of an Ex-Colored Man*, and in 1917 he cried out bitterly that Negroes must cease speaking "servile words" and must "stand erect and without fear."

III

Other factors than simple protest contributed to the generation of the New Negro. In the first place, the notions regarding the Old Negro were based on pure myth. The changes occurring at the onset of war in Europe sloughed off some of the emotional and intellectual accretions, and the Negro stood partially revealed for what he was—a fellow whose opportunities had been narrowed by historical fallacies, "a creature of moral debate," but a man pretty much as other men. The war, which made him an intersectional migrant, proved that he, too, sought more economic opportunities, the protection of laws even handedly administered, the enlargement of democracy. He, too, was a seeker for the realities in the American dream.

But when in 1917 the Negro was called upon to protect that dream with his blood, he revealed himself more fully. He asked questions and demanded answers. Whose democracy? he wanted to know; and why, and wherefore? There followed the promises, which were certainly sincerely meant in the stress of the times. Then came the fighting and dying—and, finally, came a thing called Peace. But in 1919 and after, there were the race riots in the nation's capital, in Chicago, in Chester, Pennsylvania, and in East St. Louis.

By this time the New Negro movement was already stirring massively along many fronts. In the 1920's Negroes cracked through the prejudices that had largely confined them to supernumerary roles on Broadway. *Shuffle Along* was praised as "a sparkling, all-Negro musical of unusual zest and talent." Charles Gilpin's portrayal of the Emperor Jones was the dramatic triumph of 1921. The Garvey Movement, fast getting out of bounds, swept the country like a wildfire. James Weldon Johnson published an anthology of Negro verse. The monumental historical studies of the Negro were begun by Carter Woodson. *The Gift of Black Folk*, *Color*, *Fire in the Flint*, *Weary Blues*, *Gods Trombones*, *Walls of Jericho*, and *Home to Harlem* had all been published, read, discussed, praised or damned by 1928.

Fortunately some of the talents that produced these works were genuine. Had this not been so, the New Negro movement in art and literature would surely have come to nothing. The best of Johnson, Hughes, Cullen, McKay, Fisher and Du Bois would have lived without the movement, but the movement without them would have gone the way of mah-jongg. Their work considerably furthered the interest of white writers and critics in Negro material and Negro art expression. Whatever else Eugene O'Neill,

Paul Rosenfeld and Du Bose Heyward did, they gave validity to the new concept of the Negro as material for serious artistic treatment.

Writing by Negroes beginning with this period and continuing into the early thirties had two distinct aspects. The first of these was extremely arty, self-conscious and experimental. Jean Toomer's *Cane* and the "racial-rhythm" and jazz-rhythm poetry of Hughes represent it most notably, while the magazines *Harlem* and *Fire*, which published a quantity of nonsense by writers unheard of since, were its special organs. But the times were themselves arty and experimental. That Negro writers could afford to be touched by these influences was a good sign. It was healthy for them to be blown upon by the winds of literary freedom—even of license—that blew upon e. e. cummings, Dos Passos and Hemingway. If their self-conscious experimentation proved nothing lasting, it at least worked no harm.

One searches in vain for a phrase to characterize the exact impulses behind the second aspect, which is the one best remembered. It was chock—full of many contradictory things. It showed itself naive and sophisticated, hysterical and placid, frivolous and sober, free and enslaved. It is simple enough to attribute this contrariety to the effects of the war; but the atavistic release of certain aberrant tendencies in writing by Negroes in this period cannot be matched in all the rest of contemporary writing. The period produced the poignant beauty of Johnson's *Gods Trombones* and the depressing futility of Thurman's *The Blacker the Berry*. Within a span of five years McKay wrote the wholesome *Banjo* and the pointlessly filthy *Banana Bottom*. The Hughes who wrote "I've Known Rivers" and "Mother to Son" could also find creative satisfaction in the bizarre "The Cat and the Saxophone."

The mass mind of white America fastened upon the exotic and the atavistic elements and fashioned them into a fad, the commercialized products of which were manufactured in Harlem. That that Harlem itself was largely synthetic did not seem to matter. It was "nigger heaven." There, the advertised belief was, Dullness was dethroned; Gaiety was king! The rebels from Sauk Center and Winesburg, Main Street and Park Avenue, sought carnival in Harlem. "Life," the burden of the dithyrambics ran, "had surge and sweep there, and blood-pounding savagery."

Commercialism was the bane of the Negro renaissance of the twenties. Jazz music became no longer the uninhibited expression of unlearned music-makers, but a highly sophisticated pattern of musical sounds. The "Charleston" and the "Black Bottom" went down to Broadway and Park Avenue. Losing much of its folk value, the blues became the "torch song" eloquently sung by Ruth Etting and Helen Morgan. Negro material passed into the less sincere hands of white artists, and Negro writers themselves, from a high pitch of creation, fell relatively and pathetically silent.

IV

When Richard Wright's *Uncle Tom's Children* was published in 1938, only the least aware did not realize that a powerful new pen was employing itself in stern and terrible material; when *Native Son* appeared in 1940, even the least aware realized it. The first book is a clinical study of human minds under the stress of violence; the second is a clinical study of the social being under the cumulative effects of organized repression. The two books complement each other. The theme of both is prejudice, conceptual prejudgment—the effects of this upon the human personality. For Wright deals only incidentally—and for dramatic purposes, and because of the authenticity of empiricism—with *Negro* and *white*. "Bigger Thomas was not black all the time," Wright wrote in "How Bigger Was Born." "He was white, too, and there were literally millions of him, *everywhere*.... Certain modern experiences were creating types of personalities whose existence ignored racial and national lines. ... "

Some critics have said that the wide appeal of Wright's work (it has been translated into a dozen languages) is due to the sensationalism in it, but one can have serious doubts that the sensationalism comes off well in translation. What does come off well is the concept of the primary evil of prejudice. This all peoples would understand, and a delineation of its effects, particular though it be, interests them in the same way and for the same reason that love interests them. *Black Boy*, which does not prove the point, does not deny it either. Even here it may be argued that Wright delineates and skewers home the point that "to live habitually as a superior among inferiors ... is a temptation and a hubris, inevitably deteriorating."

So Wright is a new kind of writer in the ranks of Negroes. He has extricated himself from the dilemma of writing exclusively for a Negro audience and limiting himself to a glorified and race-proud picture of Negro life, and of writing exclusively for a white audience and being trapped in the old stereotypes and fixed opinions that are bulwarks against honest creation. Negro writers traditionally have been impaled upon one or the other horn of this dilemma, sometimes in spite of their efforts to avoid it. Langston Hughes was sincere when he declared, back in the twenties, that Negro writers cared nothing for the pleasure or displeasure of either a white or a colored audience—he was sincere, but mistaken.

A writer writes for an audience. Until recently Negro writers have not believed that the white audience and the colored audience were essentially alike, because, in fact, they have not been essentially alike. They have been kept apart by a wide sociocultural gulf, by differences of concept, by cultivated fears, ignorance, race- and caste-consciousness. Now that gulf is closing, and Negro writers are finding it easier to appeal to the two audiences without being either false to the one or subservient to the other. Thus Margaret Walker, writing for the two audiences now becoming one, can carry away an important poetry prize with her book *For My People*. No longer fearing the ancient interdiction, Chester Himes in *If He Hollers Let Him Go* and *Lonely Crusade* writes of the sexual attraction a white woman feels for a Negro man. In *Knock On Any Door* Willard Motley can concern himself almost entirely with white characters. On the purely romantic and escapist side, Frank Yerby's *The Foxes of Harrow* sells over a million copies, and *The Vixens* and *The Golden Hawk* over a half-million each. Anthologists no longer think it risky to collect, edit and issue the works of Negro writers.

Facing up to the tremendous challenge of appealing to two audiences, Negro writers are extricating themselves from what has sometimes seemed a terrifying dilemma. Working honestly in the material they know best, they are creating for themselves a new freedom. Though what is happening seems very like a miracle, it has been a long, long time preparing. Writing by American Negroes has never before been in such a splendid state of health, nor had so bright and shining a future before it.

(1949)

12. What White Publishers Won't Print
白人出版人不愿印刷什么

Zora Neale Hurston

佐拉·尼尔·赫斯顿

佐拉·尼尔·赫斯顿（1891—1960），小说家、人类学家，民俗学家，1891 年 1 月 7 日出生于亚拉巴马州的诺塔萨尔加村。赫斯顿在家中八个孩子中排行第五。后来全家定居于美国第一个混合的黑人社区伊顿维尔，她在此处度过了无忧无虑的童年时光。1918—1924 年，她断断续续地在霍华德大学英语专业读书，后来到纽约，结识了休斯、卡伦、赫斯特、迈耶、威克腾等人；1926 年 9 月到伯纳德学院读书，是该校唯一的黑人学生，跟随博厄斯教授学习人类学，在博厄斯的帮助下，她获得科研资助；1927 年 2 月，离开纽约来到南方的家乡收集民间故事、灵歌、布道、劳动号子、布鲁斯与儿童游戏等；1935 年出版第一部美国黑人民间故事《骡子与人》（*Mules and Men*）。赫斯顿是哈莱姆文艺复兴时期最多产的黑人女作家，出版了四部小说，两部民俗著作，一部自传。她不仅是美国最重要的非裔美国民俗收集者，也是黑人妇女主义思想的重要先驱。

她在《白人出版人不愿印刷什么》一文中指出，盎格鲁-撒克逊人对黑人的内在生活与情感缺乏兴趣，她觉得很奇怪，因为出版社与剧院为了赚钱，会想尽办法支持那些销路好的作品，如果他们不愿意做，这只能说明，公众对此没有什么兴趣。赫斯顿认为，公众能够接受"不够典型"的白人，但是却很难接受"不够典型"的黑人，其实黑人与其他种族的人并没有什么大的区别，既不更好也不更糟，如果文学只描绘片面、"例外"与"奇怪"的黑人，那么就很难描绘美国黑人生活的真实图景，这不仅违背文学应该再现自然的伟大原则，也将最终妨碍黑人文学的健康发展。

I have been amazed by the Anglo-Saxon's lack of curiosity about the internal lives and emotions of the Negroes, and for that matter, any non-Anglo-Saxon peoples within our borders, above the class of unskilled labor.

This lack of interest is much more important than it seems at first glance. It is even more important at this time than it was in the past. The internal affairs of the nation have bearings on the international stress and strain, and this gap in the national literature now has tremendous weight in world affairs. National coherence and solidarity is implicit in a thorough understanding of the various groups within a nation, and this lack of knowledge about the internal emotions and behavior of the minorities cannot fail to bar out understanding. Man, like all the other animals fears and is repelled by that which he does not understand, and mere difference is apt to connote something malign.

The fact that there is no demand for incisive and full-dress stories around Negroes above the servant class is indicative of something of vast importance to this nation. This blank is NOT filled by the fiction built around upperclass Negroes exploiting the race problem. Rather, it tends to point it up. A college-bred Negro still is not a person like other folks, but an interesting problem, more or less. It calls to mind a story of slavery time. In this story, a master with more intellectual curiosity than usual, set out to see how much he could teach a particularly bright slave of his. When he had gotten him up to higher mathematics and to be a fluent reader of Latin, he called in a neighbor to show off his brilliant slave, and to argue that Negroes had brains just like the slave-owners had, and given the same opportunities, would turn out the same.

The visiting master of slaves looked and listened, tried to trap the literate slave in Algebra and Latin, and failing to do so in both, turned to his neighbor and said:

"Yes, he certainly knows his higher mathematics, and he can read Latin better than many white men I know, but I cannot bring myself to believe that he understands a thing that he is doing. It is all an aping of our culture. All on the outside. You are crazy if you think that it has changed him inside in the least. Turn him loose, and he will revert at once to the jungle. He is still a savage, and no amount of translating Virgil and Ovid is going to change him. In fact, all you have done is to turn a useful savage into a dangerous beast."

That was in slavery time, yes, and we have come a long, long way since then, but the troubling thing is that there are still too many who refuse to believe in the ingestion and digestion of western culture as yet. Hence the lack of literature about the higher emotions and love life of upperclass Negroes and the minorities in general.

Publishers and producers are cool to the idea. Now, do not leap to the conclusion that editors and producers constitute a special class of unbelievers. That is far from true. Publishing houses and theatrical promoters are in business to make money. They will sponsor anything that they believe will sell. They shy away from romantic stories about Negroes and Jews because they feel that they know the public indifference to such works, unless the story or play involves racial tension. It can then be offered as a study in Sociology, with the romantic side subdued. They know the skepticism in general about the complicated emotions in the minorities. The average American just cannot conceive of it, and would be apt to reject the notion, and publishers and producers take the stand that they are not in business to educate, but to make money. Sympathetic as they might be, they cannot afford to be crusaders.

In proof of this, you can note various publishers and producers edging forward a little, and ready to go even further when the trial balloons show that the public is ready for it. This public lack of interest is the nut of the matter.

The question naturally arises as to the why of this indifference, not to say skepticism, to the internal life of educated minorities.

The answer lies in what we may call THE AMERICAN MUSEUM OF UNNATURAL HISTORY. This is an intangible built on folk belief. It is assumed that all non-Anglo-Saxons are uncomplicated stereotypes. Everybody knows all about them. They are lay figures mounted in the museum where all may take them in at a glance. They are made of bent wires without insides at all. So how could anybody write a book about the nonexistent?

The American Indian is a contraption of copper wires in an eternal war-bonnet, with no equipment for laughter, expressionless face and that says "How" when spoken to. His only activity is treachery leading to massacres. Who is so dumb as not to know all about Indians, even if they have never seen one, nor talked with anyone who ever knew one?

The American Negro exhibit is a group of two. Both of these mechanical toys are built so that their feet eternally shuffle, and their eyes pop and roll. Shuffling feet and those popping, rolling eyes denote the Negro, and no characterization is genuine without this monotony. One is seated on a stump picking away on his banjo and singing and laughing. The other is a most amoral character before a sharecropper's shack mumbling about injustice. Doing this makes him out to be a Negro "intellectual." It is as simple as all that.

The whole museum is dedicated to the convenient "typical." In there is the "typical" Oriental, Jew, Yankee, Westerner, Southerner, Latin, and even out-of-favor Nordics like the German. The Englishman "I say old chappie," and the gesticulating Frenchman. The least observant American can know them all at a glance.

However，the public willingly accepts the untypical in Nordics，but feels cheated if the untypical is portrayed in others. The author of *Scarlet Sister Mary* complained to me that her neighbors objected to her book on the grounds that she had the characters thinking，"and everybody know that Nigras don't think."

But for the national welfare，it is urgent to realize that the minorities do think，and think about something other than the race problem. That they are very human and internally，according to natural endowment，are just like everybody else. So long as this is not conceived，there must remain that feeling of unsurmountable difference，and difference to the average man means something bad. If people were made right，they would be just like him.

The trouble with the purely problem arguments is that they leave too much unknown. Argue all you will or may about injustice，but as long as the majority cannot conceive of a Negro or a Jew feeling and reacting inside just as they do，the majority will keep right on believing that people who do not look like them cannot possibly feel as they do，and conform to the established pattern. It is well known that there must be a body of waived matter，let us say，things accepted and taken for granted by all in a community before there can be that commonality of feeling. The usual phrase is having things in common. Until this is thoroughly established in respect to Negroes in America，as well as of other minorities，it will remain impossible for the majority to conceive of a Negro experiencing a deep and abiding love and not just the passion of sex. That a great mass of Negroes can be stirred by the pageants of Spring and Fall；the extravaganza of summer，and the majesty of winter. That they can and do experience discovery of the numerous subtle faces as a foundation for a great and selfless love，and the diverse nuances that go to destroy that love as with others. As it is now，this capacity，this evidence of high and complicated emotions，is ruled out. Hence the lack of interest in a romance uncomplicated by the race struggle has so little appeal.

This insistence on defeat in a story where upperclass Negroes are portrayed，perhaps says something from the subconscious of the majority. Involved in western culture，the hero or the heroine，or both，must appear frustrated and go down to defeat，somehow. Our literature reeks with it. Is it the same as saying，"You can translate Virgil，and fumble with the differential calculus，but can you really comprehend it? Can you cope with our subtleties?" That brings us to the folklore of "reversion to type." This curious doctrine has such wide acceptance that it is tragic. One has only to examine the huge literature on it to be convinced. No matter how high we may *seem* to climb, put us under strain and we revert to type, that is, to the bush. Under a superficial layer of western culture, the jungle drums throb in our veins.

This ridiculous notion makes it possible for that majority who accept it to conceive of even a man like the suave and scholarly Dr. Charles S. Johnson to hide a black cat's bone on his person, and indulge in a midnight voodoo ceremony, complete with leopard skin and drums if threatened with the loss of the presidency of Fisk University, or the love of his wife. "Under the skin... better to deal with them in business, etc., but otherwise keep them at a safe distance and under control. I tell you, Carl Van Vechten, think as you like, but they are just not like us."

But the opening wedge for better understanding has been thrust into the crack. Though many Negroes denounced Carl Van Vechten's *Nigger Heaven* because of the title, and without ever reading it, the book, written in the deepest sincerity, revealed Negroes of wealth and culture to the white public. It created curiosity even when it aroused skepticism. It made folks want to know. Worth Tuttle Hedden's *The Other Room* has definitely widened the opening. Neither of these well-written works take a romance of upperclass Negro life as the central theme, but the atmosphere and the background is there. These works should be followed up by some incisive and intimate stories from the inside.

The realistic story around a Negro insurance official, dentist, general practitioner, undertaker and the like would be most revealing. Thinly disguised fiction around the well known Negro names is not the answer, either. The "exceptional" as well as the Ol' Man Rivers has been exploited all out of context already. Everybody is already resigned to the "exceptional" Negro, and willing to be entertained by the "quaint." To grasp the penetration of western civilization in a minority, it is necessary to know how the average behaves and lives. Books that deal with people like in Sinclair Lewis' *Main Street* is the necessary metier. For various reasons, the average, struggling, nonmorbid Negro is the best-kept secret in America. His revelation to the public is the thing needed to do away with that feeling of difference which inspires fear, and which ever expresses itself in dislike.

It is inevitable that this knowledge will destroy many illusions and romantic traditions which America probably likes to have around. But then, we have no record of anybody sinking into a lingering death on finding out that there was no Santa Claus. The old world will take it in its stride. The realization that Negroes are no better nor no worse, and at times just as boring as everybody else, will hardly kill off the population of the nation.

Outside of racial attitudes, there is still another reason why this literature should exist. Literature and other arts are supposed to hold up the mirror to nature. With only the fractional "exceptional" and the "quaint" portrayed, a true picture of Negro life in America cannot be. A great principle of national art has been violated.

These are the things that publishers and producers, as the accredited representatives of the American people, have not as yet taken into consideration sufficiently. Let there be light!

(1950)

13. Twentieth-Century Fiction and the Black Mask of Humanity
20 世纪小说与黑色人性面具

Ralph Ellison
拉尔夫·艾里森

拉尔夫·艾里森（1914—1994），美国小说家、学者与批评家，1914 年 3 月 1 日出生于俄克拉何马市，虽然该地当时还属于边远地区，但是种族歧视同样比较严重。1931 年艾里森高中毕业，获得奖学金，1933 年他因路费不足扒货车去塔斯基吉学院读书，学习音乐和雕塑，梦想成为一名音乐家。在学院图书馆勤工助学时，他开始阅读现代主义文学，随后对文学产生浓厚兴趣。1936 年夏天，他离开塔斯基吉到纽约打工，遇见休斯等人，在赖特的鼓励下进行创作。代表作《看不见的人》（*Invisible Man*，1952）获得美国国家图书奖，后有两部批评文集出版，《影子与行动》（*Shadow and Act*，1964）和《去高地》（*Going to the Territory*，1986）奠定其小说家与批评家的地位。他把很多著名白人作家，如艾略特、詹姆斯、马克·吐温、海明威、麦尔维尔、陀思妥耶夫斯基、福克纳等视为自己的文学祖先，把著名黑人作家赖特与休斯等视为自己的文学亲戚，体现了自己的文学趣味及其对欧美主流文学传统的认同。

艾里森的这篇文章《20 世纪小说与黑色人性面具》写于 1946 年，发表于 1953 年，在对比分析 20 世纪美国文学如何继承 19 世纪文学传统的同时，重点聚焦三位美国经典作家马克·吐温、海明威和福克纳与美国文学中的道德意识和民主传统的联系。马克·吐温笔下的哈克选择相信自己的良知而非世人认可的法律，把逃奴吉姆视为和自己一样的人，清楚表明自己的基本道德立场，成为美国文学中的宝贵遗产。相比较而言，海明威则比较忽略这层道德意识，更加重视马克·吐温实现这一目的所采取的技术手段。福克纳则接过马克·吐温留下来的这个问题，很多作品都在尝试解决 19 世纪以后受压制的道德问题。如果美国作家无视或对黑人及其他少数族裔进行刻板化处理，那终将扭曲他们自己的人性。马克·吐温相信，在美国，人性戴着黑人性的面具。

有论者指出，即便艾里森没有创作小说《看不见的人》，他的文学与文化批评成果也足以使他成为当之无愧的批评家。他超越了美国 20 世纪中叶种族逻辑的局限性，既是伟大的小说家，同时也是伟大的批评家，其论文与小说一样具有非同寻常的价值。

When this essay was published in 1953, it was prefaced with the following note:

"*When I started rewriting this essay* it *occurred* to me *that* its *value might be somewhat increased if* it *remained very much as I wrote* it *during 1946. For in that form* it is *what a young member of a minority felt about much of our writing. Thus I've left in much of the bias and short-sightedness*, *for* it *says perhaps as much about* me *as a member of a minority as* it *does about literature. I hope you still find the essay useful*, *and I'd like* to *see an editorial note stating that this* is *an unpublished piece written not long after the Second World War*."

Perhaps the most insidious and least understood form of segregation is that of the word. And by this I mean the word in all its complex formulations, from the proverb to the novel and stage play, the word with all its subtle power to suggest and foreshadow overt action while magically disguising the moral consequences of that action and providing it with symbolic and psychological justification. For if the word has the potency to revive and make us free, it has also the power to blind, imprison and destroy.

The essence of the word is its ambivalence, and in fiction it is never so effective and revealing as when both potentials are operating simultaneously, as when it mirrors both good and bad, as when it blows both hot and cold in the same breath. Thus it is unfortunate for the Negro that the most powerful formulations of modern American fictional words have been so slanted against him that when he approaches for a glimpse of himself he discovers an image drained of humanity.

Obviously the experiences of Negroes—slavery, the grueling and continuing fight for full citizenship since Emancipation, the stigma of color, the enforced alienation which constantly knifes into our natural identification with our country—have not been that of white Americans. And though as passionate believers in democracy Negroes identify themselves with the broader American ideals, their sense of reality springs, inpart, from an American experience which most white men not only have not had, but one with which they are reluctant to identify themselves even when presented in forms of the imagination. Thus when the white American, holding up most twentieth-century fiction, says, "This is American reality," the Negro tends to answer (not at all concerned that Americans tend generally to fight against any but the most flattering imaginative depictions of their lives), "Perhaps, but you've left out this, and this, and this. And most of all, what you'd have the world accept as *me* isn't even human."

Nor does he refer only to second-rate works but to those of our most representative authors. Either like Hemingway and Steinbeck (in whose joint works I recall not more than five American Negroes) they tend to ignore them, or like the early Faulkner, who distorted Negro humanity to fit his personal versions of Southern myth, they seldom conceive Negro characters possessing the full, complex ambiguity of the human. Too often what is presented as the American Negro (a most complex example of Western man) emerges an oversimplified clown, a beast or an angel. Seldom is he drawn as that sensitively focused process of opposites, of good and evil, of instinct and intellect, of passion and spirituality, which great literary art has projected as the image of man. Naturally, the attitude of Negroes toward this writing is one of great reservation. Which, indeed, bears out Richard Wright's remark that there is in progress between black and white Americans a struggle over the nature of reality.

Historically this is but a part of that larger conflict between older, dominant groups of white Americans, especially the Anglo-Saxons, on the one hand, and the newer white and nonwhite groups on the other, over the major group's attempt to impose its ideals upon the rest, insisting that its exclusive image be accepted as *the* image of the American. This conflict should not, however, be misunderstood. For despite the impact of the American idea upon the world, the "American" himself has not (fortunately for the United States, its minorities, and perhaps for the world) been finally defined. So that far from being socially undesirable this struggle between Americans as to what the American is to be is part of that democratic process through which the nation works to achieve itself. Out of this conflict the ideal American character—a type truly great enough to possess the greatness of the land, a delicately poised unity of divergencies—is slowly being born.

But we are concerned here with fiction, not history. How is it then that our naturalistic prose—one of the most vital bodies of twentieth-century fiction, perhaps the brightest instrument for recording sociological fact, physical action, the nuance of speech, yet achieved—becomes suddenly dull when confronting the Negro?

Obviously there is more in this than the mere verbal counterpart of lynching or segregation. Indeed, it represents a projection of processes lying at the very root of American culture and certainly at the central core of its twentieth-century literary forms, a matter having less to do with the mere "reflection" of white racial theories than with processes molding the attitudes, the habits of mind, the cultural atmosphere and the artistic and intellectual traditions that condition men dedicated to democracy to practice, accept and, most crucial of all, often blind themselves to the essentially undemocratic treatment of their fellow citizens.

It should be noted here that the moment criticism approaches Negro-white relationships it is plunged into problems of psychology and symbolic ritual. Psychology, because the distance between Americans, Negroes and whites, is not so much spatial as psychological; while they might dress and often look alike, seldom on deeper levels do they think alike. Ritual, because the Negroes of fiction are so consistently false to human life that we must question just what they truly represent, both in the literary work and in the inner world of the white American.

Despite their billings as images of reality, these Negroes of fiction are counterfeits. They are projected aspects of an internal symbolic process through which, like a primitive tribesman dancing himself into the group frenzy necessary for battle, the white American prepares himself emotionally to perform a social role. These fictive Negroes are not, as sometimes interpreted, simple racial cliches introduced into society by a ruling class to control political and economic realities. For although they are manipulated to that end, such an externally one-sided interpretation relieves the individual of personal responsibility for the health of democracy. Not only does it forget that a democracy is a collectivity of *individuals*, but it never suspects that the tenacity of the stereotype springs exactly from the fact that its function is no less personal than political. Color prejudice springs not from the stereotype alone, but from an internal psychological state; not from misinformation alone, but from an inner need to believe. It thrives not only on the obscene witch-doctoring of men like Jimmy Byrnes and Malan, but upon an inner craving for symbolic magic. The prejudiced individual creates his own stereotypes, very often unconsciously, by reading into situations involving Negroes those stock meanings which justify his emotional and economic needs.

Hence whatever else the Negro stereotype might be as a social instrumentality, it is also a key figure in a magic rite by which the white American seeks to resolve the dilemma arising between his democratic beliefs and certain antidemocratic practices, between his acceptance of the sacred democratic belief that all men are created equal and his treatment of every tenth man as though he were not.

Thus on the moral level I propose that we view the whole of American life as a drama acted out upon the body of a Negro giant, who, lying trussed up like Gulliver, forms the stage and the scene upon which and within which the action unfolds. If we examine the beginning of the Colonies, the application of this view is not, in its economic connotations at least, too farfetched or too difficult to see. For then the Negro's body was exploited as amorally as the soil and climate. It was later, when white men drew up a plan for a democratic way of life, that the Negro began slowly to exert an influence upon America's moral consciousness. Gradually he was recognized as the human factor placed outside the democratic master plan, a human "natural" resource who, so that white men could become more human, was elected to undergo a process of institutionalized dehumanization.

Until the Korean War this moral role had become obscured within the staggering growth of contemporary science and industry, but during the nineteenth century it flared nakedly in the American consciousness, only to be repressed after the Reconstruction. During periods of national crises, when the United States rounds a sudden curve on the pitch-black road of history, this moral awareness surges in the white American's conscience like a raging river revealed at his feet by a lightning flash. Only then is the veil of anti-Negro myths, symbols, stereotypes and taboos drawn somewhat aside. And when we look closely at our literature it is to be seen operating even when the Negro seems most patently the little man who isn't there.

I see no value either in presenting a catalogue of Negro characters appearing in twentieth-century fiction or in charting the racial attitudes of white writers. We are interested not in quantities but in qualities. And since it is impossible here to discuss the entire body of this writing, the next best thing is to select a framework in which the relationships with which we are concerned may be clearly seen. For brevity let us take three representative writers: Mark Twain, Hemingway and Faulkner. Twain for historical perspective and as an example of how a great nineteenth-century writer handled the Negro; Hemingway as the prime example of the artist who ignored the dramatic and symbolic possibilities presented by this theme; and Faulkner as an example of a writer who has confronted Negroes with such mixed motives that he has presented them in terms of both the "good nigger" and the "bad nigger" stereotypes, and who yet has explored perhaps more successfully than anyone else, either white or black, certain forms of Negro humanity.

For perspective let us begin with Mark Twain's great classic, *Huckleberry Finn*. Recall that Huckleberry has run away from his father, Miss Watson and the Widow Douglas (indeed the whole community, in relation to which he is a young outcast) and has with him as companion on the raft upon which they are sailing down the Mississippi the Widow Watson's runaway Negro slave, Jim. Recall, too, that Jim, during the critical moment of the novel, is stolen by two scoundrels and sold to another master, presenting Huck with the problem of freeing Jim once more. Two ways are open: he can rely upon his own ingenuity and "steal" Jim into freedom or he might write the Widow Watson and request reward money to have Jim returned to her. But here is a danger in this course, remember, since the angry widow might sell the slave down the river into a harsher slavery. It is this course which Huck starts to take, but as he composes the letter he wavers.

"It was a close place." [he tells us] "I took it [the letter] up, and held it in my hand. I was trembling, because I'd got to decide forever, "twixt two things, and I knowed it. I studied a minute, sort of holding my breath, and then says to myself":

"Alright, then, I'll *go* to hell—and tore it up, ... It was awful thoughts and awful words, but they was said ... And I let them stay said, and never thought no more about reforming. I shoved the whole thing out of my head and said I would take up wickedness again, which was in my line, being brung up to it, and the other warn't. And for a starter I would ... steal Jim out of slavery again ..."

And a little later, in defending his decision to Tom Sawyer, Huck comments, "I know you'll say it's dirty, low-down business but I'm low-down. And I'm going to steal him ... "

We have arrived at a key point of the novel and, by an ironic reversal, of American fiction, a pivotal moment announcing a change of direction in the plot, a reversal as well as a recognition scene (like that in which Oedipus discovers his true identity) wherein a new definition of necessity is being formulated. Huck Finn has struggled with the problem poised by the clash between property rights and human rights, between what the community considered to be the proper attitude toward an escaped slave and his knowledge of Jim's humanity, gained through their adventures as fugitives together. He has made his decision on the side of humanity. In this passage Twain has stated the basic moral issue centering around Negroes and the white American's democratic ethics. It dramatizes as well the highest point of tension generated by the clash between the direct, human relationships of the frontier and the abstract, inhuman, market-dominated relationships fostered by the rising middle class—which in Twain's day was already compromising dangerously with the most inhuman aspects of the defeated slave system. And just as politically these forces reached their sharpest tension in the outbreak of the Civil War, in *Huckleberry Finn* (both the boy and the novel) their human implications come to sharpest focus around the figure of the Negro.

Huckleberry Finn knew, as did Mark Twain, that Jim was not only a slave but a human being, a man who in some ways was to be envied, and who expressed his essential humanity in his desire for freedom, his will to possess his own labor, in his loyalty and capacity for friendship and in his love for his wife and child. Yet Twain, though guilty of the sentimentality common to humorists, does not idealize the slave. Jim is drawn in all his ignorance and superstition, with his good traits and his bad. He, like all men, is ambiguous, limited in circumstance but not in possibility. And it will be noted that when Huck makes his decision he identifies himself with Jim and accepts the judgment of his super-ego—that internalized representative of the community—that his action is evil. Like Prometheus, who for mankind stole fire from the gods, he embraces the evil implicit in his act in order to affirm his belief in humanity. Jim, therefore, is not simply a slave, he is a symbol of humanity, and in freeing Jim, Huck makes a bid to free himself of the conventionalized evil taken for civilization by the town.

This conception of the Negro as a symbol of Man—the reversal of what he represents in most contemporary thought—was organic to nineteenth-century literature. It occurs not only in Twain but in Emerson, Thoreau, Whitman and Melville (whose symbol of evil, incidentally, was white), all of whom were men publicly involved in various forms of deeply personal rebellion. And while the Negro and the color black were associated with the concept of evil and ugliness far back in the Christian era, the Negro's emergence as a symbol of value came, I believe, with Rationalism and the rise of the romantic individual of the eighteenth century. This, perhaps, because the romantic was in revolt against the old moral authority, and if he suffered a sense of guilt, his passion for personal freedom was such that he was willing to accept evil (a tragic attitude) even to identifying himself with the "noble slave"—who symbolized the darker, unknown potential side of his personality, that underground side, turgid with possibility, which might, if given a chance, toss a fistful of mud into the sky and create a "shining star."

Even that prototype of the bourgeois, Robinson Crusoe, stopped to speculate as to his slave's humanity. And the rising American industrialists of the late nineteenth century were to rediscover what their European counterparts had learned a century before: that the good man Friday was as sound an investment for Crusoe morally as he was economically, for not only did Friday allow Crusoe to achieve himself by working for him, but by functioning as a living scapegoat to contain Crusoe's guilt over breaking with the institutions and authority of the past, he made it possible to exploit even his guilt economically. The man was one of the first missionaries.

Mark Twain was alive to this irony and refused such an easy (and dangerous) way out. Huck Finn's acceptance of the evil implicit in his "emancipation" of Jim represents Twain's acceptance of his personal responsibility in the condition of society. This was the tragic face behind his comic mask.

But by the twentieth century this attitude of tragic responsibility had disappeared from our literature along with that broad conception of democracy which vitalized the work of our greatest writers. After Twain's compelling image of black and white fraternity the Negro generally disappears from fiction as a rounded human being. And if already in Twain's time a novel which was optimistic concerning a democracy which would include all men could not escape being banned from public libraries, by our day his great drama of interracial fraternity had become, for most Americans at least, an amusing boy's story and nothing more. But, while a boy, Huck Finn has become by the somersault motion of what William Empson terms "pastoral," an embodiment of the heroic, and an exponent of humanism. Indeed, the historical and artistic justification for his adolescence lies in the fact that Twain was depicting a transitional period of American life; its artistic justification is that adolescence is the time of the "great confusion" during which both individuals and nations flounder between accepting and rejecting the responsibilities of adulthood. Accordingly, Huck's relationship to Jim, the river, and all they symbolize, is that of a humanist; in his relation to the community he is an individualist. He embodies the two major conflicting drives operating in nineteenth-century America. And if humanism is man's basic attitude toward a social order which he accepts, and individualism his basic attitude toward one he rejects, one might say that Twain, by allowing these two attitudes to argue dialectically in his work of art, was as highly moral an artist as he was a believer in democracy, and vice versa.

History, however, was to bring an ironic reversal to the direction which Huckleberry Finn chose, and by our day the divided ethic of the community had won out. In contrast with Twain's humanism, individualism was thought to be the only tenable attitude for the artist.

Thus we come to Ernest Hemingway, one of the two writers whose art is based most solidly upon Mark Twain's language, and one who perhaps has done most to extend Twain's technical influence upon our fiction. It was Hemingway who pointed out that all modern American writing springs from *Huckleberry Finn*. (One might add here that equally as much of it derives from Hemingway himself.) But by the twenties the element of rejection implicit in Twain had become so dominant an attitude of the American writer that Hemingway goes on to warn us to "stop where the Nigger Jim is stolen from the boys. That is the real end. The rest is just cheating."

So thoroughly had the Negro, both as man and as a symbol of man, been pushed into the underground of the American conscience that Hemingway missed completely the structural, symbolic and moral necessity for that part of the plot in which the boys rescue Jim. Yet it is precisely this part which gives the novel its significance. Without it, except as a boy's tale, the novel is meaningless. Yet Hemingway, a great artist in his own right, speaks as a victim of that culture of which he is himself so critical, for by his time that growing rift in the ethical fabric pointed out by Twain had become completely sundered—snagged upon the irrepressible moral reality of the Negro. Instead of the single democratic ethic for every man, there now existed two: one, the idealized ethic of the Constitution and the Declaration of Independence, reserved for white men; and the other, the pragmatic ethic designed for Negroes and other minorities, which took the form of discrimination. Twain had dramatized the conflict leading to this division in its earlier historical form, but what was new here was that such a moral division, always a threat to the sensitive man, was ignored by the artist in the most general terms, as when Hemingway rails against the rhetoric of the First World War.

Hemingway's blindness to the moral values of *Huckleberry Finn* despite his sensitivity to its technical aspects duplicated the one-sided vision of the twenties. Where Twain, seeking for what Melville called "the common continent of man," drew upon the rich folklore of the frontier (not omitting the Negro's) in order to "Americanize" his idiom, thus broadening his stylistic appeal, Hemingway was alert only to Twain's technical discoveries—the flexible colloquial language, the sharp naturalism, the thematic potentialities of adolescence. Thus what for Twain was a means to a moral end became for Hemingway an end in itself. And just as the trend toward technique for the sake of technique and production for the sake of the market lead to the neglect of the human need out of which they spring, so do they lead in literature to a marvelous technical virtuosity won at the expense of a gross insensitivity to fraternal values.

It is not accidental that the disappearance of the human Negro from our fiction coincides with the disappearance of deep-probing doubt and a sense of evil. Not that doubt in some form was not always present, as the works of the lost generation, the muckrakers and the proletarian writers make very clear. But it is a shallow doubt, which seldom turns inward upon the writer's own values; almost always it focuses outward, upon some scapegoat with which he is seldom able to identify himself as Huck Finn identified himself with the scoundrels who stole Jim and with Jim himself. This particular naturalism explored everything except the nature of man.

And when the artist would no longer conjure with the major moral problem in American life, he was defeated as a manipulator of profound social passions. In the United States, as in Europe, the triumph of industrialism had repelled the artist with the blatant hypocrisy between its ideals and its acts. But while in Europe the writer became the most profound critic of these matters, in our country he either turned away or was at best halfhearted in his opposition—perhaps because any profound probing of human values, both within himself and within society, would have brought him face to face with the rigidly tabooed subject of the Negro. And now the tradition of avoiding the moral struggle had led not only to the artistic segregation of the Negro but to the segregation of real fraternal, i.e., democratic, values.

The hard-boiled school represented by Hemingway, for instance, is usually spoken of as a product of World War I disillusionment, yet it was as much the product of a tradition which arose even before the Civil War—that tradition of intellectual evasion for which Thoreau criticized Emerson in regard to the Fugitive Slave Law, and which had been growing swiftly since the failure of the ideals in whose name the Civil War was fought. The failure to resolve the problem symbolized by the Negro has contributed indirectly to the dispossession of the artist in several ways. By excluding our largest minority from the democratic process, the United States weakened all national symbols and rendered sweeping public rituals which would dramatize the American dream impossible; it robbed the artist of a body of unassailable public beliefs upon which he could base his art; it deprived him of a personal faith in the ideals upon which society supposedly rested; and it provided him with no tragic mood indigenous to his society upon which he could erect a tragic art. The result was that he responded with an attitude of rejection, which he expressed as artistic individualism. But too often both his rejection and individualism were narrow; seldom was he able to transcend the limitations of pragmatic reality, and the quality of moral imagination—the fountain head of great art—was atrophied within him.

Malraux has observed that contemporary American writing is the only important literature not created by intellectuals, and that the creators possess "neither the relative historical culture, nor the love of ideas (a prerogative of professors in the United States)" of comparable Europeans. And is there not a connection between the non-intellectual aspects of this writing (though many of the writers are far more intellectual than they admit or than Malraux would suspect) and its creators' rejection of broad social responsibility, between its nonconcern with ideas and its failure to project characters who grasp the broad sweep of American life, or who even attempt to state its fundamental problems? And has not this affected the types of heroes of this fiction, is it not a partial explanation of why it has created no characters possessing broad insight into their situations or the emotional, psychological and intellectual complexity which would allow them to possess and articulate a truly democratic world view?

It is instructive that Hemingway, born into a civilization characterized by violence, should seize upon the ritualized violence of the culturally distant Spanish bullfight as a laboratory for developing his style. For it was, for Americans, an amoral violence (though not for the Spaniards) which he was seeking. Otherwise he might have studied that ritual of violence closer to home, that ritual in which the sacrifice is that of a human scapegoat, the lynching bee. Certainly this rite is not confined to the rope as agency, nor to the South as scene, nor even to the Negro as victim.

But let us not confuse the conscious goals of twentieth-century fiction with those of the nineteenth century, let us take it on its own terms. Artists such as Hemingway were seeking a technical perfection rather than moral insight. (Or should we say that theirs was a morality of technique?) They desired a style stripped of unessentials, one that would appeal without resorting to what was considered worn-out rhetoric, or best of all without any rhetoric whatsoever. It was felt that through the default of the powers that ruled society the artist had as his major task the "pictorial presentation of the evolution of a personal problem." Instead of recreating and extending the national myth as he did this, the writer now restricted himself to elaborating his personal myth. And although naturalist in his general style, he was not interested, like Balzac, in depicting a society, or even, like Mark Twain, in portraying the moral situation of a nation. Rather he was engaged in working out a personal problem through the evocative, emotion-charged images and ritual-therapy available through the manipulation of art forms. And while art was still an instrument of freedom, it was now mainly the instrument of a questionable personal freedom for the artist, which too often served to enforce the "unfreedom" of the reader.

This because it is not within the province of the artist to determine whether his work is social or not. Art by its nature is social. And while the artist can determine within a certain narrow scope the type of social effect he wishes his art to create; here his will is definitely limited. Once introduced into society, the work of art begins to pulsate with those meanings, emotions, ideas brought to it by its audience and over which the artist has but limited control. The irony of the "lost generation" writers is that while disavowing a social role it was the fate of their works to perform a social function which re-enforced those very social values which they most violently opposed. How could this be? Because in its genesis the work of art, like the stereotype, is personal; psychologically it represents the socialization of some profoundly personal problem involving guilt (often symbolic murder—parricide, fratricide—incest, homosexuality, all problems at the base of personality) from which by expressing them along with other elements (images, memories, emotions, ideas) he seeks transcendence. To be effective as personal fulfillment, if it is to be more than dream, the work of art must simultaneously evoke images of reality and give them formal organization. And it must, since the individual's emotions are formed in society, shape them into socially meaningful patterns (even Surrealism and Dadaism depended upon their initiates). Nor, as we can see by comparing literature with reportage, is this all. The work of literature differs basically from reportage not merely in its presentation of a pattern of events, nor in its concern with emotion (for a report might well be an account of highly emotional events), but in the deep personal necessity which cries full-throated in the work of art and which seeks transcendence in the form of ritual.

Malcolm Cowley, on the basis of the rites which he believes to be the secret dynamic of Hemingway's work, has identified him with Poe, Hawthorne and Melville, "the haunted and nocturnal writers," he calls them, "the men who dealt with images that were symbols of an inner world." In Hemingway's work, he writes, "we can recognize rites of animal sacrifice ... of sexual union ... of conversion ... and of symbolic death and rebirth." I do not believe, however, that the presence of these rites in writers like Hemingway is as important as the fact that here, beneath the deadpan prose, the cadences of understatement, the anti-intellectualism, the concern with every "fundamental" of man except that which distinguishes him from the animal—that here is the twentieth-century form of that magical rite which during periods of great art has been to a large extent public and explicit. Here is the literary form by which the personal guilt of the pulverized individual of our rugged era is expatiated: not through his identification with the guilty acts of an Oedipus, a

Macbeth or a Medea, by suffering their agony and loading his sins upon their "strong and passionate shoulders," but by being gored with a bull, hooked with a fish, impaled with a grasshopper on a fishhook; not by identifying himself with human heroes, but with those who are indeed defeated.

On the social level this writing performs a function similar to that of the stereotype: it conditions the reader to accept the less worthy values of society, and it serves to justify and absolve our sins of social irresponsibility. With unconscious irony it advises stoic acceptance of those conditions of life which it so accurately describes and which it pretends to reject. And when I read the early Hemingway I seem to be in the presence of Huckleberry Finn who, instead of identifying himself with humanity and attempting to steal Jim free, chose to write the letter which sent him back into slavery. So that now he is a Huck full of regret and nostalgia, suffering a sense of guilt that fills even his noondays with nightmares, and against which, like a terrified child avoiding the cracks in the sidewalk, he seeks protection through the compulsive minor rituals of his prose.

The major difference between nineteenth- and twentieth-century writers is not in the latter's lack of personal rituals—a property of all fiction worthy of being termed literature—but in the social effect aroused within their respective readers. Melville's ritual (and his rhetoric) was based upon materials that were more easily available, say, than Hemingway's. They represented a blending of his personal myth with universal myths as traditional as any used by Shakespeare or the Bible, while until *For Whom the Bell Tolls* Hemingway's was weighted on the personal side. The difference in terms of perspective of belief is that Melville's belief could still find a public object. Whatever else his works were "about" they also managed to be about democracy. But by our day the democratic dream had become too shaky a structure to support the furious pressures of the artist's doubt. And as always when the belief which nurtures a great social myth declines, large sections of society become prey to superstition. For man without myth is Othello with Desdemona gone: chaos descends, faith vanishes and superstitions prowl in the mind.

Hard-boiled writing is said to appeal through its presentation of sheer fact, rather than through rhetoric. The writer puts nothing down but what he pragmatically "knows." But actually one "fact" itself—which in literature must be presented simultaneously as image and as event—became a rhetorical unit. And the symbolic ritual which has set off the "fact"—that is, the fact unorganized by vital social myths (which might incorporate the findings of science and still contain elements ofmystery)—is the rite of superstition. The superstitious individual responds to the capricious event, the fact that seems to explode in his face through blind fatality. For it is the creative function of myth to protect the individual from the irrational, and since it is here in the realm of the irrational that, impervious to science, the stereotype grows, we see that the Negro stereotype is really an image of the unorganized, irrational forces of American life, forces through which, by projecting them in forms of images of an easily dominated minority, the white individual seeks to be at home in the vast unknown world of America. Perhaps the object of the stereotype is not so much to crush the Negro as to console the white man.

Certainly there is justification for this view when we consider the work of William Faulkner. In Faulkner most of the relationships which we have pointed out between the Negro and contemporary writing come to focus: the social and the personal, the moral and the technical, the nineteenth-century emphasis upon morality and the modern accent upon the personal myth. And on the strictly literary level he is prolific and complex enough to speak for those Southern writers who are aggressively anti-Negro and for those younger writers who appear most sincerely interested in depicting the Negro as a rounded human being. What is more, he is the greatest artist the South has produced. While too complex to be given more than a glance in these notes, even a glance is more revealing of what lies back of the distortion of the Negro in modern writing than any attempt at a group survey might be.

Faulkner's attitude is mixed. Taking his cue from the Southern mentality in which the Negro is often dissociated into a malignant stereotype (the bad nigger) on the one hand and a benign stereotype (the good nigger) on the other, most often Faulkner presents characters embodying both. The dual function of this dissociation seems to be that of avoiding moral pain and thus to justify the South's racial code. But since such a social order harms whites no less than blacks, the sensitive Southerner, the artist, is apt to feel its effects acutely—and within the deepest levels of his personality. For not only is the social division forced upon the Negro by the ritualized ethic of discrimination, but upon the white man by the strictly enforced set of anti-Negro taboos. The conflict is always with him. Indeed, so rigidly has the recognition of Negro humanity been tabooed that the white Southerner is apt to associate any form of personal rebellion with the Negro. So that for the Southern artist the Negro becomes a symbol of his personal rebellion, his guilt and his repression of it. The Negro is thus a compelling object of fascination, and this we see very clearly in Faulkner.

Sometimes in Faulkner the Negro is simply a villain, but by an unconsciously ironic transvaluation his villainy consists, as with Loosh in *The Unvanquished*, of desiring his freedom. Or again the Negro appears benign, as with Ringo, of the same novel, who uses his talent not to seek personal freedom but to remain the loyal and resourceful retainer. Not that I criticize loyalty in itself, but that loyalty given where one's humanity is unrecognized seems a bit obscene. And yet in Faulkner's story, "The Bear," he brings us as close to the moral implication of the Negro as Twain or Melville. In the famous "difficult" fourth section, which Malcolm Cowley advises us to skip very much as Hemingway would have us skip the end of *Huckleberry Finn*, we find an argument in progress in which one voice (that of a Southern abolitionist) seeks to define Negro humanity against the other's enumeration of those stereotypes which many Southerners believe to be the Negro's basic traits. Significantly the mentor of the young hero of this story, a man of great moral stature, is socially a Negro.

Indeed, through his many novels and short stories, Faulkner fights out the moral problem which was repressed after the nineteenth century, and it was shocking for some to discover that for all his concern with the South, Faulkner was actually seeking out the nature of man. Thus we must turn to him for that continuity of moral purpose which made for the greatness of our classics. As for the Negro minority, he has been more willing perhaps than any other artist to start with the stereotype, accept it as true, and then seek out the human truth which it hides. Perhaps his is the example for our writers to follow, for in his work technique has been put once more to the task of creating value.

Which leaves these final things to be said. First, that this is meant as no plea for white writers to define Negro humanity, but to recognize the broader aspects of their own. Secondly, Negro writers and those of the other minorities have their own task of contributing to the total image of the American by depicting the experience of their own groups. Certainly theirs is the task of defining Negro humanity, as this can no more be accomplished by others than freedom, which must be won again and again each day, can be conferred upon another. A people must define itself, and minorities have the responsibility of having their ideals and images recognized as part of the composite image which is that of the still forming American people.

The other thing to be said is that while it is unlikely that American writing will ever retrace the way to the nineteenth century, it might be worthwhile to point out that for all its technical experimentation it is nevertheless an ethical instrument, and as such it might well exercise some choice in the kind of ethic it prefers to support. The artist is no freer than the society in which he lives, and in the United States the writers who stereotype or ignore the Negro and other minorities in the final analysis stereotype and distort their own humanity. Mark Twain knew that in *his* America humanity masked its face with blackness.

（1953）

14. Everybody's Protest Novel
大家的抗议小说

James Baldwin
詹姆斯·鲍德温

詹姆斯·鲍德温(1924—1987),小说家、随笔作者、剧作家,1924 年 8 月 2 日出生于纽约的哈莱姆。鲍德温很早就显露出文学才能,13 岁时就写出第一篇文章《哈莱姆:过去与现在》,发表在校报上。在 40 多年的创作生涯中,他出版了 22 部书,包括 6 部小说,8 部论文集,1 本短篇小说,2 个系列访谈,以及难以数计的文章、访谈、录音与讨论等。其非虚构作品,如结集出版的《土生子札记》(*Notes of a Native Son*,1955)、《没人知道我的名字》(*Nobody Knows My Name*,1961)、《下一次将是烈火》(*The Fire Next Time*,1963)和《街上无名》(*No Name in the Street*,1972)等,在 20 世纪中叶产生了深远的影响。但是真正为他赢得文名,乃至引起广泛争议的是他的论文《大家的抗议小说》(1949)与《千逝》(1951)等。

《大家的抗议小说》主要批评斯托夫人创作的《汤姆叔叔的小屋》,认为它非常伤感,不能忠实于生活,实际上是给压迫者带来更多的自由,强化了黑人想要谴责的对自己的压迫,无益于黑人的真正解放。而理查德·赖特(Richard Wright,1908—1960)《土生子》(*The Native Son*,1940)的主人公别格就是汤姆叔叔的后裔,他的悲剧不在于他是美国黑人,而是因为他接受了否认自己黑人生命的神学,在于他承认自己亚人类的可能性,他仿佛不得不根据那些生来就强加给他的残忍的标准,为自己的人性而战。而抗议小说的失败之处在于,它拒绝生命,拒绝人,否认自己的美、自己的力量。这种对抗议小说的总结与严厉批评深化了关于抗议小说的争论,其历史意义不容忽视。

In *Uncle Tom's Cabin*, that cornerstone of American social protest fiction, St. Clare, the kindly master, remarks to his coldly disapproving Yankee cousin, Miss Ophelia, that, so far as he is able to tell, the blacks have been turned over to the devil for the benefit of the whites in this world—however, he adds thoughtfully, it may turn out in the next. Miss Ophelia's reaction is, at least, vehemently right-minded: "This is perfectly horrible!" she exclaims. "You ought to be ashamed of yourselves!"

Miss Ophelia, as we may suppose, was speaking for the author; her exclamation is the moral, neatly framed, and incontestable like those improving mottoes sometimes found hanging on the walls of furnished rooms. And, like these mottoes, before which one invariably flinches, recognizing an insupportable, almost an indecent glibness, she and St. Clare are terribly in earnest. Neither of them questions the medieval morality from which their dialogue springs: black, white, the devil, the next world—posing its alternatives between heaven and the flames—were realities for them as, of course, they were for their creator. They spurned and were terrified of the darkness, striving mightily for the light; and considered from this aspect, Miss Ophelia's exclamation, like Mrs. Stowe's novel, achieves a bright, almost a lurid significance, like the light from a fire which consumes a witch. This is the more striking as one considers the novels of Negro oppression written in our own, more enlightened day, all of which say only: "This is perfectly horrible! You ought to be ashamed of yourselves!" (Let us ignore, for the moment, those novels of oppression written by Negroes, which add only a raging, near-paranoiac postscript to this statement and actually reinforce, as I hope to make clear later, the principles which activate the oppression they decry.)

Uncle Tom's Cabin is a very bad novel, having, in its self-righteous, virtuous sentimentality, much in common with *Little Women*. Sentimentality, the ostentatious parading of excessive and spurious emotion, is the mark of dishonesty, the inability to feel; the wet eyes of the sentimentalist betray his aversion to experience, his fear of life, his arid heart; and it is always, therefore, the signal of secret and violent inhumanity, the mask of cruelty. *Uncle Tom's Cabin*—like its multitudinous, hard-boiled descendants—is a catalogue of violence. This is explained by the nature of Mrs. Stowe's subject matter, her laudable determination to flinch from nothing in presenting the complete picture; an explanation which falters only if we pause to ask whether or not her picture is indeed complete; and what constriction or failure of perception forced her to so depend on the description of brutality—unmotivated, senseless—and to leave unanswered and unnoticed the only important question: what it was, after all, that moved her people to such deeds.

But this, let us say, was beyond Mrs. Stowe's powers; she was not so much a novelist as an impassioned pamphleteer; her book was not intended to do anything more than prove that slavery was wrong; was, in fact, perfectly horrible. This makes material for a pamphlet but it is hardly enough for a novel; and the only question left to ask is why we are bound still within the same constriction. How is it that we are so loath to make a further journey than that made by Mrs. Stowe, to discover and reveal something a little closer to the truth?

But that battered word, truth, having made its appearance here, confronts one immediately with a series of riddles and has, moreover, since so many gospels are preached, the unfortunate tendency to make one belligerent. Let us say, then, that truth, as used here, is meant to imply a devotion to the human being, his freedom and fulfillment; freedom which cannot be legislated, fulfillment which cannot be charted. This is the prime concern, the frame of reference; it is not to be confused with a devotion to Humanity which is too easily equated with a devotion to a Cause; and Causes, as we know, are notoriously blood-thirsty. We have, as it seems to me, in this most mechanical and interlocking of civilizations, attempted to lop this creature down to the status of a time-saving invention. He is not, after all, merely a member of a Society or a Group or a deplorable conundrum to be explained by Science. He is—and how old-fashioned the words sound—something more than that, something resolutely indefinable, unpredictable. In overlooking, denying, evading his complexity—which is nothing more than the disquieting complexity of ourselves—we are diminished and we perish; only within this web of ambiguity, paradox, this hunger, danger, darkness, can we find at once ourselves and the power that will free us from ourselves. It is this power of revelation which is the business of the novelist, this journey toward a more vast reality which must take precedence over all other claims. What is today parroted as his Responsibility—which seems to mean that he must make formal declaration that he is involved in, and affected by, the lives of other people and to say something improving about this somewhat self-evident fact—is, when he believes it, his corruption and our loss; moreover, it is rooted in, interlocked with and intensifies this same mechanization. Both *Gentleman's Agreement* and *The Postman Always Rings Twice* exemplify this terror of the human being, the determination to cut him down to size. And in *Uncle Tom's Cabin* we may find foreshadowing of both; the formula created by the necessity to find a lie more palatable than the truth has been handed down and memorized and persists yet with a terrible power.

It is interesting to consider one more aspect of Mrs. Stowe's novel, the method she used to solve the problem of writing about a black man at all. Apart from her lively procession of field hands, house niggers, Chloe, Topsy, etc.—who are the stock, lovable figures presenting no problem—she has only three other Negroes in the book.

These are the important ones and two of them may be dismissed immediately, since we have only the author's word that they are Negro and they are, in all other respects, as white as she can make them. The two are George and Eliza, a married couple with a wholly adorable child—whose quaintness, incidentally, and whose charm, rather put one in mind of a darky bootblack doing a buck and wing to the clatter of condescending coins. Eliza is a beautiful, pious hybrid, light enough to pass—the heroine of *Quality* might, indeed, be her reincarnation—differing from the genteel mistress who has overseered her education only in the respect that she is a servant. George is darker, but makes up for it by being a mechanical genius, and is, moreover, sufficiently un-Negroid to pass through town, a fugitive from his master, disguised as a Spanish gentleman, attracting no attention whatever beyond admiration. They are a race apart from Topsy. It transpires by the end of the novel, through one of those energetic, last-minute convolutions of the plot, that Eliza has some connection with French gentility. The figure from whom the novel takes its name, Uncle Tom, who is a figure of controversy yet, is jet-black, wooly-haired, illiterate; and he is phenomenally forbearing. He has to be; he is black; only through this forbearance can he survive or triumph. (*Cf*. Faulkner's preface to *The Sound and the Fury*: These others were not Compsons. They were black:—They endured.) His triumph is metaphysical, unearthly; since he is black, born without the light, it is only through humility, the incessant mortification of the flesh, that he can enter into communion with God or man. The virtuous rage of Mrs. Stowe is motivated by nothing so temporal as a concern for the relationship of men to one another—or even as she would have claimed, by a concern for their relationship to God—but merely by a panic of being hurled into the flames, of being caught in traffic with the devil. She embraced this merciless doctrine with all her heart, bargaining shamelessly before the throne of grace: God and salvation becoming her personal property, purchased with the coin of her virtue. Here, black equates with evil and white with grace; if, being mindful of the necessity of good works, she could not cast out the blacks—a wretched, huddled mass, apparently, claiming, like an obsession, her inner eye—she could not embrace them either without purifying them of sin. She must cover their intimidating nakedness, robe them in white, the garments of salvation; only thus could she herself be delivered from ever-present sin, only thus could she bury, as St. Paul demanded, "the carnal man, the man of the flesh." Tom, therefore, her only black man, has been robbed of his humanity and divested of his sex. It is the price for that darkness with which he has been branded.

Uncle Tom's Cabin, then, is activated by what might be called a theological terror, the terror of damnation; and the spirit that breathes in this book, hot, self-righteous, fearful, is not different from that spirit of medieval times which sought to exorcize evil by burning witches; and is not different from that terror which activates a lynch mob. One need not, indeed, search for examples so historic or so gaudy; this is a warfare waged daily in the heart, a warfare so vast, so relentless and so powerful that the interracial handshake or the interracial marriage can be as crucifying as the public hanging or the secret rape. This panic motivates our cruelty, this fear of the dark makes it impossible that our lives shall be other than superficial; this, interlocked with and feeding our glittering, mechanical, inescapable civilization which has put to death our freedom.

This, notwithstanding that the avowed aim of the American protest novel is to bring greater freedom to the oppressed. They are forgiven, on the strength of these good intentions, whatever violence they do to language, whatever excessive demands they make of credibility. It is, indeed, considered the sign of a frivolity so intense as to approach decadence to suggest that these books are both badly written and wildly improbable. One is told to put first things first, the good of society coming before niceties of style or characterization. Even if this were incontestable—for what exactly is the "good" of society? —it argues an insuperable confusion, since literature and sociology are not one and the same; it is impossible to discuss them as if they were. Our passion for categorization, life neatly fitted into pegs, has led to an unforeseen, paradoxical distress; confusion, a breakdown of meaning. Those categories which were meant to define and control the world for us have boomeranged us into chaos; in which limbo we whirl, clutching the straws of our definitions. The "protest" novel, so far from being disturbing, is an accepted and comforting aspect of the American scene, ramifying that framework we believe to be so necessary. Whatever unsettling questions are raised are evanescent, titillating; remote, for this has nothing to do with us, it is safely ensconced in the social arena, where, indeed, it has nothing to do with anyone, so that finally we receive a very definite thrill of virtue from the fact that we are reading such a book at all. This report from the pit reassures us of its reality and its darkness and of our own salvation; and "As long as such books are being published," an American liberal once said to me, "everything will be all right."

But unless one's ideal of society is a race of neatly analyzed, hard-working ciphers, one can hardly claim for the protest novels the lofty purpose they claim for themselves or share the present optimism concerning them. They emerge for what they are: a mirror of our confusion, dishonesty, panic, trapped and immobilized in the sunlit prison of the American dream. They are fantasies, connecting nowhere with reality, sentimental; in exactly the same sense that such movies as *The Best Years of Our Lives* or the works of Mr. James M. Cain are fantasies. Beneath the dazzling pyrotechnics of these current operas one may still discern, as the controlling force, the intense theological preoccupations of Mrs. Stowe, the sick vacuities of *The Rover Boys*. Finally, the aim of the protest novel becomes something very closely resembling the zeal of those alabaster missionaries to Africa to cover the nakedness of the natives, to hurry them into the pallid arms of Jesus and thence into slavery. The aim has now become to reduce all Americans to the compulsive, bloodless dimensions of a guy named Joe.

It is the peculiar triumph of society—and its loss—that it is able to convince those people to whom it has given inferior status of the reality of this decree; it has the force and the weapons to translate its dictum into fact, so that the allegedly inferior are actually made so, insofar as the societal realities are concerned. This is a more hidden phenomenon now than it was in the days of serfdom, but it is no less implacable. Now, as then, we find ourselves bound, first without, then within, by the nature of our categorization. And escape is not effected through a bitter railing against this trap; it is as though this very striving were the only motion needed to spring the trap upon us. We take our shape, it is true, within and against that cage of reality bequeathed us at our birth; and yet it is precisely through our dependence on this reality that we are most endlessly betrayed. Society is held together by our need; we bind it together with legend, myth, coercion, fearing that without it we will be hurled into that void, within which, like the earth before the Word was spoken, the foundations of society are hidden. From this void—ourselves—it is the function of society to protect us; but it is only this void, our unknown selves, demanding, forever, a new act of creation, which can save us—"from the evil that is in the world." With the same motion, at the same time, it is this toward which we endlessly struggle and from which, endlessly, we struggle to escape.

It must be remembered that the oppressed and the oppressor are bound together within the same society; they accept the same criteria, they share the same beliefs, they both alike depend on the same reality. Within this cage it is romantic, more, meaningless, to speak of a "new" society as the desire of the oppressed, for that shivering dependence on the props of reality which he shares with the *Herrenvolk* makes a truly "new" society impossible to conceive. What is meant by a new society is one in which inequalities will disappear, in which vengeance will be exacted; either there will be no oppressed at all, or the oppressed and the oppressor will change places. But, finally, as it seems to me, what the rejected desire is, is an elevation of status, acceptance within the present community. Thus, the African, exile, pagan, hurried off the auction block and into the fields, fell on his knees before that God in Whom he must now believe; who had made him, but not in His image. This tableau, this impossibility, is the heritage of the Negro in America: *Wash me*, cried the slave to his Maker, *and I shall be whiter, whiter than snow*! For black is the color of evil; only the robes of the saved are white. It is this Cry, implacable on the air and in the skull, that he must live with. Beneath the widely published catalogue of brutality—bringing to mind, somehow, an image, a memory of church-bells burdening the air—is this reality which, in the same nightmare notion, he both flees and rushes to embrace. In America, now, this country devoted to the death of the paradox—which may, therefore, be put to death by one—his lot is as ambiguous as a tableau by Kafka. To flee or not, to move or not, it is all the same; his doom is written on his forehead, it is carried in his heart. In *Native Son*, Bigger Thomas stands on a Chicago street corner watching airplanes flown by white men racing against the sun and "Goddamn" he says, the bitterness bubbling up like blood, remembering a million indignities, the terrible, rat-infested house, the humiliation of home-relief, the intense, aimless, ugly bickering, hating it; hatred smoulders through these pages like sulphur fire. All of Bigger's life is controlled, defined by his hatred and his fear. And later, his fear drives him to murder and his hatred to rape; he dies, having come, through this violence, we are told, for the first time, to a kind of life, having for the first time redeemed his manhood. Below the surface of this novel there lies, as it seems to me, a continuation, a complement of that monstrous legend it was written to destroy. Bigger is Uncle Tom's descendant, flesh of his flesh, so exactly opposite a portrait that, when the books are placed together, it seems that the contemporary Negro novelist and the dead New England woman are locked together in a deadly, timeless battle; the one uttering merciless exhortations, the other shouting curses. And, indeed, within this web of lust and fury, black and white can only thrust and counter-thrust, long for each other's slow, exquisite death; death by torture, acid, knives and burning; the thrust, the counter-thrust, the longing making the heavier that cloud which blinds and suffocates them both, so that they go down into the pit together. Thus has the cage betrayed us all, this moment, our life, turned to nothing through our terrible attempts to insure it. For Bigger's tragedy is not that he is cold or black or hungry, not even that he is

American, black; but that he has accepted a theology that denies him life, that he admits the possibility of his being sub-human and feels constrained, therefore, to battle for his humanity according to those brutal criteria bequeathed him at his birth. But our humanity is our burden, our life; we need not battle for it; we need only to do what is infinitely more difficult—that is, accept it. The failure of the protest novel lies in its rejection of life, the human being, the denial of his beauty, dread, power, in its insistence that it is his categorization alone which is real and which cannot be transcended.

(1955)

15. Integration and Race Literature
融合与种族文学

Arthur Davis
阿瑟·戴维斯

阿瑟·戴维斯(1904—1996),批评家、作家,1904 年出生于弗吉尼亚的汉普顿。戴维斯本科毕业于霍华德大学,硕士和博士毕业于哥伦比亚大学,曾分别在北卡罗来纳大学与霍华德大学任教,与其他学者合作,编辑过《黑人行旅》等重要文集。

戴维斯的文章《融合与种族文学》非常重视社会环境对文学创作的影响。他认为,为了回应美国的种族隔离政策与实践,黑人作家创作了大量的抗议小说与关注社会问题的作品,特别是 20 世纪 40 年代,受赖特的抗议小说《土生子》的影响,许多作家发表抗议小说与抗议性的诗歌,但是随着 20 世纪 50 年代美国种族融合思潮的深入人心,以及美国在法律层面废除种族隔离政策,美国黑人在很多方面开始摆脱种族隔离之苦:比如,军队开始融合,南方的白人大学开始接收黑人学生,最高法院敲响公立学校种族隔离的丧钟,南方的黑人不用再冒着生命危险参加投票,私刑已经成为历史等,这些变化极大地改变了美国的黑人文学创作。20 世纪 50 年代,很多因抗议小说闻名于世的黑人作家纷纷开始在种族框架内发现新的主题,开始重视黑人群体内部的生活,而非与外界的矛盾,要么轻描淡写要么干脆避免传统的抗议方式,反映了作者希望黑人能够融入美国社会、生活、政治、经济与文学等的思想。

戴维斯的这种想法并非个案,反映了 20 世纪 50 年代美国融合思想的影响,上承斯凯勒"黑人艺术的废话"中的主张,下接沃伦教授关于"何谓非裔美国文学"的论述,是部分非裔美国学者渴望黑人文学不再局限于"种族"问题,能够利用各自的语言,反映人类共同的美好愿望。

Integration is the most vital issue in America today. The word is on every tongue, and it has acquired all kinds of meanings and connotations. The idea—not the fact obviously—but the idea of integration threatens to split the nation into two hostile camps. As the Negro is the center of this violent controversy, his reaction to it is of supreme importance. In this paper I wish to examine one segment of that reaction—that of the Negro creative artist. How has the integration issue affected him? It is my belief that the concept of integration has already produced a major trend or change in our literature, and that as integration becomes a reality, it will transform Negro writing even more drastically. The rest of this article will be an attempt to illustrate and uphold this thesis.

But before we explore these changes, let us examine the peculiar period in which the Negro writer finds himself because of the integration movement. In the phrase of Matthew Arnold, he is actually living "between two worlds"—one not yet dead, the other not fully born. It is obvious to even the most rabid critic that racial conditions in America are far better than they have ever been before. Barriers are falling in all areas. The armed forces are integrated. Most Southern universities have Negro students, and the Supreme Court has sounded the legal death knell of segregation in public schools. The State Department and the better Northern schools are vying with each other to enlist the services of outstanding race scholars. In practically all states Negroes can now vote without risking their lives; and though the Till Case may seem to deny it, lynching is a dead practice. In short, despite the last desperate and futile efforts of frightened and panicky Southerners, the country has committed itself spiritually to integration. As yet, it is still largely a spiritual commitment, but it has changed radically the racial climate of America.

This change of climate, however, has inadvertently dealt the Negro writer a crushing blow. Up to the present decade, our literature has been predominantly a protest literature. Ironical though it may be, we have capitalized on oppression (I mean, of course, in a literary sense). Although we may deplore and condemn the cause, there is great creative motivation in a movement which brings all members of a group together and cements them in a common bond. And that is just what segregation did for the Negro, especially during the Twenties and Thirties when full segregation was not only practiced in the South but tacitly condoned by the whole nation. As long as there was this common enemy, we had a common purpose and a strong urge to transform into artistic terms our deep-rooted feelings of bitterness and scorn. When the enemy capitulated, he shattered our most fruitful literary tradition. The possibility of imminent integration has tended to destroy the protest element in Negro writing.

And one must always keep in mind the paradox involved. We do not have actual integration anywhere. We have surface integration and token integration in many areas, but the everyday pattern of life for the overwhelming majority of Negroes is unchanged, and probably will be for the next two or three decades. But we do have— and this is of the utmost importance—we do have the spiritual climate which will eventually bring about complete integration. The Negro artist recognizes and acknowledges that climate; he accepts it on good faith; and he is resolved to work with it at all costs. In the meantime, he will have to live between worlds, and that for any artist is a disturbing experience. For the present-day Negro artist—especially the writer in his middle years—it becomes almost a tragic experience because it means giving up a tradition in which he has done his apprentice and journeyman work, giving it up when he is prepared to make use of that tradition as a master craftsman.

Another disturbing factor which must be considered here is that this change of climate came about rather suddenly. Perhaps it would be more exact to say that the full awareness came suddenly because there were signs of its approach all during the Forties, and Negro writers from time to time showed that they recognized these signs. But the full awareness did not come until the present decade, and it came with some degree of abruptness. For example, all through World War II, all through the Forties, the Negro writer was still grinding out protest and Problem novels, most of them influenced by *Native Son*. The list of these works is impressive: *Blood on the Forge* (1941), *White Face* (1943), *If He Hollers* (1943), *The Street* (1946), *Taffy* (1951), and there were others—practically all of them naturalistic novels with the same message of protest against America's treatment of its black minority. The poets wrote in a similar vein. *For My People* (1942), *Freedom's Plow* (1943), *A Street in Bronzeville* (1945), and *Powerful Long Ladder* (1946) all had strong protest elements, all dealt in part with the Negro's fight against segregation and discrimination at home and in the armed forces. Noting the dates of these works, one realizes that, roughly speaking, up to 1950 the protest tradition was in full bloom, and that most of our best writers were still using it. And then with startling swiftness came this awareness of a radical change in the nation's climate; and with it the realization that the old protest themes had to be abandoned. The new climate tended to date the Problem works of the Forties as definitely as time had dated the New Negro "lynching-passing" literature of the Twenties and Thirties. In other words, protest writing has become the first casualty of the new racial climate.

Faced with the loss of his oldest and most cherished tradition, the Negro writer has been forced to seek fresh ways to use his material. First of all, he has attempted to find new themes within the racial framework. Retaining the Negro character and background, he has shifted his emphasis from the protest aspect to Negro living and placed it on the problems and conflicts within the group itself. For example, Chester Himes, pursuing this course in his latest novel, *Third Generation*, explores school life in the Deep South. His main conflict in this work is not concerned with interracial protest but with discord within a Negro family caused by color differences. The whole racial tone of this novel is quite different from that of *If He Hollers*, which, as stated above, is a typical protest work. One came out in 1943, the other in 1953. The two books are a good index to the changes which took place in the decade separating them.

In like manner, Owen Dodson and Gwendolyn Brooks in their novels, *Boy at the Window* and *Maud Martha*, respectively, show this tendency to find new themes within the racial framework. Both of these publications are "little novels," written in the current style, giving intimate and subtle vignettes of middle class living. Their main stress is on life within the group, not on conflict with outside forces. Taking a different approach, William Demby, in *Beetlecreek*, completely reversed the protest pattern by showing the black man's inhumanity to his white brother. In *The Outsider*, Richard Wright has taken an even more subtle approach. He uses a Negro main character, but by adroitly and persistently minimizing that character's racial importance, he succeeds in divorcing him from any association with the traditional protest alignment. And Langston Hughes in his latest work, *Sweet Flypaper of Life*, though using all Negro characters, does not even remotely touch on the matter of interracial protest. All of these authors, it seems to me, show their awareness of the new climate by either playing down or avoiding entirely the traditional protest approach.

Another group of writers have elected to show their awareness by avoiding the Negro character. Among them are William Gardner Smith (*Anger at Innocence*), Ann Petry (*Country Place*), Richard Wright (*Savage Holiday*), and Willard Motley (*Knock on Any Door*). None of these works has Negro main characters. With the exception of *Knock on Any Door*, each is a "second" novel, following a work written in the Forties which has Negro characters and background, and which is written in the protest vein. In each case the first work was highly popular, and yet each of these novelists elected to avoid the theme which gave him his initial success. The effect of the changed climate, it seems to me, is obvious here.

I realize that Frank Yerby with his ten or more best sellers in a row should be listed in this group. Yerby, however, has never used a Negro background or Negro principal characters for his novels. His decision not to make use of the Negro protest tradition came so early in his career, we cannot use it as a case in point at this time. But it is interesting to note that Yerby's first published work, a short story, was written in the protest tradition.

So far I have spoken only of the novelists, but the Negro poets have also sensed the change of climate in America and have reacted to it. Incidentally, several of our outstanding protest poets of the Thirties and Forties have simply dropped out of the picture as poets. I cannot say, of course, that the new climate alone has silenced them, but I do feel that it has been a contributing cause. It is hard for a mature writer to slough off the tradition in which he has worked during all of his formative years. Acquiring a new approach in any field of art is a very serious and trying experience. One must also remember that the protest tradition was no mere surface fad with the Negro writer. It was part of his self-respect, part of his philosophy of life, part of his inner being. It was almost a religious experience with those of us who came up through the dark days of the Twenties and Thirties. When a tradition so deeply ingrained is abandoned, it tends to leave a spiritual numbness—a kind of void not easily filled with new interests or motivations. Several of our ablest poets—and novelists too, for that matter—have not tried to fill that void.

But a few of our poets have met the challenge of the new climate, among them Langston Hughes, M. B. Tolson, Robert Hayden, and several others. A comparison of their early and later works will show in each case a tendency either to avoid protest themes entirely or to approach them much more subtly and obliquely. Compare, for example, Tolson's *Rendezvous with America* (1944) with a *Libretto for the Republic of Liberia* (1953). The thumping rhythms of the protest verse in the former work have given way in the latter to a new technique, one that is influenced largely by Hart Crane. With this work, Tolson has turned his back on the tradition in which he came to maturity, and he has evidently done so successfully. Concerning the work, Allen Tate feels that: "For the first time ... a Negro poet has assimilated completely the full poetic language of his time and, by implication, the language of the Anglo-American poetic tradition." A younger poet like Gwendolyn Brooks, in her poetic career, as brief as it is, also illustrates this change in attitude. There is far more racial protest in *A Street in Bronzeville* than in her latest Pulitzer-Prize-winning volume, *Annie Allen*. Moreover, the few pieces in the latter book which concern the Problem are different in approach and in technique from those in the first work. This tendency to avoid too much emphasis on Problem poetry is also seen, curiously enough, in a very recent anthology, *Lincoln University Poets*, edited by Waring Cuney, Langston Hughes, and Bruce Wright. Several of the Lincoln poets were writing during the New Negro period when the protest tradition was at its height, but these editors, two of them New Negro poets themselves, took great pains to keep the protest pieces down to the barest minimum; and those which they included are relatively mild.

Summing up then, I think we can safely say that the leaven of integration is very much at work. It has forced the Negro creative artist to play down his most cherished tradition; it has sent him in search of new themes; it has made him abandon, at least on occasion, the Negro character and background; and it has possibly helped to silence a few of the older writers now living.

The course of Negro American literature has been highlighted by a series of social and political crises over the Negro's position in America. The Abolition Movement, the Civil War, Reconstruction, World War I, and the Riot Lynching Period of the Twenties all radically influenced Negro writing. Each crisis in turn produced a new tradition in our literature; and as each crisis has passed, the Negro writer has dropped the special tradition which the occasion demanded and moved towards the mainstream of American literature. The Integration Controversy is another crisis and from it we hope that the Negro will move permanently into full participation in American life— social, economic, political and literary.

But what about the literature of this interim between two worlds—between a world of dying segregation and one of a developing integration? It is my belief that this period will produce for a while a series of "goodwill books"—novels and short stories for the most part in which the emphasis will be on what the Negro journalists now call "positive reporting." In an all-out effort to make integration become a reality, the Negro writer will tend to play down the remaining harshness in Negro American living and to emphasize the progress towards equality. This new type of work will try to do in fiction what Roi Ottley has done in *No Green Pastures*. May I say in passing that I do not imply any praise of this work. It simply illustrates for me a trend which I feel will become more and more popular during this interim period. May I also add that this type of goodwill publication will lend itself to all kinds of abuse at the hands of mercenary charlatans; it will create other stereotypes more unbelievable than those we already have, but it will be immensely popular.

During this interim there will also come into fashion another type of racial publication—racial fiction that, without using the Problem, will do for the internal life of Negroes what *Marty* has done for New York Italian-American family and group life and what a host of works in recent years have done for Irish-American life. With the pressure of segregation lightened, the Negro artist will find it easy to draw such pictures of his people. He will discover, what we all know in our objective moments, that there are many facets of Negro living—humorous, pathetic, and tragic—which are not directly touched by the outside world. Hughes' *Sweet Flypaper of Life* is, I believe, a forerunner of many more works of this type.

And when we finally reach that stage in which we can look at segregation in the same way that historians now regard the Inquisition or the Hitler Era in Germany or any other evil period of the past, we shall then do naturally and without self-consciousness what the Joyces and Dostoevskys of the world have always done—write intimately and objectively of our own people in universal human terms.

(1956)

16. The Myth of a "Negro Literature"
"黑人文学"的迷思

Amiri Baraka
埃米里·巴拉卡

埃米里·巴拉卡(1934—2014),诗人、剧作家、社会活动家,1934 年 10 月 7 日出身于新泽西州纽瓦克的一户黑人中产阶级家庭,曾在拉特格斯大学、霍华德大学与哥伦比亚大学求学。他的生平与创作极好地反映了当时美国社会的变化,20 世纪 50 年代末到 20 世纪 60 年代初,他是先锋派诗人,属于垮掉派的一员;20 世纪 60 年代末到 20 世纪 70 年代初,他是黑人艺术运动的骨干,转向黑人民族主义;20 世纪 70 年代中期,他认为民族主义已经落后,转向马列主义,倡导黑人解放运动。他的诗歌、戏剧与随笔成为反映美国社会与文化的重要文献。"9·11"事件之后,他因发表反犹诗歌,被剥夺新泽西州桂冠诗人的称号。

作为黑人艺术运动的参与者与重要推动者,巴拉卡非常重视文学的社会功能,主张以文学、诗歌为武器。在《黑人艺术》("Black Art")这篇诗歌中比较直观地呈现了文学作为"匕首"与"投枪"的战斗功能。《"黑人文学的"迷思》这篇文章发表较早,"革命性"色彩相对较弱,对美国黑人文学整体评价不太高,认为截至目前,除了图默、赖特、艾里森与鲍德温以外,优秀的美国黑人作家较少,水平一般,除了黑人音乐,对美国文化的贡献也乏善可陈。此外,巴拉卡对 20 世纪 30 和 40 年代的抗议文学颇有微词,认为虽然抗议小说家摆出某种姿态,但是基本浮在表面,未能深入问题的本质,很难从根本上揭示美国的现实。黑人作家只有不满足于模仿中产阶级思想,直面现实,真实讲述,才能获得成功。

The mediocrity of what has been called "Negro Literature" is one of the most loosely held secrets of American culture. From Phyllis Wheatley to Charles Chesnutt, to the present generation of American Negro writers, the only recognizable accretion of tradition readily attributable to the black producer of a formal literature in this country, with a few notable exceptions, has been of an almost agonizing mediocrity. In most other fields of "high art" in America, with the same few notable exceptions, the Negro contribution has been, when one existed at all, one of impressive mediocrity. Only in music, and most notably in blues, jazz, and spirituals, *i.e.*, "Negro Music," has there been a significantly profound contribution by American Negroes.

There are a great many reasons for the spectacular vapidity of the American Negro's accomplishment in other formal, serious art forms—social, economic, political, etc.—but one of the most persistent and aggravating reasons for the absence of achievement among serious Negro artists, except in Negro music, is that in most cases the Negroes who found themselves in a position to pursue some art, especially the art of literature, have been members of the Negro middle class, a group that has always gone out of its way to cultivate *any* mediocrity, as long as that mediocrity was guaranteed to prove to America, and recently to the world at large, that they were not really who they were, *i.e.*, Negroes. Negro music alone, because it drew its strengths and beauties out of the depth of the black man's soul, and because to a large extent its traditions could be carried on by the lowest classes of Negroes, has been able to survive the constant and willful dilutions of the black middle class. Blues and jazz have been the only consistent exhibitors of "Negritude" in formal American culture simply because the bearers of its tradition maintained their essential identities as Negroes; in no other art (and I will persist in calling Negro music, Art) has this been possible. Phyllis Wheatley and her pleasant imitations of 18th century English poetry are far and, finally, ludicrous departures from the huge black voices that splintered southern nights with their *hollers*, *chants*, *arwhoolies*, and *ballits*. The embarrassing and inverted paternalism of Charles Chesnutt and his "refined Afro-American" heroes are far cries from the richness and profundity of the blues. And it is impossible to mention the achievements of the Negro in any area of artistic endeavor with as much significance as in spirituals, blues and jazz. There has never been an equivalent to Duke Ellington or Louis Armstrong in Negro writing, and even the best of contemporary literature written by Negroes cannot yet be compared to the fantastic beauty of the music of Charlie Parker.

American Negro music from its inception moved logically and powerfully out of a fusion between African musical tradition and the American experience. It was, and continues to be, a natural, yet highly stylized and personal version of the Negro's life in America. It is, indeed, a chronicler of the Negro's movement, from African slave to American slave, from Freedman to Citizen. And the literature of the blues is a much more profound contribution to Western culture than any other literary contribution made by American Negroes. Moreover, it is only recently that formal literature written by American Negroes has begun to approach the literary standards of its model, *i.e.*, the literature of the white middle class. And only Jean Toomer, Richard Wright, Ralph Ellison, and James Baldwin have managed to bring off examples of writing, in this genre, that could succeed in passing themselves off as "serious" writing, in the sense that, say, the work of Somerset Maugham is "serious" writing. That is, serious, if one has never read Herman Melville or James Joyce. And it is part of the tragic naivete? Of the middle class (brow) writer that he has not.

Literature, for the Negro writer, was always an example of "culture." Not in the sense of the more impressive philosophical characteristics of a particular social group, but in the narrow sense of "cultivation" or "sophistication" by an individual within that group. The Negro artist, because of his middle-class background, carried the artificial social burden as the "best and most intelligent" of Negroes, and usually entered into the "serious" arts to exhibit his familiarity with the social graces, *i.e.*, as a method or means of displaying his participation in the "serious" aspects of American culture. To be a writer was to be "cultivated," in the stunted bourgeois sense of the word. It was also to be a "quality" black man. It had nothing to do with the investigation of the human soul. It was, and is, a social preoccupation rather than an aesthetic one. A rather daring way of status seeking. The cultivated Negro leaving those ineffectual philanthropies, Negro colleges, looked at literature merely as another way of gaining prestige in the white world for the Negro middle class. And the literary and artistic models were always those that could be socially acceptable to the white middle class, which automatically limited them to the most spiritually debilitated imitations of literature available. Negro music, to the middle class, black and white, was never socially acceptable. It was shunned by blacks ambitious of "waking up white," as low and degrading. It was shunned by their white models simply because it was produced by blacks. As one of my professors at Howard University protested one day, "It's amazing how much bad taste the blues display." Suffice it to say, it is in part exactly this "bad taste" that has continued to keep Negro music as vital as it is. The abandonment of one's local (*i.e.*, place or group) emotional attachments in favor of the abstract emotional response of what is called "the general public" (which is notoriously white and middle class) has always been the great diluter of any Negro culture. "You're acting like a nigger," was the standard disparagement. I remember being chastised severely for daring to eat a piece of watermelon on the Howard campus. "Do you realize you're sitting near the highway?" is what the man said, "This is the capstone of Negro education." And it is too, in the sense that it teaches the Negro how to make out in the white society, using the agonizing overcompensation of pretending he's also white. James Baldwin's play, *The Amen Corner*, when it appeared at the Howard Players theatre, "set the speech department back ten years," an English professor groaned to me. The play depicted the lives of poor Negroes running a store-front church. Any reference to the Negro-ness of the American Negro has always been frowned upon by the black middle class in their frenzied dash toward the precipice of the American mainstream.

High art, first of all, must reflect the experiences of the human being, the emotional predicament of the man, as he exists, in the defined world of his being. It must be produced from the legitimate emotional resources of the soul in the world. It can *never* be produced by evading these resources or pretending that they do not exist. It can never be produced by appropriating the withered emotional responses of some strictly social idea of humanity. High art, and by this I mean any art that would attempt to describe or characterize some portion of the profound meaningfulness of human life with any finality or truth, cannot be based on the superficialities of human existence. It must issue from *real* categories of human activity, *truthful* accounts of human life, and not fancied accounts of the attainment of cultural privilege by some willingly preposterous apologists for one social "order" or another. Most of the formal literature produced by Negroes in America has never fulfilled these conditions. And aside from Negro music, it is only in the "popular traditions" of the so-called lower-class Negro that these conditions are fulfilled as a basis for human life. And it is because of this "separation" between Negro life (as an emotional experience) and Negro art, that, say, Jack Johnson or Ray Robinson is a larger cultural hero than any Negro writer. It is because of this separation, even evasion, of the emotional experience of Negro life, that Jack Johnson is a more modern political symbol than most Negro writers. Johnson's life, as proposed, certainly, by his career, reflects much more accurately the symbolic yearnings for singular values among the great masses of Negroes than any black novelist has yet managed to convey. Where is the Negro-ness of a literature written in imitation of the meanest of social intelligences to be found in American culture, *i.e.*, the white middle class? How can it even begin to express the emotional predicament of black Western man? Such a literature, even if its "characters" *are* black, takes on the emotional barrenness of its model, and the blackness of the characters is like the blackness of Al Jolson, an unconvincing device. It is like using black checkers instead of white. They are still checkers.

The development of the Negro's music was, as I said, direct and instinctive. It was the one vector out of African culture impossible to eradicate completely. The appearance of blues as a native *American* music signified in many ways the appearance of American Negroes where once there were African Negroes. The emotional fabric of the music was colored by the emergence of an American Negro culture. It signified that culture's strength and vitality. In the evolution of form in Negro music it is possible to see not only the evolution of the Negro as a cultural and social element of American culture, but also the evolution of that culture itself. The "Coon Shout" proposed one version of the American Negro—and of America; Ornette Coleman proposes another. But the point is that both these versions are accurate and informed with a legitimacy of emotional concern nowhere available in what is called "Negro Literature," and certainly not in the middlebrow literature of the white American.

The artifacts of African art and sculpture were consciously eradicated by slavery. Any African art that based its validity on the production of an artifact, *i.e.*, some *material* manifestation such as a wooden statue or a woven cloth, had little chance of survival. It was only the more "abstract" aspects of African culture that could continue to exist in slave America. Africanisms still persist in the music, religion, and popular cultural traditions of American Negroes. However, it is not an African art American Negroes are responsible for, but an American one. The traditions of Africa must be utilized within the culture of the American Negro where they *actually* exist, and not because of a defensive rationalization about the *worth* of one's ancestors or an attempt to capitalize on the recent eminence of the "new" African nations. Africanisms do exist in Negro culture, but they have been so translated and transmuted by the American experience that they have become integral parts of that experience.

The American Negro has a definable and legitimate historical tradition, no matter how painful, in America, but it is the only place such a tradition exists, simply because America is the only place the American Negro exists. He is, as William Carlos Williams said, "A pure product of America." The paradox of the Negro experience in America is that it is a separate experience, but inseparable from the complete fabric of American life. The history of Western culture begins for the Negro with the importation of the slaves. It is almost as if all Western history before that must be strictly a learned concept. It is only the American experience that can be a persistent cultural catalyst for the Negro. In a sense, history for the Negro, before America, must remain an emotional abstraction. The cultural memory of Africa informs the Negro's life in America, but it is impossible to separate it from its American transformation. Thus, the Negro writer if he wanted to tap his legitimate cultural tradition should have done it by utilizing the entire spectrum of the American experience from the point of view of the emotional history of the black man in this country: as its victim and its chronicler. The soul of such a man, as it exists outside the boundaries of commercial diversion or artificial social pretense. But without a deep commitment to cultural relevance and intellectual purity this was impossible. The Negro as a writer was always a social object, whether glorifying the concept of white superiority, as a great many early Negro writers did, or in crying out against it, as exemplified by the stock "protest" literature of the thirties. He never moved into the position where he could propose his own symbols, erect his own personal myths, as any great literature must. Negro writing was always "after the fact," *i.e.*, based on known social concepts within the structure of bourgeois idealistic projections of "their America," and an emotional climate that never really existed.

The most successful fiction of most Negro writing is in its emotional content. The Negro protest novelist postures, and invents a protest quite amenable with the tradition of bourgeois American life. He never reaches the central core of the America which *can* cause such protest. The intellectual traditions of the white middle class prevent such exposure of reality, and the black imitators reflect this. The Negro writer on Negro life in America postures, and invents a Negro life, and an America to contain it. And even most of those who tried to rebel against that *invented* America were trapped because they had lost all touch with the reality of their experience within the *real* America, either because of the hidden emotional allegiance to the white middle class, or because they did not realize where the reality of their experience lay. When the serious Negro writer disdained the "middlebrow" model, as is the case with a few contemporary black American writers, he usually rushed headlong into the groves of the Academy, perhaps the most insidious and clever dispenser of middlebrow standards of excellence under the guise of "recognizable tradition." That such recognizable tradition is necessary goes without saying, but even from the great philosophies of Europe a contemporary usage must be established. No poetry has come out of England of major importance for forty years, yet there are would-be Negro poets who reject the gaudy excellence of 20th-century American poetry in favor of disembowelled Academic models of second-rate English poetry, with the notion that somehow it is the only way poetry should be written. It would be better if such a poet listened to Bessie Smith sing *Gimme a Pigfoot*, or listened to the tragic verse of a Billie Holiday, than be content to imperfectly imitate the bad poetry of the ruined minds of Europe. And again, it is this striving for *respectability* that has it so. For an American, black or white, to say that some hideous imitation of Alexander Pope means more to him, emotionally, than the blues of Ray Charles or Lightnin' Hopkins, it would be required for him to have completely disappeared into the American Academy's vision of a Europeanized and colonial American culture, or to be lying. In the end, the same emotional sterility results. It is somehow much more tragic for the black man.

A Negro literature, to be a legitimate product of the Negro experience in America, must get at that experience in exactly the terms America has proposed for it, in its most ruthless identity. Negro reaction to America is as deep a part of America as the root causes of that reaction, and it is impossible to accurately describe that reaction in terms of the American middle class; because for them, the Negro has never really existed, never been glimpsed in anything even approaching the complete reality of his humanity. The Negro writer has to go from where he actually is, completely outside of that conscious white myopia. That the Negro does exist is the point, and as an element of American culture he is completely misunderstood by Americans. The middlebrow, commercial Negro writer assures the white American that, in fact, he doesn't exist, and that if he does, he does so within the perfectly predictable fingerpainting of white bourgeois sentiment and understanding. Nothing could be further from the truth. The Creoles of New Orleans resisted "Negro" music for a time as raw and raucous, because they thought they had found a place within the white society which would preclude their being Negroes. But they were unsuccessful in their attempts to "disappear" because the whites themselves reminded them that they were still, for all their assimilation, "just coons." And this seems to me an extremely important idea, since it is precisely this bitter insistence that has kept what can be called "Negro Culture" a brilliant amalgam of diverse influences. There was always a border beyond which the Negro could not go, whether musically or socially. There was always a possible limitation to any dilution or excess of cultural or spiritual reference. The Negro could not ever become white and that was his strength; at some point, always, he could not participate in the dominant tenor of the white man's culture, yet he came to understand that culture as well as the white man. It was at this juncture that he had to make use of other resources, whether African, sub-cultural, or hermetic.

And it was this boundary, this no-man's-land, that provided the logic and beauty of his music. And this is the only way for the Negro artist to provide his version of America—from that no-man's land outside the mainstream. A no-man's-land, a black country, completely invisible to white America, but so essentially part of it as to stain its whole being an ominous gray. Were there really a Negro literature, now it could flower. At this point when the whole of Western society might go up in flames, the Negro remains an integral part of that society, but continually outside it, a figure like Melville's Bartleby. He is an American, capable of identifying emotionally with the fantastic cultural ingredients of this society, but he is also, forever, outside that culture, an invisible strength within it, an observer. If there is ever a Negro literature, it must disengage itself from the weak, heinous elements of the culture that spawned it, and use its very existence as evidence of a more profound America. But as long as the Negro writer contents himself with the imitation of the useless ugly in elegance of the stunted middle-class mind, academic or popular, and refuses to look around him and "tell it like it is"—preferring the false prestige of the black bourgeoisie or the deceitful "acceptance" of *buy and sell* America, something never included in the legitimate cultural tradition of "his people"—he will be a failure, and what is worse, not even a significant failure. Just another dead American.

(1966)

17. The Black Arts Movement
黑人艺术运动

Larry Neal
拉里·尼尔

拉里·尼尔(1937—1981),诗人、批评家,1937 年 9 月 5 日出生于佐治亚州亚特兰大市。尼尔在费城长大,本科毕业于林肯大学,硕士毕业于宾夕法尼亚大学。作为高产的随笔作家,他与埃米里·巴拉卡合作较多,共同编辑的文集《黑人的怒火》(*Black Fire*: *An Anthology of Afro-American Writing*,1968)影响较大,他不仅积极投身当时的政治活动,也坚持文学作品既要表达革命的意义也要能够体现艺术的严谨性,是黑人艺术运动的重要代表人物。

作为黑人艺术运动的代表性文献,尼尔的这篇文章明确提出,黑人艺术是黑人权力概念的美学与精神姐妹,黑人艺术运动必须重新考虑西方文化的美学这一问题。此外,黑人艺术与黑人权力这两个概念都是民族主义的,主要与非裔美国人渴望的自我决定与民族地位有关。如果说黑人权力的主要原则是以自己的方式定义这个世界,那么黑人艺术家的首要任务就是针对黑人的精神与文化需要,重新评价西方美学、作家的作用以及艺术的社会功能等。尼尔借用奈特的表述,不无极端地指出,黑人艺术家如果不创立"黑人美学",就不可能有什么未来,黑人艺术家必须创立新的形式和新的价值观,创立一种新的历史、新的象征、迷思与传说。而且他认为存在创立这种美学的基础,黑人艺术必须破坏白人美学,破坏白人的观念和他们看待世界的方式,才能让黑人艺术家在社会改革中扮演有意义的角色。这既深化了哈莱姆文艺复兴运动所倡导的黑人的自我决定与自我表达主题,也成为 20 世纪 80 年代文化战争的先声。

The Black Arts Movement is radically opposed to any concept of the artist that alienates him from his community. Black Art is the aesthetic and spiritual sister of the Black Power concept. As such, it envisions an art that speaks directly to the needs and aspirations of Black America. In order to perform this task, the Black Arts Movement proposes a radical reordering of the western cultural aesthetic. It proposes a separate symbolism, mythology, critique, and iconology. The Black Arts and the Black Power concept both relate broadly to the Afro-American's desire for self-determination and nationhood. Both concepts are nationalistic. One is concerned with the relationship between art and politics; the other with the art of politics.

Recently, these two movements have begun to merge: the political values inherent in the Black Power concept are now finding concrete expression in the aesthetics of Afro-American dramatists, poets, choreographers, musicians, and novelists. A main tenet of Black Power is the necessity for Black people to define the world in their own terms. The Black artist has made the same point in the context of aesthetics. The two movements postulate that there are in fact and in spirit two Americas—one black, one white. The Black artist takes this to mean that his primary duty is to speak to the spiritual and cultural needs of Black people. Therefore, the main thrust of this new breed of contemporary writers is to confront the contradictions arising out of the Black man's experience in the racist West. Currently, these writers are reevaluating western aesthetics, the traditional role of the writer, and the social function of art. Implicit in this reevaluation is the need to develop a "Black aesthetic." It is the opinion of many Black writers, I among them, that the Western aesthetic has run its course: it is impossible to construct anything meaningful within its decaying structure. We advocate a cultural revolution in art and ideas. The cultural values inherent in western history must either be radicalized or destroyed, and we will probably find that even radicalization is impossible. In fact, what is needed is a whole new system of ideas. Poet Don L. Lee expresses it:

> ... We must destroy Faulkner, Dick, Jane, and other perpetuators of evil. It's time for Du Bois, Nat Turner, and Kwame Nkrumah. As Frantz Fanon points out: destroy the culture and you destroy the people. This must not happen. Black artists are culture stabilizers; bringing back old values, and introducing new ones. Black Art will talk to the people and with the will of the people stop impending "protective custody."

The Black Arts Movement eschews "protest" literature. It speaks directly to Black people. Implicit in the concept of "protest" literature, as Brother Knight has made clear, is an appeal to white morality:

> Now any Black man who masters the technique of his particular art form, who adheres to the white aesthetic, and who directs his work toward a white audience is, in one sense, protesting. And implicit in the act of protest is the belief that a change will be forthcoming once the masters are aware of the protestor's "grievance" (the very word connotes begging, supplications to the gods). Only when that belief has faded and protestings end, will Black art begin.

Brother Knight also has some interesting statements about the development of a "Black aesthetic":

Unless the Black artist establishes a "Black aesthetic" he will have no future at all. To accept the white aesthetic is to accept and validate a society that will not allow him to live. The Black artist must create new forms and new values, sing new songs (or purify old ones); and along with other Black authorities, he must create a new history, new symbols, myths and legends (and purify old ones by fire). And the Black artist, in creating his own aesthetic, must be accountable for it only to the Black people. Further, he must hasten his own dissolution as an individual (in the Western sense)—painful though the process may be, having been breast-fed the poison of "individual experience."

When we speak of a "Black aesthetic" several things are meant. First, we assume that there is already in existence the basis for such an aesthetic. Essentially, it consists of an African-American cultural tradition. But this aesthetic is finally, by implication, broader than that tradition. It encompasses most of the useable elements of Third World culture. The motive behind the Black aesthetic is the destruction of the white thing, the destruction of white ideas, and white ways of looking at the world. The new aesthetic is mostly predicated on an Ethics which asks the question: whose vision of the world is finally more meaningful, ours or the white oppressors'? What is truth? Or more precisely, whose truth shall we express, that of the oppressed or of the oppressors? These are basic questions. Black intellectuals of previous decades failed to ask them. Further, national and international affairs demand that we appraise the world in terms of our own interests. It is clear that the question of human survival is at the core of contemporary experience. The Black artist must address himself to this reality in the strongest terms possible. In a context of world upheaval, ethics and aesthetics must interact positively and be consistent with the demands for a more spiritual world. Consequently, the Black Arts Movement is an ethical movement. Ethical, that is, from the viewpoint of the oppressed. And much of the oppression confronting the Third World and Black America is directly traceable to the Euro-American cultural sensibility. This sensibility, anti-human in nature, has, until recently, dominated the psyches of most Black artists and intellectuals; it must be destroyed before the Black creative artist can have a meaningful role in the transformation of society.

It is this natural reaction to an alien sensibility that informs the cultural attitudes of the Black Arts and the Black Power movement. It is a profound ethical sense that makes a Black artist question a society in which art is one thing and the actions of men another. The Black Arts Movement believes that your ethics and your aesthetics are one. That the contradictions between ethics and aesthetics in western society is symptomatic of a dying culture.

The term "Black Arts" is of ancient origin, but it was first used in a positive sense by LeRoi Jones:

We are unfair

And unfair

We are black magicians

Black arts we make

in black labs of the heart

The fairare fair

and deathly white

The day will not save them

And we own the night

There is also a section of the poem "Black Dada Nihilismus" that carries the same motif. But a fuller amplification of the nature of the new aesthetics appears in the poem "Black Art":

Poems are bullshit unless they are

teeth or trees or lemons piled

on a step. Or black ladies dying

of men leaving nickel hearts

beating them down. Fuck poems

and they are useful, would they shoot

come at you, love what you are,

breathe like wrestlers, or shudder

strangely after peeing. We want live

words of the hip world, live flesh &

coursing blood. Hearts and Brains

Souls splintering fire. We want poems

like fists beating niggers out of Jocks

or dagger poems in the slimy bellies

of the owner-jews ...

Poetry is a concrete function, an action. No more abstractions. Poems are physical entities: fists, daggers, airplane poems, and poems that shoot guns. Poems are transformed from physical objects into personal forces:

> ... Put it on him poem. Strip him naked
> to the world. Another bad poem cracking
> steel knuckles in a jewlady's mouth
> Poem scream poison gas on breasts in green berets ...

Then the poem affirms the integral relationship between Black Art and Black people:

> ... Let Black people understand
> that they are the lovers and the sons
> of lovers and warriors and sons
> of warriors Are poems & poets &
> all the loveliness here in the world

It ends with the following lines, a central assertion in both the Black Arts Movement and the philosophy of Black Power:

> We want a black poem. And a
> Black World.
> Let the world be a Black Poem
> And let All Black People Speak This Poem
> Silently
> Or LOUD

The poem comes to stand for the collective conscious and unconscious of Black America—the real impulse in back of the Black Power movement, which is the will toward self-determination and nationhood, a radical reordering of the nature and function of both art and the artist.

In the spring of 1964, LeRoi Jones, Charles Patterson, William Patterson, Clarence Reed, Johnny Moore, and a number of other Black artists opened the Black Arts Repertoire Theatre School. They produced a number of plays including Jones' *Experimental Death Unit # One*, *Black* Mass, *Jello*, and *Dutchman*. They also initiated a series of poetry readings and concerts. These activities represented the most advanced tendencies in the movement and were of excellent artistic quality the Black Arts School came under immediate attack by the New York power structure. The Establishment, fearing Black creativity, did exactly what it was expected to do—it attacked the theatre and all of its values. In the meantime, the school was granted funds by OEO through HARYOU-ACT. Lacking a cultural program itself, HARYOU turned to the only organization which addressed itself to the needs of the community.

In keeping with its "revolutionary" cultural ideas, the Black Arts Theatre took its programs into the streets of Harlem. For three months, the theatre presented plays, concerts, and poetry readings to the people of the community Plays that shattered the illusions of the American body politic, and awakened Black people to the meaning of their lives.

Then the hawks from the OEO moved in and chopped off the funds. Again, this should have been expected. The Black Acts Theatre stood in radical opposition to the feeble attitudes about culture of the "War on Poverty" bureaucrats. And later, because of internal problems, the theatre was forced to close. But the Black Arts group proved that the community could be served by a valid and dynamic art. It also proved that there was a definite need for a cultural revolution in the Black community.

With the closing of the Black Arts Theatre, the implications of what Brother Jones and his colleagues were trying to do took on even more significance. Black Art groups sprang up on the West Coast and the idea spread to Detroit, Philadelphia, Jersey City, New Orleans, and Washington, D.C. Black Arts movements began on the campuses of San Francisco State College, Fisk University, Lincoln University, Hunter College in the Bronx, Columbia University, and Oberlin College. In Watts, after the rebellion, Maulana Karenga welded the Black Arts Movement into a cohesive cultural ideology which owed much to the work of LeRoi Jones. Karenga sees culture as the most important element in the struggle for self-determination:

Culture is the basis of all ideas, images and actions. To move is to move culturally, i.e. by a set of values given to you by your culture.

Without a culture Negroes are only a set of reactions to white people. The seven criteria for culture are:

1. Mythology
2. History
3. Social Organization
4. Political Organization
5. Economic Organization
6. Creative Motif
7. Ethos

In drama, LeRoi Jones represents the most advanced aspects of the movement. He is its prime mover and chief designer. In a poetic essay entitled "The Revolutionary Theatre," he outlines the iconology of the movement:

The Revolutionary Theatre should force change: it should be change. (All their faces turned into the lights and you work on them black nigger magic, and cleanse them at having seen the ugliness. And if the beautiful see themselves, they will love themselves.) We are preaching virtue again, but by that to mean NOW, toward what seems the most constructive use of the word.

The theatre that Jones proposes is inextricably linked to the Afro-American political dynamic. And such a link is perfectly consistent with Black America's contemporary demands. For theatre is potentially the most social of all of the arts. It is an integral part of the socializing process. It exists in direct relationship to the audience it claims to serve. The decadence and inanity of the contemporary American theatre is an accurate reflection of the state of American society. Albee's *Who's Afraid of Virginia Woolf?* is very American: sick white lives in a homosexual hell hole. The theatre of white America is escapist, refusing to confront concrete reality. Into this cultural emptiness come the musicals, an up-tempo version of the same stale lives. And the use of Negroes in such plays as *Hello Dolly* and *Hallelujah Baby* does not alert their nature; it compounds the problem. These plays are simply hipper versions of the minstrel show. They present Negroes acting out the hang-ups of middle-class white America. Consequently, the American theatre is a palliative prescribed to bourgeois patients who refuse to see the world as it is. Or, more crucially, as the world sees them. It is no accident, therefore, that the most "important" plays come from Europe—Brecht, Weiss, and Ghelderode. And even these have begun to run dry.

The Black Arts theatre, the theatre of LeRoi Jones, is a radical alternative to the sterility of the American theatre. It is primarily a theatre of the Spirit, confronting the Black man in his interaction with his brothers and with the white thing.

Our theatre will show victims so that their brothers in the audience will be better able to understand that they are brothers of victims, and that they themselves are blood brothers. And what we show must cause the blood to rush, so that prerevolutionary temperaments will be bathed in this blood, and it will cause their deepest souls to move, and they will find themselves tensed and clenched, even ready to die, at what the soul has been taught. We will scream and cry, murder, run through the streets in agony, if it means some soul will be moved, moved to actual life understanding of what the world is, and what it ought to be. We are preaching virtue and feeling, and a natural sense of the self in the world. All men live in the world, and the world ought to be a place for them to live.

The victims in the world of Jones' early plays are Clay, murdered by the white bitch-goddess in *Dutchman*, and Walker Vessels, the revolutionary in *The Slave*. Both of these plays present Black men in transition. Clay, the middle-class Negro trying to get himself a little action from Lula, digs himself and his own truth only to get murdered after telling her like it really is:

> Just let me bleed you, you loud whore, and one poem vanished. A whole people neurotics, struggling to keep from being sane. And the only thing that would cure the neurosis would be your murder. Simple as that. I mean if I murdered you, then other white people would understand me. You understand? No, I guess not. If Bessie Smith had killed some white people she wouldn't needed that music. She could have talked very straight and plain about the world. Just straight two and two are four. Money. Power. Luxury. Like that. All of them. Crazy niggers turning their back on sanity. When all it needs is that simple act. Just murder. Would make us all sane.

But Lula understands, and she kills Clay first. In a perverse way it is Clay's nascent knowledge of himself that threatens the existence of Lula's idea of the world. Symbolically, and in fact, the relationship between Clay (Black America) and Lula (white America) is rooted in the historical castration of black manhood. And in the twisted psyche of white America, the Black man is both an object of love and hate. Analogous attitudes exist in most Black Americans, but for decidedly different reasons. Clay is doomed when he allows himself to participate in Lula's "fantasy" in the first place. It is the fantasy to which Frantz Fanon alludes in *The Wretched of the Earth* and *Black Skins, White Mask*: the native's belief that he can acquire the oppressor's power by acquiring his symbols, one of which is the white woman. When Clay finally digs himself it is too late.

Walker Vessels, in *The Slave*, is Clay reincarnated as the revolutionary confronting problems inherited from his contact with white culture. He returns to the home of his ex-wife, a white woman, and her husband, a literary critic. The play is essentially about Walker's attempt to destroy his white past. For it is the past, with all of its painful memories, that is really the enemy of the revolutionary. It is impossible to move until history is either recreated or comprehended. Unlike Todd, in Ralph Ellison's *Invisible Man*, Walker cannot fall outside history. Instead, Walker demands a confrontation with history, a final shattering of bullshit illusions. His only salvation lies in confronting the physical and psychological forces that have made him and his people powerless. Therefore, he comes to understand that the world must be restructured along spiritual imperatives. But in the interim it is basically a question of *who* has power:

> *Easley*. You're so wrong about everything. So terribly, sickeningly wrong. What

can you change? What do you hope to change? Do you think Negroes are better people than whites ... that they can govern a society *better* than whites? That they'll be more judicious or more tolerant? Do you think they'll make fewer mistakes? I mean really, if the Western white man has proved one thing ... it's the futility of modem society. So the have-not peoples become the haves. Even so, will that change the essential functions of the world? Will there be more love or beauty in the world ... more knowledge ... because of it?

Walker. Probably. Probably there will be more ... if more people have a chance to understand what it is. But that's not even the point. It comes down to baser human endeavor than any social-political thinking. What does it matter if there's more love or beauty? Who the fuck cares? Is that what the Western ofay thought while he was ruling ... that his rule somehow brought more love and beauty into the world? Oh, he might have thought that concomitantly, while sipping a gin rickey and scratching his ass ... but that was not ever the point. Not even on the Crusades. The point is that you had your chance, darling, now these other folks have theirs. *Quietly*. Now they have theirs.

Easley: God, what an ugly idea.

This confrontation between the black radical and the white liberal is symbolic of larger confrontations occurring between the Third World and Western society. It is a confrontation between the colonizer and the colonized, the slavemaster and the slave. Implicit in Easley's remarks is the belief that the white man is culturally and politically superior to the Black Man. Even though Western society has been traditionally violent in its relation with the Third World, it sanctimoniously deplores violence or self assertion on the part of the enslaved. And the Western mind, with clever rationalizations, equates the violence of the oppressed with the violence of the oppressor. So that when the native preaches self-determination, the Western white man cleverly misconstrues itto mean hate of *all* white men. When the Black political radical warns his people not to trust white politicians of the left and the right, but instead to organize separately on the basis of power, the white man cries: "racism in reverse." Or he will say, as many of them do today: "We deplore both white and black racism." As if the two could be equated.

There is a minor element in *The Slave* which assumes great importance in a later play entitled *Jello*. Here I refer to the emblem of Walker's army: a red-mouthed grinning field slave. The revolutionary army has taken one of the most hated symbols of the Afro-American past and radically altered its meaning. This is the supreme act of freedom, available only to those who have liberated themselves psychically. Jones amplifies this inversion of emblem and symbol in *Jello* by making Rochester (Ratfester) of the old Jack Benny (Penny) program into a revolutionary nationalist. Ratfester, ordinarily the supreme embodiment of the Uncle Tom Clown, surprises Jack Penny by turning on the other side of the nature of the Black man. He skillfully, and with an evasive black humor, robs Penny of all of his money. But Ratfester's actions are "moral." That is to say, Ratfester is getting his back pay; payment of a long overdue debt to the Black man. Ratfester's sensibilities are different from Walker's. He is *blues people* smiling and shuffling while trying to figure out how to destroy the white thing. And like the blues man, he is the master of the understatement. Or in the Afro-American folk tradition, he is the Signifying Monkey, Shine, and Stagolee all rolled into one. There are no stereotypes any more. History has killed Uncle Tom. Because even Uncle Tom has a breaking point beyond which he will not be pushed. Cut deeply enough into the most docile Negro, and you will find a conscious murderer. Behind the lyrics of the blues and the shuffling porter looms visions of white throats being cut and cities burning.

Jones' particular power as a playwright does not rest solely on his revolutionary vision, but is instead derived from his deep lyricism and spiritual outlook. In many ways, he is fundamentally more a poet than a playwright. And it is his lyricism that gives body to his plays. Two important plays in this regard are *Black Mass* and *Slave Ship*. *Black Mass* is based on the Muslim myth of Yacub. According to this myth, Yacub, a Black scientist, developed the means of grafting different colors of the Original Black Nation until a White Devil was created. In *Black Mass*, Yacub's experiments produce a raving White Beast who is condemned to the coldest regions of the North. The other magicians implore Yacub to cease his experiments. But he insists on claiming the primacy of scientific knowledge over spiritual knowledge. The sensibility of the White Devil is alien, informed by lust and sensuality. The Beast is the consummate embodiment of evil, the beginning of the historical subjugation of the spiritual world.

Black Mass takes place in some prehistorical time. In fact, the concept of time, we learn, is the creation of an alien sensibility, that of the Beast. This is a deeply weighted play, a colloquy on the nature of man, and the relationship between legitimate spiritual knowledge and scientific knowledge. It is LeRoi Jones' most important play mainly because it is informed by a mythology that is wholly the creation of the Afro-American sensibility.

Further, Yacub's creation is not merely a scientific exercise. More fundamentally, it is the aesthetic impulse gone astray. The Beast is created merely for the sake of creation. Some artists assert a similar claim about the nature of art. They argue that art need not have a function. It is against this decadent attitude toward art—ramified throughout most of Western society—that the play militates. Yacub's real crime, therefore, is the introduction of a meaningless evil into a harmonious universe. The evil of the Beast is pervasive, corrupting everything and everyone it touches. What was beautiful is twisted into an ugly screaming thing. The play ends with destruction of the holy place of the Black Magicians. Now the Beast and his descendants roam the earth. An offstage voice chants a call for the Jihad to begin. It is then that myth merges into legitimate history, and we, the audience, come to understand that all history is merely someone's version of mythology.

Slave Ship presents a more immediate confrontation with history. In a series of expressionistic tableaux it depicts the horrors and the madness of the Middle Passage. It then moves through the period of slavery, early attempts at revolt, tendencies toward Uncle Tom-like reconciliation and betrayal, and the final act of liberation. There is no definite plot (LeRoi calls it a pageant), just a continuous rush of sound, groans, screams, and souls wailing for freedom and relief from suffering. This work has special affinities with the New Music of Sun Ra, John Coltrane, Albert Ayler, and Ornette Coleman. Events are blurred, rising and falling in a stream of sound. Almost cinematically, the images flicker and fade against a heavy backdrop of rhythm. The language is spare, stripped to the essential. It is a play which almost totally eliminates the need for a text. It functions on the basis of movement and energy—the dramatic equivalent of the New Music.

LeRoi Jones is the best known and the most advanced playwright of the movement, but he is not alone. There are other excellent playwrights who express the general mood of the Black Arts ideology. Among them are Ron Milner, Ed Bullins, Ben Caldwell, Jimmy Stewart, Joe White, Charles Patterson, Charles Fuller, Aisha Hughes, Carol Freeman, and Jimmy Garrett.

Ron Milner's *Who's Got His Own* is of particular importance. It strips bare the clashing attitudes of a contemporary Afro-American family. Milner's concern is with legitimate manhood and morality. The family in *Who's Got His Own* is in search of its conscience, or more precisely its own definition of life. On the day of his father's death, Tim and his family are forced to examine the inner fabric of their lives; the lies, self-deceits, and sense of powerlessness in a white world. The basic conflict, however, is internal. It is rooted in the historical search for black manhood. Tim's mother is representative of a generation of Christian Black women who have implicitly understood the brooding violence lurking in their men. And with this understanding, they have interposed themselves between their men and the object of that violence—the white man. Thus unable to direct his violence against the oppressor, the Black man becomes more frustrated and the sense of powerlessness deepens. Lacking the strength to be a man in the white world, he turns against his family. So the oppressed, as Fanon explains, constantly dreams violence against his oppressor, while killing his brother on fast weekends.

Tim's sister represents the Negro woman's attempt to acquire what Eldridge Cleaver calls "ultrafemininity." That is, the attributes of her white upper-class counterpart. Involved here is a rejection of the body-oriented life of the working class Black man, symbolized by the mother's traditional religion. The sister has an affair with a white upper-class liberal, ending in abortion. There are hints of lesbianism, i.e. a further rejection of the body. The sister's life is a pivotal factor in the play. Much of the stripping away of falsehood initiated by Tim is directed at her life, which they have carefully kept hidden from the mother.

Tim is the product of the new Afro-American sensibility, informed by the psychological revolution now operative within Black America. He is a combination ghetto soul brother and militant intellectual, very hip and slightly flawed himself. He would change the world, but without comprehending the particular history that produced his "tyrannical" father. And he cannot be the man his father was—not until he truly understands his father. He must understand why his father allowed himself to be insulted daily by the "honky" types on the job; why he took a demeaning job in the "shit-house"; and why he spent on his family the violence that he should have directed against the white man. In short, Tim must confront the history of his family. And that is exactly what happens. Each character tells his story, exposing his falsehood to the other until a balance is reached.

Who's Got His Own is not the work of an alienated mind. Milner's main thrust is directed toward unifying the family around basic moral principles, toward bridging the "generation gap." Other Black playwrights, Jimmy Garrett for example, see the gap as unbridgeable.

Garrett's *We Own the Night* takes place during an armed insurrection. As the play opens we see the central characters defending a section of the city against attacks by white police. Johnny, the protagonist, is wounded. Some of his Brothers intermittently fire at attacking forces, while others look for medical help. A doctor arrives, forced at gun point. The wounded boy's mother also comes. She is a female Uncle Tom who berates the Brothers and their cause. She tries to get Johnny to leave. She is hysterical. The whole idea of Black people fighting white people is totally outside of her orientation. Johnny begins a vicious attack on his mother, accusing her of emasculating his father—a recurring theme in the sociology of the Black community. In Afro-American literature of previous decades the strong Black mother was the object of awe and respect. But in the new literature her status is ambivalent and laced with tension. Historically, Afro-American women have had to be the economic mainstays of the family. The oppressor allowed them to have jobs while at the same time limiting the economic mobility of the Black man. Very often, therefore, the woman's aspirations and values are closely tied to those of the white power structure and not to those of her man. Since he cannot provide for his family the way white men do, she despises his weakness, tearing into him at every opportunity until, very often, there is nothing left but a shell.

The only way out of this dilemma is through revolution. It either must be an actual blood revolution, or one that psychically redirects the energy of the oppressed. Milner is fundamentally concerned with the latter and Garrett with the former. Communication between Johnny and his mother breaks down. The revolutionary imperative demands that men step outside the legal framework. It is a question of erecting *another* morality. The old constructs do not hold up, because adhering to them means consigning oneself to the oppressive reality. Johnny's mother is involved in the old constructs. Manliness is equated with white morality. And even though she claims to love her family (her men), the overall design of her ideas are against black manhood. In Garrett's play the mother's morality manifests itself in a deep-seated hatred of Black men; while in Milner's work the mother understands, but holds her men back.

The mothers that Garrett and Milner see represent the Old Spirituality—the Faith of the Fathers of which Du Bois spoke. Johnny and Tim represent the New Spirituality. They appear to be a type produced by the upheavals of the colonial world of which Black America is a part. Johnny's assertion that he is a criminal is remarkably similar to the rebel's comments in Aime Cesaire's play, *Les Armes Miraculeuses* (*The Miraculous Weapons*). In that play the rebel, speaking to his mother, proclaims: "My name—an offense; my Christian name—humiliation; my status—a rebel; my age—the stone age." To which the mother replies: "My race—the human race. My religion—

brotherhood." The Old Spirituality is generalized. It seeks to recognize Universal Humanity. The New Spirituality is specific. It begins by seeing the world from the concise point-of-view of the colonialized. Where the Old Spirituality would live with oppression while ascribing to the oppressors an innate goodness, the New Spirituality demands a radical shift in point-of-view. The colonialized native, the oppressed must, of necessity, subscribe to a *separate* morality. One that will liberate him and his people.

The assault against the Old Spirituality can sometimes be humorous. In Ben Caldwell's play, *The Militant Preacher*, a burglar is seen slipping into the home of a wealthy minister. The preacher comes in and the burglar ducks behind a large chair. The preacher, acting out the role of the supplicant minister begins to moan, praying to De Lawd for understanding.

In the context of today's politics, the minister is an Uncle Tom, mouthing platitudes against self-defense. The preacher drones in a self-pitying monologue about the folly of protecting oneself against brutal policeman. Then the burglar begins to speak. The preacher is startled, taking the burglar's voice for the voice of God. The burglar begins to play on the preacher's old time religion. He *becomes* the voice of God insulting and goading the preacher on until the preacher's attitudes about protective violence change. The next day the preacher emerges militant, gun in hand, sounding like Reverend Cleage in Detroit. He now preaches a new gospel—the gospel of the gun, an eye for an eye. The gospel is preached in the rhythmic cadences of the old Black church. But the content is radical. Just as Jones inverted the symbols in Jello, Caldwell twists the rhythms of the Uncle Tom preacher into the language of the new militancy.

These plays are directed at problems within Black America. They begin with the premise that there is a well defined Afro-American audience. An audience that must see itself and the world in terms of its own interests. These plays, along with many others, constitute the basis for a viable movement in the theatre—a movement which takes as its task a profound reevaluation of the Black man's presence in America. The Black Arts Movement represents the flowering of a cultural nationalism that has been suppressed since the 1920s. I mean the "Harlem Renaissance"—which was essentially a failure. It did not address itself to the mythology and the lifestyles of the Black community. It failed to take roots, to link itself concretely to the struggles of that community, to become its voice and spirit. Implicit in the Black Arts Movement is the idea that Black people, however dispersed, constitute a *nation* within the belly of white America. This is not a new idea. Garvey said it and the Honorable Elijah Muhammad says it now. And it is on this idea that the concept of Black Power is predicated.

Afro-American life and history is full of creative possibilities，and the movement is just beginning to perceive them. Just beginning to understand that the most meaningful statements about the nature of Western society must come from the Third World of which Black America is a part. The thematic material is broad，ranging from folk heroes like Shine and Stagolee to historical figures like Marcus Garvey and Malcolm X. And then there is the struggle for Black survival，the coming confrontation between white America and Black America. If art is the harbinger of future possibilities，what does the future of Black America portend?

（1968）

18. Cultural Strangulation: Black Literature and the White Aesthetic
文化的窒息：黑人文学与白人美学

Addison Gayle，Jr.

艾迪森·盖尔

艾迪森·盖尔(1932—1991)，文学批评家、随笔作家和传记家，1932 年 6 月 2 日出生于弗吉尼亚。盖尔 1950 年高中毕业，1960 年在纽约城市学院读本科，1965 年取得文学学士学位，1966 年取得加州大学落山矶分校硕士学位，之后在纽约的伯纳德学院教书，直至去世。他很早就喜爱赖特的作品，渴望能够通过写作战胜贫困与种族主义，高中毕业后曾参加美国空军，并从事文学创作，曾经撰写关于邓巴(1971)、麦凯(1972)和赖特(1980)的传记，并在自传《任性的孩子》(*Wayward Child：A Personal Odyssey*，1977)中坦率而且冷静地叙述了自己的生活。他长期为富勒的《黑人世界》投稿，编选的文集有《黑人的表达》(*Black Expressions：Essays by and About Black Americans in the Greative Arts*，1969)，《黑人的状况》(*The Black Situation*，1970)，《黑人美学》(*The Black Aesthetic*，1971)和《新世界的方式》(*The Way of the New World：The Black Novel in America*，1975)，其中以《黑人美学》最具影响。他支持文化民族主义，认为黑人艺术家的核心目标就是针对社会与政治状况，并予以改善。

作为黑人美学的重要倡导者之一，盖尔的文章《文化的窒息：黑人文学与白人美学》(1971)强调"黑人美学"的重要意义。首先，他分析了为何有人反对黑人美学：因为没有所谓白人美学，美国不同种族都共享一种文化遗产，如果妄谈黑人美学，就有种族沙文主义和分离主义之嫌。其次，他梳理了西方文化与文学中的种族主义，指出在西方历史的大部分时间里，以白来定义美，把白视为美与纯洁，把黑视为丑与邪恶，进而把白人视为纯洁，把黑人视为邪恶的种族主义传统。再次，他以具体的作家、作品为例，分析英美文学中的种族主义及其负面影响。最后，他明确指出，倡导黑人美学就是要打破美国文化的偶像，确立衡量美国黑人文学与艺术的规则。

> *"This assumption that of all the hues of God，whiteness is inherently and obviously better than brownness or tan leads to curious acts."*
>
> —W. E. B. Du Bois

The expected opposition to the concept of a "Black Aesthetic" was not long in coming. In separate reviews of *Black Fire*, an anthology edited by LeRoi Jones and Larry Neal, critics from the *Saturday Review* and the *New York Review of Books* presented the expected rebuttal. Agreeing with Ralph Ellison that sociology and art are incompatible mates, these critics, nevertheless, invoked the clichés of the social ideology of the "we shall overcome" years in their attempt to steer Blacks from "the path of literary fantasy and folly."

Their major thesis is simple: There is no Black aesthetic because there is no white aesthetic. The Kerner Commission Report to the contrary, America is not two societies but one. Therefore, Americans of all races, colors and creeds share a common cultural heredity. This is to say that there is one predominant culture—the American culture—with tributary national and ethnic streams flowing into the larger river. Literature, the most important by-product of this cultural monolith, knows no parochial boundaries. To speak of a Black literature, a Black aesthetic, or a Black state, is to engage in racial chauvinism, separatist bias, and Black fantasy.

The question of a white aesthetic, however, is academic. One has neither to talk about it nor define it. Most Americans, black and white, accept the existence of a "White Aesthetic" as naturally as they accept April 15th as the deadline for paying their income tax—with far less animosity towards the former than the latter. The white aesthetic, despite the academic critics, has always been with us: for long before Diotima pointed out the way to heavenly beauty to Socrates, the poets of biblical times were discussing beauty in terms of light and dark—the essential characteristics of a white and black aesthetic—and establishing the dichotomy of superior versus inferior which would assume body and form in the eighteenth century. Therefore, more serious than a definition, is the problem of tracing the white aesthetic from its early origins and afterwards, outlining the various changes in the basic formula from culture to culture and from nation to nation. Such an undertaking would be more germane to a book than an essay; nevertheless, one may take a certain starting point and, using selective nations and cultures, make the critical point, while calling attention to the necessity of a more comprehensive study encompassing all of the nations and cultures of the world.

Let us propose Greece as the logical starting point, bearing in mind Will Durant's observation that "all of Western Civilization is but a footnote to Plato," and take Plato as the first writer to attempt a systematic aesthetic. Two documents by Plato, *The Symposium* and *The Republic*, reveal the twin components of Plato's aesthetic system.

In *The Symposium*, Plato divides the universe into spheres. In one sphere, the lower, one finds the forms of beauty; in the other, the higher, beauty, as Diotima tells Socrates, is absolute and supreme. In *The Republic*, Plato defines the poet as an imitator (a third-rate imitator—a point which modern critics have long since forgotten) who reflects the heavenly beauty in the earthly mirror. In other words, the poet recreates beauty as it exists in heaven; thus the poet, as Neo-Platonists from Aquinas to Coleridge have told us, is the custodian of beauty on earth.

However, Plato defines beauty only in ambiguous, mystical terms; leaving the problem of a more circumscribed, secular definition to philosophers, poets, and critics. During most of the history of the Western world, these aestheticians have been white; therefore, it is not surprising that, symbolically and literally, they have defined beauty in terms of whiteness. (An early contradiction to this tendency is the Marquis de Sade who inverted the symbols, making black beautiful, but demonic, and white pure, but sterile—the Marquis is considered by modern criticism to have been mentally deranged.)

The distinction between whiteness as beautiful (good) and blackness as ugly (evil) appears early in the literature of the middle ages—in the Morality Plays of England. Heavily influenced by both Platonism and Christianity, these plays set forth the distinctions which exist today. To be white was to be pure, good, universal, and beautiful; to be black was to be impure, evil, parochial, and ugly.

The characters and the plots of these plays followed this basic format. The villain is always evil, in most cases the devil; the protagonist, or hero, is always good, in most cases, angels or disciples. The plot then is simple; good (light) triumphs over the forces of evil (dark). As English literature became more sophisticated, the symbols were made to cover wider areas of the human and literary experience. To love was divine; to hate, evil. The fancied mistress of Petrarch was the purest of the pure; Grendel's mother, a creature from the "lower regions and marshes," is, like her son, a monster; the "bad" characters in Chaucer's *Canterbury Tales* tell dark stories; and the Satan of *Paradise Lost* must be vanquished by Gabriel, the angel of purity.

These ancients, as Swift might have called them, established their dichotomies as a result of the influences of Neo-Platonism and Christianity. Later, the symbols became internationalized. Robert Burton, in *The Anatomy of Melancholy*, writes of "dark despair" in the seventeenth century, and James Boswell describes melancholia, that state of mind common to intellectuals of the 17th and 18th centuries, as a dark, dreaded affliction which robbed men of their creative energies. This condition—dark despair or melancholia—was later popularized in what is referred to in English literature as its "dark period"—the period of the Grave Yard School of poets and the Gothic novels.

The symbols thus far were largely applied to conditions, although characters who symbolized evil influences were also dark. In the early stages of English literature, these characters were mythological and fictitious and not representative of people of specific racial or ethnic groups. In the eighteenth century English novel, however, the symbolism becomes ethnic and racial.

There were forerunners. As early as 1621, Shakespeare has Iago refer to Othello as that "old Black ewe," attaching the mystical sexual characteristic to blackness which would become the motive for centuries of oppressive acts by white Americans. In *The Tempest*, Shakespeare's last play, Caliban, though not ostensibly black, is nevertheless a distant cousin of the colonial Friday in Daniel Defoe's *Robinson Crusoe*.

Robinson Crusoe was published at a historically significant time. In the year 1719, the English had all but completed their colonization of Africa. The slave trade in America was on its way to becoming a booming industry; in Africa, Black people were enslaved mentally as well as physically by such strange bedfellows as criminals, businessmen, and Christians. In the social and political spheres, a rationale was needed, and help came from the artist—in this case, the novelist—in the form of *Robinson Crusoe*. In the novel, Defoe brings together both Christian and Platonic symbolism, sharpening the dichotomy between light and dark on the one hand, while on the other establishing a criterion for the inferiority of Black people as opposed to the superiority of white.

One need only compare Crusoe with Friday to validate both of these statements. Crusoe is majestic, wise, white and a colonialist; Friday is savage, ignorant, black and a colonial. Therefore, Crusoe, the colonialist, has a double task. On the one hand he must transform the island (Africa—unproductive, barren, dead) into a little England (prosperous, life-giving, fertile), and he must recreate Friday in his own image, thus bringing him as close to being an Englishman as possible. At the end of the novel, Crusoe has accomplished both undertakings; the island is a replica of "mother England"; and Friday has been transformed into a white man, now capable of immigrating to the land of the gods.

From such mystical artifacts has the literature and criticism of the Western world sprung; and based upon such narrow prejudices as those of Defoe, the art of Black people throughout the world has been described as parochial and inferior. Friday was parochial and inferior until, having denounced his own culture, he assimilated another. Once this was done, symbolically, Friday underwent a change. To deal with him after the conversion was to deal with him in terms of a character who had been civilized and therefore had moved beyond racial parochialism.

However, Defoe was merely a hack novelist, not a thinker. It was left to shrewder minds than his to apply the rules of the white aesthetic to the practical areas of the Black literary and social worlds, and no shrewder minds were at work on this problem than those of writers and critics in America. In America, the rationale for both slavery and the inferiority of Black art and culture was supplied boldly, without the trappings of eighteenth century symbolism.

In 1867, in a book entitled *Nojoque: A Question for a Continent*, Hinton Helper provided the vehicle for the cultural and social symbols of inferiority under which Blacks have labored in this country. Helper intended, as he states frankly in his preface, "to write the negro out of America." In the headings of the two major chapters of the book, the whole symbolic apparatus of the white aesthetic handed down from Plato to America is graphically revealed: the heading of one chapter reads: "Black: A Thing of Ugliness, Disease"; another heading reads: "White: A Thing of Life, Health, and Beauty."

Under the first heading, Helper argues that the color black "has always been associated with sinister things such as mourning, the devil, the darkness of night." Under the second, "White has always been associated with the light of day, divine transfiguration, the beneficent moon and stars ... the fair complexion of romantic ladies, the costumes of Romans and angels, and the white of the American flag so beautifully combined with blue and red without ever a touch of the black that has been for the flag of pirates."

Such is the American critical ethic based upon centuries of distortion of the Platonic ideal. By not adequately defining beauty, and implying at least that this was the job of the poet, Plato laid the foundation for the white aesthetic as defined by Daniel Defoe and Hinton Helper. However, the uses of that aesthetic to stifle and strangle the cultures of other nations is not to be attributed to Plato but, instead, to his hereditary brothers far from the Aegean. For Plato knew his poets. They were not, he surmised, a very trusting lot and, therefore, by adopting an ambiguous position on symbols, he limited their power in the realm of aesthetics. For Plato, there were two kinds of symbols: natural and proscriptive. Natural symbols corresponded to absolute beauty as created by God; proscriptive symbols, on the other hand, were symbols of beauty as proscribed by man, which is to say that certain symbols are said to mean such and such by man himself.

The irony of the trap in which the Black artist has found himself throughout history is apparent. Those symbols which govern his life and art are proscriptive ones, set down by minds as diseased as Hinton Helper's. In other words, beauty has been in the eyes of an earthly beholder who has stipulated that beauty conforms to such and such a definition. To return to Friday, Defoe stipulated that civilized man was what Friday had to become, proscribed certain characteristics to the term "civilized," and presto, Friday, in order not to be regarded as a "savage under Western eyes," was forced to conform to this ideal. How well have the same stipulative definitions worked in the artistic sphere! Masterpieces are made at will by each new critic who argues that the subject of his doctoral dissertation is immortal. At one period of history, John Donne, according to the critic Samuel Johnson, is a second rate poet; at another period, according to the critic T. S. Eliot, he is one of the finest poets in the language. Dickens, argues Professor Ada Nisbet, is one of England's most representative novelists, while for E. R. Leavis, Dickens' work does not warrant him a place in *The Great Tradition*.

When Black literature is the subject, the verbiage reaches the height of the ridiculous. The good "Negro Novel," we are told by Robert Bone and Herbert Hill, is that novel in which the subject matter moves beyond the limitations of narrow parochialism. Form is the most important criterion of the work of art when Black literature is evaluated, whereas form, almost nonexistent in Dostoyevsky's *Crime and Punishment*, and totally chaotic in Kafka's *The Trial*, must take second place to the supremacy of thought and message.

Richard Wright, says Theodore Gross, is not a major American novelist; while Ralph Ellison, on the strength of one novel, is. LeRoi Jones is not a major poet, Ed Bullins not a major playwright, Baldwin incapable of handling the novel form—all because white critics have said so.

Behind the symbol is the object or vehicle, and behind the vehicle is the definition. It is the definition with which we are concerned, for the extent of the cultural strangulation of Black literature by white critics has been the extent to which they have been allowed to define the terms in which the Black artist will deal with his own experience. The career of Paul Laurence Dunbar is the most striking example. Having internalized the definitions handed him by the American society, Dunbar would rather not have written about the Black experience at all, and three of his novels and most of his poetry support this argument. However, when forced to do so by his white liberal mentors, among them was the powerful critic, William Dean Howells, Dunbar deals with Blacks in terms of buffoonery, idiocy and comedy.

Like so many Black writers, past and present, Dunbar was trapped by the definitions of other men, never capable of realizing until near the end of his life, that those definitions were not god-given, but man-given; and so circumscribed by tradition and culture that they were irrelevant to an evaluation of either his life or his art.

In a literary conflict involving Christianity, Zarathustra, Friedrich Nietzsche's iconoclast, calls for "a new table of the laws." In similar iconoclastic fashion, the proponents of a Black Aesthetic, the idol smashers of America, call for a set of rules by which Black literature and art is to be judged and evaluated. For the historic practice of bowing to other men's gods and definitions has produced a crisis of the highest magnitude, and brought us, culturally, to the limits of racial armageddon. The trend must be reversed.

The acceptance of the phrase "Black is Beautiful" is the first step in the destruction of the old table of the laws and the construction of new ones, for the phrase flies in the face of the whole ethos of the white aesthetic. This step must be followed by serious scholarship and hard work; and Black critics must dig beneath the phrase and unearth the treasure of beauty lying deep in the untoured regions of the Black experience—regions where others, due to historical conditioning and cultural deprivation, cannot go.

(1971)

19. In Search of Our Mothers' Gardens
寻找我们母亲的花园

Alice Walker
爱丽丝·沃克

　　爱丽丝·沃克(1944),诗人、小说家,1944年出生于佐治亚州的一个小镇。8岁时,她的右眼意外受伤失明。1961年,沃克就读于南方的斯佩尔曼学院,然后转学北方的莎拉劳伦斯学院(1963—1965)。她不仅热心民权运动,还特别关注黑人社区与黑人家庭内部男性对女性的压迫问题,很多创作也仅仅围绕这些问题展开,当然她的这些"揭短"行为也引发一些非议。小说《紫颜色》(The Color Purple)荣登《纽约时报》畅销书榜,获得过普利策奖和美国国家图书奖。此外,她所提出的"妇女主义(womanism)"思想影响甚大,明显区别于"女性主义(feminism)"这一专注女性文化权利且流行更广的表述,体现了她能够超越性别,更加重视整个黑人民族的生存与完整的理念。而她对赫斯顿的重新发现,不仅丰富了非裔美国女性文学传统,而且深化了非裔美国文学研究。

　　作为20世纪70年代以来美国黑人文艺复兴运动的一位重要代表作家,沃克在其论文《寻找我们母亲的花园》中借用英国著名作家伍尔夫关于女性不仅需要一间自己的房间,同时需要有足够的钱维持生计的提法,分析女性作为艺术家的艰辛。相比较而言,美国普通黑人女性的遭遇更加严峻,但是她们作为"艺术家"的才能并没有被完全淹没,而是体现在日常生活中。如果说奴隶制时期没有人身自由的黑人女性(如惠特莉)尚能进行诗歌创作,那么获得解放的黑人女性在艰难度日的过程中,也能通过日常生活的审美化,展示自己的艺术趣味与追求,为当代黑人女性树立摆脱日常,进入更高审美天地的典范。

I described her own nature and temperament. Told how they needed a larger life for their expression ... I pointed out that in lieu of proper channels, her emotions had overflowed into paths that dissipated them. I talked, beautifully I thought, about an art that would be born, an art that would open the way for women the likes of her. I asked her to hope, and build up an inner life against the coming of that day. ... I sang, with a strange quiver in my voice, a promise song.

—Jean Toomer,"Avey" Cane

The poet speaking to a prostitute who falls asleep while he's talking—When the poet Jean Toomer walked through the South in the early twenties, he discovered a curious thing: black women whose spirituality was so intense, so deep, so *unconscious*, that they were themselves unaware of the richness they held. They stumbled blindly through their lives: creatures so abused and mutilated in body, so dimmed and confused by pain, that they considered themselves unworthy even of hope. In the selfless abstractions their bodies became to the men who used them, they became more than "sexual objects," more even than mere women: they became "Saints." Instead of being perceived as whole persons, their bodies became shrines: what was thought to be their minds became temples suitable for worship. These crazy Saints stared out at the world, wildly, like lunatics—or quietly, like suicides; and the "God" that was in their gaze was as mute as a great stone.

Who were these Saints? These crazy, loony, pitiful women?

Some of them, without a doubt, were our mothers and grandmothers.

In the still heat of the post-Reconstruction South, this is how they seemed to Jean Toomer: exquisite butterflies trapped in an evil honey, toiling away their lives in an era, a century, that did not acknowledge them, except as "the *mule* of the world." They dreamed dreams that no one knew—not even themselves, in any coherent fashion—and saw visions no one could understand. They wandered or sat about the countryside crooning lullabies to ghosts, and drawing the mother of Christ in charcoal on courthouse walls.

They forced their minds to desert their bodies and their striving spirits sought to rise, like frail whirlwinds from the hard red clay. And when those frail whirlwinds fell, in scattered particles, upon the ground, no one mourned. Instead, men lit candles to celebrate the emptiness that remained, as people do who enter a beautiful but vacant space to resurrect a God.

Our mothers and grandmothers, some of them: moving to music not yet written. And they waited.

They waited for a day when the unknown thing that was in them would be made known; but guessed, somehow in their darkness, that on the day of their revelation they would be long dead. Therefore to Toomer they walked, and even ran, in slow motion. For they were going nowhere immediate, and the future was not yet within their grasp. And men took our mothers and grandmothers, "but got no pleasure from it." So complex was their passion and their calm.

To Toomer, they lay vacant and fallow as autumn fields, with harvest time never in sight; and he saw them enter loveless marriages, without joy; and become prostitutes, without resistance; and become mothers of children, without fulfillment.

For these grandmothers and mothers of ours were not Saints, but Artists; driven to a numb and bleeding madness by the springs of creativity in them for which there was no release. They were Creators, who lived lives of spiritual waste, because they were so rich in spirituality—which is the basis of Art—that the strain of enduring their unused and unwanted talent drove them insane. Throwing away this spirituality was their pathetic attempt to lighten the soul to a weight their work-worn, sexually abused bodies could bear.

What did it mean for a black woman to be an artist in our grandmothers' time? In our great-grandmothers' day? It is a question with an answer cruel enough to stop the blood.

Did you have a genius of a great-great-grandmother who died under some ignorant and depraved white overseer's lash? Or was she required to bake biscuits for a lazy backwater tramp, when she cried out in her soul to paint watercolors of sunsets, or the rain falling on the green and peaceful pasture lands? Or was her body broken and forced to bear children (who were more often than not sold away from her)—eight, ten, fifteen, twenty children—when her one joy was the thought of modeling heroic figures of rebellion, in stone or clay?

How was the creativity of the black woman kept alive, year after year and century after century, when for most of the years black people have been in America, it was a punishable crime for a black person to read or write? And the freedom to paint, to sculpt, to expand the mind with action did not exist. Consider, if you can bear to imagine it, what might have been the result if singing, too, had been forbidden by law. Listen to the voices of Bessie Smith, Billie Holiday, Nina Simone, Roberta Flack, and Aretha Franklin, among others, and imagine those voices muzzled for life. Then you may begin to comprehend the lives of our "crazy," "Sainted" mothers and grandmothers. The agony of the lives of women who might have been Poets, Novelists, Essayists, and Short-Story Writers (over a period of centuries), who died with their real gifts stifled within them.

And, if this were the end of the story, we would have cause to cry out in my paraphrase of Okot p'Bitek's great poem:

O, my clanswomen

Let us all cry together!

Come,

Let us mourn the death of our mother,

    The death of a Queen

    The ash that was produced

    By a great fire!

    O, this homestead is utterly dead

    Close the gates

    With *lacari* thorns,

    For our mother

    The creator of the Stool is lost!

    And all the young women

    Have perished in the wilderness!

But this is not the end of the story, for all the young women—our mothers and grandmothers, ourselves—have not perished in the wilderness. And if we ask ourselves why, and search for and find the answer, we will know beyond all efforts to erase it from our minds, just exactly who, and of what, we black American women are.

One example, perhaps the most pathetic, most misunderstood one, can provide a backdrop for our mothers' work: Phillis Wheatley, a slave in the 1700s.

Virginia Woolf, in her book *A Room of One's Own*, wrote that in order for a woman to write fiction she must have two things, certainly: a room of her own (with key and lock) and enough money to support herself.

What then are we to make of Phillis Wheatley, a slave, who owned not even herself? This sickly; frail black girl who required a servant of her own at times—her health was so precarious—and who, had she been white, would have been easily considered the intellectual superior of all the women and most of the men in the society of her day.

Virginia Woolf wrote further, speaking of course not of our Phillis, that "any woman born with a great gift in the sixteenth century [insert "eighteenth century," insert "black woman," insert "born or made a slave"] would certainly have gone crazed, shot herself, or ended her days in some lonely cottage outside the village, half witch, half wizard [insert "Saint"], feared and mocked at. For it needs little skill and psychology to be sure that a highly gifted girl who had tried to use her gift for poetry would have been so thwarted and hindered by contrary instincts [add "chains, guns, the lash, the ownership of one's body by someone else, submission to an alien religion"], that she must have lost her health and sanity to a certainty."

The key words, as they relate to Phillis, are "contrary instincts." For when we read the poetry of Phillis Wheatley—as when we read the novels of Nella Larsen or the oddly false-sounding autobiography of that freest of all black women writers, Zora Hurston—evidence of "contrary instincts" is everywhere. Her loyalties were completely divided, as was, without question, her mind.

But how could this be otherwise? Captured at seven, a slave of wealthy, doting whites who instilled in her the "savagery" of the Africa they "rescued" her from, one wonders if she was even able to remember her homeland as she had known it, or as it really was.

Yet, because she did try to use her gift for poetry in a world that made her a slave, she was "so thwarted and hindered by ... contrary instincts, that she ... lost her health ...." In the last years of her brief life, burdened not only with the need to express her gift but also with a penniless, friendless "freedom" and several small children for whom she was forced to do strenuous work to feed, she lost her health, certainly. Suffering from malnutrition and neglect and who knows what mental agonies, Phillis Wheatley died.

So torn by "contrary instincts" was black, kidnapped, enslaved Phillis that her description of "the Goddess"—as she poetically called the Liberty she did not have—is ironically, cruelly humorous. And, in fact, has held Phillis up to ridicule for more than a century. It is usually read prior to hanging Phillis's memory as that of a fool. She wrote:

> The Goddess comes, she moves divinely fair,
>
> Olive and laurel binds her *golden* hair.
>
> Wherever shines this native of the skies,
>
> Unnumber'd charms and recent graces rise.

It is obvious that Phillis, the slave, combed the "Goddess's" hair every morning; prior, perhaps, to bringing in the milk, or fixing her mistress's lunch. She took her imagery from the one thing she saw elevated above all others.

With the benefit of hindsight we ask, "How could she?"

But at last, Phillis, we understand. No more snickering when your stiff, struggling, ambivalent lines are forced on us. We know now that you were not an idiot or a traitor; only a sickly little black girl, snatched from your home and country and made a slave; a woman who still struggled to sing the song that was your gift, although in a land of barbarians who praised you for your bewildered tongue. It is not so much what you sang, as that you kept alive, in so many of our ancestors, *the notion of song.*

Black women are called, in the folklore that so aptly identifies one's status in society, "the *mule* of the world," because we have been handed the burdens that everyone else —*everyone* else—refused to carry. We have also been called "Matriarchs," "Superwomen," and "Mean and Evil Bitches." Not to mention "Castraters" and "Sapphire's Mama." When we have pleaded for understanding, our character has been distorted; when we have asked for simple caring, we have been handed empty inspirational appellations, then stuck in the farthest corner. When we have asked for love, we have been given children. In short, even our plainer gifts, our labors of fidelity and love, have been knocked down our throats. To be an artist and a black woman, even today; lowers our status in many respects, rather than raises it: and yet, artists we will be.

Therefore we must fearlessly pull out of ourselves and look at and identify with our lives the living creativity some of our great-grandmothers were not allowed to know. I stress *some* of them because it is well known that the majority of our great-grandmothers knew, even without "knowing" it, the reality of their spirituality, even if they didn't recognize it beyond what happened in the singing at church—and they never had any intention of giving it up.

How they did it—those millions of black women who were not Phillis Wheatley, or Lucy Terry or Frances Harper or Zora Hurston or Nella Larsen or Bessie Smith; or Elizabeth Catlett, or Katherine Dunham, either—brings me to the title of this essay, "In Search of Our Mothers' Gardens," which is a personal account that is yet shared, in its theme and its meaning, by all of us. I found, while thinking about the far-reaching world of the creative black woman, that often the truest answer to a question that really matters can be found very close.

In the late 1920s my mother ran away from home to marry my father. Marriage, if not running away, was expected of seventeen-year-old girls. By the time she was twenty, she had two children and was pregnant with a third. Five children later, I was born. And this is how I came to know my mother: she seemed a large, soft, loving-eyed woman who was rarely impatient in our home. Her quick, violent temper was on view only a few times a year, when she battled with the white landlord who had the misfortune to suggest to her that her children did not need to go to school.

She made all the clothes we wore, even my brothers' overalls. She made all the towels and sheets we used. She spent the summers canning vegetables and fruits. She spent the winter evenings making quilts enough to cover all our beds.

During the "working" day, she labored beside—not behind—my father in the fields. Her day began before sunup, and did not end until late at night. There was never a moment for her to sit down, undisturbed, to unravel her own private thoughts; never a time free from interruption—by work or the noisy inquiries of her many children. And yet, it is to my mother—and all our mothers who were not famous—that I went in search of the secret of what has fed that muzzled and often mutilated, but vibrant, creative spirit that the black woman has inherited, and that pops out in wild and unlikely places to this day.

But when, you will ask, did my overworked mother have time to know or care about feeding the creative spirit?

The answer is so simple that many of us have spent years discovering it. We have constantly looked high, when we should have looked high—and low.

For example: in the Smithsonian Institution in Washington, D.C., there hangs a quilt unlike any other in the world. In fanciful, inspired, and yet simple and identifiable figures, it portrays the story of the Crucifixion. It is considered rare, beyond price. Though it follows no known pattern of quilt-making, and though it is made of bits and pieces of worthless rags, it is obviously the work of a person of powerful imagination and deep spiritual feeling. Below this quilt I saw a note that says it was made by "an anonymous Black woman in Alabama, a hundred years ago."

If we could locate this "anonymous" black woman from Alabama, she would turn out to be one of our grandmothers—an artist who left her mark in the only materials she could afford, and in the only medium her position in society allowed her to use.

As Virginia Woolf wrote further, in *A Room of One's Own*:

> Yet genius of a sort must have existed among women as it must have existed among the working class. [Change this to "slaves" and "the wives and daughters of sharecroppers."] Now and again an Emily Brontë or a Robert Burns [change this to "a Zora Hurston or a Richard Wright"] blazes out and proves its presence. But certainly it never got itself on to paper. When, however, one reads of a witch being ducked, of a woman possessed by devils [or "Sainthood"], of a wise woman selling herbs [our root workers], or even a very remarkable man who had a mother, then I

think we are on the track of a lost novelist, a suppressed poet, of some mute and inglorious Jane Austen .... Indeed, I would venture to guess that Anon, who wrote so many poems without signing them, was often a woman ....

And so our mothers and grandmothers have, more often than not anonymously, handed on the creative spark, the seed of the flower they themselves never hoped to see: or like a sealed letter they could not plainly read.

And so it is, certainly, with my own mother. Unlike "Ma" Rainey's songs, which retained their creator's name even while blasting forth from Bessie Smith's mouth, no song or poem will bear my mother's name. Yet so many of the stories that I write, that we all write, are my mother's stories. Only recently did I fully realize this: that through years of listening to my mother's stories of her life, I have absorbed not only the stories themselves, but something of the manner in which she spoke, something of the urgency that involves the knowledge that her stories—like her life—must be recorded. It is probably for this reason that so much of what I have written is about characters whose counterparts in real life are so much older than I am.

But the telling of these stories, which came from my mother's lips as naturally as breathing, was not the only way my mother showed herself as an artist. For stories, too, were subject to being distracted, to dying without conclusion. Dinners must be started, and cotton must be gathered before the big rains. The artist that was and is my mother showed itself to me only after many years. This is what I finally noticed:

Like Mem, a character in *The Third Life of Grange Copeland*, my mother adorned with flowers whatever shabby house we were forced to live in. And not just your typical straggly country stand of zinnias, either. She planted ambitious gardens—and still does—with over fifty different varieties of plants that bloom profusely from early March until late November. Before she left home for the fields, she watered her flowers, chopped up the grass, and laid out new beds. When she returned from the fields she might divide clumps of bulbs, dig a cold pit, uproot and replant roses, or prune branches from her taller bushes or trees—until night came and it was too dark to see.

Whatever she planted grew as if by magic, and her fame as a grower of flowers spread over three counties. Because of her creativity with her flowers, even my memories of poverty are seen through a screen of blooms—sunflowers, petunias, roses, dahlias, forsythia, spirea, delphiniums, verbena ... and on and on.

And I remember people coming to my mother's yard to be given cuttings from her flowers; I hear again the praise showered on her because whatever rocky soil she landed on，she turned into a garden. A garden so brilliant with colors，so original in its design，so magnificent with life and creativity，that to this day people drive by our house in Georgia—perfect strangers and imperfect strangers—and ask to stand or walk among my mother's art.

I notice that it is only when my mother is working in her flowers that she is radiant，almost to the point of being invisible—except as Creator：hand and eye. She is involved in work her soul must have. Ordering the universe in the image of her personal conception of Beauty.

Her face，as she prepares the Art that is her gift，is a legacy of respect she leaves to me，for all that illuminates and cherishes life. She has handed down respect for the possibilities—and the will to grasp them.

For her，so hindered and intruded upon in so many ways，being an artist has still been a daily part of her life. This ability to hold on，even in very simple ways，is work black women have done for a very long time.

This poem is not enough，but it is something，for the woman who literally covered the holes in our walls with sunflowers：

> They were women then
> My mama's generation
> Husky of voice—Stout of
> Step
> With fists as well as
> Hands
> How they battered down
> Doors
> And ironed
> Starched white
> Shirts
> How they led
> Armies
> Headragged Generals
> Across mined
> Fields
> Bobby-trapped
> Kitchens

To discover books

Desks

A place for us

How they knew what we

Must know

Without knowing a page

Of it

Themselves.

Guided by my heritage of a love of beauty and a respect for strength—in search of my mother's garden, I found my own.

And perhaps in Africa over two hundred years ago, there was just such a mother; perhaps she painted vivid and daring decorations in oranges and yellows and greens on the walls of her hut; perhaps she sang—in a voice like Roberta Flack's—sweetly over the compounds of her village; perhaps she wove the most stunning mats or told the most ingenious stories of all the village storytellers. Perhaps she was herself a poet— though only her daughter's name is signed to the poems that we know.

Perhaps Phillis Wheatley's mother was also an artist.

Perhaps in more than Phillis Wheatley's biological life is her mother's signature made clear.

(1972)

20. Toward a Black Feminist Criticism
论黑人女性主义批评

Barbara Smith
芭芭拉·史密斯

芭芭拉·史密斯(1946),作家、黑人女性主义、社会活动分子。史密斯出生于克利夫兰,1969年毕业于曼荷莲文理学院,获学士学位,1971年毕业于匹兹堡大学,获硕士学位。她曾在马萨诸塞大学等任过短暂的教职,主要在学术界之外工作。她高中时就热衷于民权运动,既熟悉妇女解放与民权运动的成就,也十分清楚其局限之所在。她1977年发表的论文《论黑人女性主义批评》为她赢得了广泛好评,也引发后来的诸多批评。

她在文章开始明确提出,无论是白人男性批评家还是白人女性批评家,或者是黑人男性批评家,都不知道或仿佛显得不知道黑人女作家的存在,也很少持续进行女性主义分析。黑人女性的存在,她们的经验与文化仿佛都不在白人以及/或黑人男性意识之内,变得既不可见也不可知。更令人难堪的是,那些所谓的女性主义者也无法理解黑人女性的女性特征。史密斯认为,必须审视外人如何看待黑人女性,并证明黑人女性主义批评的必要,因为如果没有黑人女性主义的批评视角,黑人女作家的作品就会遭到误解,甚至被毁掉。史密斯以莫里森的作品《秀拉》(*Sula*,1973)为例,通过具体的文本分析,指出秀拉与奈尔这两位黑人女性之间温暖的关系,为读者展示了黑人女性主义批评既关注黑人女作家作品中的性与种族政治,也关注文学作品中的政治意蕴及其与黑人女性状况的联系。

I do not know where to begin. Long before I tried to write this I realized that I was attempting something unprecedented, something dangerous merely by writing about black women writers from a feminist perspective and about black lesbian writers from any perspective at all. These things have not been done. Not by white male critics, expectedly. Not by black male critics. Not by white women critics who think of themselves as feminists. And most crucially not by black women critics who, although they pay the most attention to black women writers as a group, seldom use a consistent feminist analysis or write about black lesbian literature. All segments of the literary world—whether establishment, progressive, black, female, or lesbian—do not know, or at least act as if they do not know, that black women writers and black lesbian writers exist.

For whites, this specialized lack of knowledge is inextricably connected to their not knowing in any concrete or politically transforming way that black women of any description dwell in this place. Black women's existence, experience and culture, and the brutally complex systems of oppression which shape these, are in the 'real world' of white and/or male consciousness beneath consideration, invisible, unknown.

This invisibility, which goes beyond anything that either black men or white women experience and tell about in their writing, is one reason it is so difficult for me to know where to start. It seems overwhelming to break such a massive silence. Even more numbing, however, is the realization that so many of the women who will read this have not yet noticed us missing either from their reading matter, their politics or their lives. It is galling that ostensible feminists and acknowledged lesbians have been so blinded to the implications of any womanhood that is not white womanhood and that they have yet to struggle with the deep racism in themselves that is at the source of this blindness.

I think of the thousands and thousands of books, magazines and articles which have been devoted, by this time, to the subject of women's writing and I am filled with rage at the fraction of those pages that mention black and other Third World women. I finally do not know how to begin because in 1977 I want to be writing this for a black feminist publication, for black women who know and love these writers as I do and who, if they do not yet know their names, have at least profoundly felt the pain of their absence.

The conditions that coalesce into the impossibilities of this essay have as much to do with politics as with the practice of literature. Any discussion of Afro-American writers can rightfully begin with the fact that for most of the time we have been in this country we have been categorically denied not only literacy, but the most minimal possibility of a decent human life. In her landmark essay "In Search of Our Mothers' Gardens," Alice Walker discloses how the political, economic and social restrictions of slavery and racism have historically stunted the creative lives of black women.

At the present time I feel that the politics of feminism have a direct relationship to the state of black women's literature. A viable, autonomous black feminist movement in this country would open up the space needed for the exploration of black women's lives and the creation of consciously black woman-identified art. At the same time a redefinition of the goals and strategies of the white feminist movement would lead to much needed change in the focus and content of what is now generally accepted as women's culture.

I want to make in this essay some connections between the politics of black women's lives, what we write about and our situation as artists. In order to do this I will look at how black women have been viewed critically by outsiders, demonstrate the necessity for black feminist criticism, and try to understand what the existence or nonexistence of black lesbian writing reveals about the state of black women's culture and the intensity of *all* black women's oppression.

The role that criticism plays in making a body of literature recognizable and real hardly needs to be explained here. The necessity for nonhostile and perceptive analysis of works written by persons outside the mainstream of white/male cultural rule has been proven by the black cultural resurgence of the 1960s and 1970s and by the even more recent growth of feminist literary scholarship. For books to be real and remembered they have to be talked about. For books to be understood they must be examined in such a way that the basic intentions of the writers are at least considered. Because of racism, black literature has usually been viewed as a discrete subcategory of American literature and there have been black critics of black literature who did much to keep it alive long before it caught the attention of whites. Before the advent of specifically feminist criticism in this decade, books by white women, on the other hand, were not clearly perceived as the cultural manifestation of an oppressed people. It took the surfacing of the second wave of the North American feminist movement to expose the fact that these works contain a stunningly accurate record of the impact of patriarchal values and practice upon the lives of women and more significantly that literature by women provides essential insights into female experience.

In speaking about the current situation of black women writers, it is important to remember that the existence of a feminist movement was an essential precondition to the growth of feminist literature, criticism and women's studies, which focused at the beginning almost entirely upon investigations of literature. The fact that a parallel black feminist movement has been much slower in evolving cannot help but have impact upon the situation of black women writers and artists and explains in part why during this very same period we have been so ignored.

There is no political movement to give power or support to those who want to examine black women's experience through studying our history, literature and culture. There is no political presence that demands a minimal level of consciousness and respect from those who write or talk about our lives. Finally, there is not a developed body of black feminist political theory whose assumptions could be used in the study of black women's art. When black women's books are dealt with at all, it is usually in the context of black literature which largely ignores the implications of sexual politics. When white women look at black women's works they are of course ill-equipped to deal with the subtleties of racial politics. A black feminist approach to literature that embodies the realization that the politics of sex as well as the politics of race and class are crucially interlocking factors in the works of black women writers is an absolute necessity. Until a black feminist criticism exists we will not even know what these writers mean. The citations from a variety of critics which follow prove that without a black feminist critical perspective not only are books by black women misunderstood, they are destroyed in the process.

Jerry H. Bryant, the *Nation's* white male reviewer of Alice Walker's *In Love and Trouble: Stories of Black Women*, wrote in 1973: "The subtitle of the collection," Stories of Black Women, "is probably an attempt by the publisher to exploit not only black subjects but feminine ones. There is nothing feminist about these stories, however." Blackness and feminism are to his mind mutually exclusive and peripheral to the act of writing fiction. Bryant of course does not consider that Walker might have titled the work herself, nor did he apparently read the book which unequivocally reveals the author's feminist consciousness.

In *The Negro Novel in America*, a book that black critics recognize as one of the worst examples of white racist pseudoscholarship, Robert Bone cavalierly dismisses Ann Petry's classic, *The Street*. He perceives it to be "a superficial social analysis" of how slums victimize their black inhabitants. He further objects that:

It is an attempt to interpret slum life in terms of *Negro* experience, when a larger frame of reference is required. As Alain Locke has observed, "*Knock on Any Door* is superior to *The Street* because it designates class and environment, rather than mere race and environment, as its antagonist."

Neither Robert Bone nor Alain Locke, the black male critic he cites, can recognize that *The Street* is one of the best delineations in literature of how sex, race *and* class interact to oppress black women.

In her review of Toni Morrison's *Sula* for *The* New *York Times Book Review* in 1973, putative feminist Sara Blackburn makes similarly racist comments. She writes:

Toni Morrison is far too talented to remain only a marvelous recorder of the black side of provincial American life. If she is to maintain the large and serious audience she deserves, she is going to have to address a riskier contemporary reality than this beautiful but nevertheless distanced novel. *And if she does this, it seems to me that she might easily transcend that early and unintentionally limiting classification 'black woman writer' and take her place among the most serious, important and talented American novelists now working.*

Recognizing Morrison's exquisite gift, Blackburn unashamedly asserts that Morrison is "too talented" to deal with mere black folk, particularly those double nonentities, black women. In order to be accepted as "serious," "important," "talented" and "American," she must obviously focus her efforts upon chronicling the doings of white men.

The mishandling of black women writers by whites is paralleled more often by their not being handled at all, particularly in feminist criticism. Although Elaine Showalter in her review essay on literary criticism for *Signs* states that: "The best work being produced today [in feminist criticism] is exacting and cosmopolitan," her essay is neither. If it were, she would not have failed to mention a single black or Third World woman writer, whether "major" or "minor," to cite her questionable categories. That she also does not even hint that lesbian writers of any color exist renders her purported overview virtually meaningless. Showalter obviously thinks that the identities of being black and female are mutually exclusive, as this statement illustrates: "Furthermore, there are other literary subcultures (black American novelists, for example) whose history offers a precedent for feminist scholarship to use." The idea of critics like Showalter *using* black literature is chilling, a case of barely disguised cultural imperialism. The final insult is that she footnotes the preceding remark by pointing readers to works on black literature by white males Robert Bone and Roger Rosenblatt.

Two recent works by white women, Ellen Moers's *Literary Women: The Great Writers* and Patricia Meyer Spacks's *The Female Imagination*, evidence the same racist flaw. Moers includes the names of four black and one Puertorriquefia writer in her seventy pages of bibliographical notes and does not deal at all with Third World women in the body of her book. Spacks refers to a comparison between Negroes (sic) and women in Mary Ellmann's *Thinking About Women* under the index entry, "blacks, women and." "Black Boy (Wright)" is the preceding entry. Nothing follows. Again there is absolutely no recognition that black and female identity ever coexist, specifically in a group of black women writers. Perhaps one can assume that these women do not know who black women writers are, that they have little opportunity like most Americans to learn about them. Perhaps. Their ignorance seems suspiciously selective, however, particularly in the light of the dozens of truly obscure white women writers they are able to unearth. Spacks was herself employed at Wellesley College at the same time that Alice Walker was there teaching one of the first courses on black women writers in the country.

I am not trying to encourage racist criticism of black women writers like that of Sara Blackburn, to cite only one example. As a beginning I would at least like to see in print white women's acknowledgment of the contradictions of who and what are being left out of their research and writing.

Black male critics can also act as if they do not know that black women writers exist and are, of course, hampered by an inability to comprehend black women's experience in sexual as well as racial terms. Unfortunately there are also those who are as virulently sexist in their treatment of black women writers as their white male counterparts. Darwin Turner's discussion of Zora Neale Hurston in his *In a Minor Chord: Three Afro-American Writers and Their Search for Identity* is a frightening example of the near assassination of a great black woman writer. His descriptions of her and her work as "artful," "coy," "irrational," "superficial" and "shallow" bear no relationship to the actual quality of her achievements. Turner is completely insensitive to the sexual political dynamics of Hurston's life and writing.

In a recent interview, the notoriously misogynist writer, Ishmael Reed, comments in this way upon the low sales of his newest novel:

> but the book only sold 8000 copies. I don't mind giving out the figure: 8000. Maybe if I was one of those young *female* Afro-American writers that are so hot now, I'd sell more. You know, fill my books with ghetto women who can *do no wrong* .... But come on, I think I could have sold 8000 copies by myself.

The politics of the situation of black women are glaringly illuminated by this statement. Neither Reed nor his white male interviewer has the slightest compunction about attacking black women in print. They need not fear widespread public denunciation since Reed's statement is in perfect agreement with the values of a society that hates black people, women and black women. Finally the two of them feel free to base their actions on the premise that black women are powerless to alter either their political or their cultural oppression.

In her introduction to "A Bibliography of Works Written by American Black Women" Ora Williams quotes some of the reactions of her colleagues toward her efforts to do research on black women. She writes:

> Others have reacted negatively with such statements as, "I really don't think

you are going to find very much written." "Have 'they' written anything that is any good?" and "I wouldn't go overboard with this woman's lib thing." When discussions touched on the possibility of teaching a course in which emphasis would be on the literature by black women, one response was, "Ha, ha. That will certainly be the most nothing course ever offered!"

A remark by Alice Walker capsulizes what all the preceding examples indicate about the position of black women writers and the reasons for the damaging criticism about them. In response to her interviewer's question "Why do you think that the black woman writer has been so ignored in America? Does she have even more difficulty than the black male writer, who perhaps has just begun to gain recognition?" Walker replies:

> There are two reasons why the black woman writer is not taken as seriously as the black male writer. One is that she's a woman. Critics seem unusually ill-equipped to intelligently discuss and analyze the works of black women. Generally, they do not even make the attempt; they prefer, rather, to talk about the lives of black women writers, not about what they write. And, since black women writers are not—it would seem—very likable—until recently they were the least willing worshippers of male supremacy—comments about them tend to be cruel.

A convincing case for black feminist criticism can obviously be built solely upon the basis of the negativity of what already exists. It is far more gratifying, however, to demonstrate its necessity by showing how it can serve to reveal for the first time the profound subtleties of this particular body of literature.

Before suggesting how a black feminist approach might be used to examine a specific work I will outline some of the principles that I think a black feminist critic could use. Beginning with a primary commitment to exploring how both sexual and racial politics and black and female identity are inextricable elements in black women's writings, she would also work from the assumption that black women writers constitute an identifiable literary tradition. The breadth of her familiarity with these writers would have shown her that not only is theirs a verifiable historical tradition that parallels in time the tradition of black men and white women writing in this country, but that thematically, stylistically, aesthetically and conceptually black women writers manifest common approaches to the act of creating literature as a direct result of the specific political, social and economic experience they have been obliged to share. The way, for example, that Zora Neale Hurston, Margaret Walker, Toni Morrison and Alice Walker incorporate the traditional black female activities of rootworking, herbal medicine, conjure and midwifery into the fabric of their stories is not mere coincidence, nor is their use of specifically black female language to express their own and their characters' thoughts accidental. The use of black women's language and cultural experience in books *by* black women *about* black women results in a miraculously rich coalescing of form and content and also takes their writing far beyond the confines of white/male literary structures. The black feminist critic would find innumerable commonalities in works by black women.

Another principle which grows out of the concept of a tradition and which would also help to strengthen this tradition would be for the critic to look first for precedents and insights in interpretation within the works of other black women. In other words she would think and write out of her own identity and not try to graft the ideas or methodology of white/male literary thought upon the precious materials of black women's art. Black feminist criticism would by definition be highly innovative, embodying the daring spirit of the works themselves. The black feminist critic would be constantly aware of the political implications of her work and would assert the connections between it and the political situation of all black women. Logically developed, black feminist criticism would owe its existence to a black feminist movement while at the same time contributing ideas that women in the movement could use.

Black feminist criticism applied to a particular work can overturn previous assumptions about it and expose for the first time its actual dimensions. At the "Lesbians and Literature" discussion at the 1976 Modem Language Association convention Bertha Harris suggested that if in a woman writer's work a sentence refuses to do what it is supposed to do, if there are strong images of women and if there is a refusal to be linear, the result is innately lesbian literature. As usual, I wanted to see if these ideas might be applied to the black women writers that I know and quickly realized that many of their works were, in Harris's sense, lesbian. Not because women are lovers, but because they are the central figures, are positively portrayed and have pivotal relationships with one another. The form and language of these works are also nothing like what white patriarchal culture requires or expects.

I was particularly struck by the way in which Toni Morrison's novels *The Bluest Eye* and *Sula* could be explored from this new perspective. In both works the relationships between girls and women are essential, yet at the same time physical sexuality is overtly expressed only between men and women. Despite the apparent heterosexuality of the female characters, I discovered in re-reading *Sula* that it works as a lesbian novel not only because of the passionate friendship between Sula and Nel, but because of Morrison's consistently critical stance toward the heterosexual institutions of male/female relationships, marriage and the family. Consciously or not, Morrison's work poses both lesbian and feminist questions about black women's autonomy and their impact upon each other's lives.

Sula and Nel find each other in 1922 when each of them is 12, on the brink of puberty and the discovery of boys. Even as awakening sexuality "clotted their dreams," each girl desires "a someone" obviously female with whom to share her feelings. Morrison writes:

> for it was in dreams that the two girls had met. Long before Edna Finch's Mellow House opened, even before they marched through the chocolate halls of Garfield Primary School ... they had already made each other's acquaintance in the delirium of their noon dreams. They were solitary little girls whose loneliness was so profound it intoxicated them and sent them stumbling into Technicolored visions that always included a presence, a someone who, quite like the dreamer, shared the delight of the dream. When Nel, an only child, sat on the steps of her back porch surrounded by the high silence of her mother's incredibly orderly house, feeling the neatness pointing at her back, she studied the poplars and fell easily into a picture of herself lying on a flower bed, tangled in her own hair, waiting for some fiery prince. He approached but never quite arrived. But always, watching the dream along with her, were some smiling sympathetic eyes. Someone as interested as she herself in the flow of her imagined hair, the thickness of the mattress of flowers, the voile sleeves that closed below her elbows in gold-threaded cuffs.

> Similarly, Sula, also an only child, but wedged into a household of throbbing disorder constantly awry with things, people, voices and the slamming of doors, spent hours in the attic behind a roll of linoleum galloping through her own mind on a gray-and-white horse tasting sugar and smelling roses in full view of someone who shared both the taste and the speed.

> So when they met, first in those chocolate halls and next through the ropes of the swing, they felt the ease and comfort of old friends. Because each had discovered years before that they were neither white nor male, and that all freedom and triumph was forbidden to them, they had set about creating something else to be. Their meeting was fortunate, for it let them use each other to grow on. Daughters of distant mothers and incomprehensible fathers (Sula's because he was dead; Nel's because he wasn't), they found in each other's eyes the intimacy they were looking for. (*Sula*, 51-52)

As this beautiful passage shows, their relationship, from the very beginning, is suffused with an erotic romanticism. The dreams in which they are initially drawn to each other are actually complementary aspects of the same sensuous fairy tale. Nel imagines a "fiery prince" who never quite arrives while Sula gallops like a prince "on a gray-and-white horse." The "real world" of patriarchy requires, however, that they channel this energy away from each other to the opposite sex. Lorraine Bethel explains this dynamic in her essay "Conversations with Ourselves: Black Female Relationships in Toni Cade Bambara's *Gorilla*, *My Love* and Toni Morrison's *Sula*." She writes:

> I am not suggesting that Sula and Nel are being consciously sexual, or that their relationship has an overt lesbian nature. I am suggesting, however, that there is a certain sensuality in their interactions that is reinforced by the mirror-like nature of their relationship. Sexual exploration and coming of age is a natural part of adolescence. Sula and Nel discover men together, and though their flirtations with males are an important part of their sexual exploration, the sensuality that they experience in each other's company is equally important.

Sula and Nel must also struggle with the constrictions of racism upon their lives. The knowledge that "they were neither white nor male" is the inherent explanation of their need for each other. Morrison depicts in literature the necessary bonding that has always taken place between black women for the sake of barest survival. Together the two girls can find the courage to create themselves.

Their relationship is severed only when Nel marries Jude, an unexceptional young man who thinks of her as "the hem—the tuck and fold that hid his raveling edges" (83). Sula's inventive wildness cannot overcome social pressure or the influence of Nel's parents who "had succeeded in rubbing down to a dull glow any sparkle or splutter she had" (83). Nel falls prey to convention while Sula escapes it. Yet at the wedding which ends the first phase of their relationship, Nel's final action is to look past her husband toward Sula:

> a slim figure in blue, gliding, with just a hint of a strut, down the path towards the road ... Even from the rear Nel could tell that it was Sula and that she was smiling; that something deep down in that litheness was amused. (85)

When Sula returns ten years later, her rebelliousness full-blown, a major source of the town's suspicions stems from the fact that although she is almost thirty, she is still unmarried. Sula's grandmother, Eva, does not hesitate to bring up the matter as soon as she arrives. She asks "When you gone to get married? You need to have some babies. It'll settle you .... Ain't no woman got no business floatin' around without no man" (92). Sula replies: "I don't want to make somebody else. I want to make myself" (92). Self-definition is a dangerous activity for any women to engage in, especially a black one, and it expectedly earns Sula pariah status in Medallion.

Morrison dearly points out that it is the fact that Sula has not been tamed or broken by the exigencies of heterosexual family life which most galls the others. She writes:

> Among the weighty evidence piling up was the fact that Sula did not look her age. She was near thirty and, unlike them, had lost no teeth, suffered no bruises, developed no ring of fat at the waist or pocket at the back of her neck. (115)

In other words she is not a domestic serf, a woman run down by obligatory childbearing or a victim of battering. Sula also sleeps with the husbands of the town once and then discards them, needing them even less than her own mother did, for sexual gratification and affection. The town reacts to her disavowal of patriarchal values by becoming fanatically serious about their own family obligations, as if in this way they might counteract Sula's radical criticism of their lives.

Sula's presence in her community functions much like the presence of lesbians everywhere to expose the contradictions of supposedly normal life. The opening paragraph of the essay "Woman Identified Woman" has amazing relevance as an explanation of Sula's position and character in the novel. It asks:

> What is a lesbian? A lesbian is the rage of all women condensed to the point of explosion. She is the woman who, often beginning at an extremely early age, acts in accordance with her inner compulsion to be a more complete and freer human being than her society—perhaps then, but certainly later—cares to allow her. These needs and actions, over a period of years, bring her into painful conflict with people, situations, the accepted ways of thinking, feeling and behaving, until she is in a state of continual war with everything around her, and usually with herself. She may not be fully conscious of the political implications of what for her began as personal necessity, but on some level she has not been able to accept the limitations and oppression laid on her by the most basic role of her society—the female role.

The limitations of the *black* female role are even greater in a racist and sexist society as is the amount of courage it takes to challenge them. It is no wonder that the townspeople see Sula's independence as imminently dangerous.

Morrison is also careful to show the reader that despite their years of separation and their opposing paths, Nel and Sula's relationship retains its primacy for each of them. Nel feels transformed when Sula returns and thinks:

It was like getting the use of an eye back, having a cataract removed. Her old friend had come home. Sula. Who made her laugh, who made her see old things with new eyes, in whose presence she felt clever, gentle and a littly raunchy. (95)

Laughing together in the familiar "rib-scraping" way. Nel feels "new, soft and new" (98). Morrison uses here the visual imagery which symbolizes the women's closeness throughout the novel.

Sula fractures this closeness, however, by sleeping with Nel's husband, an act of little import according to her system of values. Nel, of course, cannot understand. Sula thinks ruefully:

Nel was the one person who had wanted nothing from her, who had accepted all aspects of her. Now she wanted everything, and all because of *that*. Nel was the first person who had been real to her, whose name she knew, who had seen as she had the slant of life that made it possible to stretch it to its limits. Now Nel was one of *them*. (119-20)

Sula also thinks at the realization of losing Nel about how unsatisfactory her relationships with men have been and admits: "She had been looking all along for a friend, and it took her a while to discover that a lover was not a comrade and could never be-for a woman" (121). The nearest that Sula comes to actually loving a man is in a brief affair with Ajax and what she values most about him is the intellectual companionship he provides, the brilliance he "allows" her to show.

Sula's feelings about sex with men are also consistent with a lesbian interpretation of the novel. Morrison writes:

She went to bed with men as frequently as she could. It was the only place where she could find what she was looking for: *misery and the ability to feel deep sorrow*. ... During the lovemaking she found and needed to find the cutting edge. When she left off cooperating with her body and began to assert herself in the act, particles of strength gathered in her like steel shavings drawn to a spacious magnetic center, forming a tight cluster that nothing, it seemed, could break. *And there was utmost irony and outrage in lying under someone, in a position of surrender, feeling her own abiding strength and* limitless *power...*. When her partner disengaged himself, she looked up at him in wonder trying to recall his name ... waiting impatiently for him to tum away ... *leaving her to the postcoital privateness in which she met herself, welcomed herself and joined herself in matchless harmony*. (122-23)

Sula uses men for sex which results not in communion with them, but in her further delving into self.

Ultimately the deepest communion and communication in the novel occurs between two women who love each other. After their last painful meeting, which does not bring reconciliation, Sula thinks as Nel leaves her:

"So she will walk on down that road, her back so straight in that old green coat ... thinking how much I have cost her and never remember the days when we were two throats and one eye and we had no price." (147)

It is difficult to imagine a more evocative metaphor for what women can be to each other, the "pricelessness" they achieve in refusing to sell themselves for male approval, the total worth that they can only find in each other's eyes. Decades later the novel concludes with Nel's final comprehension of the source of the grief that has plagued her from the time her husband walked out. Morrison writes:

"All that time, all that time, I thought I was missing Jude." And the loss pressed down on her chest and came up into her throat. "We was girls together," she said as though explaining something. "O Lord, Sula," she cried, "girl, girl, girl girl girl."

It was a fine cry—loud and long—but it had no bottom and it had no top, just circles and circles of sorrow. (174)

Again Morrison exquisitely conveys what women, black women, mean to each other. This final passage verifies the depth of Sula and Nel's relationship and its centrality to an accurate interpretation of the work.

Sula is an exceedingly lesbian novel in the emotions expressed, in the definition of female character, and in the way that the politics of heterosexuality are portrayed. The very meaning of lesbianism is being expanded in literature, just as it is being redefined through politics. The confusion that many readers have felt about *Sui* may well have a lesbian explanation. If one sees Sula's inexplicable "evil" and nonconformity as the evil of not being male-identified, many elements in the novel become clear. The work might be clearer still if Morrison had approached her subject with the consciousness that a lesbian relationship was at least a possibility for her characters. Obviously Morrison did not *intend* the reader to perceive Sula and Nel's relationship as inherently lesbian. However, this lack of intention only shows the way in which heterosexist assumptions can veil what may logically be expected to occur in a work. What I have tried to do here is not to prove that Morrison wrote something that she did not, but to point out how a black feminist critical perspective at least allows consideration of this level of the novel's meaning.

In her interview in *Conditions: One* Adrienne Rich talks about unconsummated relationships and the need to reevaluate the meaning of intense yet supposedly nonerotic connections between women. She asserts: "We need a lot more documentation about what actually happened: I think we can also imagine it, because we know it happened—we know it out of our own lives." Black women are still in the position of having to "imagine," discover and verify black lesbian literature because so little has been written from an avowedly lesbian perspective. The near nonexistence of black lesbian literature which other black lesbians and I so deeply feel has everything to do with the politics of our lives, the total suppression of identity that all black women, lesbian or not, must face. This literary silence is again intensified by the unavailability of an autonomous black feminist movement through which we could fight our oppression and also begin to name ourselves.

In a speech, "The Autonomy of Black Lesbian Women," Wilmette Brown comments upon the connection between our political reality and the literature we must invent:

> Because the isolation of Black lesbian women, given that we are superfreaks, given that our lesbianism defies both the sexual identity that capital gives us and the racial identity that capital gives us, the isolation of Black lesbian women from heterosexual Black women is very profound. Very profound. I have searched throughout Black history, Black literature, whatever, looking for some women that I could see were somehow lesbian. Now I know that in a certain sense they were all lesbian. But that was a very painful search.

Heterosexual privilege is usually the only privilege that black women have. None of us have racial or sexual privilege, almost none of us have class privilege, maintaining "straightness" is our last resort. Being out, particularly out in print, is the final renunciation of any claim to the crumbs of tolerance that nonthreatening ladylike black women are sometimes fed. I am convinced that it is our lack of privilege and power in every other sphere that allows so few black women to make the leap that many white women, particularly writers, have been able to make in this decade, not merely because they are white or have economic leverage, but because they have had the strength and support of a movement behind them.

As black lesbians we must be out not only in white society, but in the black community as well, which is at least as homophobic. That the sanctions against black lesbians are extremely high is well illustrated in this comment by black male writer Ishmael Reed. Speaking about the inroads that whites make into black culture, he asserts:

In Manhattan you find people actively trying to impede intellectual debate among Afro-Americans. The powerful "liberal/radical/existentialist" influences of the Manhattan literary and drama establishment speak through tokens, like for example that ancient notion of the *one* black ideologue (who's usually a Communist), the *one* black poetess (who's usually a feminist lesbian).

To Reed, "feminist" and "lesbian" are the most pejorative terms he can hurl at a black woman and totally invalidate anything she might say; regardless of her actual politics or sexual identity. Such accusations are quite effective for keeping black women writers who are writing with integrity and strength from any conceivable perspective in line, but especially ones who are actually feminist and lesbian. Unfortunately Reed's reactionary attitude is all too typical. A community which has not confronted sexism, because a widespread black feminist movement has not required it to, has likewise not been challenged to examine its heterosexism. Even at this moment I am not convinced that one can write explicitly as a black lesbian and live to tell about it.

Yet there are a handful of black women who have risked everything for truth. Audre Lorde, Pat Parker and Ann Allen Shockley have at least broken ground in the vast wilderness of works that do not exist. Black feminist criticism will again have an essential role not only in creating a climate in which black lesbian writers can survive, but in undertaking the total reassessment of black literature and literary history needed to reveal the black woman-identified women that Wilmette Brown and so many of us are looking for.

Although I have concentrated here upon what does not exist and what needs to be done, a few black feminist critics have already begun this work. Gloria T. Hull at the University of Delaware has discovered in her research on black women poets of the Harlem Renaissance that many of the women who are considered minor writers of the period were in constant contact with each other and provided both intellectual stimulation and psychological support for each other's work. At least one of these writers, Angelina Weld Grimke, wrote many unpublished love poems to women. Lorraine Bethel, a recent graduate of Yale College, has done substantial work on black women writers, particularly in her senior essay, "This Infinity of Conscious Pain: Blues Lyricism and Hurston's Black Female Folk Aesthetic and Cultural Sensibility in *Their Eyes Were Watching God*," in which she brilliantly defines and uses the principles of black feminist criticism. Elaine Scott at the State University of New York at Old Westbury is also involved in highly creative and politically resonant research on Hurston and other writers.

The fact that these critics are young and, except for Hull, unpublished merely indicates the impediments we face. Undoubtedly there are other women working and writing whom I do not even know, simply because there is no place to read them. As Michele Wallace states in her article "A Black Feminist's Search for Sisterhood":

> We exist as women who are Black who are feminists, each stranded for the moment, working independently because there is not yet an environment in this society remotely congenial to our struggle—[or our thoughts].

I only hope that this essay is one way of breaking our silence and our isolation, of helping us to know each other.

Just as I did not know where to start I am not sure how to end. I feel that I have tried to say too much and at the same time have left too much unsaid. What I want this essay to do is lead everyone who reads it to examine *everything* that they have ever thought and believed about feminist culture and to ask themselves how their thoughts connect to the reality of black women's writing and lives. I want to encourage in white women, as a first step, a sane accountability to all the women who write and live on this soil. I want most of all for black women and black lesbians somehow not to be so alone. This last will require the most expansive of revolutions as well as many new words to tell us how to make this revolution real. I finally want to express how much easier both my waking and my sleeping hours would be if there were one book in existence that would tell me something specific about my life. One book based in black feminist and black lesbian experience, fiction or nonfiction. Just one work to reflect the reality that I and the black women whom I love are trying to create. When such a book exists then each of us will not only know better how to live, but how to dream.

(1977)

21. The Question of Form and Judgement in Contemporary Black American Poetry: 1962—1977
当代美国诗歌的形式与判断问题

Stephen E. Henderson

斯蒂芬·亨德森

斯蒂芬·亨德森(1925—1997),非裔美国文学与文化教授。亨德森于 1925 年 10 月 13 日出生于弗罗里达州的基韦斯特,第二次世界大战快结束时曾在美军中服役两年,后就读于亚特兰大的莫尔豪斯学院,1949 年以优异成绩毕业,获得学士学位,1950 年获得威斯康辛大学英语专业硕士学位,1959 年获得英语与艺术史博士学位,后在哈佛大学进行博士后研究。他曾先后在弗吉尼亚联合大学(1950—1962)、莫尔豪斯学院(1962—1969)与霍华德大学(1971—1992)等校任教,他的著作《理解新黑人诗歌》(*Understanding the New Black Poetry*:*Black Speech and Black Music as Poetic References*,1973)对黑人语言与黑人音乐的重视预示着后来学者,如贝克与盖茨等人的理论化研究之路,具有开拓性的意义。

亨德森的文章《当代美国诗歌的形式与判断问题》对非裔美国诗歌的评价比较具有代表性,入选多部非裔美国文学批评文集,在非裔美国文学批评界产生了比较广泛的影响,反映了特定时期非裔美国文学批评的理念。他所提出的几大问题,诸如"如何评价黑人诗歌","谁来评价黑人诗歌"等不仅具有方法论的意义,而且反映了美国黑人文学批评的原则。他认为,必须明确何谓"黑人诗歌",而且要具体考虑"经典""诗人""读者"以及"标准与评价"这四个方面的因素,才能很好地回答这两个问题。为更好地阐释自己的思想,他逐条予以分析,不仅追溯了非裔美国诗歌的源起与发展,而且回顾了非裔美国诗人的论述,并特别强调读者的反映对非裔美国诗歌发展的作用,以及诗歌的标准与评价中所蕴含的种族意识形态思想。

For one reason or another, the question of how to judge a Black poem has been fudged, blurred, evaded, or ignored. Now that the spectacular Black Arts Movement seems to have run its course, the question of evaluation takes on crucial importance. Among the signs that the movement is over, or is entering a new phase, are the demise of *Black World* magazine, the most important cultural periodical of the Black Consciousness Movement; the intensified sniping by scholars, Black and white, who disagreed with the idea of a Black Aesthetic; the systematic efforts by white scholars either to blunt, appropriate, or discredit the artistic achievements of the sixties, and their attendant critical justifications; and the defection of important writers to other camps, both aesthetic and political.

Although sniping at the Black Aesthetic is not new, its critics have not relented. In some instances, the concern is largely scholarly, as in the case of Arthur P. Davis, for example. In others, it is essentially polemical. Whether scholarly or not, reactions to the Black Aesthetic rest overtly or implicitly on a political base. At any rate, no one can accuse Prof. Davis of inconsistency, for throughout his long and distinguished career he has made plain his views on integration, on American literature, and the role which Black writers have played in shaping that literature. Yet the achievement of *From the Dark Tower*, 1974, his recent admirable history, is marred by his failure to grapple with the hard issues raised by the Black Aesthetic. He lumps all of the critics together, calls them honorable men, but asserts that to date they have failed either to destroy the white aesthetic or to erect another in its place. So, then, the question remains a matter of ranking authors according to their craftsmanship, their thematic concerns, in historical and social context, or the size of their output. Prof. Davis solves the problem of judgment by avoidance or oversimplification.

Another example of scholarly fudging is found in Robert Rosenblatt's recent book *Black Fiction*. He disposes of the problem of judgment by a retreat into formalism. The social issues are not important—technique is technique and pattern is pattern. Although he discusses fiction, not poetry, many of the issues are the same. Professor Rosenblatt solves the problem of judgment by ignoring it.

In Helen Vendler's review of a series of Broadside books for the *New York Times Book Review*, September 29, 1974, liberal sympathy is tempered by unconscious liberal condescension which reveals an essential ignorance of the issues involved in the Black Aesthetic in general and in the evaluation of Black poetry in particular. After praising the range and variety of Black "verse" and the pioneering role of Dudley Randall, she expresses the fond hope that in the future some single giant Black poet will unite all of those varied threads and themes in one single giant voice—as Whitman did, for example, for the American nation. What she fails to realize is that the Black epic voice is collective and communal, and it has already achieved what she speaks of, though in forms, perhaps, which she doesn't understand or recognize—in the tales and the spirituals especially, but also in the worksongs and the blues. Prof. Vendler also solves the problem of judgment by oversimplification.

Not so the editors of the *Saturday Review*. They solve it by overkill. In their infamous issue of November 15, 1975, devoted to "The Arts in Black America," the intent is clearly political, clearly designed to give a *coup de grace* to the Black Arts Movement. The article, written by Robert F. Moss, describes the state of the arts in Black America in pathological and racist terms. It links the political problems of FESTAC and the Nigerian government with the author's views on Black art in general. Of the Black Aesthetic, he predicts that it seems "destined to produce more heat than light." But one important by-product, he asserts, has been the building of Black audiences, presumably for legitimate art, that by whites or based on white models. Matters of "form and style" in Black art, he states, "have not really been ignored so much as they have been translated into ethnic terms, and in some cases thoroughly politicized. Black verse is perhaps the most obvious example." (p. 15) He continues: "The elder statesmen among black poets—notably Robert Hayden, Melvin B. Tolson, and Gwendolyn Brooks—achieved recognition from the literary establishment by adjusting their timbre and rhythms, their style and vocabulary, to the requirements of mainstream verse, although their subject matter was sometimes racial. Perhaps the last important 'accommodationist' was Baraka, a competent beat poet who was beached by the receding currents of that short-lived movement in the early sixties. Taking the techniques of Ginsberg & Company—a declamatory voice, deliberate formlessness, street language—and fusing them to virulent outbursts of racial protest, Baraka was able to found a new school of black poetry." (pp. 15, 16.)

It should be apparent that Moss would not think very highly of that poetry. Speaking of technical matters, Moss states:

> Baraka-ites such as Don L. Lee, Nikki Giovanni, Sonia Sanchez, and David Anderson profess to have tossed every scrap of whitey's *ars poetica* —along with his "diseased civilization"—onto the cultural bonfire. In its place they have introduced black consciousness, carefully equipped with a black literary technique to articulate it correctly. In practice this usually means a free use of obscenities (especially the omnipresent m-f), ghetto slang, phonetic spellings, typographical hijinks *a la* Cummings, a striving after oral effects, and a tone of voice pitched at megaphone level. (p. 16)

After examining examples of "verse" that he disagrees with from Carolyn Rodgers, Don Lee and Baraka, Moss concludes his observations on Black literary technique with the following:

> Beyond this, there is a taste for black word games like "playing the Dozens"

and "Signifying." Such is the route favored by Ishmael Reed, though he is better known as a novelist than as a poet. A devout follower of William Burroughs' comic surrealism with generous helpings of black folklore, pop culture, and ghetto sociology. Despite its imitativeness, his writing has a creative energy and a stylistic reach that is beyond most black writers today.(p. 17)

An analysis of these views and others will be made later in this essay. Suffice it to say at present that Prof. Moss repeats most of the cliches which critics of Black art, especially of the poetry, have made for some time. He adds a special virulence couched in the self-satisfaction of one who feels that he has done his homework and who knows, in addition, that his views have the editorial support of a powerful and influential periodical. That does not, of course, make them either accurate or important.

A further sign of reaction to the Black Consciousness Movement can be seen in another recent book by a white scholar—*Folklore in Nigerian Literature*, 1973, by Bernth Lindfors. Lindfors' book is relevant to our discussion for several reasons: (a) the aggressive, defensive tone of the introduction; (b) the rejection of white critics of their literature by both African and Afro-American critics; and (c) the theoretical implications of some of the chapters, especially the two listed under "Critical Perspectives" (p. 6, p. 23) and the one under "Rhetoric," entitled "Characteristics of Yoruba and Ibo Prose Styles in English." (p. 153)

Like numerous other white critics of "black" literature, Lindfors is concerned about the "territorial imperative" which Black critics asserted during the sixties. Lindfors quotes a statement which I made in *The Militant Black Writer*, 1969, that "despite the proliferation of 'experts,' whites are unable to evaluate the Black Experience, and, consequently, any work of art derived from it or addressed to those who live it." He adds: "Whites should therefore abandon the field to blacks, who are innately better qualified to understand and appreciate their own literature." (p. 1)

Lindfors calls attention to a similar rejection of white critics by African writers. Then he proceeds to some tacky logic and linguistic sleight of hand. "While these statements condemning the incompetence of white critics are not as extreme as those heard in America today, they do point in the same racial direction: black critics are acclaimed as the best possible interpreters of their own literature." (p. 1) And Prof. Lindfors gives what he calls the "standard reply" to these views.

A favorite tactic is to reverse the argument by asking "Should all the black critics—and this includes Africans as well as Afro-Americans and teachers and professors of literature throughout the world—be given a similar 'hands off' ultimatum on nonblack writing?"

"An affirmative answer to this question," Lindfors concludes, "would be very hard to justify." And, one might add, hardly worth the time.

The reactions cited above have one important common factor: They substitute for the question "How does one judge a Black poem?" the related, question "*Who* is to judge a Black poem?" While the substitution reveals a great deal about those who make it, it nonetheless leaves the prior question unanswered. To repeat, then, "How does one judge a Black poem?"

Curiously, very few answers were given to that question during the sixties. The responses among Blacks tended to be mystical, ideological, defensive, or hostile. Among whites, they tended and still tend to be condescending, defensive or preemptive, when not narrowly or naively academic. At any rate, there has been poor and uninformed criticism written by Blacks and whites alike. And, conversely, there has been on occasion, some useful criticism by Blacks, less frequently by whites. (A major exception is the important study of Baraka, *The Renegade and the Mask*, 1976, by Kimberly Benston.) Older Black poets and poets who are not Nationalists have stated that they would rather be reviewed by a good white critic than by a poor Black one. And writers as diverse as Frank Marshall Davis, Robert Hayden, and Clarence Major have said that they were not especially writing for a Black audience.

To begin with, the question of judgment is tied up with the question of definition. What is a Black poem? What is Black poetry? In *Understanding the New Black Poetry*, Morrow, 1973, I made an approach to that question in a series of statements, which I repeat below. These statements may be approached in an historical or empirical manner. In either case, one could say with varying degrees of validity that Black poetry is chiefly:

Any poetry by any person or group of persons of known Black African ancestry, whether the poetry is designated Black or not.

Poetry which is somehow *structurally* Black, irrespective of authorship.

Poetry by any person or group of known Black African ancestry, which is *also identifiably* Black, in terms of structure, theme or other characteristics.

Poetry by any identifiably Black person who can be classed as a "poet" by Black people. Judgment may or may not coincide with judgments of whites.

Poetry by any identifiably Black person whose ideological stance vis-a-vis history and the aspirations of his people since slavery is adjudged by them to be "correct."(p. 7)

Since an empirical approach has the advantage of historical anchorage and verifiability, let us place that perspective on the foregoing statements. Again, since I have discussed the implications of these statements in *Understanding the New Black Poetry*, I shall not pursue them here. Nevertheless, when the statements are examined from this perspective one must consider the following items: (a) *What the record or canon says*, (b) *What the poets say*, (c) *What the reader/audience/critic says*, and (d) *The notion of standards and evaluation*. In the following pages, I shall address each of these items in some detail.

a. *What the record reveals* is a rich tradition of both oral and written poetry which is usefully designated the folk and the formal. In the United States the oral traditions go back to the emergence of distinctive Afro-American verbal expression—the field cries and hollers, work songs, ballads, spirituals, sermons and blues. The size of this literature though not so complex as that of the West Indies or Africa is enormous. John Lovell, Jr. estimates the number of spirituals alone at over 10,000, with no way of knowing how many were not recorded. The tradition continues today in children's songs, in rapping, the dozens and its contemporary descendants, in the sermon, and in gospel and pop songs at their best. But gospel and pop songs are individually composed and written down, so here the oral tradition merges with that of the formal literary tradition. The literary tradition itself dates back to Lucy Terry's *Bars Fight*, 1746, a long ballad of historical rather than literary merit, and to Jupiter Hammon and Phillis Wheatley.

The nineteenth century produced dozens of published poets, some of significant talent. Notable among them were George Moses Horton, Charles L. Reason, Frances E. W. Harper, and Alberry A. Whitman. An introduction to these writers can be obtained from Benjamin Brawley's *Early American Negro Writers*; William H. Robinson's *Early Black American Poets*; Sterling A. Brown's *Negro Poetry and Drama*, and *The Negro Caravan* edited with Arthur P. Davis and Ulysses Lee. An important work in this area is Joan Sherman's recent book *The Invisible Poets*. In addition, there are individual volumes which are listed in Sherman's bibliographies and in checklists by Arthur Schomburg and Dorothy L. Porter.

Paul Laurence Dunbar, W. E. B. Du Bois, and James Weldon Johnson open the twentieth century. Their work was followed by Langston Hughes, Claude McKay, Jean Toomer, Sterling Brown, Countee Cullen, and the various poets of the New

Negro Movement. The next generation produced Margaret Walker, Owen Dodson, Gwendolyn Brooks, Robert Hayden, and others. Some of these poets were active in the fifties and the sixties. And, of course, the 1960's produced a veritable explosion of Black poetry, with such notable names as Amiri Baraka, Larry Neal, Sonia Sanchez, Nikki Giovanni, Don L. Lee(Haki Madhubuti) and others. Much of the work of this period has probably never been published so no one has a complete picture of the phenomenon. Notwithstanding, one can easily acquaint himself with this poetry by reading the individual volumes published by Broadside Press, Paul Bremen Press, and by major publications such as *The Journal of Black Poetry*; *Liberator*; *Negro Digest/Black World*; *Soul Book*; *Black Creations*, and *Umbra*. Some journals had limited, regional circulation, such as college publications like *Ex Umbra*. Some poets printed their works themselves. Many of these are listed in *Negro Digest/Black World*. Other sources include useful anthologies such as *Soul Script*, June Jordan; *Dices and Black Bones*, Adam David Miller; *Natural Process*, Tom Weatherly and Ted Willenz; *Understanding the New Black Poetry*, S. E. Henderson; *The Black Poets*, Dudley Randall; *The New Black Poetry*, Clarence Major. Current publishers of Black poetry include *First World*, *Essence*, *Black Arts South*, *Yardbird Reader*, *Black Books Bulletin*, etc. In addition, Black poetry is being published at workshops, on campuses, etc., as well as by white publishers. At any rate, this brief account merely hints at the corpus of poetry produced by Black Americans. To this (if one were talking about the entire range of modern Black poetry) could be added the poetry published in English by Caribbean and African poets living in the United States. Less tenable, but logical, would be the addition of all poetry in English by Africans on the continent and in the Dispersion. While that could be done and, eventually, must be done, the problem of focus would thereby be greatly increased. Thus for the purpose of this study, Black poetry must be studied in historical context—with Black people in the United States as the focus. The justification for this is simple. Modern Black formal poetry has existed longer in the United States than it has in Africa or the West Indies (Cf. Jahn, *Neo-African Literature*, p. 50, Table 1). In addition, the poetry of the Harlem Renaissance helped stimulate the flowering of modern Black Poetry in Africa, Europe and the West Indies, during the Negritude Movement. With that in mind, one could still benefit from studying work produced in Africa and the West Indies, not only in English, but in Portuguese, French, Dutch, Spanish as well as the various African languages. Conversely, any serious and extended study of the oral tradition of Afro-American poetry must recognize the vast resources of that tradition in Africa and the

West Indies. This includes not only traditional materials but popular contemporary expression as well.

b. *What the poets say*. Historically, the question of what constitutes a Black poem or how to judge one does not really come to a head until the 1960's and the promulgation of the Black Aesthetic in literature and the other arts. In a special sense, then, "Black" poetry was invented in the 1960's along with the radicalization of the word "Black" and the emergence of the Black Power philosophy. From the beginning, however, there were problems of definition, contradiction, ideology, and taste, resulting from differences in personal background and in political and cultural orientation. In the January, 1968 issue of *Negro Digest*, Hoyt Fuller, the Executive Editor, conducted a survey of the opinions of 38 Black writers on some 25 questions which included the following:

Do you see any future at all for the school of black writers which seeks to establish "a black aesthetic"?

Do you believe that the black writer's journey toward "Art" should lead consciously and deliberately through exploitation of "the black experience"?

Should black writers direct their work toward black audiences?

Some older writers, like Robert Hayden, felt that a writer's chief concern should be with the truth of all people everywhere. Others stressed craftsmanship and felt that writers should write to be read. Others felt enthusiastically that they should write about what they knew best, themselves and their people. There was, in effect, no simple consensus as to what Black writing was, could be, or should be, though there was fairly general agreement that Black writers should write about Black people, for Black people, and sometimes for sympathetic whites. Some younger writers were immersed in the self-consciousness of other "modern" writers; others still were rigidly nationalistic. The split among the younger writers was best exemplified in an exchange between Ron Karenga, of US and James Cunningham, of OBAC. Their views were polar. Karenga set forth his famous and influential dicta that literature must be functional, collective, and committing, and must support the Revolution. Cunningham felt that the writer should be free to express himself.

Perhaps the most insightful statement in the *Negro Digest* survey was made by Larry Neal. On the question of the Black Aesthetic, he said:

There is no need to establish a "black aesthetic." Rather, it is important to understand that one already exists. The question is: where does it exist? And what do we do with it. Further, there is something distasteful about a formalized aesthetic. This is what the so-called New Critics never understood. Essentially, art is relevant when it makes you stronger.(p. 35)

In that opening statement Neal not only demonstrated an understanding of the aesthetic questions under discussion but also an extensive grasp of the roots of Afro-American art, thereby linking up with a tradition of "criticism" which includes James Weldon Johnson, W. E. B. Du Bois, Alain Locke, and Sterling Brown. That was an important linkage, for it not only insured historical continuity but kept the field of discussion open to a wide range of approaches. At the same time that it claimed for the poet much of the personal freedom which Cunningham advocated, it insisted on the wider dedication advocated by Ron Karenga. But this was done with a greater degree of subtlety, as, for example in his sensitive understanding of the blues and the central importance of the Black Church.

c. *The Reader/Critic/Audience*. Specifically, the question of the poet's audience was crucial to the sixties. It was encapsulated in the *Negro Digest* survey. The response ranged from Karenga's paraphrase of Senghor that art is "functional, collective and committing or committed," to Gwendolyn Brooks' shrewd comment that Black writers "should concern themselves with TRUTH." Truth should be put upon paper. That phrase, 'direct their work,' she said in reference to the questionnaire, "suggests a secret contempt for the intelligence of the black audience" (p. 29). Some other writers hedged their bets, writing for ideal audiences, or for anyone who would buy their books. But the question was not altogether new, nor the consciousness. Langston Hughes had said to a similar question posed in 1927 by *Crisis* magazine, "We younger Negro artists who create now intend to express our individual dark-skinned selves without fear or shame. If white people are pleased we are glad. If they are not, it doesn't matter. We know we are beautiful. And ugly too. The tom-tom cries and the tom-tom laughs. If colored people are pleased we are glad. If they are not, their displeasure doesn't matter either. We build our temples for tomorrow, strong as we know how, and we stand on top of the mountain, free within ourselves" ("The Negro Artist and the Racial Mountain"). What is often overlooked in this passage is an individualism that borders on "Art for Art's Sake."

But Langston Hughes also pioneered some of the techniques of direct audience communication which were to become popular in the sixties. His readings with jazz accompaniment, his strong sense of the aural tradition, of the preacher and the musician, of the oral tradition of the raconteur and the rapper, provided a strong model. So that Larry Neal was to say in the sixties:

To explore the black experience means that we do not deny the reality and the power of the slave culture; the culture that produced the blues, spirituals, folk songs, work songs, and "jazz." It means that Afro-American life and its myriad of styles are expressed and examined in the fullest, most truthful manner possible. The models for what Black literature should be are found primarily in our folk culture, especially in the blues and jazz. Further models exist in the word-magic of James Brown, Wilson Pickett, Stevie Wonder, Sam Cooke, and Aretha Franklin. Have you ever heard a Black poet scream like James Brown? I mean, we should want to have that kind of energy in our work. The kind of energy that informs the music of John Coltrane, Cecil Taylor, Albert Ayler, and Sun Ra—the modern equivalent of the ancient ritual energy. An energy that demands to be heard, and which no one can ignore. Energy to shake us out of our lethargy and free our bodies and minds, opening us to unrealized possibilities. (*Negro Digest*, p. 81)

Again at this point one sees Neal's understanding of and linkage to the tradition of W. E. B. Du Bois, James Weldon Johnson, Langston Hughes, Sterling Brown, and Richard Wright. He adds two dimensions: popular music and African ritual. The crucial insight is the realization of Black oral expression as a continuum—in fact, oral expression as part of the larger global continuum of Black expressive culture.

Central to that continuum are music and dance. Small wonder then that when Black poets described what they were trying to do they used the language of these arts. Small wonder still that readers who conceived of poetry in Euro-American terms were unable to come to grips with the new Black poetry. This was true of some older Blacks as well as many white professional critics. Again, that should have surprised no one, for the history of the criticism of Black music and dance is a systematic attempt to deny the originality, the power, and the ultimate worth of those forms also. Thus Robert Moss and the others have their tradition too, of denial, presumption, subversion, and neglect.

The beauty and power of Black American poetry, notwithstanding these negative views, have long been recognized. Among the first to bring the oral tradition to national attention was Colonel Thomas Wentworth Higginson, in an article which appeared in the *Atlantic Monthly*, June, 1867, entitled "Negro Spirituals." He points out the verbal as well as the musical beauty of the songs. His reaction to one of the songs has been quoted by W. E. B. Du Bois, James Weldon Johnson, Sterling Brown and John Lovell, Jr. It is worth quoting again. He stated:

But of all the "spirituals" that which surprised me the most, I think—perhaps because it was that in which external nature furnished the images most directly—was this. With all my experience of their ideal ways of speech, I was startled when first I came on such a flower of poetry in that dark soil:

XVII. I Know Moon-Rise

I know moon-rise, I know star-rise,
Lay dis body down.
I walk in de moonlight, I walk in de starlight,
To lay dis body down.
I'll walk in de graveyard, I'll walk through de graveyard,
To lay dis body down.
I'll lie in de grave and stretch out my arms;
Lay dis body down.
I go to de judgment in de evenin' of de day,
When I lay dis body down;
And my soul and your soul will meet in de day
When I lay dis body down.

"I'll lie in de grave and stretch out my arms." Never, it seems to me, since man first lived and suffered, was his infinite longing for peace uttered more plaintively than in that line.

Note Higginson's expression—"their ideal ways of speech." It not only furnishes a corrective to the stereotypes created by the minstrel tradition, but provides an important literary insight. For speech is a chief element of anybody's poetry. And here the manner of the speech is noted in a useful way. We shall return later to this point.

Frequently the words of these songs are referred to as poems, as they are in this study. Their composers are also referred to as poets, by Blacks and whites alike. This practice is found not only in Higginson and others who appreciated the slaves' "ideal ways of speech," but by those who satirized the songs on the minstrel stage, and even, as John Lovell brings to our attention, on the concert stage.

At any rate, the language posed a challenge to the serious collector and the casual listener alike. There were problems of intelligibility and of transcription. Regarding the latter, V. S. Nathanson recounts his difficulty in transcribing a refrain which imitates a wild turkey's gobble. He concludes that "I am aware that no words can express the rich, unctuous, guttural flow of the line, when uttered in perfect time by a full gang at their corn-shucking task."

In "Song of the Slaves," John Mason Brown observes:

To convey a correct idea of negro pronunciation by ordinary rules of orthography is almost impossible. Combinations that would satisfy the ear would be grotesquely absurd to the eye. The habits of the negro in his pronunciation of English words are not such as minstrelsy would indicate. Just as the French and German characters in our comedies have passed into a conventional form of mispronunciation which the bulk of playgoers firmly believe to be lifelike and true, so have minstrels given permanency to very great mistakes in reproducing negro pronunciation. (*Lippincott's Magazine*, II, Philadelphia, December, 1868, 617-623).

The problem confronted Black scholars and poets also, just as it was to confront poets of the 1960's and the present decade. Paul Laurence Dunbar, for example, wrote in a dialect tradition popularized by whites, although his orthography was more idealized than satirical or fanciful. James Weldon Johnson wrote "coon songs" in the white manner of his time, but later turned to a serious confrontation of the problem of rendering the sounds of Black speech and song. In his two collections of Negro spirituals, *The Book of American Negro Spirituals*, 1925, and *The Second Book of Negro Spirituals*, 1926, he indicated the importance of preserving the original pronunciation of the words, and in the preface to the first volume, he discussed serious questions of dialect, voice timbre, and poetry, with informed sensitivity. Like John Mason Brown before him, he attacks visual grotesqueries masquerading as speech.

Negro dialect is for many people made unintelligible on the printed page by the absurd practice of devising a clumsy, outlandish, so-called phonetic spelling for words in a dialect story or poem when the regular English spelling represents the very same sound. Paul Laurance Dunbar did a great deal to reform the writing down of dialect, but since it is more a matter of ear than of rules those who are not intimately familiar with the sounds continue to make the same blunders. (*The Books of American Negro Spirituals*, James Weldon Johnson and J. Rosamond Johnson. Viking Press, 1940, p. 38.)

Later, Johnson spoke thus of his intent and method in his volume *God's Trombones*, 1927. These poems were sermons in the folk manner. He wanted to go beyond the limitations of dialect with its twin stops of pathos and humor. What he wanted was "a form that will express the racial spirit by symbols from within rather than by symbols from without, such as the mere mutilation of English spelling and pronunciation." The form would be "freer and larger than dialect, but which will still hold the racial flavor; a form expressing the imagery, the idioms, the peculiar turns of thought, and the distinctive humor and pathos, too, of the Negro, but which will also be capable of voicing the deepest and highest emotions and aspirations, and allow of the widest range of subjects and the widest scope of treatment." (*The Book of American Negro Poetry*, pp. 41 – 42).

But Johnson, like others, was acutely aware of the difficulties involved in developing this form. Earlier, he had said of the spirituals:

> What can be said about the poetry of the texts of the Spirituals? Naturally, not so much as can be said about the music. In the use of the English language both the bards and the group worked under limitations that might appear to be hopeless. Many of the lines are less than trite, and irrelevant repetition often becomes tiresome. They are often saved alone by their naivete. And yet there is poetry, and a surprising deal of it in the Spirituals. There is more than ought to be reasonably expected from a forcedly ignorant people working in an absolutely alien language. (*The Book of American Negro Spirituals*, p. 38)

And Thomas W. Talley makes the point with a Black anecdote. Speaking of the secular rhymes, he observes:

> When critically measured by the laws and usages governing the best English poetry, Negro Folk Rhymes will probably remind readers of the story of the good brother, who arose solemnly in a Christian praise meeting, and thanked God that he had broken all of the Commandments, but had kept his religion. (*Negro Folk Rhymes*, p. 228.)

Note Johnson's use of the terms "racial spirit" and "racial flavor" as well as the more explicit reference to "imagery," "idioms," and "peculiar turns of thought." Note, too, the humorous but meaningful use of the term "religion" by Talley. To this one might add a remark by an experienced preacher from the folk tradition. When his language was questioned by his self-consciously academic brothers in the seminary, he stated: "A verb is like a nut. You got to crack it to get the goodie out of it." And Sterling Brown reports an encounter with a young minister at Virginia Seminary, in 1923, when he took his first job, teaching English. He was so exacting in his grading that the students called him a "red ink man." The exasperated seminarian said to him one day, "Prof., you run them verbs, and I'll drive the thought." And Brown concedes, "He could drive the thought."

And a few years later James Weldon Johnson wrote the preface to Sterling Brown's masterly first volume of poems *Southern Road*. He said:

> He infused his poetry with genuine characteristic flavor by adopting as his medium the common, racy, living speech of the Negro in certain phases of *real* life. For his raw material he dug down into the deep mine of Negro folk poetry. He found the unfailing sources from which sprang the Negro folk epics and ballads such as "Stagolee," "John Henry," "Casey Jones," "Long Gone John" and others.
>
> But as I said in commenting on his work in *The Book of American Negro Poetry*: he has made more than mere transcriptions of folk poetry, and he has done more than bring to it mere artistry; he has deepened its meanings and multiplied its implications. He has actually absorbed the spirit of his material, made it his own; and without diluting its primitive frankness and raciness, truly re-expressed it with artistry and magnified power. In a word, he has taken this raw material and worked it into original authentic poetry.

In other words, Sterling Brown had achieved the kind of form that Johnson himself had spoken of and had experimented with in *God's Trombones*.

Johnson had singled out other young poets for special mention. Among them were Claude McKay, Jean Toomer, Countee Cullen, and Langston Hughes. Even a cursory examination of their work would reveal a wide range of styles, technique, subject matter, and tone, from the Romantic sonorities of Cullen to the jazzy rhythms of Hughes. Yet they had something in common, their concern with "race" and their response to it. Johnson states, "In their approach to 'race' they are less direct and obvious, less didactic or imploratory; and, too, they are less regardful of the approval or disapprobation of their white environment." ("Preface" to *SR*, xxxvi.)

These statements of Johnson's, taken together with other observations of his, pose most of the larger critical questions of Black poetry, questions of *range*, *theme*, *form* and *structure*, and *judgment*. As far as the theme is concerned, that which makes it Black is "race," in his words, "the principal motive of poetry written by Negroes ..." (xxvi). As for form and structure, they are found in "the deep mine of Negro folk poetry" (xxxvi). Yet he includes the sonnets of Claude McKay and Countee Cullen and the free verse odes of Jean Toomer, all written in "standard English." And we may recall some of the difficulty which Johnson experienced with the language of the spirituals, a difficulty not really unlike that encountered by the white collector John Mason Brown. Not merely the problem of orthography, but of poetic expression.

Notwithstanding the beauty of the music, the difficulty of working in an unfamiliar language caused the slaves to produce many lines which "are less than trite, and irrelevant repetition often becomes tiresome. They are often saved alone by their naivete." Yet Johnson makes critical judgments, both of the spirituals, and, as we have seen, of the formal poets, of whom the "Younger Group" received his special blessings.

On what basis was Johnson able to distinguish the excellent from the trite in this vastly varied body of material? Obviously he had some means, some measure, some touchstone that would allow him to accept both the Keatsean lushness of Cullen, the sonorous language of the sermons, and the transcendent simplicity of the spirituals. Johnson himself suggests something of his mechanism, his method, and his consideration in several places, among them the two works previously cited and in his *Autobiography of an Ex-Coloured Man*. The mechanism included a reliance upon the ear rather than the eye, for example, and he states:

> Paul Laurence Dunbar did a great deal to reform the writing down of dialect, but since it is more a matter of ear than of rules those who are not intimately familiar with the sounds continue to make the same blunders.

This reliance upon the ear includes a deep and sympathetic and sensitive knowledge and love of music, not only that of his own people but of other cultures as well. He could thus say with complete assurance of the motif of the spiritual "Go Down Moses" ("Preface," *The Book of American Negro Spirituals*, 13):

> I have termed this music noble, and I do so without qualifications. Take, for example, *Go Down Moses*: there is not a nobler theme in the whole musical literature of the world. If the Negro had voiced himself in only that one song, it would have been evidence of his nobility of soul.

And his knowledge of Black music ran the gamut, from the worksongs and the spirituals to ragtime and the newly emergent jazz. Black music, he says in effect, is the touchstone of Black art. And the touchstone can be applied also to the creative work of other cultures. This is implicit in the statement above. It is more explicit in his poetic statement in "O Black and Unknown Bards."

But Johnson certainly did not slight the verbal component of the songs. He recognized the poetry in their very titles. Although later scholarship has demonstrated that he overstated his case for the originality of the spirituals, it is still essentially correct.

> The white people among whom the slaves lived did not originate anything

comparable even to the mere titles of the Spirituals. In truth, the power to frame the poetic phrases that make the titles of so many of the Spirituals betokens the power to create the songs. Consider the sheer magic of:

> Swing Low Sweet Chariot
>
> I've Got to Walk my Lonesome Valley
>
> Steal Away to Jesus
>
> Singing With a Sword in My Hand
>
> Rule Death in His Arms
>
> Ride on King Jesus
>
> We Shall Walk Through the Valley in Peace
>
> The Blood Came Twinklin' Down
>
> Deep River
>
> Death's Goin' to Lay His Cold, Icy Hand on Me

And confess that none but an artistically endowed people could have evoked it.

No one has even expressed a doubt that the poetry of the titles and text of the Spirituals is Negro in character and origin, no one else has dared to lay claim to it; why then doubt the music? ("Preface," pp. 15, 16.)

Of course, even the texts were later disputed by George Pullen Jackson. And Johnson's protege, the young Sterling Brown, was to make the final point with his characteristic wit:

> In bringing forth proof that in words and melody many Negro spirituals are traceable to white songs, southern white scholars have succeeded in disproving the romantic theory of completely African origin for the spirituals. All of those who assiduously collect evidence grant, however, that now the Negro song is definitely the Negro's regardless of ultimate origin, and one of them writes as follows: "The words of the best White Spirituals cannot compare as poetry with the words of the best Negro spirituals." It remains to be said that for the best Negro spirituals, camp-meeting models remain to be discovered. (*Negro Poetry & Drama*, 17.)

d. *The notion of standards and evaluation*. I have taken thus long to suggest the outlines of this argument on the originality and the power of Black folk poetry for two reasons: (1) the poets of the sixties claim a kinship with this poetry and music; and (2) the questions raised cast some light on the latter body of poetry, some of the disputes, some of the achievement, and some of the promise.

Some of the dispute over recent Black poetry is traceable to the experimental nature of much of it, and it follows that this dispute is not necessarily racial in character. For example, Robert F. Moss's reference to the "typographical hijinks" of

e. e. cummings, or W. E. Farrison's peevish dismissal of similar experimentation in his review of Beatrice Murphy's anthology of young Negro poets. White critics, of course, have dismissed white writers in much the same manner. And, of course, one remembers the furor raised over Alan Ginsberg's "Howl" and, earlier, over Walt Whitman's *Leaves of Grass*, to name two works at random.

But the reaction goes deeper than mere resistance to change and experimentation. It seems rooted in white America's perception of the lives and culture of Black Americans, which has been marked by distortion, and by a continuing and systematic attempt to ridicule, to deny, to absorb, or to appropriate that culture. Specifically, both traditions of Afro-American poetry have long been under siege, and just to mention Black poetry is to evoke a history of white critical condescension and snobbery, and more recently, outright pathological ignorance and fear. The roots of this reaction are deep and pervasive. They are entwined in nineteenth-century attempts to justify slavery by proving the innate inferiority of the African slave. They are entwined in the African's supposed inability to master the "difficult" European languages. They are entwined in the questioning of the African's very humanity. (cf. Thomas Jefferson on the African and Greek verb, or on Benjamin Banneker.) They are likewise entwined in European conceptions of the poet and poetry—the poet as maker, or prophet, or divine madman; the poetry as sacred text or as edifying verbal diversion, producing pleasure.

Since a poem is made of words and since the slave was incapable of mastering the "difficult" English tongue, how could one take seriously the idea of a Black American poet? Most did not. A few did, as the history of the early poets, Jupiter Hammond, Phillis Wheatley, and George Moses Horton attests. But essentially they were curiosities. Phillis Wheatley was a successful experiment to test the strength of nurture vs. nature; and Hammond and Horton were sports of nature (which was, indeed, one eighteenth century definition of genius).

Other early poets took as their central aim the vindication of their race from calumny and, indeed, the larger task of Liberation through appealing to the conscience of the ruling whites. This appeal ranged from direct protest to demonstrations of worthiness as evinced by learning and by mastery of the craft of poetry. Thus Alberry A. Whitman justifies his use of the difficult Spenserian stanza, the "'stately verse,' mastered only by Spenser, Byron, and a very few other great poets," because, "Some negro is sure to do everything that anyone else has ever done, and as none of that race have ever executed a poem in the 'stately verse,' I simply venture in" (quoted by J. Sherman, p. 12).

This emphasis on craftsmanship is historically quite important. It shows the Black poet reflecting the same kind of concerns as other gifted Black individuals. It also shows a continuing need to test oneself according to white standards, and sometimes to receive white praise. Whitman treasured the praise he received from Bryant, just as Phillis Wheatley had treasured the praise of the literati of her day. And decades later, W. D. Howells was to praise Paul Laurence Dunbar in the same liberal manner. Later still Gwendolyn Brooks was awarded a Pulitzer prize for her technical mastery of the forms of Modernist poetry, and Karl Shapiro and Allen Tate were to praise Melvin B. Tolson for having assimilated the language of the Anglo-Saxon poetic tradition and for writing in "Negro" at the same time.

All of this was the recognition of individuals, not of a tradition. Indeed, the attempt has been from the outset to ignore, absorb, or to destroy the tradition in both its folk and formal dimensions. Despite this, however, the beauty and power of the tradition have been recognized by many, even though grudgingly at times.

As I have suggested, a good deal of the confusion comes from the variety of the poetry itself. Some comes from the desire of certain poets to be free from racial identification which implied inferiority of achievement or judgment by less rigorous standards. Some too comes from certain poets' unwillingness to be limited to writing on racial themes. One certainly thinks of Cullen, Hayden, Oden, Major and others.

The central concern seems to be the assumption that poetry which can be identified as Black is "racist" or inferior or un-American, so that one pretends that race is unimportant or that Black poetry is merely a fad or a bad imitation of experimental white poetry (as the Robert Moss analysis states). All of this, of course, is nonsense. Black poetry can and should be judged by the same standards that any other poetry is judged by—by those standards which validly arise out of the culture. Some of it is good, some excellent, and some downright bad. Much of this awareness has been expressed by the poets themselves, some of whom are excellent critics, like Lance Jeffers, Ethelbert Miller, Sarah Fabio, June Jordan, Margaret Walker, and Carolyn Rodgers to name but a few.

At any rate, scattered throughout their interviews, their essays, and their conversations, there are many critical pronouncements by Black poets themselves. Similarly, there are the pronouncements and preferences of their readers and their audiences, including professional scholars and critics, white, Black and other. Whether the poets approve or not is now certainly irrelevant since their work has become part of the general consciousness. And that consciousness has been formed by the media, both the national institutions and myths, and by the educational system, both public and private. That, of course, is obvious. What is less obvious is the extent to which the Black reader/audience/poet has been shaped by these forces and, further still, and more important, how they have created and synthesized a special consciousness out of their special history and experience.

Thus we have the phenomenon of Tolsonout-Pounding Pound and critics and scholars employing constructs derived from English, European, or American literature to evaluate Black literature. There is nothing necessarily wrong with this. Intellectually, we are to a large extent what we read. And we certainly need not ignore non-Black writing and criticism. Indeed, we do so at our own risk.

Nevertheless, the question, in a practical sense is whether Black poetry can most effectively be understood, experienced, explicated and encouraged by complete or even major reliance upon methodologies and standards that have evolved out of the larger Euro-American Society. To the extent that we share those values and concerns, then perhaps it should be, for the sake of efficiency and simplicity, especially for those readers who are university trained. Yet we all know that even those of us who are so trained and are accustomed to think in certain academic patterns also react in complex ways to the cultural referents and forms which arise from our Black Experience. Since the poetry often consciously or unconsciously draws upon this dual heritage one would expect a useful critical method to do likewise. Accordingly, if one were to approach the work of the past fifteen years one could begin at whatever intellectual locus he may inhabit and push toward the central experience of the poem. Easily a good deal of the work is approachable in this way, much of early Baraka, for example.

Notwithstanding, we are soon confronted with the ambiguities and densities which make up a wide range of the poems, which make up, in effect, the *blackness* of the poems. Some of these elements can be explicated through historical and cultural study. Others have to be experienced because they are "saturated" in Black Experience and these may include some which are written in so-called "Standard English."

Let us recall that there are two large categories of Black poetry of this period: (a) the political poetry of Black Power, and (b) the cultural poetry of the Black Experience. Although these categories overlap, they are by no means congruent, and writers shift from one to the other, sometimes without much clarify.

At any rate, purpose is important. The object of a Black Power poem is to raise

Black people's consciousness. The classic statement is given by Ron Karenga in his paraphrase of Leopold Senghor and in Baraka's "Black Art." These poems were often frankly propagandistic and, technically speaking, quite often not very interesting. They were meant to be "throw-away" poems. Perhaps then, they should be examined in this light—they were raps for the occasion, and the occasion was the Revolution.

But all of these were not raps, and certainly not deficient either in execution or in delivery. Excellent examples can be found in Touré, Baraka, Neal, Lee, Sanchez, the Last Poets, Ahmed A. Alhamisi and elsewhere. And one needs to observe that many great poems of the West were highly political in their time, among them the *Divine Comedy* and *Paradise Lost*. So it does not follow that Black Power poems had to be shoddy or trite. In fact, there is a "revolutionary obligation" to make the poem as good as one can. Too, many of these poems were written by non-poets, by ordinary people in a state of excitement and fervor which they felt compelled to express. This was not a function of education or class necessarily, though many were obviously written by college students. In a word, then, one should judge these poems in historical context, even that of specific readings and performances where records are available. Did the poet "get over"? That was the criterion. That was all he was trying to do.

The other category of poems was generally more sophisticated and ambitious. They not only wanted to raise consciousness, they also wanted to do it with style, to celebrate Black life and culture, to seek a larger cosmic consciousness, which, at any rate, was black, the Original Blackness.

And they wanted to do this with the energy and subtlety and precision of a John Coltrane or with the people-reaching power of a James Brown. In this regard they were certainly following in a long tradition extending formally back to Dunbar and James Weldon Johnson on one hand and to the spirituals and blues on the other. And behind that to Mother Africa.

The more astute among those poets realized that they were seeking interior models, not archeological revivals of older musical/poetic forms. But what were those forms to be like? How were they to be transmitted, created? They spoke by necessity in metaphoric terms, as Neal's mention of "the modern equivalent of the ancient ritual energy" or "word-magic" or Stanley Crouch's "The Big Feeling." And the object of all of this is, again in Neal's words, "to shake us out of our lethargy and free our bodies and minds, opening us to unrealized possibilities." These "unrealized possibilities," as suggested by the work of Baraka, Dumas, June Jordan, Alhamisi and many others, go far beyond the narrow political concerns of Black Power to a concern (no less rooted in history) with ultimate philosophical and spiritual questions.

How did the poets approach these problems in terms of craft? How successful have they been? As I have stated in this essay, and at considerable length in others, they employed a wide variety of language, at times drawn from Black speech patterns, at times not. They also through a variety of means—some clever, some clumsy— sought to tap the resources latent in Black music. These are structural considerations, and when they are successful, they form the most striking features of the recent Black poetry.

But again, how successful have these works been? And how do we judge? Essentially on the terms posed by the individual poem. If a love poem is written in blues style, it can be judged against thousands of such poems—from the urban and folk traditions, as well as from the literary versions of Hughes and Sterling Brown. There are individual blues poems which stand up under any critical examination—such as Son House's "Death Letter." For drama, for lyrical intensity and sensual precision it competes favorably with many literary poems. Blues lovers, Black, white and Japanese, know the traditionally great blues songs—the masterpieces, the legendary sessions, the mind melting lines. Any love poem written in the blues manner has to be measured against the bitter humor of: "I asked her for water and she gave me gasoline." Or the pathos of "I folded by arms, I slowly walked away/She's a good old girl—gotta lay there till judgment day." And the self destructive despair of Tommy Johnson's lines—"Canned heat, canned heat, sure, Lord, killin' me." And the poet's *Angst* has be measured against "the blues ain't nothin' but a low-down shakey chill." Henry Dumas measured against this standard is successful.

But just as jazz musicians have explored and extended the blues experience through technical means, one must ask whether in an analogous way the poets of the sixties were able to extend the achievement of Langston Hughes and Sterling Brown; or better still, whether they have been able to build on the stylistic dynamics of Black language styles (in speech and song) to create the "word-magic" that they aspired to. Intuitively, I know that some like June Jordan, like Baraka, like Neal, like Jayne Cortez, like Carolyn Rodgers, like Sonia—intuitively, I know that they have. However, in criticism intuition, though vital, is not enough. The canons, the categories, the dynamics must be as clear and as reasoned as possible. These must rest on a sound empirical base. Beneath Larry Neal's "word-magic" lie many subtle and useful linguistic patterns which merit some critical description and organization, not to restrict the poet's freedom to invent and to discover, but to serve as a guide, a framework against which these discoveries may be understood and appreciated. And in the final analysis, the issue is still the problem of definition and the problem of control, not only in literature, but in the life which it refracts and reflects.

(1977)

22. Generational Shifts and the Recent Criticism of Afro-American Literature
世代递嬗与近来的非裔美国文学批评

Houston A. Baker, Jr.
休斯敦·贝克

休斯敦·贝克(1943),批评家、诗人与编辑。贝克出生于肯塔基州的路易斯维尔,在霍华德大学以优等生成绩毕业,1968 年获得加州大学洛杉矶分校博士学位。他著述颇丰,20 世纪 70 年代以来,陆续撰写、编辑出版多部非裔美国文学与文化研究著作,如《黑人长歌》(*Long Black Song*: *Essays in Black American Literature and Culture*,1972),《归途迢迢》(*The Journey Back*: *Issues in Black Literature and Criticism*,1980),《布鲁斯、意识形态与非裔美国文学:黑人本土理论》(*Blues*,*Ideology*,*and Afro-American Literature*: *A Vernacular*,1984),《现代主义与哈莱姆文艺复兴》(*Modernism and the Harlem Renaissance*,1987),《非裔美国诗学:反思哈莱姆与黑人美学》(*Afro-American Poetics*: *Revisions of Harlem and the Black Aesthetic*,1988),《精神的活动:非裔美国女性创作诗学》(*Workings of the Spirit*: *The Poetics of Afro-American Women's Writing*,1991),《背叛:黑人知识分子是如何放弃民权时代理想的》(*Betrayal*: *How Black Intellectuals Have Abandoned the Ideals of the Civil Rights Era*,2008)等,入选“50 位重要文学理论家”。他所提出的“艺术人类学”“世代递嬗”“黑人本土理论”等概念,不仅对深入了解、把握非裔美国文学批评有指导意义,也可为其他民族、其他地区的文学批评提供借鉴。

贝克的论文《世代递嬗与近来的非裔美国文学批评》通过简要梳理过去四十来年非裔美国文学批评方面出现的变化,回顾了“融合诗学”“黑人美学”与“课程的重构”等主要批评思想,指出当下非裔美国文学批评中注重语言系统,利用语言构筑“现实”的新趋势。另外,他借用库恩的“范式”概念,采取“点面结合”的方式,重点分析了亨德森与盖茨的文学批评实践,特别是后者利用后结构主义思想进行文学批评的新尝试,为读者了解当代非裔美国文学批评的嬗变描绘了比较全面、深入的图景。

I

There exist any number of possible ways to describe changes that have occurred in Afro-American literary criticism during the past four decades. If one assumes a philosophical orientation, one can trace a movement from democratic pluralism ("integrationist poetics") through romantic Marxism (the "Black Aesthetic") to a version of Aristotelian metaphysics (the "Reconstruction of Instruction"). From another perspective, one can describe the ascendant class interests that have characterized Afro-America since World War II, forcing scholars, in one instance, to assess Afro-American expressive culture at a mass level and, in another instance, to engage in a kind of critical "professionalism" that seems contrary to mass interests. One can survey, on yet another level, transformations in the recent criticism of Afro-American literature from a perspective in the philosophy of science; from this vantage point, one can explore conceptual, or "paradigm," changes that have marked the critical enterprise in recent years. These various levels of analysis can be combined, I think, in the notion of the "generational shift."

A "generational shift" can be defined as an ideologically motivated movement overseen by young or newly-emergent intellectuals who are dedicated to refuting the work of their intellectual predecessors and to establishing a new framework of intellectual inquiry. The affective component of such shifts is described by Lewis Feuer: "Every birth or revival of an ideology is borne by a new generational wave; in its experience, each such new intellectual generation feels everything is being born anew, that the past is meaningless, or irrelevant, or nonexistent." The new generation's break with the past is normally signaled by its adoption of what the philosopher of science Thomas S. Kuhn (to whose work I shall return later) designates a new "paradigm"; i.e., a new set of guiding assumptions that unifies the intellectual community.

In the recent criticism of Afro-American literature, there have been two distinct generational shifts. Both have involved ideological and aesthetic reorientations, and both have been accompanied by shifts in literary-critical and literary-theoretical paradigms. The first such shift occurred during the mid-1960s. It led to the displacement of what might be described as integrationist poetics and gave birth to a new object or scholarly investigation.

II

The dominant critical perspective on Afro-American literature during the late 1950s and early 1960s might be called the poetics of integrationism. Richard Wright's essay "The Literature of the Negro in the United States," which appears in his 1957 collection entitled *White Man, Listen!*, offers an illustration of integrationist poetics. Wright optimistically predicts that Afro-American literature may soon be indistinguishable from the mainstream of American arts and letters. The basis for his optimism is the Supreme Court's decision in *Brown vs. Topeka Board of Education* (1954), in which the Court ruled that the doctrine "separate but equal" was inherently unequal. According to Wright, this ruling ensures a future "equality" in the experiences of black and white Americans, and this equality of *social* experience will translate in the literary domain as a homogeneity of *represented* experience (103-105). When Afro-American writers have achieved such equality and homogeneity, they will stand at one with the majority culture—in a relationship that Wright terms "entity" (72).

But the foregoing stipulations apply only to what Wright calls the "Narcissistic Level"—i.e., the self-consciously literate level—of Afro-American culture (84-85). At the folk, or mass, level the relationship between Afro-American and the majority culture has always been one of "identity" (as in "the black person's quest for identity"), or separateness (72). And though Wright argues that the self-consciously literate products of Afro-America that signify a division between cultures (e.g., "protest" poems and novels) may disappear relatively quickly under the influence of the Brown decision, he is not so optimistic with regard to the "Forms of Things Unknown" (83) i. e., the expressive products of the black American masses. For blues, jazz, work songs, and verbal forms such as folktales, boasts, toasts, and dozens are functions of the black masses' relationship of "identity" with the mainstream culture. They Signal, that is to say, *an absence of equality* and represent a *sensualization* of the masses' ongoing suffering (83). They are, according to Wright, improvisational forms filled "with a content wrung from a bleak and barren environment, an environment that stung, crushed, all but killed" (84). Only when the "Forms of Things Unknown" have disappeared altogether, or when conditions have been realized that enable them to be raised to a level of self-conscious art, will one be able to argue that an egalitarian ideal has been achieved in American life and art. The only course leading to such a positive goal, Wright implies, is momentous social action like that represented by the 1954 Supreme Court decision.

Hence, the black spokesman who champions a poetics of integrationism is constantly in search of social indicators (such as the Brown decision) that signal a democratic pluralism in American life. The implicit goal of this philosophical orientation is a raceless, classless community of men and women living in perfect harmony (105). The integrationist critic, as Wright demonstrates, founds his predictions of a future, homogeneous body of American creative expression on such social *evidence* as the Emancipation Proclamation, Constitutional amendments, Supreme Court decisions, or any one of many other documented claims that suggest that America is moving toward a pluralistic ideal. The tone that such critics adopt is always one of optimism.

Arthur P. Davis offers a striking example of an Afro-American critic who has repeatedly sought to discover evidence to support his arguments that a oneness of all Americans and a harmonious merger of disparate forms of American creative expression are impending American social realities. What seems implicit in Davis's critical formulations is a call for Afro-American writers to speed the emergence of such realities by offering genuine, *artistic* contributions to the kind of classless, raceless literature that he and other integrationist critics assume will carry the future. An injunction of this type can be inferred, for example, from the 1941 "Introduction" to *The Negro Caravan*, the influential anthology of Afro-American expression that Davis coedited with Sterling Brown and Ulysses Lee:

> The editors ... do not believe that the expression "Negro literature" is an accurate one, and in spite of its convenient brevity, they have avoided using it. "Negro literature" has no application if it means *structural peculiarity*, or a Negro school of writing. The Negro writes in the forms evolved in English and American literature. ... The editors consider Negro writers to be American writers, and literature by American Negroes to be a segment of American literature. ... The chief cause for objection to the term is that "Negro literature" is too easily placed by certain critics, white and Negro, in an alcove apart. The next step is a double standard of judgment, which is dangerous for the future of Negro writers.

In the 1950s and 1960s, Davis continued to champion the poetics implicit in such earlier work as *The Negro Caravan*. His essay "Integration and Race Literature," which he presented to the first conference of Afro-American writers sponsored by the American Society of African Culture in 1959, states:

The course of Negro American literature has been highlighted by a series of social and political crises over the Negro's position in America. The Abolition Movement, the Civil War, Reconstruction, World War I, and the riot-lynching period of the twenties all radically influenced Negro writing. Each crisis in turn produced a new tradition in our literature; and as each crisis has passed, the Negro writer has dropped the social tradition which the occasion demanded and moved towards the mainstream of American literature. The integration controversy is another crisis, and from it we hope that the Negro will move permanently into full participation in American life-social, economic, political, and literary.

The stirring drama implied here of black writers finding their way through various "little" traditions to the glory of the "great" mainstream is a function of Davis's solid faith in American pluralistic ideals. He regards history and society from a specific philosophical and ideological standpoint: Afro-Americans and their expressive traditions, like other minority cultures, have always moved unceasingly toward a unity with American majority culture. He thus predicts—like Wright—the eventual disappearance of social conditions that produce literary works of art that are identifiable (in terms of "structural peculiarity") as "Negro" or "Afro-American" literature.

Wright and Davis represent a generation whose philosophy, ideology, and attendant poetics support the vanishing of Afro-American literature qua *Afro-American* literature. I shall examine this proposition at greater length in the next section. At this point, I simply want to suggest that the consequences of this generational position for literary-critical axiology can be inferred from the "Introduction" to *The Negro Caravan*. The editors of that work assert: "They [Afro-American writers] must ask that their books be judged as books, without sentimental allowances. In their own defense they must demand a single standard of criticism" (7). This assertion suggests that black writers should construct their works in ways that make them acceptable in the sight of those who mold a "single standard of criticism" in America. These standard bearers were for many years, however, a small, exclusive community of individuals labelled by black spokesmen of the sixties as the "white, literary-critical establishment." And only a poetics buttressed by a philosophical viewpoint that augured the eventual unification of *all* talented creative men and women as judges could have prompted such able spokesmen as Wright, Brown, and Davis to consider that works of Afro-American literature and verbal art be subjected to a "single standard" of American literary-critical judgment.

III

The generational shift that displaced the integrationist poetics just described brought forth a group of intellectuals most clearly distinguished from its predecessors by its different ideological and philosophical posture vis-à-vis American egalitarian ideals. After the arrests, bombings, and assassinations that comprised the white South's reaction to nonviolent, direct-action protests by hundreds of thousands of civil rights workers from the late fifties to the mid-sixties, it was difficult for even the most committed optimist to feel that integration was an impending American social reality Rather than searching for documentary evidence and the indelible faith necessary to argue for an undemonstrated American egalitarianism, the emerging generation set itself the task of analyzing the nature, aims, ends, and arts of those hundreds of thousands of their own people who were assaulting America's manifest structures of exclusion.

The Afro-American masses demonstrated through their violent acts ("urban riots") in Harlem, Watts, and other communities throughout the nation that they were intent on black social and political sovereignty in America. Their acts signaled the birth of a new ideology, one that received its proper name in 1966, when Stokely Carmichael designated it "Black Power":

> [Black Power] is a call for black people in this country to unite, to recognize their heritage, to build a sense of community. It is a call for black people to begin to define their own goals, to lead their own organizations and to support those organizations. It is a call to reject the racist institutions and values of [American] society.

This definition, drawn from Carmichael and Charles Hamilton's work entitled *Black Power*, expresses a clear imperative for Afro-Americans to focus their social efforts and political vision on their *own* self-interests. This particularity of Black Power—its sharp emphasis on the immediate concerns of Afro-Americans themselves—was a direct counterthrust by an emergent generation to the call for a general, raceless, classless community of men and women central to an earlier integrationist framework. The community that was of interest to the emergent generation was not a future generation of integrated Americans, but rather a present, vibrant group of men and women who constituted the heart of Afro-America. The Afro-American masses became, in the late sixties and early seventies, both subject and audience for the utterances of black political spokesmen moved by a new ideology.

The poetics accompanying the new ideological orientation were first suggested by Amiri Baraka (LeRoi Jones) in an address entitled "The Myth of a 'Negro Literature,'" which he presented to the American Society of African Culture in 1962:

> Where is the Negro-ness of a literature written in imitation of the meanest of social intelligences to be found in American culture, i.e., the white middle class? How can it even begin to express the emotional predicament of black Western man? Such a literature, even if its "characters" *are* black, takes on the emotional barrenness of its model, and the blackness of the characters is like the blackness of Al Jolson, an unconvincing device. It is like using black checkers instead of white. They are still checkers.

At the self-consciously literate level of Afro-American expression, the passage implies, black spokesmen have deserted the genuine emotional referents and the authentic experiential categories of black life in America. The homogeneity between their representations of experience and those of the white mainstream are a cause for disgust rather than an occasion for rejoicing. Finally, the quoted passage implies that the enervating merger of black and white expression at the "Narcissistic" level (to use Wright's phrase) of Afro-American life is a result of the black writer's acceptance of a "single standard of criticism" molded by white America. Baraka, thus, inverts the literary-critical optimism and axiology of an earlier generation, rejecting entirely the notion that "Negro Literature" should not stand apart as a unique body of expression. It is precisely the desertion by black writers of those aspects of Afro-American life that foster the uniqueness and authenticity of black expression that Baraka condemns most severely in his essay.

But where, then, does one discover in Afro-America genuine reflections of the true emotional referents and experiential categories of black life if not in its self-consciously literate works of art? Like the more avowedly political spokesmen of his day, Baraka turned to the world of the masses, and there he discovered the "forms of things unknown" (Wright's designation for black, folk expressive forms):

> Negro music alone, because it drew its strengths and beauties out of the depth of the black man's soul, and because to a large extent its traditions could be carried on by the lowest classes of Negroes, has been able to survive the constant and willful dilutions of the black middle class. Blues and jazz have been the only consistent exhibitors of "Negritude" in formal American culture simply because the bearers of its tradition maintained their essential identities as Negroes; in no other art (and I

will persist in calling Negro music Art) has this been possible. (165-166)

In this statement, Baraka seems to parallel the Richard Wright of an earlier generation. But while Wright felt that the disappearance of the "forms of things unknown" would signal a positive stage in the integration of American life and art, Baraka established the Harlem Black Arts Repertory Theatre/ School in 1965 as an enterprise devoted to the continuance, development, and strengthening of the "coon shout," blues, jazz, holler, and other expressive forms of the "lowest classes of Negroes." He, and other artists who contributed to the establishment of the school, felt that the perpetuation of such forms would help give birth to a new black nation. Larry Neal, who worked with Baraka during the mid-sixties, delineates both the complementarity of the Black Arts and Black Power movements and the affective component of a generational shift in his often-quoted essay "The Black Arts Movement":

Black Art is the aesthetic and spiritual sister of the Black Power concept. As such, it envisions an art that speaks directly to the needs and aspirations of Black America. In order to perform this task, the Black Arts Movement proposes a radical reordering of the western cultural aesthetic. It proposes a separate symbolism, mythology, critique, and iconology.

The Black Arts Movement, therefore, like its ideological counterpart Black Power, was concerned with the articulation of experiences (and the satisfaction of audience demands) that found their essential character among the black urban masses. The guiding assumption of the movement was that if a literary-critical investigator looked to the characteristic musical and verbal forms of the masses, he would discover unique aspects of Afro-American creative expression—aspects of form and performance—that lay closest to the veritable emotional referents and experiential categories of Afro-American culture. The result of such critical investigations, according to Neal and other spokesmen such as Baraka and Addison Gayle, Jr. (to name but three prominent advocates for the Black Arts), would be the discovery of a "Black Aesthetic"—i.e., a distinctive code for the creation and evaluation of black art. From an assumed "structural peculiarity" of Afro-American expressive culture, the emergent generation of intellectuals proceeded to assert a *sui generis* tradition of Afro-American art and a unique "standard of criticism" suitable for its elucidation.

Stephen Henderson's essay entitled "The Forms of Things Unknown," which stands as the introduction to his anthology *Understanding the New Black Poetry*, offers one of the most suggestive illustrations of this discovery process at work. Henderson's formulations mark a high point in the first generational shift in the recent criticism of Afro-American literature because he is a spokesman *par excellence* for what emerged from his generation as a new object of literary-critical and literary-theoretical investigation. Before turning to the specifics of his arguments, however, I want to focus for a moment on the work of Thomas Kuhn to clarify what I mean by a "new object" of investigation.

...

VII

Discussing the manner of progression of a new philosophical posture born of a generational shift, Feuer comments:

> ... from its point of origin with an insurgent generational group, the new emotional standpoint, the new perspective, the new imagery, the new metaphors and idioms spread to the more conventional sections of their own generation, then to their slightly older opponents and their relative elders. Thus, by the time that conservative Americans spoke of themselves as 'pragmatic,' and virtually every American politician defined himself as a 'pragmatist,' the word 'pragmatist' had become a cliche, and its span as a movement was done. A new insurgent generation would perforce have to explore novel emotions, images, and idioms in order to define its own independent character, its own 'revolutionary' aims against the elders.

One might substitute "Black Aesthetic" and "Black Aesthetician" for the implied "pragmatism" and the explicit "pragmatist" of the foregoing remarks. For by the end of the 1970s, the notion of a uniquely Afro-American field of aesthetic experience marked by unique works of verbal and literary art had become a commonplace in American literary criticism. The philosophical tenets that supported early manifestations of this notion, however, had been discredited by the failure of revolutionary black social and political groups to achieve their desired ends. "Black Power," that is to say, as a motivating philosophy for the Black Aesthetic, was deemed an ideological failure by the mid-seventies because it had failed to give birth to a sovereign Afro-American state within the United States. Hence, those who adopted fundamental postulates of the Black Aesthetic as givens in the late seventies did so without a corresponding acceptance of its initial philosophical buttresses.

The "imagery" of a new and resplendent nation of Afro-Americans invested with Black Power, like the "emotional standpoint" which insisted that this hypothetical nation should have a collective and functional literature and criticism, gave way in the late seventies to a new idiom. In defining its independent character, a new group of intellectuals found it *de rigueur* to separate the language of criticism from the vocabulary of political ideology. Their supporting philosophical posture for this separation was a dualism predicated on a distinction between "literary" and "extraliterary" realms of human behavior. Their proclaimed mission was to "reconstruct" the pedagogy and study of Afro-American literature so that it would reflect the most advanced thinking of a contemporary universe of literary-theoretical discourse. This goal was similar in some respects to the revisionist efforts of Neal and Henderson discussed in the preceding section. Like their immediate forerunners, the "reconstructionists" were interested in establishing a sound theoretical framework for the future study of Afro-American literature. In their attempts to achieve this goal, however, some spokesmen for the new generation (whose work I shall discuss shortly) were hampered by a literary-critical "professionalism" that was a function of their emergent class interests.

At the outset of the present essay, I implied that the notion "generational shifts" was sufficient to offer some account of the "ascendant class interests that have characterized Afro-America since World War II." The emergence of a mass, black audience, which was so important for the Black Power and Black Arts movements, was the first instance that I had in mind. But the vertical mobility of Afro-Americans prompted by black political activism during the sixties and early seventies also resulted in the emergence during the 1970s of what has been called a "new black middle class." The opening of the doors, personnel rosters, and coffers of the white academy to minority groups effected by the radical politics of the past two decades provided the conditions of possibility for the appearance of Afro-American critics who have adopted postures, standards, and vocabularies of their white compeers. The disappearance of a mass black audience for both literary-critical and revolutionary-political discourse brought about by the billions of dollars and countless man-hours spent to suppress the American radical left in recent years has been ironically accompanied, therefore, by the emergence of Afro-American spokesmen whose class status (new, black middle-class) and privileges are, in fact, contingent upon their adherence to accepted (i.e., white) standards of their profession. Bernard Anderson's reflections on the situation of black corporate middle-managers who assumed positions in the late sixties and early seventies serve as well to describe the situation of a new group of Afro-American literary critics:

> As pioneers in a career-development process, these [black] managers face challenges and uncertainties unknown to most white managers. Many feel an extra responsibility to maintain high performance levels, and most recognize an environment of competition that will tolerate only slight failure ... Some black middle managers feel the need to conform to a value system alien to the experience of most black Americans but essential for success in professional management.

One result of a class-oriented professionalism among Afro-American literary critics has been a sometimes uncritical imposition upon Afro-American culture of literary theories borrowed from prominent white scholars.

When such borrowings have occurred among the generation that displaced the Black Aesthetic, the outcome has sometimes been disastrous for the course of Afro-American literary study. For instead of developing the mode of analysis suggested by the higher-order arguments of a previous generation, the emergent generation has chosen to distinguish Afro-American literature as an autonomous cultural domain and to criticize it in terms "alien" to the implied cultural-anthropological approach of the Black Aesthetic. Rather than attempting to assess the merits of the Black Aesthetic's methodological assumptions, that is to say, the new generation has adopted the "professional" assumptions (and attendant jargon) that mark the world of white academic literary critics. A positive outcome to the emergent generation's endeavors has been a strong and continuing emphasis on the necessity for an adequate the oretical framework for the study of Afro-American literature. The negative results of their efforts have been an unfortunate burdening of the universe of discourse surrounding Afro-American culture with meaningless jargon and the articulation of a variety of lamentably confused utterances on language, literature, and culture. The emergent generation is fundamentally correct, I feel, in its call for serious literary study of Afro-American literature. But it is misguided, I believe, in its wholesale adoption of terminology and implicit assumptions of white, "professional" critics. A view of essays by principal spokesmen for the new theoretical prospect will serve to clarify these judgments. The essays appear in the handbook of the new generation entitled *Afro-American Literature: The Reconstruction of Instruction* (1979).

Edited by Dexter Fisher and Robert B. Stepto, *Afro-American Literature* "grew out of the lectures and course design workshops of the 1977 Modem Language Association/National Endowment for the Humanities Summer Seminar on Afro-

American Literature" (p. 1). The volume sets forth basic tenets of a new paradigm. The guiding assumption—i.e., that a literature known as "Afro-American" exists in the world—is stated as follows by Stepto in his "Introduction": "[Afro-American] literature fills bookstore shelves and, increasingly, the stacks of libraries; symposia and seminars on the literature are regularly held; prominent contemporary black writers give scores of readings; and so the question of the literature's existence, at this juncture in literary studies, is not at issue" (1). The second, fundamental assumption—i.e., that literature consists in "written art" (3)—is implied by Stepto later in the same "Introduction" when he is describing the unit of *Afro-American Literature* devoted to "Afro-American folklore *and* Afro-American literature as well as Afro-American folklore in Afro-American literature" (3-4). According to the editor, folklore can be transformed into a "written art" that may, in turn, comprise "fiction" (4). Further, he suggests that the "folk" roots of a work like Frederick Douglass's *Narrative of the Life of Frederick Douglass* are to be distinguished from its "literary roots" (5). The condition signaled by "written" seems at first glance, therefore, a necessary one for "literary" and "literature" in Stepto's thinking.

There is, however, some indication in the "Introduction" that the new generation does not wish to confine its definition of the "literary" exclusively to what is "written." At the midpoint of his opening remarks, Stepto asserts that there are "discrete literary texts that are inherently interdisciplinary (e.g., blues) and often multigeneric (dialect voicings in all written art forms)" (3). If "blues" and "dialect voicings" constitute, respectively, a literary text and a genre, then it would appear to follow that *any distinctly Afro-American expressive form* (not merely *written* ones) can be encompassed by the "literary" domain. The boundaries of the new generation's theoretical inquiries, therefore, can apparently be expanded at will to include whatever seems distinctly expressive in Afro-America. Stepto suggests, for example, that "a methodology for an integrated study of *Afro-American folklore* and literature" (4) should form part of the scholar-teacher's tools. And he goes on to propose that there are "various ways in which an instructor ... can present a *collection of art forms* and still respond to the literary qualities of many of those forms in the course of the presentation" (3). On one hand, then, the new prospect implies a rejection of modes of inquiry that are sociological in character or that seek to explore ranges of experience lying beyond the transactions of an exclusive sphere of written art: "central ... to this volume as a whole" is a rejection of "extraliterary values, ideas, and pedagogical constructions that have plagued the teaching of ... [Afro-American] literature" (2). On the other hand, the new prospect attempts to preserve a concern for the "forms of things unknown" (e.g., blues) by reading them under the aspect of a Procrustean definition of "literary." Similarly; it attempts to maintain certain manifestations of Afro-American ordinary discourse (e. g., dialect voicings) as legitimate areas of study by reading them as literary genre. Finally, the new prospect, as defined by Stepto, implies that the entire realm of the Afro-American arts can be subsumed by the "literary" since any collection of black art forms can be explicated in terms of its "literary qualities." Such qualities, under the terms of the new prospect, take on the character of sacrosanct, cultural universals (a point to which I shall return shortly).

Kuhn points out that a paradigmatic shift in a community's conception of the physical world results in "the whole conceptual web whose strands are space, time, matter, force and so on" being shifted and "laid down again on nature whole" (149). While the earlier Black Aesthetic was concerned to determine how the commodity of "blackness" shaped the Afro-American artistic domain, the emergent theoretical prospect attempts to discover how the qualities of a "literary" domain shape Afro-American life as a whole. There is, thus, a movement from the whole culture to the part Signaled by the most recent generational shift in Afro-American literary criticism. For what the new group seeks to specify is a new "literary" conceptual scheme for apprehending Afro-American culture. This project constitutes its main theoretical goal. Two of *Afro-American Literature*'s most important essays—Stepto's "Teaching Afro-American Literature: Surveyor Tradition: The Reconstruction of Instruction" and Henry Louis Gates, Jr.'s "Preface to Blackness: Text and Pretext"—are devoted to this goal.

Stepto's basic premise in "Teaching Afro-American Literature" is that the typical (i.e., normative) teacher of Afro-American literature is a harried, irresponsible pedagogue ignorant of the "inner" workings of the Afro-American literary domain. It follows from this proposition that pedagogy surrounding the literature must be reconstructed on a sound basis by someone familiar with the "myriad cultural metaphors," "coded structures," and "poetic rhetoric" of Afro-America (9). Stepto asserts that only a person who has learned *to read* the discrete literary texts of Afro-America in ways that ensure a proximity and "intimacy, with writers and texts outside the normal boundaries of nonliterary structures" (16) can achieve this required familiarity. According to the author, moreover, it is a specific form of "literacy"—of proficient reading—that leads to the reconstruction of instruction.

Understandably, given the author's earlier claims, this literacy is not based on a comprehension or study of "extraliterary" structures. Its epistemological foundation is, instead, the instructor's apprehension and comprehension of what Stepto calls the "Afro-American canonical story or pregeneric myth, the particular historicity of the Afro-American literary tradition, and the Afro-American landscape or *genius loci*" (18). This "pregeneric myth," according to Stepto, is "the quest for freedom *and* literacy" (18), and he further asserts that the myth is an "aesthetic and rhetorical principle" that can serve as the basis for constructing a proper course in Afro-American literature (17). The Afro-American "pregeneric myth" is, therefore, (at one and the same instant) somehow a prelinguistic reality, a quest, and a pedagogical discovery principle.

It is at this point in Stepto's specifications that what I earlier referred to as an "unfortunate burdening" of the universe of discourse surrounding Afro-American culture with jargon becomes apparent. For the author's formulations on a "pregeneric myth" reflect his metaphysical leanings far more clearly than they project a desirable methodological competence. They signal, in fact, what I called at the outset of this essay a "version of Aristotelian metaphysics." Stepto's pregeneric myth has the character of prime matter capable of assuming an unceasing variety of forms. Just as for Aristotle "the elements are the simplest physical things, and within them the distinction of matter and form can only be made by an abstraction of thought," so for Stepto the pregeneric myth is *informed matter* that serves as the core and essence of that which is "literary" in Afro-America. It is the substance out of which all black expression molds itself: "The quest for freedom and literacy is found in every major text … " (18). Further: "If an Afro-American literary tradition exists, it does so not because there is a sizeable chronology of authors and texts but because those authors and texts seek collectively their own literary forms—their own admixture of genre—bound historically and linguistically to a shared pregeneric myth" (19).

A simplifed statement of the conceptual scheme implied by Stepto's notion of cultural evolution would be: The various *structures* of a culture derive from the informed matter of myth. The principal difficulty with this notion is that the author fails to make clear the mode of being of a "myth" that is not only *pregeneric*, but also, it would seem, *prelinguistic*. "Nonliterary structures,"

Stepto tells us, evolve "almost exclusively from freedom myths devoid of linguistic properties" (18). Such structures, we are further told, "speak rarely to questions of freedom *and* literacy" (18). The question one must pose in light of such assertions is: Are "nonliterary structures" indeed devoid of linguistic properties? If so, then "literacy" and "freedom" can scarcely function as dependent variables in a single, generative myth. For under conditions of mutual inclusiveness (where the variables are, *ab initio*, functions of one another) the structures generated from the myth could not logically be devoid of that which is essential to literacy, i.e., *linguistic properties*. It is important to note, for example, that the "nonliterary" structure known as the *African Methodist Episcopal Church* preserves in its name, and particularly in the linguistic sign "African," a marker of the structure's cultural origin and orientation. And it is difficult to imagine the kind of cognition that would be required to summon to consciousness *cultural structures* devoid of all linguistic properties such as a name, a written history, or a controlling interest in the semantic field of a culture's language. But, perhaps, what Stepto actually meant to suggest by his statement was that "freedom myths" are devoid of linguistic properties. Under this interpretation of his statement, however, one would have to adopt a philosophically idealistic conception of myth that seems contrary to the larger enterprise of the reconstructionists. For Stepto insists that the "reconstruction" of Afro-American literary instruction is contingent upon the discoverability through "literacy" (a process of *linguistic transaction*) of the Afro-American pregeneric myth. And how could such a goal be achieved if myths existed only as *prelinguistic*, philosophical ideals? In sum, Stepto seems to have adopted a critical rhetoric that plays him false. Having assumed some intrinsic merit and inherent clarity in the notion "pregeneric myth," he fails to analytically delineate the mode of existence of such a myth or to clarify the manner in which it is capable of generating two *distinct kinds* of cultural structures.

One sign of the problematical status of this myth in Stepto's formulations is the apparent "agentlessness" of its operations. According to the author, the pregeneric myth is simply "set in motion" (20), and one can observe its "motion through both chronological and linguistic time" (19). Yet, the efficacy of motion suggested here seems to have no historically based community of agents or agencies for its origination or perpetuation. The myth and its operations, therefore, are finally reduced in Stepto's thinking to an aberrant version of Aristotle's "unmoved mover." For Aristotle specifies that the force which moves the "first heaven" has "no contingency; it is not subject even to minimal change (spatial motion in a circle), since that is what it originates." Stepto, however, wants both to posit an "unmoved" substance as his pregeneric myth *and* to claim that this myth *moves* as "literary history." In fact, he designates the shape of its literary-historical movement as a circle—a "magic circle" or *temenos*—representing one kind of ideal harmony, or perfection of motion.

At this point in his description, Stepto (not surprisingly) feels compelled to illustrate his formulations with examples drawn from the Afro-American literary tradition. He first asserts that the phrase "the black belt" is one of Afro-America's metaphors for the *genius loci* (a term borrowed from Geoffrey Hartman signifying "spirit of place") that resides within the interior of the "magic circle" previously mentioned (20). Employing this metaphor, the late-nineteenth-century founder and president of Tuskegee Institute, Booker T. Washington, wrote:

> So far as I can learn the term was first used to designate a part of the country which was distinguished by the colour of the soil. The part of the country possessing this thick, dark soil was, of course, the part of the south where the slaves were most profitable, and consequently they were taken there in the largest numbers. Later, and especially since the war, the term seems to be used wholly in a political sense— that is, to designate the counties where the black people out number the white.

Stepto feels that this description comprises an act of disingenuity on Washington's part. However, when he proceeds to demonstrate that Washington's statement is a "literary offense" (something akin to a sin of shallowness in the reading of metaphor) vis-a-vis the metaphor "the black belt," Stepto does not summon logical, rhetorical, or linguistic criteria. In condemning Washington for describing only geological and political dimensions of the black belt rather than historical and symbolic dimensions, Stepto summons "extraliterary" criteria, insisting that the turn-of-the-century black leader's "offense" was committed in order to insure his success in soliciting philanthropic funds for Tuskegee. The author of *Up From Slavery*, in Stepto's view, merely glossed the metaphor "the black belt" in order to keep his white, potential benefactors happy.

We, thus, find ourselves thrust into the historical dust and heat of turn-of-the-century white philanthropy in America. And what Stepto calls a "geographical metaphor" (i.e., "the black belt") becomes, in his own reading, simply a sign for one American region where such philanthropy had its greatest impact. Contrary to his earlier injunction, therefore, Stepto allows a "nonliterary structure" to become central to his own "reading of art" (20). He assumes, however, that he has achieved his interpretation of Washington solely on the basis of his own "literacy" in regard to the black leader's employment of metaphor. He further assumes that when he contrasts W. E. B. Du Bois's employment of "the black belt" with Washington's usage that he is engaged in a purely "literary" act of "reading within tradition" (21). But if the "tradition" that he has in mind requires a comprehension of turn-of-the-century white philanthropy where Washington is concerned, then surely Stepto does his reader a disservice when he fails to reveal that Du Bois's "rhetorical journey into the soul of a race" (21) in fact curtailed white philanthropy to Atlanta University, cost Du Bois his teaching position at the same university, and led the author of *The Souls of Black Folk* to an even deeper engagement with the metaphor "the black belt." In his attempt to maintain the exclusively "literary" affiliations of a pregeneric myth and its operations, Stepto introduces historical and sociological structures into his reading only where they will not seem to conflict dramatically with his claim that all necessary keys for literacy in the tradition generated by the pregeneric myth are linguistically situated within the texts of black authors themselves. Such reading is, at best, an exercise in the positing of cultural metaphors followed by attempts to fit such metaphors into a needlessly narrow framework of interpretation. Yet, Stepto asserts "it is reading of this sorth that our instructor's new pedagogy should both emulate and promote" (21).

Rather than offering additional examples of such reading, Stepto turns to a consideration of what one early-twentieth-century critic called the relationship between "tradition and the individual talent." For Stepto, this relationship is described as the tension between "Genius and *genius loci*" and between *temenos* and *genius loci*. And the mediation between these facets of Afro-American culture constitutes what the author calls "modal improvisation." Although his borrowed terminology is almost hopelessly confusing here, what Stepto seems to suggest is that the Afro-American literature instructor must engage in "literate" communion with the inner dynamics of the region of Afro-America comprised by a pregeneric myth and its myriad forms and operations. The instructor's pedagogical "genius" consists in his ability to comprehend the "eternal landscape" (22) that is the pregeneric myth—i.e., the sacred domain of the "literary" in Afro-American culture.

An "eternal landscape" (without beginning or end and agentless in its creation and motions) is but another means of denoting for Stepto what he describes earlier in his essay as the "various dimensions of literacy achieved within the *deeper recesses* of the art form" (my italics, 13). At another point in "Teaching Afro-American Literature," the author speaks of an "*immersion* in the multiple images and landscapes of metaphor" (my italics, 15). This cumulative employment of images of a sacred interiority seems to suggest that Stepto believes there is an inner sanctum of pregeneric, mythic, literary "intimacy" resident in works of Afro-American art. Further, he seems to feel that entrance to this sanctum can be gained only by the initiated. One might posit, therefore, that what is presented by "Teaching Afro-American Literature" is a scheme of mystical literacy that finally comprises what might be called a *theology of literacy*. For the "conceptual web" laid upon Afro-America by Stepto's essay asserts the primacy and sacredness among cultural activities of the literary-critical and literary-theoretical enterprise. The argument of the essay is, in the end, a religious interpretation *manque*, complete with an unmoved mover, a priestly class of "literate" initiates, and an eternal landscape of cultural metaphor that can be obtained by those who are free of literary "offense." And the "qualities" that derive from such a landscape (since they are coextensive with the generation of cultural structure) operate as "universals."

The articulation of such a literary-critical orthodoxy is scarcely a new departure in the history of literary criticism. In his "General Introduction" to *The English Poets* published in 1880, Matthew Arnold wrote: "More and more mankind will discover that we have to turn to poetry to interpret life for us, to console us, to sustain us. Without poetry, our science will appear incomplete; and most of what now passes for religion and philosophy will be replaced by poetry." As a function of this conceptualization of the "higher uses" of poetry, Arnold confidently proclaimed: "In poetry, which is thought and art in one, it is the glory, the eternal honour, that charlatanism shall have no entrance; that this noble sphere be kept inviolate and inviolable" (3). Stepto's assumption that his "reconstructed" scheme for teaching Afro-American literature may "nuture literacy in the academy" (23) is certainly akin to Arnold's formulations on the exalted mission of poetry. And his zeal in preserving "inviolate" the sacred domain of the literary surely constitutes a modem, Arnoldian instance of a theology of literacy. As a function of this zeal, Stepto condemns with fierce self-righteousness any pedagogical contextualization of Afro-American literature that might lead a student to ascribe to, say, a Langston Hughes poem, a use-value, or meaning, in opposition to the kind of linguistic and rhetorical values made available by the reconstruction of instruction.

The author of "Teaching Afro-American Literature" emerges as a person incapable of acknowledging that the decision to investigate the material bases of the society that provided enabling conditions for Hughes's metaphors is a sound literary-theoretical decision. Semantic and pragmatic considerations of metaphor suggest that the information communicated by metaphor is hardly localized in a given image on a given page (or, exclusively within the confines of a "magical" literary circle). Rather, the communication process is a function of myriad factors; e.g., a native speaker's ability to recognize ungrammatical sentences, the vast store of encyclopedic knowledge constituting a speech community's common knowledge of objects and concepts, relevant information supplied by the verbal context of a specific metaphoric text, and, finally, the relevant knowledge brought to bear by an "introjecting" listener or reader. Conceived under these terms, metaphoric communication may actually be more fittingly comprehended by an investigation of the material bases of society than by an initiate's passage "from metaphor to metaphor and from image to image of the same metaphor in order to locate the Afro-American *genius loci*" (21). Hughes is, perhaps, more comprehensible, for example, within the framework of Afro-American verbal and musical *performance* than within the borrowed framework for the description of *written* inscriptions of cultural metaphor adduced by Stepto. Only a full investigation of Afro-American metaphor—an analysis based on the best theoretical models available—will enable a student to decide.

The zeal that forced Stepto to adopt a narrow, "literary" conception of metaphor should not be totally condemned. For it is correct (and fair) to point out that a kind of sacred crusade did seem in order by the mid-seventies to modify or "reconstruct" the instruction and study of Afro-American literature that were not then based on sound theoretical foundations. While I do not think the type of mediocre instruction and misguided criticism that Stepto describes were, in fact, as prevalent as he assumes, I do feel that there were enough charlatans about in the mid-seventies to justify renewed vigilance and effort. But though one comes away from "Teaching Afro-American Literature" with a fine sense of these villains, one does not depart the essay (or others in *Afro-American Literature*) with a sense that the reconstructionists are either broad-minded or well-informed in their preachments. In fact, I think the instructor who seeks to model his course on the formulations of Stepto might find himself as nonplused as the critic who attempts to pattern his investigative strategies on the model implicit in Gates's "Preface to Blackness: Text and Pretext."

Just as Stepto's work begins with the assumption that the pedagogy surrounding Afro-American literature rests on a mistake, so Gates's essay commences with the notion that the criticism of Afro-American literature (prior to 1975) rested upon a mistake. This mistake, according to Gates, consisted in the assumption by past critics that a "determining formal relation" exists between "literature" and "social institutions."

The idea of a determining formal relation between literature and social institutions does not in itself explain the sense of urgency that has, at least since the publication in 1760 of *A Narrative of the Uncommon Sufferings and Surprising Deliverance of Briton Hammon, a Negro Man*, characterized nearly the whole of Afro-American writing. This idea has often encouraged a posture that belabors the social and documentary status of black art, and indeed the earliest discrete examples of written discourse by slave and ex-slave came under a scrutiny not primarily literary. (235)

For Gates, "social institutions" is an omnibus category equivalent to Stepto's "nonliterary structures." Such institutions include: the philosophical musings of the Enlightenment on the "African Mind," eighteenth-century debates concerning the African's place in the great chain of being, the politics of abolitionism, or (more recently) the economics, politics, and sociology of the Afro-American liberation struggle in the twentieth century. Gates contends that Afro-American literature has repeatedly been interpreted and evaluated according to criteria derived from such "institutions."

As a case in point, he surveys the critical response that marked the publication of Phillis Wheatley's *Poems on Various Subjects, Religious and Moral*, discovering that "almost immediately after its publication in London in 1773," the black Boston poet's collection became "the international antislavery movement's most salient argument for the African's innate mental equality" (236). Gates goes on to point out that "literally scores of public figures" provided prefatory signatures, polemical reviews, or "authenticating" remarks dedicated to proving that Wheatley's verse was (or was not, as the case may be) truly the product of an African imagination. Such responses were useless in the office of criticism, however, because "virtually no one," according to Gates, "discusses ... [Wheatley's collection] as poetry" (236). Hence: "The documentary status of black art assumed priority over mere literary judgment; criticism rehearsed content to justify one notion of origins or another" (236).

Thomas Jefferson's condemnation (on "extra-literary" grounds) of Wheatley and of the black eighteenth-century epistler Ignatius Sancho set an influential model for the discussion of Afro-American literature that, in Gates's view, "exerted a prescriptive influence over the criticism of the writings of blacks for the next 150 years" (237). Jefferson's recourse to philosophical, political, religious, economic and other cultural systems for descriptive and evaluative terms in which to discuss black writing was, in short, a *mistake* that has been replicated through the decades by both white and Afro-American commentators. William Dean Howells, the writers of the Harlem Renaissance, and, most recently, according to Gates, spokesmen for the

Black Aesthetic have repeated the critical offense of Jefferson. They have assumed that there is, in fact, a determining formal relation between literature and other cultural institutions and that various dimensions of these other institutions constitute areas of knowledge relevant to literary criticism. Gates says, "No," in thunder, to such assumptions. For as he reviews the "prefaces" affixed to various Afro-American texts through the decades, he finds no useful criteria for the practice of literary criticism. He discovers only introductory remarks that are "pretexts" for discussing African humanity, or for displaying "artifacts of the sable mind" (239), or for chronicling the prefacer's own "attitude toward being black in white America" (252).

Like Larry Neal, Gates concludes that such "pretexts" and the lamentable critical situation that they imply are functions of the powerful influence of "race" as a variable in all spheres of American intellectual endeavor related to Afro-America. And like Neal, he states that racial considerations have been substituted for "class" as a category in the thinking of those who have attempted to criticize Afro-American literature, resulting in what he calls "race and superstructure" criticism: "blacks borrowed whole the Marxist notion of base and superstructure and made of it, if you will, race and superstructure" (245). Gates also believes that Afro-American creative writers have fallen prey to the mode of thought that marks "race and superstructure" criticism. For these writers have shaped their work on polemical, documentary lines designed to prove the equality of Afro-Americans or to argue a case for their humanity. And in the process, they have neglected the "literary" engagement that results in true art.

What, then, is the path that leads beyond the critical and creative failings of the past? According to Gates, it lies in a semiotic understanding of literature as a "system" of signs that stand in an "arbitrary" relationship to social reality (250-252). Having drawn a semiotic circle around literature, however, he moves rapidly to disclaim the notion that literature as a "system" is radically distinct from other domains of culture:

> It is not, of course, that literature is unrelated to culture, to other disciplines, or even to other arts; it is not that words and usage somehow exist in a vacuum or that the literary work of art occupies an ideal or reified, privileged status, that province of some elite cult of culture. It is just that the literary work of art is a system of signs that may be decoded with various methods, all of which assume the fundamental unity of form and content and all of which demand close reading. (251-252)

The epistemology on which this description rests is stated as follows:

... perceptions of reality are in no sense absolute; reality is a function of our senses. Writers present models of reality, rather than a description of it, though obviously the two may be related variously. In fact, fiction often contributes to cognition by providing models that highlight the nature of things precisely by their failure to coincide with it. Such certainly is the case in science fiction. (253)

The semiotic notion of literature and culture implied by Gates seems to combine empiricism (reality as a "function of our senses") with an ontology of the sign that suggests that signs are somehow "natural" or "inherent" to human beings. For if "reality" is, indeed, a function of our senses, then observation and study of these physiological capacities should yield some comprehension of a subject's "reality." In truth, however, it is not these physiological processes in themselves that interest Gates, but rather the operation of such processes under the conditions of "models" of cognition, which, of course, is a very different thing. For if one begins not with the senses, but with cognition, then one is required to ask: How are "models" of cognition conceived, articulated, and transmitted in human cultures? Certainly, one of the obvious answers here is *not* that human beings are endowed at birth with a "system of signs," but rather that *models of cognition are conceived in, articulated through, and transmitted by language*. And like other systems of culture, language is a "social institution." Hence, if cognitive "models" of "fiction" differ from those of other spheres of human behavior, they do not do so because fiction is somehow discontinuous with social institutions. In fact, it is the attempt to understand the coextensiveness of language *as a social institution* and literature *as a system within it* that constitutes what is, perhaps, the defining process of literary-theoretical study in our day.

When, therefore, Gates proposes metaphysical and behavioral models that suggest that a literature, or even a single text (254), exists as a structured "world" ("a system of signs") that can be comprehended without reference to "social institutions," he seems misguided in his claims and only vaguely aware of recent developments in literary study, symbolic anthropology, linguistics, the psychology of perception, and other related areas of intellectual inquiry. He seems, in fact, to have adopted, without qualification, a theory of the literary sign (of the "word" in a literary text) that presupposes a privileged status for the creative writer: "The black writer is the point of consciousness of his language" (254). What this assertion means to Gates is that a writer is more capable than others in society of producing a "complex structure of meanings"—a linguistic structure that (presumably) corresponds more closely than those produced by non-writers—to the organizing principles by which a group's world view operates in consciousness (254).

One might be at a loss to understand how a writer can achieve this end unless he is fully aware of language *as a social institution* and of the relationship that language bears to other institutions that create, shape, maintain, and transmit a society's "organizing principles." Surely, Gates does not mean to suggest that the mind of the writer is an autonomous semantic domain where complex structures are conceived and maintained "nonlinguistically." On the other hand, if such structures of meaning are, in fact, "complex" *because* they are linguistically maintained, then so, too, are similar structures that are conceived by nonwriters.

That is to say, Gates renders but small service to the office of theoretical distinction when he states that "a poem is above all atemporal and must cohere at a symbolic level, if it coheres at all" (248), or when he posits that "literature approaches its richest development when its 'presentational symbolism' (as opposed by Suzanne Langer to its 'literal discourse') cannot be reduced to the form of a literal proposition" (253). The reason such sober generalities contribute little to our understanding of literature, of course, is that Gates provides no just notion of the nature of "literal discourse," failing to admit both its social-institutional status and its fundamental existence as a symbolic system. On what basis, then, except a somewhat naive belief in the explanatory power of semiotics can he suggest a radical disjunction between literature and other modes of linguistic behavior in a culture? The critic who attempted to pattern his work on Gates's model would find himself confronted by a theory of language, literature, and culture that suggests that "literary" meanings are conceived in a nonsocial, non-institutional manner by the "point of consciousness" of a language and are maintained and transmitted in an agentless fashion within a closed circle of "intertextuality" (254). It does seem, therefore, that despite his disclaimer, Gates feels that "literature is unrelated to culture." For culture consists in the interplay of various human symbolic systems, an interplay that is essential to the production and comprehension of meaning. Gates's independent literary domain, which produces meanings from some mysteriously nonsocial, noninstitutional medium, bears no relationship to such a process.

One reason Gates fails to articulate an adequate theory of literary semantics in his essay, I think, is that he allots an inordinate amount of space to the castigation of his critical forebears. And his attacks are often restatements of shortcomings that his predecessors had recognized and discussed by the later seventies. Yet Gates provides elaborate detail in, for example, his analysis of the Black Aesthetic.

Among the many charges that he levels against Stephen Henderson, Addison Gayle, Jr., and the present author is the accusation that the spokesmen for a Black Aesthetic assumed they could "achieve an intimate knowledge of a literary text by recreating it from the inside: Critical thought must become the thought criticized" (253). Though Gates employs familiar terminology here, what he seems to object to in the work of Black Aesthetic spokesmen is their treatment of the text as subject. He levels the charge, in short, that these spokesmen postulated a tautological, literary-critical circle, assuming that the thought of an Afro-American literary text was "black thought" and, hence, could be "re-thought" only by a black critic. And while there is some merit in this charge (as Henderson's and Neal's previously mentioned reconsiderations of their initial critical postures make clear), it is scarcely true, as Gates argues, that Black Aestheticians did nothing in their work but reiterate presuppositions about "black thought" and then interpret Afro-American writing in accord with the entailments of such presuppositions. For the insular vision that would have resulted from this strategy would not have enabled Black Aestheticians to discuss and interpret Afro-American verbal behavior in the holistic ways conceived by Henderson, Neal, Gayle, and the present author. Spokesmen for the Black Aesthetic seldom conceived of the "text" as a *closed* enterprise. Instead, they normally thought (at the higher level of their arguments) of the text as an occasion for transactions between writer and reader, between performer and audience. And far from insisting that the written text is, in itself, a repository of inviolable "black thought" to be preserved at all costs, they called for the "destruction of the text"—for an open-endedness of performance and response that created conditions of possibility for the emergence of both new meanings and new strategies of verbal transaction. True, such spokesmen never saw the text as discontinuous with its social origins, but then they also never conceived of these "origins" as somehow divorced from the semantics of the metaphorical instances represented in black "artistic" texts. In short, they never thought of culture under the terms of a semiotic analysis that restricted its formulations to the literary domain alone.

On the other hand, they were certainly never so innocent as Gates would have one believe. Their semantics were never so crude as to permit them to accept the notion that the words of a literary text stand in a one-to-one relationship to the "things" of Afro-American culture. In fact, they were so intent on discovering the full dimensions of the artistic "word" that they attempted to situate its various manifestations within a continuum of verbal behavior in Afro-American culture as a whole. Further, they sought to understand this continuum within the complex webs of interacting cultural systems that ultimately gave meaning to such words.

Rather than a referential semantics, therefore, what was implicit in the higher-order arguments of Black Aesthetic spokesmen (as I have attempted to demonstrate in my earlier discussions) was an anthropological approach to Afro-American art. I think, in fact, that Gates recognizes this and is, finally, unwilling to accept the kind of critical responsibilities signaled by such an enterprise. For though he spends a great deal of energy arguing with Henderson's and my own assumptions on Afro-American culture, he refuses (not without some disingenuity) to acknowledge our *actual readings of Afro-American texts*. The reason for this refusal, I think, is that our readings bring together, in what one hopes are useful ways, our knowledge of various social institutions, or cultural systems (including language), in our attempts to reveal the *sui generis* character of Afro-American artistic texts. Gates's formulations, however, imply an ideal critic whose readings would summon knowledge *only* from the literary system of Afro-America. The semantics endorsed by his ideal critic would *not* be those of a culture. They would constitute, instead, the specially consecrated meanings of an intertextual world of "written art."

The emphasis on "close reading" (252) in Gates's formulations, therefore, might justifiably be designated a call for a "closed" reading of selected Afro-American written texts. In fact, the author implies that the very defining criteria of a culture may be extrapolated from selected written, literary texts rather than vice-versa (250). For example, if any Afro-American literary artist has entertained the notion of "frontier," then Gates feels the notion must have defining force in Afro-American culture (251). Only by ignoring the mass level of Afro-America and holding up the "message" of literary works of art by Ralph Ellison and Ishmael Reed as "normative" utterances in Afro-American culture can Gates support such a claim. His claim is, thus, a function of the privileged status he grants to the writer and the elitist status that he bestows on "literary uses of language" (250).

But if it is true that scholarly investigations of an Afro-American expressive tradition must begin at a mass level—at the level of the "forms of things unknown"—then Gates's claim that the notion of "frontier" has defining force in Afro-America would have to be supported by the testimony of, say, the blues, work songs, or early folktales of Afro-America. And I think that an emphasis on frontier, in the sense intended by Frederick Jackson Turner, is scarcely to be discerned in these cultural manifests.

Gates, however, is interested only in what *writers* (as "points of consciousness") have to say, and he seems to feel no obligation to turn to Afro-American folklore. In fact, when he comments on Henderson's formulations on Afro-American folk language, or vernacular, he reveals not only a lack of interest in folk processes, but also some profound misconceptions about the nature of Afro-American language.

Henderson attempts to establish a verbal and musical continuum of expressive behavior in Afro-American culture as an analytical category. In this process, he encounters certain verbal items that seem to claim (through usage) expansive territory in the Afro-American "sign field." Gates mistakenly assumes that Henderson is setting such items (e.g., "jook," "jelly") apart from a canon of "ordinary" usage as "poetic discourse." This assumption is a function of Gates's critical methodology, which is predicated on a distinction between ordinary and poetic discourse. And the assumption compels him to cast aspersions on the originality of Henderson's work by asserting that "practical critics" since the 1920s (249) have been engaged in actions similar to those of the Black Aesthetic spokesman.

The fault here is that Gates fails to recognize that Henderson is *not* seeking to isolate a lexicon of Afro-American "poetic" usages, nor to demonstrate how such usages "superimpose" a "grammar" (Gates's notion) on "nonliterary discourse" (249). Henderson is concerned, instead, to demonstrate that Afro-American ordinary discourse is, in fact, continuous with Afro-American artistic discourse and that an investigation of the black oral tradition would finally concern itself not simply with a lexicon, but also with a "grammar" adequate to describe the syntax and phonology of *all* Afro-American speech.

Gates is incapable of understanding this notion, however, because he believes that the artistic domain is unrelated to ordinary, "social" modes of behavior. Hence, he is enamored of the written, literary work, suggesting that a mere dictionary of black "poetic" words and their "specific signification" would lead to an understanding of how "Black English" departs from "general usage" (249). This view of language is coextensive with his views of literature and culture. For it concentrates solely on words as "artistic" words and ignores the complexities of the syntax and phonology that give resonance to such words. "A literary text," Gates writes, "is a linguistic event; its explication must be an activity of close textual analysis" (254).

It is not, however, the "text" that constitutes an "event" (if by this Gates means a process of linguistic transaction). It is rather the reading or performance by human beings of a kind of score, or graphemic record, if you will, that constitutes *the event* and, in the process, produces (or reproduces) the meaningful text. And the observer or critic who wishes to "analyze" such a text must have a knowledge of far more than the mere words of the performers. He should, it seems to me, have some theoretically adequate notions of the entire array of cultural forces which shape the performers' or readers' cognition and allow them to actualize the text as an instance of a distinctive cultural semantics. Gates has no such notions to bring to bear. And his later essay in *Afro-American Literature* entitled "Dis and Dat: Dialect and the Descent" reveals some confusion on issues of both language and culture.

Briefly, we are told by Gates that "culture is imprisoned in a linguistic contour that no longer matches ... the changing landscape of fact" (92). This appears a mild form of Whorfianism until one asks: How do "facts" achieve a nonlinguistic existence? The answer is that *they do not achieve such an existence*. Placed in proper perspective, Gates's statement simply means that different communities of speakers of the same language have differential access to "modern" ideas. But in his efforts to preserve language apart from the other social institutions, Gates ignores agents or speakers until he wishes to add further mystery and distinctiveness to his own conceptions of language. When he finally comes to reflect on speakers, he invokes the notion of "privacy," insisting that lying and remaining silent both offer instances of the employment of a "personal" thesaurus by a speaker (93). Now, this conception stands in contrast to Gates's earlier Whorfianism. And, to my knowledge, it possesses little support in the literature of linguistics or semiotics.

The notions that Gates advocates presuppose uniquely "personal" meanings for lexical items that form part of a culture's "public discourse." But what is unique, or personal, about these items is surely their difference from public discourse; their very identity, that is to say, is a function of public discourse. Further, the ability to use such lexical items to lie, or to misinform, scarcely constitutes an argument for privacy. Umberto Eco, for example, writes:

> A sign is everything which can be taken as significantly substituting for something else. This something else does not necessarily have to exist or to actually be somewhere at the moment in which a sign stands for it. Thus *semiotics is in principle the discipline studying everything which can be used in order to lie*. If something cannot be used to tell a lie, conversely it cannot be used to tell the truth: it cannot in fact be used "to tell" at all.

The *word*, in short, becomes a sign by being able *to tell*, and unless Gates means to propose the idealistic notion that each human mind generates its own system of meaningful, nonpublic signs, it is difficult to understand how he conceives of sign usage in lying as an instance of "private" usage of language. His goal in "Dis and Dat" (an unfortunate choice of lexical items for his title since the phonological feature *d* for *th* is not unique to Black English Vernacular, but rather can be found in other nonstandard language varieties) is to define Afro-American "dialect" as a kind of "private," subconscious code signifying a "hermetic closed world" (94). The problem with this very suggestive notion, however, is that Gates not only seems to misunderstand the issue of privacy in language and philosophy, but also seems to fail to comprehend the nature of Black English Vernacular as a natural language.

He bases his understanding of this language on a nineteenth-century magazine article by a writer named James A. Harrison, who asserted that "the poetic and multiform messages which nature sends him [the Afro-American] through his auditory nerve" are reproduced, in words, by the Afro-American (95). Gates takes Harrison's claims seriously, assuming that there is a fundamental physiological difference between the linguistic behavior of Afro-Americans and other human beings: "One did not believe one's eyes, were one black; one believed [presumably on the basis of the Afro-American's direct auditory contact with nature] ... one's ears" (109). On the basis of such problematical linguistic and cultural assumptions as the foregoing, Gates proposes that Black English Vernacular was essentially musical, poetical, spoken discourse generated by means other than those employed to generate standard English and maintained by Afro-Americans as a code of symbolic inversion.

There are reasons for studying the process of symbolic, linguistic inversion in Afro-American culture, and, indeed, for studying the relationship between the tonal characteristics of African languages (which is what both Harrison and Gates have in mind when they say "musical") in relationship to Afro-American speech. Such study, however, should not be grounded on the assertions of Wole Soyinka, Derek Walcott, or James A. Harrison (Gates's sources). It should be a matter of careful, holistic cultural analysis that summons as evidence a large, historical body of informed comment and scholarship on Black English Vernacular. A beginning has been made in this direction by Henderson in his previously-mentioned essay "The Question of Form and Judgment," which commences with the assumption that a discussion of Afro-American poetry (whether written in "dialect" or in standard English) must be based on sound historical notions of Black English Vernacular resulting from detailed research.

Neither Gates nor Stepto, who are the principal spokesmen for the new theoretical prospect in *Afro-American Literature*, has undertaken the detailed research in various domains of Afro-American culture that leads to adequate theoretical formulations. Stepto's stipulations on the ontology of a pregeneric myth from which all Afro-American cultural "structures" originate are just as problematical as Gates's notions of a generative, artistic "point of consciousness" whose "literary uses of language" are independent of "social institutions." The narrowness of Stepto's conception of the "literary" forces him to adopt "nonliterary" criteria in his reading of *Up From Slavery*. And the instability of Gates's views of language and culture forces him to relinquish his advocacy for a synchronic, close reading of literary utterances when he comes to discuss Afro-American dialect poetry. Social institutions, and far more than "literary" criteria, are implied when he asserts:

> When using aword we wake into resonance, as it were, its entire previous history. A text is embedded in specific historical time; it has what linguists call a diachronic structure. To read fully is to restore all that one can of the immediacies of value and intent in which speech actually occurs. (114)

Here, contextualization, rethinking the "intent" of the speaker, and "institutional" considerations are all advocated in a way that hardly seems opposed to the critical strategies of the Black Aesthetic.

To concentrate exclusively on the shortcomings and contradictions of Stepto and Gates, however, is to minimize their achievements. For both writers have suggested, in stimulating ways, that Afro-American literature can be incorporated into a contemporary universe of literary-theoretical discourse. True, the terms on which they propose incorporation amount in one instance to a theology of literacy and, in another, to a mysterious semiotics of literary consciousness. Nonetheless, the very act of proposing that a sound, theoretical orientation toward an Afro-American literary tradition is necessary constitutes a logical second step after the paradigmatic establishment of that tradition by the Black Aesthetic.

Furthermore, Stepto and Gates are both better critics than theoreticians. Hence, they provide interpretations of texts that are, at times, quite striking. (Gates's reflections on structuralism and his structuralist reading of the *Narrative of the Life of Frederick Douglass* are quite provocative.) In addition, neither is so imprisoned by his theoretical claims that he refuses to acknowledge the claims of radically competing theories. For example, the essay by Sherley Anne Williams entitled "The Blues Roots of Contemporary Afro-American Poetry" (72-87) that appears in *Afro-American*

Literature is based on the work of Henderson and stands in direct contrast in its methodology to the stipulations on written, non-institutional, literary art adduced by Stepto and Gates. And although Robert Hemenway, in his fine essay on Zora Neale Hurston's relationship to Afro-American folk processes (122-152), makes a gallant attempt to join the camp of Stepto and Gates, his work finally suggests the type of linguistic, expressive continuum implied by Henderson rather than the segmented model of Gates. Finally, Robert O'Meally's brilliant essay on Frederick Douglass's *Narrative* (192-211) is antithetical at every turn to Stepto's notion that critical "literacy" is a function of the reader's understanding of written "metaphor," or inscribed instances of "poetic rhetoric *in isolatio*" (9). For it is O'Meally's agile contextualizing of Douglass's work within the continuum of Afro-American verbal behavior that enables him to provide a reading of the work that suggests "intertextual" possibilities that are far more engaging than those suggested by Stepto's own reading of the *Narrative* (178-191).

In his editorial capacity, therefore, Stepto has rendered a service to the scholarly community by refusing to allow his theory of the "literary" to foreclose the inclusion of essays that contradict, or sharply qualify, his own explicit claims. Unfortunately, he and his coeditor did not work as effectively in their choice of course designs—the models of "reconstructed" instruction toward which the whole of *Afro-American Literature* is directed (if we are to believe the volume's title). Briefly, the section entitled "Afro-American Literature Course Designs" reflects all of the theoretical confusions that have been surveyed heretofore. There are models for courses based on weak distinctions between "literary" and "socio-historical" principles (237); the assumption that literature is an "act of language" (234); the notion that the "oral tradition is ... a language with a grammar, a syntax, and standards of eloquence of its own" (237); the idea that folk forms are "literary" genres (246); and, finally, the assumption that "interdisciplinary" status can be achieved merely by bringing together different forms of art rather than by summoning methods and models from an array of intellectual disciplines (250-255). The concluding course designs, thus, capture the novelty and promise, as well as the shortcomings, of the new theoretical prospect. The types of distinctions, concerns, and endeavors they suggest are, indeed, significant for the future study of Afro-American literature and verbal art. What they lack—i.e., sound theories of ordinary and literary discourse, an adequate theory of semantics, and a comprehensive theory of reading—will, one hopes, be provided in time by scholars of Afro-American literature who are as persuaded as the reconstructionists that the Afro-American literary tradition can, indeed, withstand sharp critical scrutiny and can survive (as a subject of study) the limitations of early attempts at its literary-theoretical comprehension.

VIII

In *Ideology and Utopia*, Karl Mannheim writes:

To-day we have arrived at the point where we can see clearly that there are differences in modes of thought, not only in different historical periods but also in different cultures. Slowly it dawns upon us that not only does the content of thought change but also its categorical structure. Only very recently has it become possible to investigate the hypothesis that, in the past as well as the present, the dominant modes of thought are supplanted by new categories when the social basis of the group of which these thought-forms are characteristic disintegrates or is transformed under the impact of social change.

The generational shifts discussed in the preceding pages attest the accuracy of Mannheim's observation. The notion of "generational shift," as I have defined it, begins with the assumption that changes in the "categorical structure" of thought are coextensive with social change. The literary-theoretical goal of an analysis deriving from the concept of generational shifts is a "systematic and total formulation" of problems of Afro-American literary study. For only by investigating the guiding assumptions (the "categories" of thought, as it were) of recent Afro-American literary criticism can one gain a sense of the virtues and limitations of what have stood during the past four decades as opposing generational paradigms. What emerges from such an investigation is, first, a realization of the socially- and generationally-conditioned selectivity, or partiality, of such paradigms. They can be as meetly defined by their exclusions as by their manifest content. The quasi-political rhetoric of the Black Aesthetic seems to compete (at its weakest points) with the quasi-religious and semiotic jargon of the reconstructionists for a kind of flawed critical ascendancy.

Yet what also emerges from an investigation of generational shifts in recent Afro-American literary criticism is the sense that this criticism has progressed during the past forty years to a point where some "systematic" formulation of theoretical problems is possible. The extremism and shortsightedness of recent generations have been counterbalanced, that is to say, by their serious dedication to the analysis of an object that did not even exist in the world prior to the mid-sixties. The perceptual reorientations of recent generations have served as enabling conditions for a "mode of thought" that takes the theoretical investigation of a unique tradition of *Afro-American literature* as a normative enterprise.

Given the foregoing discussion, it is perhaps clear that my own preference where such theoretical investigation is concerned is the kind of holistic, cultural-anthropological approach that is implicit in the work of Henderson and other spokesmen for the Black Aesthetic. This does not mean, however, that I seek to minimize the importance of the necessary and forceful call that the reconstructionists have issued for serious literary-theoretical endeavors on the part of Afro-Americanists. Still, I am persuaded that at this juncture in the progress of critical generations the theoretical prospect that I call the "anthropology of art" is the most realistic and fruitful approach to the future study of Afro-American literature and culture. The guiding assumption of the anthropology of art is coextensive with basic tenets of the Black Aesthetic insofar as both prospects assert that works of Afro-American literature and verbal art can not be adequately understood unless they are contextualized within the interdependent systems of Afro-American culture. But the anthropology of art *departs from both the Black Aesthetic and the reconstructionist prospects in* its *assumption that art can not be studied without serious attention to the methods and models of many disciplines*. The contextualization of a work of literary or verbal art, from the perspective of the anthropology of art, is an "interdisciplinary" enterprise in the most contemporary sense of that word. Rather than ignoring (or denigrating) the research and insights of scholars in the nature, social, and behavioral sciences, the anthropology of art views such efforts as positive, rational attempts to comprehend the full dimensions of human behavior. And such efforts serve the literary-theoretical investigator as guides and contributions to an understanding of the symbolic dimensions of human behavior that comprise Afro-American literature and verbal art.

In his essay "Ideology as a Cultural System," Clifford Geertz writes: "The sociology of knowledge ought to be called the sociology of meaning, for what is socially determined is not the nature of conception but the vehicles of conception." I think the anthropology of art stands today not only as a "vehicle of conception" rich in theoretical possibilities, but also as a "categorical structure" that may signal a next generational shift in the criticism of Afro-American literature.

(1981)

23. The Race for Theory
理论的角逐

Barbara Christian
芭芭拉·克里斯琴

芭芭拉·克里斯琴(1943—2000),教授、批评家。克里斯琴 1943 年出生于英属维尔京群岛的圣托马斯,1963 年以优异成绩毕业于马凯特大学,获学士学位,1964 年和 1971 年分别获得哥伦比亚大学硕士和博士学位。1971 年开始她在加州大学伯克利分校任教,直至去世,是该校第一位获得终身教职的黑人女性。

随着 20 世纪 60 年代末欧洲的后结构主义思潮在美国登陆,各种批评理论竞相登场,对文学批评实践产生越来越大的影响。非裔美国文学研究领域也越来越重视引介欧陆各种批评思想,并用于分析非裔美国文学文本与文化现象。在此基础上,关于文学批评理论与文学之间关系的探讨也越来越深入。克里斯琴在其论文《理论的角逐》(1987)中毫不掩饰自己对各种"文学理论"的拒斥,认为很多批评语言丑陋、概念模糊、故弄玄虚、味同嚼蜡,明确反对非裔美国文学批评的"理论化"尝试,认为必须明确"我们为谁而作文学批评",确定这个目标后,才能确定我们使用什么样的语言,想达到什么样的目标。对克里斯琴而言,文学批评必须能够有助于提升文学的价值,加深对文学的理解。鉴于很多非裔美国作家被忽略,很多作品被埋没,文学批评应该积极回应这些文化现象,才能维系非裔美国文学传统。乔伊斯与盖茨及贝克关于非裔美国文学批评的后结构主义之争,更为直观地反映了非裔美国文学批评与西方文学理论之间的争端。

I have seized this occasion to break the silence among those of us, critics, as we are now called, who have been intimidated, devalued by what I call the race for theory I have become convinced that there has been a takeover in the literary world by Western philosophers from the old literary elite, the neutral humanists. Philosophers have been able to effect such a takeover because so much of the literature of the West has become pallid, laden with despair, self-indulgent, and disconnected. The New philosophers, eager to understand a world that is today fast escaping their political control, have redefined literature so that the distinctions implied by that term, that is, the distinctions between everything written and those things written to evoke feeling as well as to express thought, have been blurred. They have changed literary critical language to suit their own purposes as philosophers, and they have reinvented the meaning of theory.

My first response to this realization was to ignore it. Perhaps, in spite of the egocentrism of this trend, some good might come of it. I had, I felt, more pressing and interesting things to do, such as reading and studying the history and literature of black women, a history that had been totally ignored, a contemporary literature bursting with originality, passion, insight, and beauty. But unfortunately it is difficult to ignore this new takeover, theory has become a commodity because that helps determine whether we are hired or promoted in academic institutions—worse, whether we are heard at all. Due to this new orientation, works (a word which evokes labor) have become texts. Critics are no longer concerned with literature, but with other critics' texts, for the critic yearning for attention has displaced the writer and has conceived of himself as the center. Interestingly in the first part of this century, at least in England and America, the critic was usually also a writer of poetry, plays, or novels. But today, as a new generation of professionals develops, he or she is increasingly an academic. Activities such as teaching or writing one's response to specific works of literature have, among this group, become subordinated to one primary thrust, that moment when one creates a theory, thus fixing a constellation of ideas for a time at least, a fixing which no doubt will be replaced in another month or so by somebody else's competing theory as the race accelerates. Perhaps because those who have effected the takeover have the power (although they deny it) first of all to be published, and thereby to determine the ideas which are deemed valuable, some of our most daring and potentially radical critics (and by *our* I mean black, women, Third World) have been influenced, even co-opted, into speaking a language and defining their discussion in terms alien to and opposed to our needs and orientation. At least so far, the creative writers I study have resisted this language.

For people of color have always theorized—but in forms quite different from the Western form of abstract logic. And I am inclined to say that our theorizing (and I intentionally use the verb rather than the noun) is often in narrative forms, in the stories we create, in riddles and proverbs, in the play with language, since dynamic rather than fixed ideas seem more to our liking. How else have we managed to survive with such spiritedness the assault on our bodies, social institutions, countries, our very humanity? And women, at least the women I grew up around, continuously speculated about the nature of life through pithy language that unmasked the power relations of their world. It is this language, and the grace and pleasure with which they played with it, that I find celebrated, refined, critiqued in the works of writers like Toni Morrison and Alice Walker. My folk, in other words, have always been a race of theory—though more in the form of the hieroglyph, a written figure which is both sensual and abstract, both beautiful and communicative. In my own work I try to illuminate and explain these hieroglyphs, which is, I think, an activity quite different from the creating of the hieroglyphs themselves. As the Buddhists would say, the finger pointing at the moon is not the moon.

In this discussion, however, I am more concerned with the issue raised by my first use of the term, *the race of theory*, in relation to its academic hegemony, and possibly of its inappropriateness to the energetic emerging literatures in the world today. The pervasiveness of this academic hegemony is an issue continually spoken about—but usually in hidden groups, lest we, who are disturbed by it, appear ignorant to the reigning academic elite. Among the folk who speak in muted tones are people of color, feminists, radical critics, creative writers, who have struggled for much longer than a decade to make their voices, their various voices, heard, and for whom literature is not an occasion for discourse among critics but is necessary nourishment for their people and one way by which they come to understand their lives better. Cliched though this may be, it bears, I think, repeating here.

The race for theory, with its linguistic jargon, its emphasis on quoting its prophets, its tendency towards "Biblical" exegesis, its refusal even to mention specific works of creative writers, far less contemporary ones, its preoccupations with mechanical analyses of language, graphs, algebraic equations, its gross generalizations about culture, has silenced many of us to the extent that some of us feel we can no longer discuss our own literature, while others have developed intense writing blocks and are puzzled by the incomprehensibility of the language set adrift in literary circles. There have been, in the last year, any number of occasions on which I had to convince literary critics who have pioneered entire new areas of critical inquiry that they did have something to say. Some of us are continually harassed to invent wholesale theories regardless of the complexity of the literature we study I, for one, am tired of being asked to produce a black feminist literary theory as if I were a mechanical man. For I believe such theory is prescriptive—it ought to have some relationship to practice. Since I can count on one hand the number of people attempting to be black feminist literary critics in the world today, I consider it presumptuous of me to invent a theory of how we *ought* to read. Instead, I think we need to read the works of our writers in our various ways and remain open to the intricacies of the intersection of language, class, race, and gender in the literature. And it would help if we share our process, that is, our practice, as much as possible since, finally, our work is a collective endeavor.

The insidious quality of this race for theory is symbolized for me by a term like "Minority Discourse"—a label that is borrowed from the reigning theory of the day but which is untrue to the literatures being produced by our writers, for many of our literatures (certainly Afro-American literature) are central, not minor. I have used the passive voice in my last sentence construction, contrary to the rules of Black English, which like all languages has a particular value system, since I have not placed responsibility on any particular person or group. But that is precisely because this new ideology has become so prevalent among us that it behaves like so many of the other ideologies with which we have had to contend. It appears to have neither head nor center. At the least, though, we can say that the terms "minority" and "discourse" are located firmly in a Western dualistic or "binary" frame which sees the rest of the world as minor, and tries to convince the rest of the world that it is major, usually through force and then through language, even as it claims many of the ideas that we, its "historical" other, have known and spoken about for so long. For many of us have never conceived of ourselves only as somebody's *other*.

Let me not give the impression that by objecting to the race for theory I ally myself with or agree with the neutral humanists who see literature as pure expression and will not admit to the obvious control of its production, value, and distribution by those who have power, who deny, in other words, that literature is, of necessity, political. I am studying an entire body of literature that has been denigrated for centuries by such terms as *political*. For an entire century Afro-American writers, from Charles Chestnutt [*sic*] in the nineteenth century through Richard Wright in the 1930s, Imamu Baraka in the 1960s, Alice Walker in the 1970S, have protested the literary hierarchy of dominance which declares when literature is literature, when literature is great, depending on what it thinks is to its advantage. The Black Arts Movement of the 1960s, out of which Black Studies, the Feminist Literary Movement of the 1970s, and Women's Studies grew, articulated precisely those issues, which came *not* from the declarations of the New Western Philosophers but from these groups' reflections on their own lives. That Western scholars have long believed their ideas to be universal has been strongly opposed by many such groups. Some of my colleagues do not see black critical writers of previous decades as eloquent enough.

Clearly they have not read Wright's "A Blueprint for Negro Writing," Ellison's *Shadow and Act*, Chesnutt's resignation from being a writer, or Alice Walker's "In search of Zora Neale Hurston." There are two reasons for this general ignorance of what our writer-critics have said. One is that black writing has been generally ignored in the USA. Since we, as Toni Morrison has put it, are seen as a discredited people, it is no surprise, then, that our creations are also discredited. But this is also due to the fact that until recently, dominant critics in the Western world have also been creative writers who have had access to the upper-middle-class institutions of education and, until recently, our writers have decidedly been excluded from these institutions and in fact have often been opposed to them. Because of the academic world's general ignorance about the literature of black people, and of women, whose work too has been discredited, it is not surprising that so many of our critics think that the position arguing that literature is political begins with these New Philosophers. Unfortunately, many of our young critics do not investigate the reasons *why* that statement— literature is political—is now acceptable when before it was not; nor do we look to our own antecedents for the sophisticated arguments upon which we can build in order to change the tendency of any established Western idea to become hegemonic.

For I feel that the new emphasis on literary critical theory is as hegemonic as the world which it attacks. I see the language it creates as one which mystifies rather than clarifies our condition, making it possible for a few people who know that particular language to control the critical scene—that language surfaced, interestingly enough, just when the literature of peoples of color, of black women, of Latin Americans, of Africans, began to move to "the center." Such words as *center* and *periphery* are themselves instructive. *Discourse*, *canon*, *texts*, words as Latinate as the tradition from which they come, are quite familiar to me. Because I went to a Catholic Mission school in the West Indies I must confess that I cannot hear the word "canon" without smelling incense, that the word "text" immediately brings back agonizing memories of Biblical exegesis, that "discourse" reeks for me of metaphysics forced down my throat in those courses that traced *world* philosophy from Aristotle through Thomas Aquinas to Heidegger. "Periphery" too is a word I heard throughout my childhood, for if anything was seen as being at the periphery, it was those small Caribbean islands which had neither land mass nor military power. Still I noted how intensely important this periphery was, for US troups were continually invading one island or another if any change in political control even seemed to be occurring. As I lived among folk for whom language was an absolutely necessary way of validating our existence, I was told that the minds of the world lived only in the small continent of Europe. The metaphysical language of the New Philosophy, then, I must admit, is repulsive to me and is one reason why I raced from philosophy to literature, since the latter seemed to me to have the possibilities of rendering the world as large and as complicated as I experienced it, as sensual as I knew it was. In literature I sensed the possibility of the integration of feeling/knowledge, rather than the split between the abstract and the emotional in which Western philosophy inevitably indulged.

Now I am being told that philosophers are the ones who write literature, that authors are dead, irrelevant, mere vessels through which their narratives ooze, that they do not work nor have they the faintest idea what they are doing; rather, they produce texts as disembodied as the angels. I am frankly astonished that scholars who call themselves Marxists or post-Marxists could seriously use such metaphysical language even as they attempt to deconstruct the philosophical tradition from which their language comes. And as a student of literature, I am appalled by the sheer ugliness of the language, its lack of clarity, its unnecessarily complicated sentence constructions, its lack of pleasurableness, its alienating quality. It is the kind of writing for which composition teachers would give a freshman a resounding F.

Because I am a curious person, however, I postponed readings of black women writers I was working on and read some of the prophets of this new literary orientation. These writers did announce their dissatisfaction with some of the cornerstone ideas of their own tradition, a dissatisfaction with which I was born. But in their attempt to change the orientation of Western scholarship, they, as usual, concentrated on themselves and were not in the slightest interested in the worlds they had ignored or controlled. Again I was supposed to know *them*, while they were not at all interested in knowing *me*. Instead they sought to "deconstruct" the tradition to which they belonged even as they used the same forms, style, language of that tradition, forms that necessarily embody its values. And increasingly as I read them and saw their substitution of their philosophical writings for literary ones, I began to have the uneasy feeling that their folk were not producing any literature worth mentioning. For they always harkened back to the masterpieces of the past, again reifying the very texts they said they were deconstructing. Increasingly; as *their* way, *their* terms, *their* approaches remained central and became the means by which one defined literary critics, many of my own peers who had previously been concentrating on dealing with the other side of the equation, the reclamation and discussion of past and *present* Third World literatures, were diverted into continually discussing the new literary theory.

From my point of view as a critic of contemporary Afro-American women's writing, this orientation is extremely problematic. In attempting to find the deep structures in the literary tradition, a major preoccupation of the new New Criticism, many of us have become obsessed with the nature of reading itself to the extent that we have stopped writing about literature being written today. Since I am slightly paranoid, it has begun to occur to me that the literature being produced is precisely one of the reasons why this new philosophical-literary-critical theory of relativity is so prominent. In other words, the literature of blacks, women of South America and Africa, etc., as overtly "political" literature, was being preempted by a new Western concept which proclaimed that reality does not exist, that everything is relative, and that every text is silent about something—which indeed it must necessarily be.

There is, of course, much to be learned from exploring how we know what we know, how we read what we read, an exploration which, of necessity; can have no end. But there also has to be a "what," and that "what," when it is even mentioned by the New Philosophers, are texts of the past, primarily Western male texts, whose norms are again being transferred onto Third World, female texts as theories of reading proliferate. Inevitably a hierarchy has now developed between what is called theoretical criticism and practical criticism, as mind is deemed superior to matter. I have no quarrel with those who wish to philosophize about how we know what we know. But I do resent the fact that this particular orientation is so privileged and has diverted so many of us from doing the first readings of the literature being written today as well as of past works about which nothing has been written. I note, for example, that there is little work done on Gloria Naylor, that most of Alice Walker's works have not been commented on—despite the rage around *The Color Purple* —that there has yet to be an in-depth study of Frances Harper, the nineteenth-century abolitionist poet and novelist. If our emphasis on theoretical criticism continues, critics of the future may have to reclaim the writers we are now ignoring, that is, if they are even aware these artists exist.

I am particularly perturbed by the movement to exalt theory, as well, because of my own adult history. I was an active member, of the Black Arts Movement of the 1960s and know how dangerous theory can become. Manytoday may not be aware of this, but the Black Arts Movement tried to create Black Literary Theory and in doing so became prescriptive. My fear is that when Theory is not rooted in practice, it becomes prescriptive, exclusive, elitist.

An example of this prescriptiveness is the approach the Black Arts Movement took towards language. For it, blackness resided in the use of black talk which they defined as hip urban language. So that when Nikki Giovanni reviewed Paule Marshall's *Chosen Place, Timeless People*, she criticized the novel on the grounds that it was not black, for the language was too elegant, too white. Blacks, she said, did not speak that way. Having come from the West Indies where we do, some of the time, speak that way, I was amazed by the narrowness of her vision. The emphasis on *one way* to be black resulted in the works of Southern writers being seen as non-black since the black talk of Georgia does not sound like the black talk of Philadelphia. Because the ideologues, like Baraka, came from the urban centers, they tended to privilege their way of speaking, thinking, writing, and to condemn other kinds of writing as not being black enough. Whole areas of the canon were assessed according to the dictum of the Black Arts Nationalist point of view, as in Addison Gayle's *The Way of the New World*, while other works were ignored because they did not fit the scheme of cultural nationalism. Older writers like Ralph Ellison and James Baldwin were condemned because they saw that the intersection of Western and African influences resulted in a new Afro-American culture, a position with which many of the Black Nationalist ideologues disagreed. Writers were told that writing love poems was not being black. Further examples abound.

It is true that the Black Arts Movement resulted in a necessary and important critique both of previous Afro-American literature and of the white-established literary world. But in attempting to take over power, it, as Ishmael Reed satirizes so well in *Mumbo Jumbo*, became much like its opponent, monolithic and downright repressive.

It is this tendency towards the monolithic, monotheistic, and so on, that worries me about the race for theory. Constructs like the *center* and the *periphery* reveal that tendency to want to make the world less complex by organizing it according to one principle, to fix it through an idea which is really an ideal. Many of us are particularly sensitive to monolithism because one major element of ideologies of dominance, such as sexism and racism, is to dehumanize people by stereotyping them, by denying them their variousness and complexity. Inevitably, monolithism becomes a metasystem, in which there is a controlling ideal, especially in relation to pleasure. Language as one form of pleasure is immediately restricted, and becomes heavy, abstract, prescriptive, monotonous.

Variety, multiplicity, eroticismare difficult to control. And it may very well be that these are the reasons why writers are often seen as *persona non grata* by political states, whatever form they take, since writers/artists have a tendency to refuse to give up their way of seeing the world and of playing with possibilities; in fact, their very expression relies on that insistence. Perhaps that is why creative literature, even when written by politically reactionary people, can be so freeing, for in having to embody ideas and recreate the world, writers cannot merely produce "one way."

The characteristics of the Black Arts Movement are, I am afraid, being repeated again today, certainly in the other area to which I am especially tuned. In the race for theory, feminists, eager to enter the halls of power, have attempted their own prescriptions. So often I have read books on feminist literary theory that restrict the definition of what *feminist* means and overgeneralize about so much of the world that most women as well as men are excluded. Seldom do feminist theorists take into account the complexity of life—that women are of many races and ethnic backgrounds with different histories and cultures and that as a rule women belong to different classes that have different concerns. Seldom do they note these distinctions, because if they did they could not articulate a theory. Often as a way of clearing themselves they do acknowledge that women of color, for example, do exist, then go on to do what they were going to do anyway, which is to invent a theory that has little relevance for us.

That tendency towards monolithism is precisely how I see the French feminist theorists. They concentrate on the female body as the means to creating a female language, since language, they say, is male and necessarily conceives of woman as other. Clearly many of them have been irritated by the theories of Lacan for whom language is phallic. But suppose there arc peoples in the world whose language was invented primarily in relation to women, who after all are the ones who relate to children and teach language. Some Native American languages, for example, use female pronouns when speaking about non-gender-specific activity. Who knows who, according to gender, created languages. Further, by positing the body as the source of everything French feminists return to the old myth that biology determines everything and ignore the fact that gender is a social rather than a biological construct.

I could go on critiquing the positions of French feminists who are themselves more various in their points of view than the label which is used to describe them, but that is not my point. What I am concerned about is the authority this school now has in feminist scholarship—the way it has become *authoritative discourse*, monologic, which occurs precisely because it does have access to the means of promulgating its ideas. The Black Arts Movement was able to do this for a time because of the political movements of the 1960s—so too with the French feminists who could not be inventing "theory" if a space had not been created by the women's movement. In both cases, both groups posited a theory that excluded many of the people who made that space possible. Hence one of the reasons for the surge of Afro-American women's writing during the 1970s and its emphasis on sexism in the black community is precisely that when the ideologues of the 1960s said *black*, they meant *black male*.

I and many of my sisters do not see the world as being so simple. And perhaps that is why we have not rushed to create abstract theories. For we know there are countless women of color, both in America and in the rest of the world, to whom our singular ideas would be applied. There is, therefore, a caution we feel about pronouncing black feminist theory that might be seen as a decisive statement about Third World women. This is not to say we are not theorizing. Certainly our literature is an indication of the ways in which our theorizing, of necessity, is based on our multiplicity of experiences.

There is at least one other lesson I learned from the Black Arts Movement. One reason for its monolithic approach had to do with its desire to destroy the power which controlled black people, but it was a power which many of its ideologues wished to achieve. The nature of our context today is such that an approach which desires power single-mindedly must of necessity become like that which it wishes to destroy. Rather than wanting to change the whole model, many of us want to be at the center. It is this point of view that writers like June Jordan and Audre Lorde continually critique even as they call for empowerment, as they emphasize the fear of difference among us and our need for leaders rather than a reliance on ourselves.

For one must distinguish the desire for power from the need to become empowered—that is, seeing oneself as capable of and having the right to determine one's life. Such empowerment is partially derived from a knowledge of history. The Black Arts Movement did result in the creation of Afro-American Studies as a concept, thus giving it a place in the university where one might engage in the reclamation of Afro-American history and culture and pass it on to others. I am particularly concerned that institutions such as black studies and women's studies, fought for with such vigor and at some sacrifice, are not often seen as important by many of our black or women scholars precisely because the old hierarchy of traditional departments is seen as superior to these "marginal" groups. Yet, it is in this context that many others of us are discovering the extent of our complexity, the interrelationships of different areas of knowledge in relation to a distinctly Afro-

American or female experience. Rather than having to view our world as subordinate to others, or rather than having to work as if we were hybrids, we can pursue ourselves as subjects.

My major objection to the race for theory, as some readers have probably guessed by now, really hinges on the question, "For whom are we doing what we are doing when we do literary criticism?" It is, I think, the central question today, especially for the few of us who have infiltrated academia enough to be wooed by it. The answer to that question determines what orientation we take in our work, the language we use, the purposes for which it is intended.

I can only speak for myself. But what I write and how I write is done in order to save my own life. And I mean that literally. For me literature is a way of knowing that I am not hallucinating, that whatever I feel/know is. It is an affirmation that sensuality is intelligence, that sensual language is language that makes sense. My response, then, is directed to those who write what I read and to those who read what I read—put conconcretely—to Toni Morrison and to people who read Toni Morrison (among whom I would count few academics). That number is increasing, as is the readership of Walker and Marshall. But in no way is the literature Morrison, Marshall, or Walker create supported by the academic world. Nor given the political context of our society, do I expect that to change soon. For there is no reason, given who controls these institutions, for them to be anything other than threatened by these writers.

My readings do presuppose a need, a desire among folk who like me also want to save their own lives. My concern, then, is a passionate one, for the literature of people who are not in power has always been in danger of extinction or of co-optation, not because we do not theorize, but because what we can even imagine, far less who we can reach, is constantly limited by societal structures. For me, literary criticism is promotion as well as understanding, a response to the writer to whom there is often no response, to folk who need the writing as much as they need anything. I know, from literary history, that writing disappears unless there is a response to it. Because I write about writers who are now writing, I hope to help ensure that their tradition has continuity and survives.

So my "method," to use a new "lit. crit." word, is not fixed but relates to what I read and to the historical context of the writers I read *and* to the many critical activities in which I am engaged, which mayor may not involve writing. It is a learning from the language of creative writers, which is one of surprise, so that I might discover what language I might use. For my language is very much based on what I read and how it affects me, that is, on the surprise that comes from reading something that compels you to read differently, as I believe literature does. I, therefore, have no set method, another prerequisite of the new theory, since for me every work suggests a new approach. As risky as that might seem, it is, I believe, what intelligence means—a tuned sensitivity to that which is alive and therefore cannot be known until it is known. Audre Lorde puts it in a far more succinct and sensual way in her essay "Poetry is not a luxury":

> As they become known to and accepted by us, our feelings and the honest exploration of them become sanctuaries and spawning grounds for the most radical and daring of ideas. They become a safe-house for that difference so necessary to change and the conceptualization of any meaningful action. Right now, I could name at least ten ideas I would have found intolerable or incomprehensible and frightening, except as they came after dreams and poems. This is not idle fantasy, but a disciplined attention to the true meaning of 'it feels right to me.' We can train ourselves to respect our feelings and to transpose them into a language so they can be shared. And where that language does not yet exist, it is our poetry which helps to fashion it. Poetry is not only dream and vision; it is the skeleton architecture of our lives. It lays the foundations for a future of change, a bridge across our fears of what has never been before.

(1987)

24. The Site of Memory
记忆之场

Toni Morrison

托尼·莫里森

托尼·莫里森(1931—2019),小说家、编辑、批评家。莫里森 1931 年 2 月 18 日出生于俄亥俄州洛兰市,1953 年毕业于霍华德大学,获得学士学位;1955 年毕业于康奈尔大学,获得硕士学位;其硕士学位论文研究的是福克纳与伍尔夫作品中的自杀主题。毕业后,她在得克萨斯南部大学与霍华德大学等校任教,后来在耶鲁大学等校就职。1968 年她来到纽约,任兰登书屋的高级编辑,编辑了《黑人之书》(*The Black Book*,1974)等,发掘了很多被埋没的黑人女作家的作品以及黑人历史与文化中的重要文献,很多材料成为她后来小说创作的极好素材。她出版了 11 部长篇小说与多部批评文集,是成功的小说家和批评家,特别是她在哈佛大学的系列演讲文集《在黑暗中嬉戏:白人性与文学想象》(*Playing in the Dark*:*Whiteness and the Literary Imagination*,1992),深入剖析美国历史与文化中的种族主义及其在美国文学作品中的体现,其对美国文学经典的反思,以及对文化记忆的重视影响甚大。

《记忆之场》这篇论文以读者和批评家对 19 世纪奴隶叙事代表作品的接受与评价为基础,比较深入地分析了以往批评界对黑人内在生活与情感世界有意无意的忽略,明确提出自己有意揭开蒙在奴隶叙事之上的面纱,弥补奴隶叙事留下的空白——因各种因素的限制,奴隶叙事无法深入描绘黑人(奴隶)遭受的各种非人待遇、揭示她们的内心世界。对莫里森而言,创作是一种文学考古,她要从一些意象入手,通过想象,构建一种新的更加完整的奴隶世界,体现文化记忆与想象的力量。

MY INCLUSION in a series of talks on autobiography and memoir is not entirely a misalliance. Although it's probably true that a fiction writer thinks of his or her work as alien in that company, what I have to say may suggest why I'm not completely out of place here. For one thing, I might throw into relief the differences between self-recollection (memoir) and fiction, and also some of the similarities—the places where those two crafts embrace and where that embrace is symbiotic.

But the authenticity of my presence here lies in the fact that a very large part of my own literary heritage is the autobiography. In this country the print origins of black literature (as distinguished from the oral origins) were slave narratives. These book-length narratives (autobiographies, recollections, memoirs), of which well over a hundred were published, are familiar texts to historians and students of black history. They range from the adventure-packed life of Olaudah Equiano's *The Interesting Narrative of the Life of Olaudah Equiano, or Gustavus Vassa, the African, Written by Himself* (1769) to the quiet desperation of *Incidents in the Life of a Slave Girl: Written by Herself* (1861), in which Harriet Jacobs ("Linda Brent") records hiding for seven years in a room too small to stand up in; from the political savvy of Frederick Douglass's *Narrative of the Life of Frederick Douglass, an American Slave, Written by Himself* (1845) to the subtlety and modesty of Henry Bibb, whose voice, in *Narrative of the Life and Adventures of Henry Bibb, an American Slave, Written by Himself* (1849), is surrounded by ("loaded with" is a better phrase) documents attesting to its authenticity. Bibb is careful to note that his formal schooling (three weeks) was short, but that he was "educated in the school of adversity, whips, and chains." Born in Kentucky, he put aside his plans to escape in order to marry. But when he learned that he was the father of a slave and watched the degradation of his wife and child, he reactivated those plans.

Whatever the style and circumstances of these narratives, they were written to say principally two things. (1) "This is my historical life—my singular, special example that is personal, but that also represents the race." (2) "I write this text to persuade other people—you, the reader, who is probably not black—that we are human beings worthy of God's grace and the immediate abandonment of slavery." With these two missions in mind, the narratives were clearly pointed.

In Equiano's account, the purpose is quite up-front. Born in 1745 near the Niger River and captured at the age of ten, he survived the Middle Passage, American plantation slavery, wars in Canada and the Mediterranean; learned navigation and clerking from a Quaker named Robert King; and bought his freedom at twenty-one. He lived as a free servant, traveling widely and living most of his later life in England. Here he is speaking to the British without equivocation: "I hope to have the satisfaction of seeing the renovation of liberty and justice, resting on the British government... I hope and expect the attention of gentlemen in power.... May the time come—at least the speculation to me is pleasing—when the sable people shall gratefully commemorate the auspicious era of extensive freedom." With typically eighteenth-century reticence he records his singular and representative life for one purpose: to change things. In fact, he and his coauthors did change things. Their works gave fuel to the fires that abolitionists were setting everywhere.

More difficult was getting the fair appraisal of literary critics. The writings of church martyrs and confessors are and were read for the eloquence of their message as well as their experience of redemption, but the American slaves' autobiographical narratives were frequently scorned as "biased," "inflammatory," and "improbable." These attacks are particularly difficult to understand in view of the fact that it was extremely important, as you can imagine, for the writers of these narratives to appear as objective as possible—not to offend the reader by being too angry, or by showing too much outrage, or by calling the reader names. As recently as 1966, Paul Edwards, who edited and abridged Equiano's story, praises the narrative for its refusal to be "inflammatory."

"As a rule," Edwards writes, "he [Equiano] puts no emotional pressure on the reader other than that which the situation itself contains—his language does not strain after our sympathy, but expects it to be given naturally and at the proper time. This quiet avoidance of emotional display produces many of the best passages in the book." Similarly, an 1836 review of Charles Bell's *Life and Adventures of a Fugitive Slave*, which appeared in the "Quarterly Anti-Slavery Magazine," praised Bell's account for its objectivity. "We rejoice in the book the more, because it is not a partisan work... It broaches no theory in regard to [slavery], nor proposes any mode of time of emancipation."

As determined as these black writers were to persuade the reader of the evil of slavery, they also complimented him by assuming his nobility of heart and his high-mindedness. They tried to summon up his finer nature in order to encourage him to employ it. They knew that their readers were the people who could make a difference in terminating slavery. Their stories—of brutality, adversity, and deliverance—had great popularity in spite of critical hostility in many quarters and patronizing sympathy in others. There was a time when the hunger for "slave stories" was difficult to quiet, as sales figures show. Douglass's *Narrative* sold five thousand copies in four months; by 1847 it had sold eleven thousand copies. Equiano's book had thirty-six editions between 1789 and 1850. Moses Roper's book had ten editions from 1837 to 1856; William Wells Brown's was reprinted four times in its first year. Solomon Northup's book sold twenty-seven thousand copies before two years had passed. A book by Josiah Henson (argued by some to be the model for the Tom of Harriet Beecher Stowe's *Uncle Tom's Cabin*) had a prepublication sale of five thousand.

In addition to using their own lives to expose the horrors of slavery, they had a companion motive for their efforts. The prohibition against teaching a slave to read and write (which in many southern states carried severe punishment) and against a slave's learning to read and write had to be scuttled at all costs. These writers knew that literacy was power. Voting, after all, was inextricably connected to the ability to read; literacy was a way of assuming and proving the "humanity" that the Constitution denied them. That is why the narratives carry the subtitle "written by himself," or "herself," and include introductions and prefaces by white sympathizers to authenticate them. Other narratives, "edited by" such well-known antislavery figures as Lydia Maria Child and John Greenleaf Whittier, contain prefaces to assure the reader how little editing was needed. A literate slave was supposed to be a contradiction in terms.

One has to remember that the climate in which they wrote reflected not only the Age of Enlightenment but its twin, born at the same time, the Age of Scientific Racism. David Hume, Immanuel Kant, and Thomas Jefferson, to mention only a few, had documented their conclusions that blacks were incapable of intelligence. Frederick Douglass knew otherwise, and he wrote refutations of what Jefferson said in *Notes on the State of Virginia*: "Never yet could I find that a black had uttered a thought above the level of plain narration; never see even an elementary trait of painting or sculpture." A sentence that I have always thought ought to be engraved at the door to the Rockefeller Collection of African Art. Hegel, in 1813, had said that Africans had no "history" and couldn't write in modern languages. Kant disregarded a perceptive observation by a black man by saying, "This fellow was quite black from head to foot, a clear proof that what he said was stupid."

Yet no slave society in the history of the world wrote more—or more thoughtfully—about its own enslavement. The milieu, however, dictated the purpose and the style. The narratives are instructive, moral, and obviously representative. Some of them are patterned after the sentimental novel that was in vogue at the time. But whatever the level of eloquence or the form, popular taste discouraged the writers from dwelling too long or too carefully on the more sordid details of their experience. Whenever there was an unusually violent incident, or a scatological one, or something "excessive," one finds the writer taking refuge in the literary conventions of the day. "I was left in a state of distraction not to be described" (Equiano). "But let us now leave the rough usage of the field ... and turn our attention to the less repulsive slave life as it existed in the home of my childhood" (Douglass). "I am not about to harrow the feelings of my readers by a terrific representation of the untold horrors of that fearful system of oppression ... It is not my purpose to descend deeply into the dark and noisome caverns of the hell of slavery" (Henry Box Brown).

Over and over, the writers pull the narrative up short with a phrase such as, "But let us drop a veil over these proceedings too terrible to relate." In shaping the experience to make it palatable to those who were in a position to alleviate it, they were silent about many things, and they "forgot" many other things. There was a careful selection of the instances that they would record and a careful rendering of those that they chose to describe. Lydia Maria Child identified the problem in her introduction to "Linda Brent's" tale of sexual abuse: "I am well aware that many will accuse me of indecorum for presenting these pages to the public; for the experiences of this intelligent and much-injured woman belong to a class which some call delicate subjects, and others indelicate. This peculiar phase of Slavery has generally been kept veiled; but the public ought to be made acquainted with its monstrous features, and I willingly take the responsibility of presenting them with the veil drawn [aside]."

But most importantly—at least for me—there was no mention of their interior life.

For me—a writer in the last quarter of the twentieth century, not much more than a hundred years after Emancipation, a writer who is black and a woman—the exercise is very different. My job becomes how to rip that veil drawn over "proceedings too terrible to relate." The exercise is also critical for any person who is black, or who belongs to any marginalized category, for, historically, we were seldom invited to participate in the discourse even when we were its topic.

Moving that veil aside requires, therefore, certain things. First of all, I must trust my own recollections. I must also depend on the recollections of others. Thus memory weighs heavily in what I write, in how I begin, and in what I find to be significant. Zora Neale Hurston said, "Like the dead-seeming, cold rocks, I have memories within that came out of the material that went to make me." These "memories within" are the subsoil of my work. But memories and recollections won't give me total access to the unwritten interior life of these people. Only the act of the imagination can help me.

If writing is thinking and discovery and selection and order and meaning, it is also awe and reverence and mystery and magic. I suppose I could dispense with the last four if I were not so deadly serious about fidelity to the milieu out of which I write and in which my ancestors actually lived. Infidelity to that milieu—the absence of the interior life, the deliberate excising of it from the records that the slaves themselves told—is precisely the problem in the discourse that proceeded without us. How I gain access to that interior life is what drives me and is the part of this talk that both distinguishes my fiction from autobiographical strategies and that also embraces certain autobiographical strategies. It's a kind of literary archaeology: on the basis of some information and a little bit of guesswork you journey to a site to see what remains were left behind and to reconstruct the world that these remains imply. What makes it fiction is the nature of the imaginative act: my reliance on the image—on the remains—in addition to recollection, to yield up a kind of a truth. By "image," of course, I don't mean "symbol"; I simply mean "picture" and the feelings that accompany the picture.

Fiction, by definition, is distinct from fact. Presumably it's the product of imagination—invention—and it claims the freedom to dispense with "what really happened," or where it really happened, or when it really happened, and nothing in it needs to be publicly verifiable, although much in it can be verified. By contrast, the scholarship of the biographer and the literary critic seems to us only trustworthy when the events of fiction can be traced to some publicly verifiable fact. It's the research of the "Oh, yes, this is where he or she got it from" school, which gets its own credibility from excavating the credibility of the sources of the imagination, not the nature of the imagination.

The work that I do frequently falls, in the minds of most people, into that realm of fiction called fantastic, or mythic, or magical, or unbelievable. I'm not comfortable with these labels. I consider that my single gravest responsibility (in spite of that magic) is not to lie. When I hear someone say, "Truth is stranger than fiction," I think that old chestnut is truer than we know, because it doesn't say that truth is truer than fiction; just that it's stranger, meaning that it's odd. It may be excessive, it may be more interesting, but the important thing is that it's random—and fiction is not random.

Therefore the crucial distinction for me is not the difference between fact and fiction, but the distinction between fact and truth. Because facts can exist without human intelligence, but truth cannot. So if I'm looking to find and expose a truth about the interior life of people who didn't write it (which doesn't mean that they didn't have it); if I'm trying to fill in the blanks that the slave narratives left—to part the veil that was so frequently drawn, to implement the stories that I heard—then the approach that's most productive and most trustworthy for me is the recollection that moves from the image to the text. Not from the text to the image.

Simone de Beauvoir, in *A Very Easy Death*, says, "I don't know why I was so shocked by my mother's death." When she heard her mother's name being called at the funeral by the priest, she says, "Emotion seized [me] by the throat....'Françoise de Beauvoir'; the words brought her to life; they summed up her history, from birth to marriage, to widowhood, to the grave; Françoise de Beauvoir—that retiring woman, so rarely named—became an *important* person." The book becomes an exploration both into her own grief and into the images in which the grief lay buried.

Unlike Mme. de Beauvoir, Frederick Douglass asks the reader's patience for spending about half a page on the death of his grandmother—easily the most profound loss he had suffered—and he apologizes by saying, in effect, "It really was very important to me. I hope you aren't bored by my indulgence." He makes no attempt to explore that death, its images or its meaning. His narrative is as close to factual as he can make it, which leaves no room for subjective speculation. James Baldwin, on the other hand, in *Notes of a Native Son*, says, in recording his father's life and his own relationship to his father, "All of my father's texts and songs, which I had decided were meaningless, were arranged before me at his death like empty bottles, waiting to hold the meaning which life would give them for me." And then his text fills those bottles. Like Simone de Beauvoir, he moves from the event to the image that it left. My route is the reverse: the image comes first and tells me what the "memory" is about.

I can't tell you how I felt when my father died. But I was able to write *Song of Solomon* and imagine, not him, not his specific interior life, but the world that he inhabited and the private or interior life of the people in it. And I can't tell you how I felt reading to my grandmother while she was turning over and over in her bed (because she was dying, and she was not comfortable), but I could try to reconstruct the world that she lived in. And I have suspected, more often than not, that I know more than she did, that I know more than my grandfather and my great-grandmother did, but I also know that I'm no wiser than they were. And whenever I have tried earnestly to diminish their vision and prove to myself that I know more, and when I have tried to speculate on their interior life and match it up with my own, I have been overwhelmed every time by the richness of theirs compared to my own. Like Frederick Douglass talking about his grandmother, and James Baldwin talking about his father, and Simone de Beauvoir talking about her mother, these people are my access to me;

they are my entrance into my own interior life. Which is why the images that float around them—the remains, so to speak, at the archaeological site—surface first, and they surface so vividly and so compellingly that I acknowledge them as my route to a reconstruction of a world, to an exploration of an interior life that was not written, and to the revelation of a kind of truth.

So the nature of my research begins with something as ineffable and as flexible as a dimly recalled figure, the corner of a room, a voice. I began to write my second book, which was called Sula, because of my preoccupation with a picture of a woman and the way in which I heard her name pronounced. Her name was Hannah, and I think she was a friend of my mother's. I don't remember seeing her very much, but what I do remember is the color around her—a kind of violet, a suffusion of something violet—and her eyes, which appeared to be half closed. But what I remember most is how the women said her name: how they said "Hannah Peace" and smiled to themselves, and there was some secret about her that they knew, which they didn't talk about, at least not in my hearing, but it seemed loaded in the way in which they said her name. And I suspected that she was a little bit of an outlaw but that they approved in some way.

And then, thinking about their relationship to her and the way in which they talked about her, the way in which they articulated her name, made me think about friendship between women. What is it that they forgive each other for? And what is it that is unforgivable in the world of women? I don't want to know any more about Miss Hannah Peace, and I'm not going to ask my mother who she really was and what did she do and what were you laughing about and why were you smiling? Because my experience when I do this with my mother is so crushing: she will give you the most pedestrian information you ever heard, and I would like to keep all of my remains and my images intact in their mystery when I begin. Later I will get to the facts. That way I can explore two worlds—the actual and the possible.

What I want to do this evening is to track an image from picture to meaning to text—a journey that appears in the novel that I'm writing now, which is called *Beloved*.

I'm trying to write a particular kind of scene, and I see corn on the cob. To "see" corn on the cob doesn't mean that it suddenly hovers; it only means that it keeps coming back. And in trying to figure out "What is all this corn doing?" I discover what it *is* doing.

I see the house where I grew up in Lorain, Ohio. My parents had a garden some distance away from our house, and they didn't welcome me and my sister there, when we were young, because we were not able to distinguish between the things that they wanted to grow and the things that they didn't, so we were not able to hoe, or weed, until much later.

I see them walking, together, away from me. I'm looking at their backs and what they're carrying in their arms: their tools, and maybe a peck basket. Sometimes when they walk away from me they hold hands, and they go to this other place in the garden. They have to cross some railroad tracks to get there.

I also am aware that my mother and father sleep at odd hours because my father works many jobs and works at night. And these naps are times of pleasure for me and my sister because nobody's giving us chores, or telling us what to do, or nagging us in any way. In addition to which, there is some feeling of pleasure in them that I'm only vaguely aware of. They're very rested when they take these naps.

And later on in the summer we have an opportunity to eat corn, which is the one plant that I can distinguish from the others, and which is the harvest that I like the best; the others are the food that no child likes—the collards, the okra, the strong, violent vegetables that I would give a great deal for now. But I do like the corn because it's sweet, and because we all sit down to eat it, and it's finger food, and it's hot, and it's even good cold, and there are neighbors in, and there are uncles in, and it's easy, and it's nice.

The picture of the corn and the nimbus of emotion surrounding it became a powerful one in the manuscript I'm now completing.

Authors arrive at text and subtext in thousands of ways, learning each time they begin anew how to recognize a valuable idea and how to render the texture that accompanies, reveals, or displays it to its best advantage. The process by which this is accomplished is endlessly fascinating to me. I have always thought that as an editor for twenty years I understood writers better than their most careful critics, because in examining the manuscript in each of its subsequent stages I knew the author's process, how his or her mind worked, what was effortless, what took time, where the "solution" to a problem came from. The end result—the book—was all that the critic had to go on.

Still, for me, that was the least important aspect of the work. Because, no matter how "fictional" the account of these writers, or how much it was a product of invention, the act of imagination is bound up with memory. You know, they straightened out the Mississippi River in places, to make room for houses and livable acreage. Occasionally the river floods these places. "Floods" is the word they use, but in fact it is not flooding; it is remembering. Remembering where it used to be. All water has a perfect memory and is forever trying to get back to where it was. Writers are like that: remembering where we were, what valley we ran through, what the banks were like, the light that was there and the route back to our original place. It is emotional memory—what the nerves and the skin remember as well as how it appeared. And a rush of imagination is our "flooding."

Along with personal recollection, the matrix of the work I do is the wish to extend, fill in, and complement slave autobiographical narratives. But only the matrix. What comes of all that is dictated by other concerns, not least among them the novel's own integrity. Still, like water, I remember where I was before I was "straightened out."

Q: *I would like to ask about your point of view as a novelist. Is it a vision, or are you taking the part of the particular characters?*

A: I try sometimes to have genuinely minor characters just walk through, like a walk-on actor. But I get easily distracted by them, because a novelist's imagination goes like that: every little road looks to me like an adventure, and once you begin to claim it and describe it, it looks like more, and you invent more and more and more. I don't mind doing that in my first draft, but afterward I have to cut back. I have seen myself get distracted, and people have loomed much larger than I had planned, and minor characters have seemed a little bit more interesting than they need to be for the purposes of the book. In that case I try to endow them: if there are little pieces of information that I want to reveal, I let them do some of the work. But I try not to get carried away; I try to restrain it, so that, finally, the texture is consistent and nothing is wasted; there are no words in the final text that are unnecessary, and no people who are not absolutely necessary.

As for the point of view, there should be the illusion that it's the characters' point of view, when in fact it isn't; it's really the narrator who is there but who doesn't make herself (in my case) known in that role. I like the feeling of a *told* story, where you hear a voice but you can't identify it, and you think it's your own voice. It's a comfortable voice, and it's a guiding voice, and it's alarmed by the same things that the reader is alarmed by, and it doesn't know what's going to happen next either. So you have this sort of guide. But that guide can't have a personality; it can only have a sound, and you have to feel comfortable with this voice, and then this voice can easily abandon itself and reveal the interior dialogue of a character. So it's a combination of using the point of view of various characters but still retaining the power to slide in and out, provided that when I'm "out" the reader doesn't see little fingers pointing to what's in the text.

What I really want is that intimacy in which the reader is under the impression that he isn't really reading this; that he is participating in it as he goes along. It's unfolding, and he's always two beats ahead of the characters and right on target.

Q: *You have said that writing is a solitary activity. Do you go into steady seclusion when you're writing, so that your feelings are sort of contained, or do you have to get away, and go out shopping and …?*

A: I do all of it. I've been at this book for three years. I go out shopping, and I stare, and I do whatever. It goes away. Sometimes it's very intense and I walk—I mean, I write a sentence and I jump up and run outside or something; it sort of beats you up. And sometimes I don't. Sometimes I write long hours every day. I get up at five thirty and just go do it, and if I don't like it the next day, I throw it away. But I sit down and do it. By now I know how to get to that place where something is working. I didn't always know; I thought every thought I had was interesting— because it was mine. Now I know better how to throw away things that are not useful. I can stand around and do other things and think about it at the same time. I don't mind not writing every minute; I'm not so terrified.

When you first start writing—and I think it's true for a lot of beginning writers— you're scared to death that if you don't get that sentence right that minute it's never going to show up again. And it isn't. But it doesn't matter—another one will, and it'll probably be better. And I don't mind writing badly for a couple of days because I know I can fix it—and fix it again and again and again, and it will be better. I don't have the hysteria that used to accompany some of those dazzling passages that I thought the world was just dying for me to remember. I'm a little more sanguine about it now. Because the best part of it all, the absolutely most delicious part, is finishing it and then doing it over. That's the thrill of a lifetime for me: if I can just get done with that first phase and then have infinite time to fix it and change it. I rewrite a lot, over and over again, so that it looks like I never did. I try to make it look like I never touched it, and that takes a lot of time and a lot of sweat.

Q: *In Song of Solomon, what was the relationship between your memories and* *what you made up? Was it very tenuous?*

A: Yes, it was tenuous. For the first time I was writing a book in which the central stage was occupied by men, and that had something to do with my loss, or my perception of loss, of a man (my father) and the world that disappeared with him. (It didn't, but I *felt* that it did.) So I was re-creating a time period that was his—not biographically his life or anything in it; I use whatever's around. But it seemed to me that there was this big void after he died, and I filled it with a book that was about men because my two previous books had had women as the central characters. So in that sense it was about my memories and the need to invent. I had to do something. I was in such a rage because my father was dead. The connections between us were threads that I either mined for a lot of strength or they were purely invention. But I created a male world and inhabited it and it had this quest—a journey from stupidity to epiphany, of a man, a complete man. It was my way of exploring all that, of trying to figure out what he may have known.

(1987)

25. The Signifying Monkey and the Language of Signifyin(g): Rhetorical Difference and the Orders of Meaning

表意的猴子与讽喻的语言

Henry Louis Gates, Jr.
亨利·路易斯·盖茨

亨利·路易斯·盖茨(1950),批评家、学者、编辑。盖茨 1950 年 9 月 16 日出生于西弗吉尼亚的凯泽,1968 年高中毕业后,在地方专科学校读书,后转学至耶鲁大学攻读历史专业,1973 年获得学士学位;同年进入剑桥大学的克莱尔学院改修文学,1979 年获得英语语言文学博士学位。他曾先后在耶鲁大学、康奈尔大学、杜克大学以及哈佛大学任教。盖茨教授著述颇丰,做了很多"文学考古"工作,在非裔美国文学与文化研究领域做了许多开创性的工作,他在《黑色之喻:词语、符号与"种族"自我》(*Figures in Black：Words，Signs，and the "Racial" Self*,1987)和《表意的猴子:非裔美国文学批评理论》(*The Signifying Monkey：A Theory of African American Literary Criticism*,1988)中提出的表意(signifying)概念影响深远,对深化非裔美国文学研究贡献巨大。此外,他编辑的文集,如《"种族",书写与差异》("*Race"，Writing，and Difference*,1986),《经典奴隶叙事》(*The Classic Slave Narratives*,1987),《牛津—朔姆堡 19 世纪黑人女作家系列丛书》(*Oxford-Schomburg Library of Nineteenth Century Black Women Writers*,1991)和《诺顿非裔美国文学选集》(*The Norton Anthology of African American Literature*,1996)等都在学术界产生了广泛且深远的影响。

盖茨提出的核心概念是与标准英语"表意"(signifying)相对应的"讽喻"[signifyin(g)]。他在《表意的猴子》的第二章,简要叙述了"表意的猴子"的故事,分析了学界对"表意"的不同认识,在归纳学界定义、阐释的基础上,结合很多具体例证,重点分析了"讽喻"的双声特征及其言此意彼的特点,是了解"讽喻"特点的重要章节。此外,盖茨所引用的丰富例证对分析"讽喻"的使用及其文化意义具有方法论的意义。

Some of the best dozens players were girls... before you can signify you got to be able to rap.... Signifying allowed you a choice—you could either make a cat feel good or bad. If you had just destroyed someone or if they were down already, signifying could help them over. Signifying was also a way of expressing your own feelings... Signifying at its best can be heard when the brothers are exchanging tales.

H. Rap Brown

And they asked me right at Christmas

If my blackness, would it rub off?

I said, ask your Mama.

Langston Hughes

I

If Esu-Elegbara stands as the central figure of the Ifa system of interpretation, then his Afro-American relative, the Signifying Monkey, stands as the rhetorical principle in Afro-American vernacular discourse. Whereas my concern in Chapter 1 was with the elaboration of an indigenous black hermeneutical principle, my concern in this chapter is to define a carefully structured system of rhetoric, traditional Afro-American figures of signification, and then to show how a curious figure becomes the trope of literary revision itself. My movement, then, is from hermeneutics to rhetoric and semantics, only to return to hermeneutics once again.

Thinking about the black concept of Signifyin(g) is a bit like stumbling unaware into a hall of mirrors: the sign itself appears to be doubled, at the very least, and (re) doubled upon ever closer examination. It is not the sign itself, however, which has multiplied. If orientation prevails over madness, we soon realize that only the signifier has been doubled and (re)doubled, a signifier in this instance that is silent, a "sound-image" as Saussure defines the signifier, but a "sound-image" sans the sound. The difficulty that we experience when thinking about the nature of the visual (re) doubling at work in a hall of mirrors is analogous to the difficulty we shall encounter in relating the black linguistic sign, "Signification," to the standard English sign, "signification." This level of conceptual difficulty stems from—indeed, seems to have been intentionally inscribed within—the selection of the signifier "Signification" to represent a concept remarkably distinct from that concept represented by the standard English signifier, "signification." For the standard English word is a homonym of the Afro-American vernacular word. And, to compound the dizziness and the giddiness that we must experience in the vertiginous movement between these two "identical" signifiers, these two homonyms have everything to do with each other and, then again, absolutely nothing.

In the extraordinarily complex relationship between the two homonyms, we both enact and recapitulate the received, classic confrontation between Afro-American culture and American culture. This confrontation is both political and metaphysical. We might profit somewhat by thinking of the curiously ironic relationship between these signifiers as a confrontation defined by the politics of semantics, semantics here defined as the study of the classification of changes in the signification of words, and more especially the relationships between theories of denotation and naming, as well as connotation and ambiguity. The relationship that black "Signification" bears to the English "signification" is, paradoxically, a relation of difference inscribed within a relation of identity. That, it seems to me, is inherent in the nature of metaphorical substitution and the pun, particularly those rhetorical tropes dependent on the repetition of a word with a change denoted by a difference in sound or in a letter (agnominatio), and in homonymic puns (antanaclasis). These tropes luxuriate in the chaos of ambiguity that repetition and difference (be that apparent difference centered in the signifier or in the signified, in the "sound-image" or in the concept) yield in either an aural or a visual pun.

This dreaded, if playful, condition of ambiguity would, of course, disappear in the instance at hand if the two signs under examination did not bear the same signifier. If the two signs were designated by two different signifiers, we could escape our sense of vertigo handily. We cannot, however, precisely because the antanaclasis that I am describing turns upon the very identity of these signifiers, and the play of differences generated by the unrelated concepts (the signifieds) for which they stand.

What we are privileged to witness here is the (political, semantic) confrontation between two parallel discursive universes: the black American linguistic circle and the white. We see here the most subtle and perhaps the most profound trace of an extended engagement between two separate and distinct yet profoundly—even inextricably—related orders of meaning dependent precisely as much for their confrontation on relations of identity, manifested in the signifier, as on their relations of difference, manifested at the level of the signified. We bear witness here to a protracted argument over the nature of the sign itself, with the black vernacular discourse proffering its critique of the sign as the difference that blackness makes within the larger political culture and its historical unconscious.

"Signification" and "signification" create a noisy disturbance in silence, at the level of the signifier. Derrida's neologism, "differance," in its relation to "difference," is a marvelous example of agnominatio, or repetition of a word with an alteration of both one letter and a sound. In this clever manner, Derrida's term resists reduction to self-identical meaning. The curiously suspended relationship between the

French verbs to differ and to defer both defines Derrida's revision of Saussure's notion of language as a relation of differences and embodies his revision which "in its own unstable meaning [is] a graphic example of the process at work."

I have encountered great difficulty in arriving at a suitably similar gesture. I have decided to signify the difference between these two signifiers by writing the black signifier in upper case ("Signification") and the white signifier in lower case ("signification"). Similarly, I have selected to write the black term with a bracketed final g ("Signifyin(g)") and the white term as "signifying." The bracketed g enables me to connote the fact that this word is, more often than not, spoken by black people without the final g as "signifyin'." This arbitrary and idiosyncratic convention also enables me to recall the fact that whatever historical community of Afro-Americans coined this usage did so in the vernacular as spoken, in contradistinction to the literate written usages of the standard English "shadowed" term. The bracketed or aurally erased g, like the discourse of black English and dialect poetry generally, stands as the trace of black difference in a remarkably sophisticated and fascinating (renaming ritual graphically in evidence here. Perhaps replacing with a visual sign the g erased in the black vernacular shall, like Derrida's neologism, serve both to avoid confusion and the reduction of these two distinct sets of homonyms to a false identity and to stand as the sign of a (black) Signifyin(g) difference itself. The absent g is a figure for the Signifyin(g) black difference.

Let me attempt to account for the complexities of this (re)naming ritual, which apparently took place anonymously and unrecorded in antebellum America. Some black genius or a community of witty and sensitive speakers emptied the signifier "signification" of its received concepts and filled this empty signifier with their own concepts. By doing so, by supplanting the received, standard English concept associated by (white) convention with this particular signifier, they (un)wittingly disrupted the nature of the sign = signified/signifier equation itself. I bracket wittingly with a negation precisely because origins are always occasions for speculation. Nevertheless, I tend to think, or I wish to believe, that this guerrilla action occurred intentionally on this term, because of the very concept with which it is associated in standard English.

"Signification," in standard English, denotes the meaning that a term conveys, or is intended to convey. It is a fundamental term in the standard English semantic order. Since Saussure, at least, the three terms signification, signifier, signified have been fundamental to our thinking about general linguistics and, of late, about criticism specifically. These neologisms in the academic-critical community are homonyms of terms in the black vernacular tradition perhaps two centuries old. By supplanting the received term's associated concept, the black vernacular tradition created a homonymic pun of the profoundest sort, thereby marking its sense of difference from the rest of the English community of speakers. Their complex act of language Signifies upon both formal language use and its conventions, conventions established, at least officially, by middle-class white people.

This political offensive could have been mounted against all sorts of standard English terms—and, indeed, it was. I am thinking here of terms such as *down*, *nigger*, *baby*, and *cool*, which snobbishly tend to be written about as "dialect" words or "slang." There are scores of such revised words. But to revise the term signification is to select a term that represents the nature of the process of meaning-creation and its representation. Few other selections could have been so dramatic, or so meaningful. We are witnessing here a profound disruption at the level of the signifier, precisely because of the relationship of identity that obtains between the two apparently equivalent terms. This disturbance, of course, has been effected at the level of the conceptual, or the signified. How accidental, unconscious, or unintentional (or any other code-word substitution for the absence of reason) could such a brilliant challenge at the semantic level be? To revise the received sign (quotient) literally accounted for in the relation represented by *signified/signifier* at its most apparently denotative level is to critique the nature of (white) meaning itself, to challenge through a literal critique of the sign the meaning of meaning. What did/do black people signify in a society in which they were intentionally introduced as the subjugated, as the enslaved cipher? Nothing on the x axis of white signification, and everything on the *y* axis of blackness.

It is not sufficient merely to reveal that black people colonized a white sign. A level of meta-discourse is at work in this process. If the signifier stands disrupted by the shift in concepts denoted and connoted, then we are engaged at the level of meaning itself, at the semantic register. Black people vacated this signifier, then— incredibly—substituted as its concept a signified that stands for the system of rhetorical strategies peculiar to their own vernacular tradition. Rhetoric, then, has supplanted semantics in this most literal meta-confrontation within the structure of the sign. Some historical black community of speakers most certainly struck directly at the heart of the matter, on the ground of the referent itself, thereby demonstrating that even (or especially) the concepts signified by the signifier are themselves arbitrary. By an act of will, some historically nameless community of remarkably self-conscious speakers of English defined their ontological status as one of profound difference vis-à-vis the rest of society. What's more, they undertook this act of self-definition, implicit in a (re)naming ritual, within the process of signification that the English language had inscribed for itself. Contrary to an assertion that Saussure makes in his *Course*, "the masses" did indeed "have [a] voice in the matter" and replaced the sign "chosen by language." We shall return to Saussure's discussion of the "Immutability and Mutability of the Sign" below.

Before critiquing Saussure's discussion of signification, however, perhaps I can help to clarify an inherently confusing discussion by representing the black critique of the sign, the replacement of the semantic register by the rhetorical, in Figure 1.

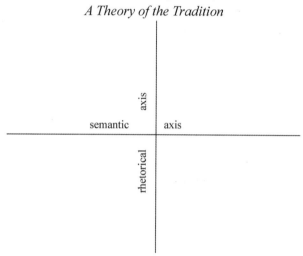

Figure 1   The Sign, "Signification"

Whereas in standard English usage signification can be represented *signified/signifier* and that which is signified is a concept, or concepts, in the black homonym, this relation of semantics has been supplanted by a relation of rhetoric, wherein the signifier "Signification" is associated with a concept that stands for the rhetorical structures of the black vernacular, the trope of tropes that is Signifyin (g). Accordingly, if in standard English

$$Signification = \frac{signified}{signifier} = \frac{concept}{sound\text{-}image},$$

then in the black vernacular,

$$Signification = \frac{rhetorical\ figures}{signifier}$$

In other words, the relation of signification itself has been critiqued by a black act of (re)doubling. The black term of *Signifyin(g)* has as its associated concept all of the rhetorical figures subsumed in the term *Signify*. To Signify, in other words, is to engage in certain rhetorical games, which I shall define and then compare to standard Western figures below.

It would be erroneous even to suggest that a concept can be erased from its relation to a signifier. A signifier is never, ultimately, able to escape its received meanings, or concepts, no matter how dramatically such concepts might change through time. In fact, homonymic puns, antanaclasis, turn precisely upon received meanings and their deferral by a vertical substitution. All homonyms depend on the absent presence of received concepts associated with a signifier.

The Signifying Monkey and the Language of Signifyin(g)

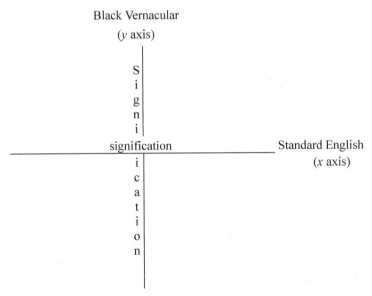

Figure 2   Black and Standard English

What does this mean in the instance of the black homonym *Signifyin(g)*, the shadowy revision of the white term? It means, it seems to me, that the signifier "Signification" has remained identical in spelling to its white counterpart to demonstrate, first, that a simultaneous, but negated, parallel discursive (ontological, political) universe exists within the larger white discursive universe, like the matter-and-antimatter fabulations so common to science fiction. It also seems apparent that retaining the identical signifier argues strongly that the most poignant level of black-white differences is that of meaning, of "signification" in the most literal sense. The play of doubles here occurs precisely on the axes, on the threshold or at Esu's crossroads, where black and white semantic fields collide. We can imagine the relationship of these two discursive universes as depicted in Figure 2. Parallel universes, then, is an inappropriate metaphor; *perpendicular* universes is perhaps a more accurate visual description.

The English-language use of *signification* refers to the chain of signifiers that configure horizontally, on the syntagmatic axis. Whereas signification operates and can be represented on a syntagmatic or horizontal axis, Signifyin(g) operates and can be represented on a paradigmatic or vertical axis. Signifyin(g) concerns itself with that which is suspended, vertically: the chaos of what Saussure calls "associative relations," which we can represent as the playful puns on a word that occupy the paradigmatic axis of language and which a speaker draws on for figurative substitutions. These substitutions in Signifyin(g) tend to be humorous, or function to name a person or a situation in a telling manner. Whereas signification depends for order and coherence on the exclusion of unconscious associations which any given word yields at any given time, Signification luxuriates in the inclusion of the free play of these associative rhetorical and semantic relations. Jacques Lacan calls these vertically suspended associations "a whole articulation of relevant contexts," by which he means all of the associations that a signifier carries from other contexts, which must be deleted, ignored, or censored "for this signifier to be lined up with a signified to produce a specific meaning." Everything that must be excluded for meaning to remain coherent and linear comes to bear in the process of Signifyin(g). As Anthony Easthope puts the matter in *Poetry as Discourse*,

> all of these absences and dependencies which have to be barred in order for
> meaning to take place constitute what Lacan designates as the *Other*. The presence
> of meaning along the syntagmatic chain necessarily depends upon the absence of the
> Other, the rest of language, from the syntagmatic chain.

Signifyin(g), in Lacan's sense, is the Other of discourse; but it also constitutes the black Other's discourse as its rhetoric. Ironically, rather than a proclamation of emancipation from the white person's standard English, the symbiotic relationship between the black and white, between the syntagmatic and paradigmatic axes, between black vernacular discourse and standard English discourse, is underscored here, and signified, by the vertiginous relationship between the terms *signification* and *Signification*, each of which is dependent on the other. We can, then, think of American discourse as both the opposition between and the ironic identity of the movement, the very vertigo, that we encounter in a mental shift between the two terms.

The process of semantic appropriation in evidence in the relation of Signification to signification has been aptly described by Mikhail Bakhtin as a double-voiced word, that is, a word or utterance, in this context, decolonized for the black's purposes "by inserting a new semantic orientation into a word which already has—and retains—its own orientation." Although I shall return later in this chapter to a fuller consideration of this notion of double-voiced words and double-voiced discourse, Gary Saul Morson's elaboration on Bakhtin's concept helps to clarify what Bakhtin implies:

> The audience of a double-voiced word is therefore meant to hear both a version of the original utterance as the embodiment of its speaker's point of view (or "semantic position") *and* the second speaker's evaluation of that utterance from a different point of view. I find it helpful to picture a double-voiced word as a special sort of palimpsest in which the uppermost inscription is a commentary on the one beneath it, which the reader (or audience) can know only by reading through the commentary that obscures in the very process of evaluating.

The motivated troping effect of the disruption of the semantic orientation of signification by the black vernacular depends on the homonymic relation of the white term to the black. The sign, in other words, has been demonstrated to be mutable.

Bakhtin's notion, then, implicitly critiques Saussure's position that the signifier ... is fixed, not free, with respect to the linguistic community that uses it. The masses have no voice in the matter, and the signifier chosen by language could be replaced by no other... [The] community itself cannot control so much as a single word; it is bound to the existing language.

Saussure, of course, proceeds to account for "shift(s) in the relationship between the signified and the signifier," shifts in time that result directly from "the arbitrary nature of the sign." But, simultaneously, Saussure denies what he terms to be "arbitrary substitution": "A particular language-state is always the product of historical forces, and these forces explain why the sign is unchangeable, i.e. why it resists any arbitrary substitution." The double-voiced relation of the two terms under analysis here argues forcefully that "the masses," especially in a multiethnic society, draw on "arbitrary substitution" freely, to disrupt the signifier by displacing its signified in an intentional act of will. Signifyin(g) is black double-voicedness; because it always entails formal revision and an intertextual relation, and because of Esu's double-voiced representation in art, I find it an ideal metaphor for black literary criticism, for the formal manner in which texts seem concerned to address their antecedents. Repetition, with a signal difference, is fundamental to the nature of Signifying(g), as we shall see.

II. *The Poetry of Signification*

The literature or tales of the Signifying Monkey and his peculiar language, Signifyin(g), is both extensive and polemical, involving as it does assertions and counterassertions about the relationship that Signifyin(g) bears to several other black tropes. I am not interested in either recapitulating or contributing to this highly specialized debate over whether or not speech act *x* is an example of this black trope or that. On the contrary, I wish to argue that Signifyin(g) is the black trope of tropes, the figure for black rhetorical figures. I wish to do so because this represents my understanding of the value assigned to Signifyin(g) by the members of the Afro-American speech community, of which I have been a signifier for quite some time. While the role of a certain aspect of linguistics study is to discern the shape and function of each tree that stands in the verbal terrain, my role as a critic, in this book at least, is to define the contours of the discursive forest or, perhaps more appropriately, of the jungle.

Tales of the Signifying Monkey seem to have had their origins in slavery. Hundreds of these have been recorded since the early twentieth century. In black music, Jazz Gillum, Count Basie, Oscar Peterson, the Big Three Trio, Oscar Brown, Jr., Little Willie Dixon, Snatch and the Poontangs, Otis Redding, Wilson Pickett, Smokey Joe Whitfield, and Johnny Otis—among others—have recorded songs about either the Signifying Monkey or, simply, Signifyin(g). The theory of Signifyin(g) is arrived at by explicating these black cultural forms. Signifyin(g) in jazz performances and in the play of black language games is a mode of formal revision, it depends for its effects on troping, it is often characterized by pastiche, and, most crucially, it turns on repetition of formal structures and their differences. Learning how to Signify is often part of our adolescent education.

Of the many colorful figures that appear in black vernacular tales, perhaps only Tar Baby is as enigmatic and compelling as is that oxymoron, the Signifying Monkey. The ironic reversal of a received racist image of the black as simianlike, the Signifying Monkey, he who dwells at the margins of discourse, ever punning, ever troping, ever embodying the ambiguities of language, is our trope for repetition and revision, indeed our trope of chiasmus, repeating and reversing simultaneously as he does in one deft discursive act. If Vico and Burke, or Nietzsche, de Man, and Bloom, are correct in identifying four and six "master tropes," then we might think of these as the "master's tropes," and of Signifyin(g) as the slave's trope, the trope of tropes, as Bloom characterizes metalepsis, "a trope-reversing trope, a figure of a figure." Signifyin(g) is a trope in which are subsumed several other rhetorical tropes, including metaphor, metonymy, synecdoche, and irony (the master tropes), and also hyperbole, litotes, and metalepsis (Bloom's supplement to Burke). To this list we could easily add aporia, chiasmus, and catechresis, all of which are used in the ritual of Signifyin(g).

Signifyin(g), it is clear, means in black discourse modes of figuration themselves. When one Signifies, as Kimberly W. Benston puns, one "tropes-a-dope." Indeed, the black tradition itself has its own subdivisions of Signifyin(g), which we could readily identify with the figures of signification received from classical and medieval rhetoric, as Bloom has done with his "map of misprision" and which we could, appropriately enough, label a "rap of misprision." The black rhetorical tropes, subsumed under Signifyin(g), would include marking, loud-talking, testifying, calling out (of one's name), sounding, rapping, playing the dozens, and so on. [See Chart 4.]

The Esu figures, among the Yoruba systems of thought in Benin and Nigeria, Brazil and Cuba, Haiti and New Orleans, are divine: they are gods who function in sacred myths, as do characters in a narrative. Esu's functional equivalent in Afro-American profane discourse is the Signifying Monkey, a figure who would seem to be distinctly Afro-American, probably derived from Cuban mythology which generally depicts Echu-Elegua with a monkey at his side. Unlike his Pan-African Esu cousins, the Signifying Monkey exists not primarily as a character in a narrative but rather as a vehicle for narration itself. Like Esu, however, the Signifying Monkey stands as the figure of an oral writing within black vernacular language rituals. It is from the corpus of mythological narratives that Signifyin(g) derives. The Afro-American rhetorical strategy of Signifyin(g) is a rhetorical practice that is not engaged in the game of information-giving, as Wittgenstein said of poetry. Signifyin(g) turns on the play and chain of signifiers, and not on some supposedly transcendent signified. As anthropologists demonstrate, the Signifying Monkey is often called the Signifier, he who wreaks havoc upon the Signified. One is signified upon by the signifier. He is indeed the "signifier as such," in Kristeva's phrase, "a presence that precedes the signification of object or emotion."

Alan Dundes's suggestion that the origins of Signifyin(g) could "lie in African rhetoric" is not as far-fetched as one might think. I have argued for a consideration of a line of descent for the Signifying Monkey from his Pan-African cousin, Esu-Elegbara. I have done so not because I have unearthed archeological evidence of a transmission process, but because of their functional equivalency as figures of rhetorical strategies and of interpretation. Esu, as I have attempted to show in Chapter 1, is the Yoruba figure of writing within an oral system. Like Esu, the Signifying Monkey exists, or is figured, in a densely structured discursive universe, one absolutely dependent on the play of differences. The poetry in which the Monkey's antics unfold is a signifying system: in marked contrast to the supposed transparency of normal speech, the poetry of these tales turns upon the free play of language itself, upon the displacement of meanings, precisely because it draws attention to its rhetorical structures and strategies and thereby draws attention to the force of the signifier.

In opposition to the apparent transparency of speech, this poetry calls attention to itself as an extended linguistic sign, one composed of various forms of the signifiers peculiar to the black vernacular. Meaning, in these poems, is not proffered; it is deferred, and it is deferred because the relationship between intent and meaning, between the speech act and its comprehension, is skewed by the figures of rhetoric or signification of which these poems consist. This set of skewed relationships creates a measure of undecidability within the discourse, such that it must be interpreted or decoded by careful attention to its play of differences. Never can this interpretation be definitive, given the ambiguity at work in its rhetorical structures. The speech of the Monkey exists as a sequence of signifiers, effecting meanings through their differential relation and calling attention to itself by rhyming, repetition, and several of the rhetorical figures used in larger cultural language games. *Signifying*) epitomizes all of the rhetorical play in the black vernacular. Its self-consciously open rhetorical status, then, functions as a kind of writing, wherein rhetoric is the writing of speech, of oral discourse. If Esu is the figure of writing in Ifa, the Signifying Monkey is the figure of a black rhetoric in the Afro-American speech community. He exists to embody the figures of speech characteristic to the black vernacular. He is the principle of self-consciousness in the black vernacular, the meta-figure itself. Given the play of doubles at work in the black appropriation of the English-language term that denotes relations of meaning, the Signifying Monkey and his language of Signifyin(g) are extraordinary conventions, with Signification standing as the term for black rhetoric, the obscuring of apparent meaning.

Scholars have for some time commented on the peculiar use of the word *Signifyin(g)* in black discourse. Though sharing some connotations with the standard English-language word, *Signifyin(g)* has rather unique definitions in black discourse. While we shall consider these definitions later in this chapter, it is useful to look briefly at one suggested by Roger D. Abrahams:

> Signifying seems to be a Negro term, in use if not in origin. It can mean any of a number of things; in the case of the toast about the signifying monkey, it certainly refers to the trickster's ability to talk with great innuendo, to carp, cajole, needle, and lie. It can mean in other instances the propensity to talk around a subject, never quite coming to the point. It can mean making fun of a person or situation. Also it can denote speaking with the hands and eyes, and in this respect encompasses a whole complex of expressions and gestures. Thus it is signifying to stir up a fight between neighbors by telling stories; it is signifying to make fun of a policeman by parodying his motions behind his back; it is signifying to ask for a piece of cake by saying, "my brother needs a piece a cake."

Essentially, Abrahams continues, Signifyin(g) is a " *technique* of indirect argument or persuasion," "a language of implication," "to imply, goad, beg, boast, by *indirect* verbal or gestural means." "The name 'signifying,'" he concludes, "shows the monkey to be a trickster, signifying being the language of trickery, that set of words or gestures achieving Hamlet's 'direction through indirection.'" The Monkey, in short, is not only a master of technique, as Abrahams concludes; he is technique, or style, or the literariness of literary language; he is the great Signifier. In this sense, one does not signify something; rather, one signifies in *some way*.

The Signifying Monkey poems, like the *ese* of the Yoruba *Odu*, reward careful explication; this sort of extensive practical criticism, however, is outside the scope of this book, as fascinating as it might be. The stanzaic form of this poetry can vary a great deal, as is readily apparent from the selections listed in this book's appendix. The most common structure is the rhyming couplet in an a-a-b-b pattern. Even within the same poem, however, this pattern can be modified, as in the stanzas cited below, where an a-a-b-c-b and an a-b-c-b pattern obtain (followed in the latter example by an a-b-a concluding "moral"). Rhyming is extraordinarily important in the production of the humorous effect that these poems have and has become the signal indication of expertise among the street poets who narrate them. The rhythm of the poems is also crucial to the desired effect, an effect in part reinforced by their quasi-musical nature of delivery.

The Monkey tales generally have been recorded from male poets, in predominantly male settings such as barrooms, pool halls, and street corners. Accordingly, given their nature as rituals of insult and naming, recorded versions have a phallocentric bias. As we shall see below, however, Signifyin(g) itself can be, and is, undertaken with equal facility and effect by women as well as men. Whereas only a relatively small number of people are accomplished narrators of Signifying Monkey tales, a remarkably large number of Afro-Americans are familiar with, and practice, modes of Signifyin(g), defined in this instance as the rubric for various sorts of playful language games, some aimed at reconstituting the subject while others are aimed at demystifying a subject. The poems are of interest to my argument primarily in three ways: as the source of the rhetorical act of Signification, as examples of the black tropes subsumed within the trope of Signifyin(g), and, crucially, as evidence for the valorization of the signifier. One of these subsumed tropes is concerned with repetition and difference; it is this trope, that of naming, which I have drawn upon as a metaphor for black intertextuality and, therefore, for formal literary history. Before discussing this process of revision, however, it is useful to demonstrate the formulaic structure of the Monkey tales and then to compare several attempts by linguists to define the nature and function of Signifyin(g). While other scholars have interpreted the Monkey tales against the binary opposition between black and white in American society, to do so is to ignore the *trinary* forces of the Monkey, the Lion, and the Elephant. To read the Monkey tales as a simple allegory of the black's political oppression is to ignore the hulking presence of the Elephant, the crucial third term of the depicted action. To note this is not to argue that the tales are not allegorical or that their import is not political. Rather, this is to note that to reduce such complex structures of meaning to a simple two-term opposition (white versus black) is to fail to account for the strength of the Elephant.

There are many versions of the toasts of the Signifying Monkey, most of which commence with a variant of the following formulaic lines:

> Deep down in the jungle so they say
>
> There's a signifying monkey down the way
>
> There hadn't been no disturbin' in the jungle for quite a bit,
>
> For up jumped the monkey in the tree one day and laughed
>
> "I guess I'll start some shit."

Endings, too, tend toward the formulaic, as in the following:

"Monkey," said the Lion,

Beat to his unbooted knees,

"You and your signifying children

Better stay up in the trees."

Which is why today

Monkey does his signifying

A-way-up out of the way.

In the narrative poems, the Signifying Monkey invariably repeats to his friend, the Lion, some insult purportedly generated by their mutual friend, the Elephant. The Monkey, however, speaks figuratively. The Lion, indignant and outraged, demands an apology of the Elephant, who refuses and then trounces the Lion. The Lion, realizing that his mistake was to take the Monkey literally, returns to trounce the Monkey. It is this relationship between the literal and the figurative, and the dire consequences of their confusion, which is the most striking repeated element of these tales. The Monkey's trick depends on the Lion's inability to mediate between these two poles of signification, of meaning. There is a profound lesson about reading here. While we cannot undertake a full reading of the poetry of the Signifying Monkey, we can, however, identify the implications for black vernacular discourse that are encoded in this poetic diction.

Signifyin(g) as a rhetorical strategy emanates directly from the Signifying Monkey tales. The relationship between these poems and the related, but independent, mode of formal language use must be made clear. The action represented in Monkey tales turns upon the action of three stock characters—the Monkey, the Lion, and the Elephant—who are bound together in a trinary relationship. The Monkey—a trickster figure, like Esu, who is full of guile, who tells lies, and who is a rhetorical genius—is intent on demystifying the Lion's self-imposed status as King of the Jungle. The Monkey, clearly, is no match for the Lion's physical prowess; the Elephant is, however. The Monkey's task, then, is to trick the Lion into tangling with the Elephant, who is the true King of the Jungle for everyone else in the animal kingdom. This the Monkey does with a rhetorical trick, a trick of mediation. Indeed, the Monkey is a term of (anti)mediation, as are all trickster figures, between two forces he seeks to oppose for his own contentious purposes, and then to reconcile.

The Monkey's trick of mediation—or, more properly, antimediation—is a play on language use. He succeeds in reversing the Lion's status by supposedly repeating aseries of insults purportedly uttered by the Elephant about the Lion's closest relatives (his wife, his "mama," his "grandmama, too!"). These intimations of sexual use, abuse, and violation constitute one well-known and commonly used mode of *Signifyin*(*g*). The Lion, who perceives his shaky, self-imposed status as having been challenged, rushes off in outrage to find the Elephant so that he might redress his grievances and preserve appearances. The self-confident but unassuming Elephant, after politely suggesting to the Lion that he must be mistaken, proceeds to trounce the Lion firmly. The Lion, clearly defeated and dethroned from his self-claimed title, returns to find the Monkey so that he can at the very least exact some sort of physical satisfaction and thereby restore his image somehat as the impregnable fortress-in-waiting that he so urgently wishes to be.

...

Like the ballad, "vocabulary and phrasing" of the Monkey poems is "colloquial, monosyllabic and everyday." Even more important to our discussion of language use in the Monkey poems, however, are the three aspects thatEast-hope locates in the operation of the ballad's syntagmatic chain. These are intertextuality, stanzaic units, and incremental repetition.

Intertextuality

As is apparent from even a cursory reading of the Signifying Monkey poems that I have listed in the appendix, each poem refers to other poems of the same genre. The artistry of the oral narrator of these poems does not depend on his or her capacity to dream up new characters or events that define the actions depicted; rather, it depends on his or her display of the ability to group together two lines that end in words that sound alike, that bear a phonetic similarity to each other. This challenge is greater when key terms are fixed, such as the three characters' identities and their received relationship to each other. Accordingly, all sorts of formulaic phrases recur across these poems, but (re)placed in distinct parts of a discrete poem.

One example demonstrates this clearly, especially if we recall that intertextuality represents a process of repetition and revision, by definition. A number of shared structural elements are repeated, with differences that suggest familiarity with other texts of the Monkey. For example, the placement of the figure "forty-four" is an instance of a formulaic phrase being repeated from poem to poem—because it has achieved a formulaic insistency—but repeated in distinct ways. For instance, the following lines in one poem:

> The Lion jumped back with a mighty roar,
>
> his tail stuck out like a forty-four,
>
> he breezed down through the jungle in a hell of a breeze,
>
> knockin' giraffes to their knees. (p.162)

are refigured in another poem in this way:

> And the Lion knew that he didn't play the Dozens
>
> and he knew the Elephant wasn't none of his cousins,
>
> so he went through the jungle with a mighty roar,
>
> poppin' his tail like a forty-four,
>
> knockin' giraffes to their knees
>
> and knockin' coconuts from the trees. (p. 164)

and in another poem in this way:

> The Lion got so mad he jump up trimmin' the trees,
>
> chopped baby giraffes, monkeys down on their knees.
>
> He went on down the jungle way a jumpin' and pawin'
>
> poppin' his tail worse in' a forty-four. (p. 166)

It is as if a received structure of crucial elements provides a base for poeisis, and the narrator's technique, his or her craft, is to be gauged by the creative (re)placement of these expected or anticipated formulaic phrases and formulaic events, rendered anew in unexpected ways. Precisely because the concepts represented in the poem are shared, repeated, and familiar to the poet's audience, meaning is devalued while the signifier is valorized. Value, in this art of poeisis, lies in its foregrounding rather than in the invention of a novel signified. We shall see how the nature of the rhyme scheme also stresses the materiality and the priority of the signifier. Let me add first, however, that all other common structural elements are repeated with variations across the texts that, together, comprise the text of the Monkey. In other words, there is no fixed text of these poems; they exist as a play of differences.

Stanzaic Units

Every Signifying Monkey poem is characterized by at least two predominant features of stanzaic structure: an introductory formulaic frame and a concluding formulaic frame, as well as a progression of rhyming couplets, each of which usually relates to the next in a binary pattern of a-a-b-b rhyme, although occasionally a pattern of a-a-b-b-c or a-a-b-c-c appears, especially to include a particularly vivid (visual) or startling (aural) combination of signifies. The frame consists of a variation of the following:

> Say deep down in the jungle in the coconut grove
>
> lay the Signifying Monkey in his one-button roll.
>
> Now the hat he wore was on the Esquire fold,
>
> his shoes was on a triple-A last.
>
> You could tell that he was a pimping motherfucker
>
> by the way his hair was gassed, (p.162)
>
> He said, "Well, Brother Lion, the day have come at last,
>
> that I have found a limb to fit your ass."
>
> He said, "You might as well stop, there ain't no use tryin',
>
> because no motherfucker is gonna stop me from signifyin." (p. 163)

I shall turn to the nature of the rhyme scheme and its import below.

Incremental Repetition

Incremental repetition in these poems assumes the form of the repeated binary structure of rhyming couplets, which function as narrative units in isolation or with a second or third set of couplets, and as larger narrative units in a tertiary relation that is contained within the binary frame described above. The frame defines a problem, the Monkey's irritation at the Lion's roaring, which disturbs the Monkey's connubial habits, and ends with some sort of resolution of that problem. The tertiary relation of the intervening narrative units turns upon the repetition of confrontation and engagement: the Monkey engages the Lion by repeating insults purportedly said by the Elephant; next, the Lion rushes off helter-skelter and challenges the Elephant to a confrontation that the Lion loses; finally, the Lion returns to the scene of the crime, the Monkey's tree, and engages the Monkey, who insults the Lion, slips from his protective branch, then usually escapes certain defeat by tricking the Lion again with a Signifyin(g) challenge, such as the following:

> The Monkey said, "I know you think you raisin' hell,
>
> but everybody seen me when I slipped and fell.

But if you let me get my nuts up out of this sand

I'll fight you just like a natural man."

This tertiary repetition of confrontation-engagement-resolution occurs in representations of direct speech. The Lion's combat with the Elephant is balanced by the Lion's combat with the Monkey. Stasis is relieved by the Monkey's trick of mediation, his rhetorical play on the Lion's incapacity to read his utterance, a flaw that enables the Monkey to scramble back to his protective limb, only to continue to Signify.

The most important aspect of language use in these poems, however, is the nature of its rhymes. Here we can draw upon Wimsatt's analysis of the rhymes of Pope and Easthope's analysis of the feudal ballad to elucidate the import of the rhyme in the Monkey tales.

...

What does such a foregrounding of the signifier imply for black vernacular discourse? We must remember that the Signifying Monkey tales are the repositories of the black vernacular tradition's rhetorical principles, coded dictionaries of black tropes. First, the Monkey "tropes-a-dope," the Lion, by representing a figurative statement as a literal statement, depending on the Lion's thickness to misread the difference. Second, the ensuing depiction of action depends on the stress of phonetic similarity between signifiers. These poems flaunt the role of the signifier in relation to the signified, allowing it its full status as an equal in their relationship, if not the superior partner. Where meaning is constant, the (re)production of this fixed meaning, by definition, foregrounds the play of the signifier. Signifyin(g), then, is the sign of rule in the kingdom of Signification: neither the Lion nor the Elephant—both Signifieds, those Signified upon—is the King of the Jungle; rather, the Monkey is King, the Monkey as Signifier.

If the rhyme pattern of the poems depends on coincidence more often than subordination, then the Monkey's process of Signifyin(g) turns upon repetition and difference, or repetition and reversal. There are so many examples of Signifyin(g) in jazz that one could write a formal history of its development on this basis alone. One early example is relatively familiar: Jelly Roll Morton's 1938 recording entitled "Maple Leaf Rag (A Transformation)" Signifies upon Scott Joplin's signature composition, "Maple Leaf Rag," recorded in 1916. Whereas Joplin played its contrasting themes and their repetitions in the form of AABBACCDD, Morton "embellishes the piece two-handedly, with a swinging introduction (borrowed from the ending to A), followed by ABACCD (a hint of the tango here) D (a real New

Orleans 'stomp' variation)," as Martin Williams observes. Morton's piano imitates "a trumpet-clarinet right hand and a trombone-rhythm left hand." Morton's composition does not "surpass" or "destroy" Joplin's; it complexly extends and tropes figures present in the original. Morton's Signification is a gesture of admiration and respect. It is this aspect of Signifyin(g) that is inscribed in the black musical tradition in jazz compositions such as Oscar Peterson's "Signify" and Count Basie's "Signifyin".

In these compositions, the formal history of solo piano styles in jazz is recapitulated, delightfully, whereby one piano style follows its chronological predecessor in the composition itself, so that boogie-woogie, stride, and blues piano styles—and so on—are represented in one composition as histories of the solo jazz piano, histories of its internal repetition and revision process. Improvisation, of course, so fundamental to the very idea of jazz, is "nothing more" than repetition and revision. In this sort of revision, again where meaning is fixed, it is the realignment of the signifier that is the signal trait of expressive genius. The more mundane the fixed text ("April in Paris" by Charlie Parker, "My Favorite Things" by John Coltrane), the more dramatic is the Signifying) revision. It is this principle of repetition and difference, this practice of intertextuality, which has been so crucial to the black vernacular forms of Signifyin(g), jazz—and even its antecedents, the blues, the spirituals, and ragtime—and which is the source of my trope for black intertextuality in the Afro-American formal literary tradition. I shall return to this idea at the end of Chapter 3.

III. *Signifyin(g): Definitions*

Signifyin(g) is so fundamentally black, that is, it is such a familiar rhetorical practice, that one encounters the great resistance of inertia when writing about it. By inertia I am thinking here of the difficulty of rendering the implications of a concept that is so shared in one's culture as to have long ago become second nature to its users. The critic is bound to encounter Ralph Ellison's "Little Man at Chehaw Station."

Who is he? Ellison tells a marvelous story about himself when he was a student of music at Tuskegee. Having failed at an attempt to compensate for a lack of practice with a virtuoso style of performance, Ellison had sought some solace from the brilliant Hazel Harrison, one of his professors, with whom he had a sustained personal relationship. Instead of solace, however, his friend and mentor greeted his solicitation with a riddle.

...

The language of blackness encodes and names its sense of independence through a rhetorical process that we might think of as the Signifyin(g) black difference. As early as the eighteenth century, commentators recorded black usages of Signification. Nicholas Cresswell, writing between 1774 and 1777, made the following entry in his journal: "In [the blacks'] songs they generally relate the usage they have received from their Masters or Mistresses in a very satirical stile [sic] and manner." Cresswell strikes at the heart of the matter when he makes explicit "the usage" that the black slaves "have received," for black people frequently "enounce" their sense of difference by repetition with a signal difference. The eighteenth century abounds in comments from philosophers such as David Hume in "Of National Characters" and statesmen such as Thomas Jefferson in *Notes on the State of Virginia*, who argued that blacks were "imitative" rather than "creative." All along, however, black people were merely Signifyin(g) through a motivated repetition.

Frederick Douglass, a masterful Signifier himself, discusses this use of troping in his *Narrative* of 1845. Douglass, writing some seventy years after Cresswell, was an even more acute observer. Writing about the genesis of the lyrics of black song, Douglass noted the crucial role of the signifier in the determination of meaning:

> [The slaves] would compose and sing as they went along, consulting neither time nor tune. The thought that came up, came out—if not in the *word*, in the *sound*;—and as frequently in the one as in the other ... they would sing, as a chorus, to words which to many seem *unmeaning jargon*, but which, nevertheless, were *full of meaning* to themselves.

Meaning, Douglass writes, was as determined by sound as by sense, whereby phonetic substitutions determined the shape of the songs. Moreover, the neologisms that Douglass's friends created, "unmeaning jargon" to standard English speakers, were "full of meaning" to the blacks, who were literally defining themselves in language, just as did Douglass andhundreds of other slave narrators. This, of course, is an example of both sorts of signification, black vernacular and standard English. Douglass continues his discussion by maintaining that his fellow slaves "would sing the most pathetic sentiment in the most rapturous tone, and the most rapturous sentiment in the most pathetic tone," a set of oppositions which led to the song's misreading by non-slaves. As Douglass admits,

> I have often been utterly astonished, since I came to the north, to find persons

who could speak of the singing, among slaves, as evidence of their contentment and happiness. It is impossible to conceive of a greater mistake.

This great mistake of interpretation occurred because the blacks were using antiphonal structures to reverse their apparent meaning, as a mode of encoding for self-preservation. Whereas black people under Cresswell's gaze Signified openly, those Douglass knew Signified protectively, leading to the misreading against which Douglass rails. As Douglass writes in his second autobiography, however, blacks often Signified directly, as in the following lyrics:

> We raise de wheat,
>
> Dey gib us de corn;
>
> We bake de bread,
>
> Dey gib us de cruss;
>
> We sif de meal,
>
> Dey gib us de huss;
>
> We peal de meat,
>
> Dey gib us de skin
>
> And dat's de way
>
> Dey takes us in.

As William Faux wrote in 1819, slaves commonly used lyrics to Signify upon their oppressors: "Their verse was their own, and abounding either in praise or satire intended for kind and unkind masters."

I cite these early references to motivated language use only to emphasize that black people have been Signifyin(g), without explicitly calling it that, since slavery, as we might expect. One ex-slave, Wash Wilson, in an interview he granted a member of the Federal Writers Project in the 1930s, implies that "sig'fication" was an especial term and practice for the slaves:

When de niggers go round singin' "Steal Away to Jesus," dat mean dere gwine be a' ligious meetin' dat night. Dat de *sig'fication* of a meetin'. De masters'fore and after freedom didn't like dem'ligious meetin's, so us natcherly slips off at night, down in de bottoms or somewheres. Sometimes us sing and pray all night.

This usage, while close to its standard English shadow, recalls the sense of Signification as an indirect form of communication, as a troping. The report of Wilson's usage overlaps with Zora Neale Hurston's definition of *signify* in *Mules and Men*, published in 1935. These two usages of the words are among the earliest recorded; Wilson's usage argues for an origin of "sig'fication" in slavery, as does the allegorical structure of the Monkey poems and the nature of their figuration, both of which suggest a nineteenth-century provenance. I shall defer a fuller examination of Hurston's sense of Signification to Chapter 5. I wish to explore, in the remainder of this section of this chapter, received definitions of Signifyin(g) before elaborating my own use of this practice in literary criticism.

We can gain some appreciation of the complexity of Signifyin(g) by examining various definitions of the concept. Dictionary definitions give us an idea of how unstable the concepts are that can be signified by Signifyin(g). Clarence Major's *Dictionary of Afro-American Slang* says that "Signify" is the "same as the Dirty Dozens; to censure in 12 or fewer statements," and advises the reader to see "Cap on." The "Dirty Dozens" he defines as "a very elaborate game traditionally played by black boys, in which the participants insult each other's relatives, especially their mothers. The object of the game is to test emotional strength. The first person to give in to anger is the loser." To "Cap on" is "to censure," in the manner of the dozens. For Major, then, to Signify is to be engaged in a highly motivated rhetorical act, aimed at figurative, ritual insult.

Hermese E. Roberts, writing in *The Third Ear: A Black Glossary*, combines Major's emphasis on insult and Roger D. Abrahams's emphasis on implication. Roberts defines "signifying," or "siggin(g)," as "language behavior that makes direct or indirect implications of baiting or boasting, the essence of which is making fun of another's appearance, relatives, or situation." For Roberts, then, a signal aspect of Signifyin(g) is "making fun of" as a mode of "baiting" or "boasting." It is curious to me how very many definitions of Signifyin(g) share this stress on what we might think of as the black person's symbolic aggression, enacted in language, rather than upon the play of language itself, the meta-rhetorical structures in evidence. "Making fun of" is a long way from "making fun," and it is the latter that defines Signifyin(g).

Roberts lists as subcategories of Signifyin(g) the following figures: "joning, playing the dozens, screaming on, sounding." Under "joning" and "sounding," Roberts asks the reader to "See signifying." "Screaming on" is defined as "telling someone off; i.e. to get on someone's case," "case" meaning among other things "an imaginary region of the mind in which is centered one's vulnerable points, eccentricities, and sensitivities." "Screaming on" also means "embarrassing someone publicly." "Playing the dozens" Roberts defines as "making derogatory, often obscene, remarks about another's mother, parents, or family members. ('Yo' mama' is an expression used as retribution for previous vituperation.)" Roberts, in other words, consistently groups Signifyin(g) under those tropes of contention wherein aggression and conflict predominate. Despite this refusal to transcend surface meaning to define its latent meaning, Roberts's decision to group joning, playing the dozens, screaming on, and sounding as synonyms of Signifyin(g) is exemplary for suggesting that Signifyin(g) is the trope of tropes in the black vernacular.

Mezz Mezzrow, the well-known jazz musician, defines "Signify" in the glossary of his autobiography, *Really the Blues*, as "hint, to put on an act, boast, make a gesture." In the body of his text, however, Mezzrow implicitly defines signifying as the homonymic pun. In an episode in which some black people in a bar let some white gangsters know that their identity as murderers is common knowledge, the blacks, apparently describing a musical performance, use homonyms such as "killer" and "murder" to Signify upon the criminals. As Mezzrow describes the event:

> He could have been talking about the music, but everybody in the room knew different. Right quick another cat spoke up real loud, saying, "That's *murder* man, really murder," and his eyes were *signifying* too. All these gunmen began to shift from foot to foot, fixing their ties and scratching their noses, faces red and Adam's apples jumping. Before we knew it they had gulped their drinks and beat it out the door, saying good-bye to the bartender with their hats way down over their eyebrows and their eyes gunning the ground. That's what Harlem thought of the white underworld.

Signifying here connotes the play of language—both spoken and body language—drawn upon to name something figuratively.

Mezzrow's definitions are both perceptive and subtle. Signifyin(g) for him is one mode of "verbal horseplay," designed to train the subject "to think faster and be more nimble-witted." Mezzrow, then, is able to penetrate the content of this black verbal horseplay to analyze the significance of the rhetorical structures that transcend any fixed form of Signifyin(g), such as the verbal insult rituals called the dozens. Indeed, Mezzrow was one of the first commentators to recognize that Signifyin(g) as a structure of performance could apply equally to verbal texts and musical texts. As he summarizes:

> Through all these friendly but lively competitions you could see the Negro's appreciation of real talent and merit, his demand for fair play, and his ardor for the best man wins and don't you come around here with no jive. Boasting doesn't cut any ice; if you think you've got something, don't waste time talking yourself up, go to work and prove it. If you have the stuff the other cats will recognize it frankly, with

solid admiration. That's especially true in the field of music, which has a double importance to the Negro because that's where he really shines, where his inventiveness and artistry come through in full force. The colored boys prove their musical talents in those competitions called cutting contests, and there it really is the best man wins, because the Negro audience is extra critical when it comes to music and won't accept anything second-rate. These cutting contests are just a musical version of the verbal duels. They're staged to see which performer can snag and cap all the others *musically*. And by the way, these battles have helped to produce some of the race's greatest musicians.

Signifyin(g) for Mezzrow is not what is played or said; it is rather a form of rhetorical training, an on-the-streets exercise in the use of troping, in which the play is the thing—not specifically what is said, but how. All definitions of Signifyin(g) that do not distinguish between manner and matter succumb, like the Lion, to serious misreading.

Malachi Andrews and Paul T. Owens, in *Black Language*, acutely recognize two crucial aspects of Signifyin(g): first, that the signifier invents a myth to commence the ritual and, second, that in the Monkey tales at least, trinary structure prevails over binary structure. "To Signify," they write,

> is to tease, to provoke into anger. The *signifier* creates a myth about someone and tells him a *third* person started it. The *signified* person is aroused and seeks that person.... Signifying is completely successful when the *signifier* convinces the chump he is working on, that what he is saying is true and that it gets him angered to wrath.

Andrews and Owen's definition sticks fairly closely to the action of the Signifying Monkey tales. While Signifyin(g) can, and indeed does, occur between two people, the three terms of the traditional mythic structure serve to dispel a simple relation of identity between the allegorical figures of the poem and the binary political relationship, outside the text, between black and white. The third term both critiques the idea of the binary opposition and demonstrates that Signifyin(g) itself encompasses a larger domain than merely the political. It is a game of language, independent of reaction to white racism or even to collective black wish-fulfillment vis-à-vis white racism. I cannot stress too much the import of the presence of this third term, or in Hermese E. Roberts's extraordinarily suggestive phrase, "The Third Ear," an intraracial ear through which encoded vernacular language is deciphered.

J. L. Dillard, who along with William Labov and William A. Stewart is one of the most sensitive observers of black language use, defines Signifyin(g) as "a familiar discourse device from the inner city, [which] tends to mean 'communicating (often an obscene or ridiculing message) by indirection.'" Dillard here is elaborating somewhat upon Zora Neale Hurston's gloss printed in *Mules and Men*, where she writes that to signify is to "show off." This definition seems to be an anomalous one, unless we supply Hurston's missing, or implied, terms: to show off *with language use*. Dillard, however, is more concerned with the dozens than he is with Signifyin(g). In an especially perceptive chapter entitled "Discourse Distribution and Semantic Difference in Homophonous Items," Dillard ignores the homophone *signify* but suggests that so-called inner-city verbal rituals, such as the dozens, could well be contemporary revisions of "the 'lies' told by Florida Blacks studied by Hurston and the Anansi stories of the southern plantations," sans the "sex and scatology." "Put those elements back," Dillard continues, "and you have something like the rhymed 'toasts' of the inner city." The "toasts," as Bruce Jackson has shown, include among their types the Signifying Monkey tales. There can be little doubt that Signifyin(g) was found by linguists in the black urban neighborhoods in the fifties and sixties because black people from the South migrated there and passed the tradition along to subsequent generations.

We can see the extremes of dictionary and glossary definitions of *Signify* in two final examples, one taken from *The Psychology of Black Language*, by Jim Haskins and Hugh F. Butts, and the other from the *Dictionary of American Slang*, compiled by Harold Wentworth and Stuart Berg Flexner. Haskins and Butts, in a glossary appended to their text, define "to signify" as "To berate, degrade." In their text, however, they define "signifying" as "a more humane form of verbal bantering" than the dozens, admitting, however, that Signifyin(g) "has many meanings," including meanings that contradict their own glossary listing: "It is, again, the clever and humorous use of words, but it can be used for many purposes—'putting down' another person, making another person feel better, or simply expressing one's feelings." Haskins and Butts's longer definition seems to contradict their glossary listing—unless we recall that Signifyin(g) can mean all of these meanings, and more, precisely because so many black tropes are subsumed within it. Signifyin(g) does not, on the other hand, mean "To pretend to have knowledge; to pretend to be hip, esp. when such pretentions cause one to trifle with an important matter," as Wentworth and Flexner would have it. Indeed, this definition sounds like a classic black Signification, in which a black informant, as it were, Signified upon either

Wentworth or Flexner, or lexicographers in general who "pretend to have knowledge."

There are several other dictionary definitions that I could cite here. My intention, however, has been to suggest the various ways in which Signifyin(g) is (mis)understood, primarily because few scholars have succeeded in defining it as a full concept. Rather, they often have taken the part—one of its several tropes—as its whole. The delightfully "dirty" lines of the dozens seem to have generated far more interest from scholars than has Signifyin(g), and perhaps far more heat than light. The dozens are an especially compelling subset of Signifyin(g), and its name quite probably derives from an eighteenth-century meaning of the verb *dozen*, "to stun, stupefy, daze," in the black sense, through language. Let us examine more substantive definitions of Signifyin(g) by H. Rap Brown, Roger D. Abrahams, Thomas Kochman, Claudia Mitchell-Kernan, Geneva Smitherman, and Ralph Ellison, before exploring examples of the definition of Signifyin(g) that I shall employ in the remainder of this book.

H. Rap Brown earned his byname because he was a master of black vernacular rhetorical games and their attendant well-defined rhetorical strategies. Brown's understanding of Signifyin(g) is unsurpassed by that of any scholar. In the second chapter of his autobiography, *Die Nigger Die!*, Brown represents the scenes of instruction by which he received his byname. "I learned to talk in the street," he writes, "not from reading about Dick and Jane going to the zoo and all that simple shit." Rather, Brown continues, "we exercised our minds," not by studying arithmetic but "by playing the Dozens":

> I fucked your mama
> Till she went blind.
> Her breath smells bad,
> But she sure can grind.

> I fucked your mama
> For a solid hour.
> Baby came out
> Screaming, Black Power.

> Elephant and the Baboon
> Learning to screw.
> Baby came out looking
> Like Spiro Agnew.

Brown argues that his teachers sought to teach him "poetry," meaning poems from the Western tradition, when he and his fellows were *making* poetry in the streets. "If anybody needed to study poetry," he maintains, "my teacher needed to study mine. We played the Dozens," he concludes, "like white folks play Scrabble." "[They] call me Rap," he writes humorously if tautologically, "'cause I could rap." To rap is to use the vernacular with great dexterity. Brown, judging from his poetry printed in this chapter of his autobiography, most certainly earned his byname.

Brown's definitions and examples are as witty as they are telling. He insists, as does Claudia Mitchell-Kernan, that both men and women can play the dozens and Signify: "Some of the best Dozens players," he writes, "were girls." Whereas the dozens were an unrelentingly "mean game because what you try to do is totally destroy somebody else with words," Signifyin(g) was "more humane": "Instead of coming down on somebody's mother, you come down on them." Brown's account of the process of Signifyin(g) is especially accurate:

> A session would start maybe by a brother
> saying, "Man, before you mess with me
> you'd rather run rabbits, eat shit and
> bark at the moon." Then, if he was talking
> to me, I'd tell him:
>
> Man, you must don't know who I am.
> I'm sweet peeter jeeter the womb beater
> The baby maker the cradle shaker
> The deerslayer the buckbinder the women finder
>
> Known from the Gold Coast to the rocky shores of Maine
> Rap is my name and love is my game.
> I'm the bed tucker the cock plucker the motherfucker
> The milkshaker the record breaker the population maker
> The gun-slinger the baby bringer
> The hum-dinger the pussy ringer
> The man with the terrible middle finger.
> The hard hitter the bullshitter the poly-nussy getter
> The beast from the East the Judge the sludge
> The women's pet the men's fret and the punks' pin-up boy.
> They call me Rap the dicker the ass kicker

The cherry picker the city slicker the titty licker

And I ain't giving up nothing but bubble gum and hard times and I'm fresh out of bubble gum.

I'm giving up wooden nickles 'cause I know they won't spend

And I got a pocketful of splinter change.

I'm a member of the bathtub club: I'm seeing a whole lot of ass but I ain't taking no shit.

I'm the man who walked the water and tied the whale's tail in a knot

Taught the little fishes how to swim

Crossed the burning sands and shook the devil's hand

Rode round the world on the back of a snail carrying a sack saying AIR MAIL.

Walked 49 miles of barbwire and used a Cobra snake for a necktie

And got a brand new house on the roadside made from a cracker's hide,

Got a brand new chimney setting on top made from the cracker's skull

Took a hammer and nail and built the world and calls it "THE BUCKET OF BLOOD."

Yes, I'm hemp the demp the women's pimp

Women fight for my delight.

I'm a bad motherfucker. Rap the rip-saw the devil's brother'n law.

I roam the world I'm known to wander and this .45 is where I get my thunder.

I'm the only man in the world who knows why white milk makes yellow butter.

I know where the lights go when you cut the switch off.

I might not be the best in the world, but I'm in the top two and my brother's getting old.

And ain't nothing bad 'bout you but your breath.

Whereas the dozens were structured to make one's subject feel bad, "Signifying allowed you a choice—you could either make a cat feel good or bad. If you had just destroyed someone [verbally] or if they were just down already, signifying could help them over."

Few scholars have recognized this level of complexity in Signifyin(g) which Brown argues implicitly to be the rhetorical structures at work in the discourse, rather than a specific content uttered. In addition to making "a cat feel good or bad," Brown continues, "Signifying was also a way of expressing your own feelings," as in the following example:

Man, I can't win for losing.

If it wasn't for bad luck, I wouldn't have no luck at all.

I been having buzzard luck

Can't kill nothing and won't nothing die

I'm living on the welfare and things is stormy

They borrowing their shit from the Salvation Army

But things bound to get better 'cause they can't get no worse

I'm just like the blind man, standing by a broken window

I don't feel no pain.

But it's your world

You the man I pay rent to

If I had you hands I'd give 'way both my arms.

Cause I could do without them

I'm the man but you the main man

I read the books you write

You set the pace in the race I run

Why, you always in good form

You got more foam than Alka Seltzer ...

Signifyin(g), then, for Brown, is an especially expressive mode of discourse that turns upon forms of figuration rather than intent or content. Signifyin(g), to cite Brown, is "what the white folks call verbal skills. We learn how to throw them words together." Signifying, "at its best," Brown concludes, "can be heard when brothers are exchanging tales." It is this sense of storytelling, repeated and often shared (almost communal canonical stories, or on-the-spot recountings of current events) in which Signifyin(g) as a rhetorical strategy can most clearly be seen. We shall return to Brown's definition in the next section of this chapter.

One of the most sustained attempts to define Signifyin(g) is that of Roger D. Abrahams, a well-known and highly regarded literary critic, linguist, and anthropologist. Abrahams's work in this area is seminal, as defined here as a work against which subsequent works must, in some way, react. Between 1962 and 1976, Abrahams published several significant studies of Signifyin (g). To tract Abrahams's interpretative evolution helps us to understand the complexities of this rhetorical strategy but is outside the scope of this book.

Abrahams in 1962 brilliantly defines Signifyin (g) in terms that he and other subsequent scholars shall repeat:

The name "Signifying Monkey" shows [the hero] to be a trickster, "signifying" being the language of trickery, that set of words or gestures which arrives at "direction through indirection."

Signifyin(g), Abrahams argues implicitly, is the black person's use of figurative modes of language use. The word *indirection* hereafter recurs in the literature with great, if often unacknowledged, frequency. Abrahams expanded on this theory of Signifyin(g) in two editions of *Deep Down in the Jungle* (1964, 1970). It is useful to list the signal aspects of his extensive definitions:

1. Signifyin(g) "can mean any number of things."
2. It is a black term and a black rhetorical device.
3. It can mean the "ability to talk with great innuendo."
4. It can mean "to carp, cajole, needle, and lie."
5. It can mean "the propensity to talk around a subject, never quite coming to the point."
6. It can mean "making fun of a person or situation."
7. It can "also denote speaking with the hands and eyes."
8. It is "the language of trickery, that set of words achieving Hamlet's 'direction through indirection.'"
9. The Monkey "is a 'signifier,' and the Lion, therefore, is the signified."

Finally, in his appended glossary of "Unusual Terms and Expressions," Abrahams defines "Signify" as "To imply, goad, beg, boast by indirect verbal or gestural means. A language of implication."

These definitions are exemplary insofar as they emphasize "indirection" and "implication," which we can read as synonyms of *figurative*. Abrahams was the first scholar, to my knowledge, to define Signifyin(g) as a language, by which he means a particular rhetorical strategy. Whereas he writes that the Monkey is a master of this technique, it is even more accurate to write that he is technique, the literariness of language, the ultimate source for black people of the figures of signification. If we think of rhetoric as the "writing" of spoken discourse, then the Monkey's role as the source and encoded keeper of Signifyin(g) helps to reveal his functional equivalency with his Pan-African cousin, *Esu-Elegbara*, the figure of writing in Ifa.

Abrahams's work helps us to understand that Signifyin(g) is an adult ritual, which black people learn as adolescents, almost exactly like children learned the traditional figures of signification in classically structured Western primary and secondard schools, training one hopes shall be returned to contemporary education. As we shall see below, Claudia Mitchell-Kernan, an anthropologist-linguist, shares an anecdote that demonstrates, first, how Signifyin(g) truly is a conscious rhetorical strategy and, second, how adult black people implicitly instruct a mature child in its most profound and subtle uses by an indirect mode of narration only implicitly related in form to the Monkey tales, perhaps as extract relates to the vanilla bean, or as sand relates to the pearl, or, as Esu might add, as palm wine relates to the palm tree. Black adults teach their children this exceptionally complex system of rhetoric, almost exactly like Richard A. Lanham describes a generic portrait of the teaching of the rhetorical *paideia to* Western schoolchildren. The mastery of Signifyin(g) creates *homo rhetoricus Africanus*, allowing—through the manipulation of these classic black figures of Signification—the black person to move freely between two discursive universes. This is an excellent example of what I call linguistic masking, the verbal sign of the mask of blackness that demarcates the boundary between the white linguistic realm and the black, two domains that exist side by side in a homonymic relation signified by the very concept of Signification. To learn to manipulate language in such a way as to facilitate the smooth navigation between these two realms has been the challenge of black parenthood, and remains so even today. Teaching one's children the fine art of Signifyin(g) is to teach them about this mode of linguistic circumnavigation, to teach them a second language that they can share with other black people. Black adolescents engaged in the dozens and in Signifyin(g) rituals to learn the classic black figures of Signification. As H. Rap Brown declares passionately, his true school was the street. Richard Lanham's wonderful depiction of the student passing through the rhetorical *paideia* reads like a description of vernacular black language training:

Start your student young. Teach him a minute concentration on the word, how to write it, speak it, remember it.... From the beginning, stress behavior as performance, reading aloud, speaking with gesture, a full range of histrionic adornment.... Develop elaborate memory schemes to keep them readily at hand. Teach, as theory of personality, a corresponding set of accepted personality types, a taxonomy of impersonation.... Nourish an acute sense of social situation.... Stress, too, the need for improvisation, ad-lib quickness, the coaxing of chance. Hold always before the student rhetoric's practical purpose: to win, to persuade. But train for this purpose with continual verbal play, rehearsal for the sake of rehearsal.

Use the "case" method.... Practice this re-creation always in an agonistic context. The aim is scoring. Urge the student to go into the world and observe its doings from this perspective. And urge him to continue his rehearsal method all his life, forever rehearsing a spontaneous real life.... Training in the word thus becomes a badge, as well as a diversion, of the leisure class.

This reads very much like a black person's training in Signifyin(g). Lanham's key words—among which are "a taxonomy of impersonation," "improvisation," "ad-lib quickness," "to win," "to persuade," "continual verbal play," "the 'case' method," "the aim is scoring"—echo exactly the training of blacks to Signify. Even Lanham's concept of a "leisure" class applies ironically here, since blacks tend in capitalist societies to occupy a disproportionate part of the "idle" unemployed, a leisure-class with a difference. To Signify, then, is to master the figures of black Signification.

Few black adults can recite an entire Monkey tale; black adults, on the other hand, can—and do—Signify. The mastering of the Monkey tales corresponds to this early part of Lanham's account of Western rhetorical training. Words are looked at in the Monkey tales because the test of this form of poeisis is to arrive at a phonetic coincidence of similar parts of speech, as I have shown above. The splendid example of Signifyin(g) that I have cited in Ralph Ellison's anecdote about Hazel Harrison, and the anecdote of Claudia Mitchell-Kernan's that I shall discuss below, conform to Lanham's apt description of the mature capacity to look through words for their full meaning. Learning the Monkey tales, then, is somewhat akin to attending troping school, where one learns to "trope-a-dope."

The Monkey is a hero of black myth, a sign of the triumph of wit and reason, his language of Signifyin(g) standing as the linguistic sign of the ultimate triumph of self-consciously formal language use. The black person's capacity to create this rich poetry and to derive from these rituals a complex attitude toward attempts at domination, which can be transcended in and through language, is a sign of their originality, of their extreme consciousness of the metaphysical. Abrahams makes these matters clear.

In *Talking Black*, published in 1976, Abrahams's analysis of Signifyin(g) as an act of language is even more subtle than his earlier interpretations. Abrahams repeats his insightful definition that Signifyin(g) turns upon indirection. Black women, he maintains, and "to a certain extent children," utilize "more indirect methods of signifying." His examples are relevant ones:

> These range from the most obvious kinds of indirection, like using an unexpected pronoun in discourse ("Didn't we come to shine, today?" or "Who thinks his drawers don't stink?"), to the more subtle technique, of *louding or loud-*

talking in a different sense from the one above. A person is loud-talking when he says something of someone just loud enough for that person to hear, but indirectly, so he cannot properly respond (Mitchell-Kernan). Another technique of signifying through indirection is making reference to a person or group not present, in order to start trouble between someone present and the ones who are not. An example of this technique is the famous toast, "The Signifying Monkey."

These examples are salient for two reasons: first, because he has understood that adults use the modes of signification commonly, even if they cannot recite even one couplet from the Monkey tales, and, second, because he has realized that other tropes, such as loud-talking, are subtropes of Signifyin(g). His emphasis on the mature forms of Signifyin(g)—that is, the indirect modes—as more common among women and children does not agree with my observations. Indeed, I have found that black men and women use indirection with each other to the same degree.

Next, Abrahams states that Signifyin(g) can also be used "in recurrent black-white encounters as masking behavior." Since the full effectiveness of Signifyin(g) turns upon all speakers possessing the mastery of reading, what Abrahams calls "intergroup" Signifyin(g) is difficult to effect, if only because the inherent irony of discourse most probably will not be understood. Still, Signifyin(g) is one significant mode of verbal masking or troping.

Abrahams's most important contribution to the literature on Signifyin(g) is his discovery that Signifyin(g) is primarily a term for rhetorical strategies, which often is called by other names depending on which of its several forms it takes. As he concludes, "with *signifying* we have a term not only for a way of speaking but for a rhetorical strategy that may be characteristic of a number of other designated events." I would add to this statement that, for black adults, Signifyin(g) is the name for the figures of rhetoric themselves, the figure of the figure. Abrahams lists the following terms as synonyms of Signifyin(g), as derived from several other scholars, and which I am defining to be black tropes as subsumed within the trope of Signifyin(g): *talking shit*, *woofing*, *spouting*, *muckty muck*, *boogerbang*, *beating your gums*, *talking smart*, *putting down*, *putting on*, *playing*, *sounding*, *telling lies*, *shag-lag*, *marking*, *shucking*, *jiving*, *jitterbugging*, *bugging*, *mounting*, *charging*, *cracking*, *harping*, *rapping*, *bookooing*, *low-rating*, *hoorawing*, *sweet-talking*, *smart-talking*, and no doubt a few others that I have omitted. This is a crucial contribution to our understanding of this figure because it transcends the disagreements, among linguists, about whether trope *x* or *y* is evidenced by speech act *a* or *b*. What's more, Abrahams reveals, by listing its synonyms, that black people can mean at least twenty-eight figures when they call something Signifyin(g). He represents a few of the figures embedded in Signifyin (g) in Table 1:

Table 1 Roger D. Abrahams's Figure 1 in Talking Black, p. 46

conversation on the streets; ways of speaking between equals			
informational; content focus *running it down*	aggressive, witty performance talk *signifying*		
	serious, clever conflict talk "me-and-you and no one else" focus *talking smart*		nonserious contest talk "any of us here" focus *talking shit*
	overtly aggressive talk *putting down*	covertly aggressive, manipulative talk *putting on*	nondirective *playing*	directive *sounding*

going deep; talking bad

conversational (apparently spontaneous)	arises within conversational context, yet judged in performance (stylistic) terms	performance interaction, yet built on model of conver- sational back-and-forth

He could have listed several others. When black people say that "Signification is the Nigger's occupation," we can readily see what they mean, since mastering all of these figures of Signification is a lifetime's work!

When a black person speaks of Signifyin(g), he or she means a "style-focused message ... styling which is *foregrounded* by the devices of making a point by indirection and wit." What is foregrounded, of course, is the signifier itself, as we have seen in the rhyme scheme of the Monkey tales. The Monkey is called the signifier because he foregrounds the signifier in his use of language. Signifyin(g), in other words, turns on the sheer play of the signifier. It does not refer primarily to the signified; rather, it refers to the style of language, to that which transforms ordinary discourse into literature. Again, one does not Signify some thing; one Signifies in *some way*.

The import of this observation for the study of black literature is manifold. When I wrote earlier that the black tradition theorized about itself in the vernacular, this is what I meant in part. Signifyin(g) is the black rhetorical difference that negotiates the language user through several orders of meaning. In formal literature, what we commonly call figuration corresponds to Signification. Again, the originality of so much of the black tradition emphasizes refiguration, or repetition and difference, or troping, underscoring the foregrounding of the chain of signifiers, rather than the mimetic representation of a novel content. Critics of Afro-American, Caribbean, and African literatures, however, have far more often than not directed their attention to the signified, often at the expense of the signifier, as if the latter were transparent. This functions contrary to the principles of criticism inherent in the concept of Signifyin(g).

Thomas Kochman's contribution to the literature on Signifyin(g) is the recognition that the Monkey is the Signifier, and that one common form of this rhetorical practice turns upon repetition and difference. Kochman also draws an important distinction between directive and expressive modes of Signification. Directive Signifyin(g), paradoxically, turns upon an indirective strategy:

> ... when the function of signifying is *directive*, and the *tactic* which is employed is one of *indirection* —i.e., the signifier reports or repeats what someone has said about the listener; the "report" is couched in plausible language designed to compel belief and arouse feelings of anger and hostility.

Kochman argues that the function of this sort of claim to repetition is to challenge and reverse the status quo:

> There is also the implication that if the listener fails to do anything about it— what has to be "done" is usually quite clear—his status will be seriously compromised. Thus the lion is compelled to vindicate the honor of his family by fighting or else leave the impression that he is afraid, and that he is not "king of the jungle." When used to direct action, signifying is like shucking in also being deceptive and subtle in approach and depending for success on the naïveté or gullibility of the person being put on.

Kochman's definition of expressive Signifyin(g), while useful, is less inclusive than that proposed by H. Rap Brown, including as it does only negative intentions: "to arouse feelings of embarrassment, shame, frustration, or futility, for the purpose of diminishing someone's status, but without directive implication." Expressive Signifyin(g), Kochman continues, employs "direct" speech tactics "in the form of a taunt, as in the ... example where the monkey is making fun of the lion." For Kochman, Signifyin(g) implies an aggressive mode of rhetoric, a form of symbolic action that yields catharsis.

While several other scholars have discussed the nature and function of Signifyin (g)，the theories of Claudia Mitchell-Kernan and Geneva Smitherman are especially useful for the theory of revision that I am outlining in this chapter. Mitchell-Kernan's theory of Signifyin(g) is among the most thorough and the most subtle in the linguistic literature，while Smitherman's work connects linguistic analysis with the Afro-American literary tradition. I shall examine Mitchell-Kernan's work first and then discuss Smitherman's work in Chapter 3.

Mitchell-Kernan is quick to demonstrate that Signifyin(g) has received most scholarly attention as "a tactic employed in game activity—verbal dueling—which is engaged in as an end in itself," as if this one aspect of the rhetorical concept amounted to its whole. In fact，however，"*Signifying* ... also refers to a way of encoding messages or meanings which involves，in most cases，an element of indirection." This alternative definition amounts to nothing less than a polite critique of the linguistic studies of Signifyin(g)，since the subtleties of this rhetorical strategy somehow escaped most other scholars before Mitchell-Kernan. As she expands her definition，"This kind of *signifying* might be best viewed as an alternative message form，selected for its artistic merit，and may occur embedded in a variety of discourse. Such *signifying* is not focal to the linguistic interaction in the sense that it does not define the entire speech event."

I cannot stress too much the importance of this definition，for it shows that Signifyin(g) is a pervasive mode of language use rather than merely one specific verbal game，an observation that somehow escaped the notice of every other scholar before Mitchell-Kernan. This definition alone serves as a corrective to what I think of as the tendency among linguists who have fixed their gaze upon the aggressive ritual part and thereby avoided seeing the concept as a whole. What's more，Mitchell-Kernan's definition points to the implicit parallels between Signifyin(g) and the use of language that we broadly define to be figurative，by which I mean in this context an intentional deviation from the ordinary form or syntactical relation of words.

Signifyin(g)，in other words，is synonymous with figuration. Mitchell-Kernan's work is so rich because she studied the language behavior of adults as well as adolescents，and of women as well as men. Whereas her colleagues studied lower-class male language use，then generalized from this strictly limited sample，Mitchell-Kernan's data are derived from a sample more representative of the black speech community. Hers is a sample that does not undermine her data because it accounts for the role of age and sex as variables in language use. In addition，Mitchell-Kernan refused to be captivated by the verbal insult rituals，such as sounding，playing the dozens, and Signifyin(g), as ritual speech events, unlike other linguists whose work suffers from an undue attention to the use of words such as *motherfucker*, to insults that turn on sexual assertions about someone's mama, and to supposed Oedipal complexes that arise in the literature only because the linguist is reading the figurative as a literal statement, like our friend, the Signified Lion.

These scholars, unlike Mitchell-Kernan, have mistaken the language games of adolescents as an end rather than as the drills common to classical rhetorical study as suggested in Lanham's hypothetical synopsis quoted earlier in this chapter. As Mitchell-Kernan concludes, both the sex and the age of the linguist's informants "may slant interpretation, particularly because the insult dimension [of Signifyin(g)] looms large in contexts where verbal dueling is focal." In the neighborhood in which she was raised, she argues, whereas "*Sounding* and *Playing the Dozens* categorically involved verbal insult (typically joking behavior); signifying did not." Mitchell-Kernan is declaring, most unobtrusively, that, for whatever reasons, linguists have misunderstood what Signifyin(g) means to black people who practice it. While she admits that one relatively minor aspect of this rhetorical principle involves the ritual of insult, the concept is much more profound than merely this. Indeed, Signifyin(g) alone serves to underscore the uniqueness of the black community's use of language: "the terminological use of *signifying* to refer to a particular kind of language specialization defines the Black community as a speech community in contrast to non-Black communities." Mitchell-Kernan here both critiques the work of other linguists who have wrestled unsuccessfully with this difficult concept (specifically Abrahams and Kochman) and provides an urgently needed corrective by defining Signifyin(g) as a way of figuring language. Mitchell-Kernan's penetrating work enables Signifyin(g) to be even further elaborated upon for use in literary theory.

Because it is difficult to arrive at a consensus of definitions of Signifyin(g), as this chapter already has made clear, Mitchell-Kernan proceeds "by way of analogy to inform the reader of its various meanings as applied in interpretation." This difficulty of definition is a direct result of the fact that Signifyin(g) is the black term for what in classical European rhetoric are called the figures of signification. Because to Signify is to be figurative, to define it in practice is to define it through any number of its embedded tropes. No wonder even Mitchell-Kernan could not arrive at a consensus among her informants—except for what turns out to be the most crucial shared aspects of all figures of speech, an indirect use of words that changes the meaning of a word or words. Or, as Quintilian put it, figuration turns on some sort of "change in signification." While linguists who disagree about what it means to Signify all repeat the role of indirection in this rhetorical strategy, none of them seems to have understood that the ensuing alteration or deviation of meaning makes Signifyin(g) the black trope for all other tropes, the trope of tropes, the figure of figures. Signifyin(g) *is* troping.

Mitchell-Kernan begins her elaboration of the concept by pointing to the unique usage of the word in black discourse:

What is unique in Black English usage is the way in which signifying is extended to cover a range of meanings and events which are not covered in its Standard English usage. In the Black community it is possible to say, "He is signifying" and "Stop signifying"—sentences which would be anomalous elsewhere.

Because in standard English signification denotes meaning and in the black tradition it denotes ways of meaning, Mitchell-Kernan argues for discrepancies between meanings of the same term in two distinct discourses:

The Black concept of *signifying* incorporates essentially a folk notion that dictionary entries for words are not always sufficient for interpreting meanings or messages, or that meaning goes beyond such interpretations. Complimentary remarks may be delivered in a left-handed fashion. A particular utterance may be an insult in one context and not another. What pretends to be informative may intend to be persuasive. The hearer is thus constrained to attend to all potential meaning carrying symbolic systems in speech events—the total universe of discourse.

Signifyin(g), in other words, is the figurative difference between the literal and the metaphorical, between surface and latent meaning. Mitchell-Kernan calls this feature of discourse an "implicit content or function, which is potentially obscured by the surface content or function." Finally, Signifyin(g) presupposes an "encoded" intention to say one thing but to mean quite another.

Mitchell-Kernan presents several examples of Signifyin(g), as she is defining it. Her first example is a conversation among three women about the meal to be served at dinner. One woman asks the other two to join her for dinner, that is, if they are willingto eat "chit'lins." She ends her invitation with a pointed rhetorical question: "Or are you one of those Negroes who don't eat chit'lins?" The third person, the woman not addressed, responds with a long defense of why she prefers "prime rib and T-bone" to "chit'lins," ending with a traditional ultimate appeal to special pleading, a call to unity within the ranks to defeat white racism. Then she leaves. After she has gone, the initial speaker replies to her original addressee in this fashion: "Well, I wasn't signifying at her, but like I always say, if the shoe fits wear it." Mitchell-Kernan concludes that while the manifest subject of this exchange was dinner, the latent subject was the political orientation of two black people vis-à-vis cultural assimilation or cultural nationalism, since many middle-class blacks refuse to eat this item from the traditional black cuisine. Mitchell-Kernan labels this form of Signifyin (g) "allegory," because "the significance or meaning of the words must be derived from known symbolic values."

This mode of Signifyin (g) is commonly practiced by Afro-American adults. It is functionally equivalent to one of its embedded tropes, often called louding or loud-talking, which as we might expect connotes exactly the opposite of that which it denotes: one successfully loud-talks by speaking to a second person remarks in fact directed to a third person, at a level just audible to the third person. A sign of the success of this practice is an indignant "What?" from the third person, to which the speaker responds, "I wasn't talking to you." Of course, the speaker was, yet simultaneously was not. Loud-talking is related to Mitchell-Kernan's second figure of Signification, which she calls "obscuring the addressee" and which I shall call naming. Her example is one commonly used in the tradition, in which "the remark is, on the surface, directed toward no one in particular":

I saw a woman the other day in a pair of stretch pants, she must have weighed 300 pounds. If she knew how she looked she would burn those things.

If a member of the speaker's audience is overweight and frequently wears stretch pants, then this message could well be intended for her. If she protests, the speaker is free to maintain that she was speaking about someone else and to ask why her auditor is so paranoid. Alternatively, the speaker can say, "if the shoe fits... Mitchell-Kernan says that a characteristic of this form of Signifyin(g) is the selection of a subject that is "selectively relevant to the speaker's audience." I once heard a black minister name the illicit behavior of specific members of his congregation by performing a magnificent reading of "The Text of the Dry Bones," which is a reading or gloss upon Ezekiel 37: 1-14. Following this sermon, a prayer was offered by Lin Allen. As "Mr. Lin," as we called him, said, "Dear Lord, go with the gambling man ... not forgetting the gamblingwoman," the little church's eerie silence was shattered by the loud-talking voice of one of my father's friends (Ben Fisher, rest his soul), whom the congregation "overheard" saying, "Got *you* that time, Gates, got *you* that time, Newtsy!" My father and one of our neighbors, Miss Newtsy, had been Signified upon.

Mitchell-Kernan presents several examples of Signifyin(g) that elaborate on its subtypes. Her conclusion is crucial to the place of her research in the literature on Signification. "*Signifying*" she declares as conclusion, "does not ... always have negative valuations attached to it; it is clearly thought of as a kind of art—a clever way of conveying messages." A literary critic might call this troping, an interpretation or mis-taking of meaning, to paraphrase Harold Bloom, because, as Mitchell-Kernan maintains, "*signifying* ... alludes to and implies things which are never made explicit." Let me cite two brief examples. In the first, "Grace" introduces the exchange by defining its context:

(After I had my little boy, I swore I was not having any more babies. I thought four kids was a nice-sized family. But it didn't turn out that way. I was a little bit disgusted and didn't tell anybody when I discovered I was pregnant. My sister came over one day and I had started to show by that time.) ...

Rochelle: Girl, you sure do need to join the Metrecal for lunch bunch.

Grace: (non-committally) Yes, I guess I am putting on a little weight.

Rochelle: Now look here, girl, we both standing here soaking wet and you still trying to tell me it ain't raining.

This form of Signifyin(g) is obviously a long way from the sort usually defined by scholars. One final example of the amusing, troping exchange follows, again cited by Mitchell-Kernan:

I: Man, when you gon pay me my five dollars?

II: Soon as I get it.

I: (to audience) Anybody want to buy afive dollar nigger? I got one to sell.

II: Man, if I gave you your five dollars, you wouldn't have nothing to signify about.

I: Nigger, long as you don't change, I'll always have me a subject.

This sort of exchange is common in the black community and represents Signifyin(g) at its more evolved levels than the more obvious examples (characterized by confrontation and insult) discussed by linguists other than Mitchell-Kernan.

The highly evolved form of Signifyin(g) that H. Rap Brown defines and that Ralph Ellison's anecdote about Hazel Harrison epitomizes is represented in a wonderful anecdote that Mitchell-Kernan narrates. This tale bears repeating to demonstrate how black adults teach their children to "hold a conversation":

At the age of seven or eight I encountered what I believe was a version of the tale of the "Signifying Monkey." In this story a monkey reports to a lion that an elephant has been maligning the lion and his family. This stirs the lion into attempting to impose sanctions against the elephant. A battle ensues in which the elephant is victor and the lion returns extremely chafed at the monkey. In this instance, the recounting of this story is a case of signifying for directive purposes. I was sitting on the stoop of a neighbor who was telling me about his adventures as a big game hunter in Africa, a favorite tall-tale topic, unrecognized by me as tall-tale at the time. A neighboring woman called to me from her porch and asked me to go to the store for her. I refused, saying that my mother had told me not to, a lie which Mr. Waters recognized and asked me about. Rather than simply saying I wanted to listen to his stories, I replied that I had refused to go because I hated the woman. Being pressured for a reason for my dislike, and sensing Mr. Water's disapproval, I countered with another lie, "I hate her because shesay you were lazy," attempting, I suppose, to regain his favor by arousing ire toward someone else. Although I had heard someone say that he was lazy, it had not been this woman. He explained to me that he was not lazy and that he didn't work because he had been laid-off from his job and couldn't find work elsewhere, and that if the lady had said what I reported, she had not done so out of meanness but because she didn't understand. Guilt-ridden, I went to fetch the can of Milnot milk. Upon returning, the tale of the "Signifying Monkey" was told to me, a censored prose version in which the monkey is rather brutally beaten by the lion after having suffered a similar fate in the hands of the elephant. I liked the story very much and righteously approved of its ending, not realizing at the time that he was *signifying* at me. Mr. Waters reacted to my response with a great deal of amusement. It was several days later in the context of retelling the tale to another child that I understood its timely telling. My apology and admission of lying were met by affectionate humor, and I was told that I was finally getting to the age where I could "hold a conversation," i.e., understand and appreciate implications.

Black people call this kind of lesson "schooling," and this label denotes its function. The child must learn to hold a conversation. We cannot but recall Richard Lanham'sideal presentation of rhetorical training and conclude that what Mr. Waters says to the child, Claudia, is analogous to an adult teacher of rhetoric attempting to show his pupils how to employ the tropes that they have memorized in an act of communication and its interpretation. This subtle process of instruction in the levels of Signification is related to, but far removed from, adolescent males insulting each other with the Signifying Monkey tales. The language of Signifyin(g), in other words, is a strategy of black figurative language use.

I have been drawing a distinction between the ritual of Signifyin(g), epitomized in the Monkey tales, and the language of Signifyin(g), which is the vernacular term for the figurative use of language. These terms correspond to what Mitchell-Kernan calls "third-party signifying" and "metaphorical signifying." Mitchell-Kernan defines their distinction as follows:

> In the metaphorical type of *signifying*, the speaker attempts to transmit his message indirectly and it is only by virtue of the hearers defining the utterance as *signifying* that the speaker's intent (to convey a particular message) is realized. In third-party signifying, the speaker may realize his aim only when the converse is true, that is, if the addressee fails to recognize the speech act as *signifying*. In [the Signifying Monkey toast] the monkey succeeds in goading the lion into a rash act because the lion does not define the monkey's message as *signifying*.

In other words, these two dominant modes of Signification function conversely, another sign of the maturation process demanded to move, as it were, from the repetition of tropes to their application.

The Monkey tales inscribe a dictum about interpretation, whereas the language of Signifyin(g) addresses the nature and application of rhetoric. The import of the Monkey tales for the interpretation of literature is that the Monkey dethrones the Lion only because the Lion cannot read the nature of his discourse. As Mitchell-Kernan argues cogently, "There seems something of symbolic relevance from the perspective of language in this poem. The monkey and lion do not speak the same language; the lion is not able to interpret the monkey's use of language, he is an outsider, un-hip, in a word." In other words, the Monkey speaks figuratively, while the Lion reads his discourse literally. For his act of misinterpretation, he suffers grave consequences. This valorization of the figurative is perhaps the most important moral of these poems, although the Monkey's mastery of figuration has made him one of the canonical heroes in the Afro-American mythic tradition, a point underscored by Mitchell-Kernan.

Mitchell-Kernan's summary of the defining characteristics of "Signifying as a Form of Verbal Art" helps to clarify this most difficult, and elusive, mode of rhetoric. We can outline these characteristics for convenience. The most important defining features of Signifyin(g) are "indirect intent" and "metaphorical reference." This aspect of indirection is a formal device, and "appears to be almost purely stylistic"; moreover, "its art characteristics remain in the forefront." Signifyin(g), in other words, turns upon the foregrounding of the Signifier. By "indirection" Mitchell-

Kernan means

> that the correct semantic (referential interpretation) or signification of the utterance cannot be arrived at by a consideration of the dictionary meaning of the lexical items involved and the syntactic rules for their combination alone. The apparent significance of the message differs from its real significance. *The apparent meaning of the sentence signifies its actual meaning.*

The relationship between latent and manifest meaning is a curious one, as determined by the formal properties of the Signifyin(g) utterance. In one of several ways, manifest meaning directs attention away from itself to another, latent level of meaning. We might compare this relationship to that which obtains between the two parts of a metaphor, tenor (the inner meaning) and vehicle (the outer meaning).

Signifyin(g), according to Mitchell-Kernan, operates so delightfully because "apparent meaning serves as a key which directs hearers to some shared knowledge, attitudes, and values or signals that reference must be produced metaphorically." The decoding of the figurative, she continues, depends "upon shared knowledge ... and this shared knowledge operates on two levels." One of these two levels is that the speaker and his audience realize that "*signifying* is occurring and that the dictionary-syntactical meaning of the utterance is to be ignored." In addition, a silent second text, as it were, which corresponds rightly to what Mitchell-Kernan is calling "shared knowledge," must be brought to bear upon the manifest content of the speech act and "employed in the reinterpretation of the utterance." Indeed, this element is of the utmost importance in the esthetics of Signifyin(g), for "it is the cleverness used in directing the attention of the hearer and audience to this shared knowledge upon which a speaker's artistic talent is judged." Signifyin(g), in other words, depends on the success of the signifier at invoking an absent meaning ambiguously "present" in a carefully wrought statement.

As I have attempted to show, there is much confusion and disagreement among linguists about the names and functions of the classical black tropes. While the specific terminology may vary from scholar to scholar, city to city, or generation to generation, however, the rhetorical functions of these tropes remain consistent. It is a fairly straightforward exercise to compare the black slave tropes to the master tropes identified by Vico, Nietzsche, Burke, and Bloom, and to map a black speech act, such as Signifyin(g), into its component Western tropes. Table 2 is intended to Signify upon Harold Bloom's "map of misprision." I echo the essence of this map here, adding columns that list the Yoruba and Afro-American tropes that correspond to their

Western counterparts.

We can, furthermore, chart our own map, in which we graph the separate lines of a "Signifyin(g) Riff," as follows:

> Slave Trope of Tropes, Signifyin(g)
>
> Your mama's a man　（metaphor）
>
> Your daddy's one too　（irony）
>
> They live in a tin can　（metonymy）
>
> That smells like a zoo　（synecdoche）

Table 2　The Figures of Signification

Rhetorical Trope	Bloom's Revisionary Ratio	Afro-American Signifyin(g) Trope	Classical Yoruba	Lexically Borrowed Yoruba
Irony	Clinamen	Signifyin(g) ("Nigger business" in the West Indies)	Ríràn (èràn)	Áiróni
Synecdoche	Tessera	Calling out of one's name		Mètóními
Metonymy	Kenosis			
Hyperbole, litotes	Daemonization	Stylin' or woofing ("Flash in the West Indies)	Ìhàlè (Èpộn)	
Metaphor	Askesis	Naming	Àfiwé (elélòó)	Métáfò (indirect "naming")*
			Àfwé gaan	Simili (direct "naming")*
Metalepsis	Apophrades	Capping	Afikún; Àjámộ; Ènì	

* N.B. "Naming" is an especially rich trope in Yoruba. Positive naming is called Oriki, while negative naming is called Inagije. Naming is also an especially luxurious (if potentially volatile) trope in the Afro-American vernacular tradition. "Naming" someone and "Calling [someone] Out of [his] name" are among the most commonly used tropes in Afro-American vernacular discourse. Scores of proverbs and epigrams in the black tradition turn upon figures for naming.

The fact that the street rhymes of blacks and their received rhetorical tropes configure into the categories of classical Western rhetoric should come as no surprise. Indeed, this aspect of black language use recalls Montaigne's statement, in "Of the Vanity of Words," that "When you hear people talk about metonymy, metaphor, allegory, and other such names in grammar, doesn't it seem that they mean some rare and exotic form of language?" Rather, Montaigne concludes, "They are terms that apply to the babble of your chambermaid." We can add that these terms also apply to the rapping of black kids on street corners, who recite and thereby preserve the classical black rhetorical structures.

Signification is a complex rhetorical device that has elicited various, even contradictory, definitions from linguists, as should be apparent from this summary of its various definitions. While many of its manifestations and possibilities are figured in the tales of the Signifying Monkey, most people who Signify do not engage in the narration of these tales. Rather, the Monkey tales stand as the canonical poems from which what I am calling the language of Signifyin(g) extends. The degree to which the figure of the Monkey is anthropologically related to the figure of the Pan-African trickster, Esu-Elegbara, shall most probably remain a matter of speculation.

Nevertheless, the two figures are related as functional equivalents because each in its own way stands as a moment of consciousness of black formal language use, of rhetorical structures and their appropriate modes of interpretation. As I have argued, both figures connote what we might think of as the writing implicit in an oral literature, and both figures function as repositories for a tradition's declarations about how and why formal literary language departs from ordinary language use. The metaphor of a double-voiced Esu-Elegbara corresponds to the double-voiced nature of the Signifyin(g) utterance. When one text Signifies upon another text, by tropological revision or repetition and difference, the double-voiced utterance allows us to chart discrete formal relationships in Afro-American literary history. Signifyin(g), then, is a metaphor for textual revision.

(1988)

26. African-American Autobiography Criticism: Retrospect and Prospect
非裔美国人自传批评：回顾与展望

William L. Andrews
威廉·安德鲁斯

威廉·安德鲁斯(1946)，教授、奴隶叙事与非裔美国人自传研究专家，20世纪80年代以来撰写、编辑40多部非裔美国文学与文化研究著作。安德鲁斯1968年毕业于戴维森学院，获得学士学位，1973年毕业于北卡罗来纳大学教堂山分校，先后获得硕士和博士学位。他在美国多所大学任教，如得克萨斯理工大学(1973—1977)，威斯康星大学麦迪逊分校(1977—1988)，堪萨斯大学(1989—1996)，1997年以后在北卡罗来纳大学教堂山分校任教，直至退休。

安德鲁斯教授的学术生涯主要围绕三大重点展开：(1)非裔美国作家对美国文学的重要贡献；(2)18世纪和19世纪的非裔美国文学创作表达的丰富；(3)非裔美国奴隶叙事传统既是非裔美国文学的基石，也是18世纪末以来全面了解美国文学与文化的根本。在他1973年读研期间，这三大主题都还没有被视为美国文学；20世纪70年代，对18世纪和19世纪非裔美国文学创作方面的研究还十分有限，仿佛除了少数几位杰出人物，非裔美国人直到20世纪哈莱姆文艺复兴时才开始进行文学创作。80年代初，在威斯康辛大学麦迪逊分校教书期间，他开始研究18世纪和19世纪北美非洲人后裔的自传。在美国国家人文与学者委员会的资助下，他出版了最具影响力的两本书《讲述自由的故事：1760—1865年的非裔美国人自传》(*To Tell a Free Story*：*The First Century of Afro-American Autobiography*，1760—1865，1986)和《精神姐妹：19世纪三位黑人女性自传》(*Sisters of the Spirit*：*Three Black Women's Autobiographies of the Nineteenth Century*，1986)。1986—2011年，他主编或与人合编了24卷关于非裔美国文学前一百年主要作家的作品，包括道格拉斯(Frederick Douglass)，布朗(William Wells Brown)，雅各布斯(Harriet Jacobs)，与考林斯(Julia C. Collins)等，其中1997年出版的三部书最具影响力：《诺顿非裔美国文学选集》《牛津非裔美国文学指南》和《诺顿美国南方文学》。此外，他与北卡罗来纳大学教堂山分校的图书馆合作，建设一个获奖的数字化项目"北美奴隶叙事"，这个完全线上的电子资源，呈现了1760—1930年奴隶创作的自传作品。2018年，安德鲁斯荣获美国文学协会授予的美国文学研究终身成就奖。2019年他出版了《美国南方的种族与阶级：一代人的奴隶叙事证言(1840—1865)》(*Slavery and Class in the American South*：*A Generation of Slave Narrative Testimony*，1840—1865）。

《非裔美国人自传批评》一文对非裔美国人自传研究进行了全方位的梳理,分析了非裔美国人自传研究中的几个重要时段,完整地反映了 20 世纪非裔美国人自传研究从 1948 年开始到 20 世纪 90 年代的发展及其变化。本文的有些论点特别值得学界关注,如美国人自传研究晚于非裔美国人自传研究,非裔美国人自传越来越具有战斗性,以及非裔美国人自传研究中的理论化倾向等。安德鲁斯指出,塞尔在 1988 年重印《自我的审视》(1964)时坦言,自己当时撰写这部自传研究的开创性著作时对黑人自传几乎一无所知,而巴顿的《见证自由》(1948)则概括性地分析了从道格拉斯的《生平与时代》(1892)到汤普森的《美国女儿》(1946)在内的二十多部美国黑人自传,特别重视"黑人视角"。巴顿强调道格拉斯自传的文学价值,并预言黑人自传将越来越具有战斗性,20 世纪 60 年代马尔科姆、克利夫、杰克逊等人的自传就是极好的例证。此外,安德鲁斯总结了 20 世纪 60 年代以来的奴隶叙事研究,认为美国内战前的奴隶叙事不仅有效地纠正了南方文学与历史中的种植园迷思,而且成为 60 和 70 年代富有革命与战斗气息的黑人自传研究的文学与政治先驱。70 年代以后,非裔美国人自传研究既注重历史挖掘,更注重吸收后结构主义批评思想,其中贝克与盖茨在研究主题与研究方法方面的探索尤其令人称道。

It may be a little surprising as well as instructive to begin this discussion by noting that the first book-length study of African-American autobiography in the United Stateswas published a generation earlier than its ground-breaking counterpart in American autobiography. Yet，as Robert F. Sayre candidly admits in his new introduction to the 1988 reprint of *The Examined Self*：*Benjamin Franklin*，*Henry Adams*，*Henry James*（1964），he "knew little or nothing" about black autobiography when he wrote his pioneering book. More than likely he had also not heard of Rebecca Chalmers Barton's *Witnesses for Freedom*：*Negro Americans in Autobiography*（1948），the first major critical analysis of African-American—and thus，one might argue，of American—autobiography. To offer this observation is not to fault Sayre. It is rather to suggest that unless we regard African-American autobiography as somehow distinct from American autobiography，we cannot escape the fact that the history of American autobiography criticism begins not with a study of the classics of what academe used to call "the American experience" but with an examination of what Barton called "the Negro point of view"（ⅺ）. *Witnesses for Freedom* may not have quickened the scholarly interest in white American autobiography that emerged in the 1960s. Nevertheless，to historicize American autobiography criticism without noting the precedence of Barton's book would deny us something crucial，namely，an awareness of black autobiography's prior claim to the agenda of American autobiography criticism.

"The problem of the Twentieth Century is the problem of the color line," prophesied W. E. B. Du Bois in *The Souls of Black Folk* (1903). When the United States finally started to come to grips with these words in the post-World War II era, Rebecca Chalmers Barton marshaled the autobiographies of twenty-three American blacks to interpret the significance of and possible solutions to what Gunnar Myrdal called *An American Dilemma*: *The Negro Problem and Modern Democracy* in 1944. As she read African-American autobiography from Frederick Douglass's *Life and Times* (1892) to Era Bell Thompson's *American Daughter* (1946), Barton found a variety and richness of matter and manner that refuted stereotypes about black experience, attitudes, and capabilities. She found in black autobiography "literary merit" commensurate with the "vigor and versatility of expression" that, she claimed presciently, "guarantees them [the autobiographies] an integral place in American letters" (274). Yet to Barton these texts "achieve their final importance by their special insights into the complexities of race" (274). Thus *Witnesses for Freedom* ends with a didactic chapter entitled "Values for Intergroup Living," in which the author extrapolates from modern black autobiography certain intellectual and ethical standards that would facilitate, in her view, the integration of American society. "The Negro Americans who come to life in these pages display the same variety of taste, temperament, and purpose as any other segment of the population" (282), Barton concludes. She goes on to urge that whites accept the "like-mindedness" of modern black autobiographers as the key to "an improved social order." Should white America continue to refuse to recognize like-mindedness between blacks and whites, Barton warns of dirc consequences. The "militancy" of recent black autobiographers whom she classifies as "Protesters for a New Freedom"—writers like Angelo Herndon, Du Bois, and Richard Wright—is "no chance occurrence" (281). Because "suppressed people will not remain so," the rising voices of militant black autobiographers "point to danger signals on the social horizon. Let him who will not heed become chaff on the wind" (281).

Barton's anticipation of an accelerating militancy in modern black autobiography was borne out in the 1960s when figures like Malcolm X and Eldridge Cleaver forged their first-person narratives in the political flame of Black Power. More articulately and cogently than any book before it, *The Autobiography of Malcolm X* (1964) exemplified the concept of black identity as necessarily distinct from and morally superior to the corporate white identity that dominated the cultural and socio-political ethos of America. This concept of blackness as the *sine qua non* of African-American identity in the 1960s inspired a new generation of self-styled black revolutionaries to give voice to their own life stories and political opinions, which liberal white America, highly sensitized by the Civil Rights Movement, bought, read, and reviewed assiduously. Cleaver's *Soul on Ice* (1968), H. Rap Brown's *Die Nigger Die* (1969), George Jackson's *Soledad Brother* (1970), Julius Lester's *Search for the New Land* (1970), and Bobby Seale's *Seize the Time* (1970) were among the best-selling of the revolutionary narratives of the 1960s. Scholars and critics of American literature felt challenged to account for these seemingly unprecedented works of black rage and radical political consciousness. Where did these autobiographies belong in the history of American—or African-American—literature, assuming one could speak of them as literature at all?

Responding to this question led scholars in two directions. Barely two years after Malcolm's *Autobiography* was published, Robert Penn Warren became the first of several distinguished critics, including Carol Ohmann, Warner Berthoff, and Barrett John Mandel, to try to locate the most widely read black autobiography of the sixties in relation to well-established white literary traditions such as Alger myth, the Benjamin Franklin success story, and the narrative of conversion exemplified by St. Augustine's *Confessions*. To those who were unsatisfied with this kind of domestication of literary blackness, however, the antebellum slave narrator seemed a more likely progenitor of Malcolm X and his successors. In *Studies in Black Literature*, *Phylon*, and other journals open to the controversial discipline of Black Studies, some of the earliest scholarship on the slave narrative and its largely unacknowledged importance to American literary history was first published. This criticism depended heavily on the pioneering research of Marion Wilson Starling and Charles H. Nichols, in whose dissertations (completed in 1946 and 1948, respectively) the first extensive literary study of the slave narrative appears.

After publishing in the 1950s a series of articles based on his research, Nichols was able to get his dissertation published in 1963 under the auspices of the Amerika-Institut of the Free University of Berlin. *Many Thousand Gone: The Ex-Slave's Account of Their Bondage and Freedom* was designed primarily to let the slaves have their say on a subject that had become of central concern to American historians by the early 1960s—the nature of slavery and its effect on African-Americans. Rather than concentrate on the merits of a few autobiographies, Nicholas chose to create a composite portrait of the slave experience by blending the life stories of many former slaves into a single overarching narrative pattern. The result was more of a summary and a celebration of the message of the slave narrators than a critical analysis of the means by which they achieved their rhetorical goals. Yet Nichols was among the first to use the slave narratives as a necessary corrective to the plantation myth of Southern literature and history and to suggest the historical continuity between Frederick Douglass and Martin Luther King, Jr. Nichols's research pointed the way for those who believed that the antebellum slave narrators were the literary and political antecedents of the revolutionary black autobiographers of the 1960s and early 1970s.

It is not coincidental that during the 1960s the *Narrative of the Life of Frederick Douglass, an American Slave* (1845) began its rise to preeminence among all black American autobiographers of the nineteenth century. The persona and rhetorical posture that Douglass assumed in his first autobiography strongly appealed to the mood of the sixties and to the search for a useable past that impelled Black Studies scholars into the slave narrative in the first place. In 1960 Benjamin Quarles, anticipating this need, rescued the *Narrative* from decades of out-of-print oblivion and edited it for the Belknap Press of Harvard University. Soon paperback reprints of the *Narrative* appeared, closely followed by reprints of Douglass's second and third autobiographies, *My Bondage and My Freedom* (1855) and *Life and Times of Frederick Douglass* (1892). By the end of the 1960s, the inclusion of Quarles's brief essay on the *Narrative* in Hennig Cohen's *Landmarks of American Writing* (1969) indicated that the *Narrative* was well on its way to inclusion in the canon of American literature.

The 1960s also saw the reprinting of dozens of long out-of-print black autobiographies, especially slave narratives, by numerous reprint houses, such as the Arno Press of the *New York Times* and Negro Universities Press. Some of these reprints were ably introduced by noted scholars such as Arna Bontemps, Larry Gara, and Robin Winks. Gilbert Osofsky's "Puttin' on Ole Massa: The Significance of Slave Narratives," which introduces *Puttin' on Ole Massa* (1968), Osofsky's edition of the narratives of Henry Bibb, William Wells Brown, and Solomon Northup, is the most detailed and valuable of the criticism that appeared in connection with reprinted texts. Unfortunately, few of the nineteenth-century slave narratives brought into print with the wave of interest in Black Studies during the 1960s remain in print today. Thanks to the herculean effort of George P. Rawick, however, the entirety of the more than two thousand interviews with ex-slaves conducted by the Federal Writers' Project between 1936 and 1938 have been compiled and reprinted in *The American Slave: A Composite Autobiography* (1972).

By the end of the 1960s, the primary texts of African-American autobiography were back in print, in some cases for the first time in many decades. Not surprisingly, the most important criticism of the 1970s attempted to create literary histories of black autobiography in America using the recent celebrities and newly reprinted texts of the 1960s as their touchstones. Stephen Butterfield's *Black Autobiography in America* (1974) is the first and still the most comprehensive literary history of African-American autobiography. In an often trenchant and vigorously polemical analysis of about fifty autobiographies published between 1830 and 1972, Butterfield set a standard for those who wished to take seriously the rhetorical art and literary import of black autobiography. Beginning with "the Slave Narrative Period, 1831—1895," Butterfield offers sustained analyses of point of view, irony, parody, and the influence of white autobiographical discourse on the slave narrators. He singles out Frederick Douglass's *Narrative* and *Life and Times* as epitomizing, in both subject matter and style, the strength of the first era of black autobiography.

Butterfield detects a certain malaise in many texts from the second era of black American autobiography, the "Period of Search," which extends from 1901, when *Up from Slavery* first appeared, to 1961, when James Baldwin's *Nobody Knows My Name* signaled the advent of a new consciousness and sense of identity among black autobiographers. The search was for a viable sense of identity for blacks in a new era, when the blandishments of the "Negro bourgeoisie" and the "white American mainstream" lure the successful black person away from the "black masses" and hence, in Butterfield's view, away from the only valid source of identity for blacks who desire a historically meaningful existence. The end of this search took black autobiographers of the middle period into a renewed sense of black pride, which led black autobiography "back into direct political struggle" (107), the theme of the third part of Butterfield's book, "the Period of Rebirth," treating autobiographies of the 1960s and early 1970s. Here Butterfield celebrates "the growth of a new radicalism" in Baldwin and "the revolutionary self" in the work of Malcolm X, Cleaver, Jackson, Lester, Brown, and Seale. Butterfield also devotes a chapter to the contributions of Ida B. Wells, Maya Angelou, and Anne Moody to the tradition, although he has difficulty reconciling the sense of self represented in Angelou and Moody to the "revolutionary self" that he offers as a paradigm of the new generation of black autobiographers. He concludes that the "strongest books" of the contemporary period—*Soul on Ice*, *Search for a New Land*, and *Soledad Brother*—are those "that most successfully assimilate and unify personal narrative and political message" (274).

As both a literary history and a work of polemic, *Black Autobiography in America* reads almost like a period piece today. No scholar since Butterfield has attempted to put the history of African-American autobiography between the covers of a single book. The politics of canon-formation, which would certainly have problematized Butterfield's enterprise, does not demand his attention, nor does the problematic nature of historical reconstruction itself trouble him—Butterfield did his work before these theoretical concerns came to the fore in autobiography criticism. One can almost be thankful that Butterfield was not inhibited by these issues, since his sense of freedom allowed him to explore and map a literary frontier with singular clarity, conciseness, and confidence. Yet to enforce his sense of historical progression and political relevance in black autobiography, Butterfield had to submit each text of this tradition to an ideological test. He candidly acknowledges his preference for works that seem to him "revolutionary narratives." He declares that "the appeal of black autobiographies is in their political awareness" (3) first and foremost. What Butterfield means by "political awareness" is never specified in his book, but one thing seems clear. Any autobiography that could be classified as a "middle-class success story" is *ipso facto* not politically aware. In keeping with the tenor of the 1960s, Butterfield's book argues that black autobiographers who did not take a stand against the American Dream usually were co-opted by it, though in their self-portraits one can find evidence of interior struggles with this condition. The problem with this dismissive attitude toward the many "middle-class success stories" of African-American autobiography is that it fails to recognize the political, and indeed, sometimes the revolutionary, significance of the black middle-class autobiographer, who proudly laid claim to a status that American racism denied him and her and whose historical role of leadership in the battle for racial integration made middle-class autobiographies potent texts in the black community.

Sidonie Smith's *Where I'm Bound: Patterns of Slavery and Freedom in Black American Autobiography* (1974) is less comprehensive but also less tendentious than Butterfield's book. Smith is interested in the patterns that structure the plots of ten black autobiographies, beginning with the antebellum slave narrative of William Wells Brown and concluding with Claude Brown's *Manchild in the Promised Land* (1965). She finds in the slave narrative a pattern of breaking "*away from* an enslaving community" in search of the chance to "break *into* a community that allowed authentic self-expression and fulfillment in a social role" (ix). Since the antebellum era, she argues, black autobiographies have manifested these patterns of flight and immersion in increasingly complex ways, depending on the autobiographer's sense of whether authentic self-expression is possible in communal roles. In the autobiographies of Cleaver, Angelou, Horace Cayton, and Claude Brown, Smith perceptively analyzes the function of the act of autobiography-writing itself in the search for liberation beyond communal identification and social roles. Unlike Butterfield, who regards the achievement of individual black identity and fulfillment apart from the black community as an impossibility, Smith argues cogently that many black autobiographies suggest that "the ultimate place of freedom lies within the self, which alone must be content to create its own 'free' consciousness" (75).

Since 1974, the trend of black autobiography criticism has been more in the direction of Smith's concept of the significance of the autobiographical act rather than Butterfield's. Many critics who address the knotty problem of what constitutes "freedom" in black autobiography have taken seriously Smith's analysis of the importance of highly subjective, individualistic acts of writing as means of achieving and expressing an elusive sense of liberation. Butterfield grants that the "subjective experience" and street-wise expressiveness of a Malcolm X or a Rap Brown is an index to the progress of the revolution, but only in the service of black militancy does an individual autobiographical act take on positive significance. A more flexible concept of the relationship between individual and community in black first-person narratives appears in Elizabeth Schultz's discussion of "the blues genre" in African-American autobiography, in which she probes the cultural traditions that enable black autobiographers to transmit the social significance of their experience through a processof creating and articulating a sense of self that draws on both the style and substance of the blues.

1974 saw the publication of a third major book on African-American autobiography, Russell C. Brignano's *Black Americans in Autobiography*, an annotated bibliography of autobiographical writing since the Civil War. Revised and updated in 1984, Brignano's bibliography is the best bibliographical work ever done on black American autobiography. It not only provides reliable information on the publishing circumstances and history of 424 black autobiographies; it also offers a brief comment on the subject matter of each text and lists the libraries in the United States that possess a copy of each text. In addition Brignano lists more than 200 "autobiographical books" by blacks, in which the author's life story is treated in sufficient detail to warrant attention from students of autobiography. Although *Black Americans in Autobiography* only lists modern reprints of antebellum autobiographies, it can be supplemented by the more thorough bibliographies that append the work of Davis and Gates (1985) and Andrews's *To Tell a Free Story* (1986). In combination, these bibliographies constitute a virtually definitive inventory of African-American autobiography. For bibliographies of black autobiography criticism, researchers have had to wait until the 1980s, when Gregory S. Sojka's checklist of works on the slave narrative and Joe Weixlmann's thoroughgoing bibliographical study of twentieth-century African-American autobiography began the process of mapping the intellectual terrain.

The black autobiography that received the most scholarly attention in the 1970s was Richard Wright's *Black Boy*. Three timely books on Wright, Dan McCall's *The Example of Richard Wright* (1969), Edward Margolies's *The Art of Richard Wright* (1969), and Michel Fabre's *The Unfinished Quest of Richard Wright* (1973), offered early readings of Wright's autobiography in light of his achievements in fiction. McCall and Margolies confess to a certain disappointment with the rhetoric of *Black Boy*, though they try to offer explanations for what they regard as the stylistic inadequacy of the book. Fabre's biographical approach to *Black Boy* makes a more lasting contribution to scholarship. Fabre judiciously notes some of the differences between the image of Wright's childhood in *Black Boy* and the facts of his youth and family situation as the biographer's research revealed them. Since Fabre's identification of these discrepancies, one of the chief topics of criticism on *Black Boy* has been the significance of discrepancies between the life and perspective of Richard Wright and that of the "black boy" whose story is not necessarily Wright's, nor perhaps even intended by Wright to represent him alone. From Claudia Tate's "*Black Boy* : Richard Wright's 'Tragic Sense of Life'" (1976) and James Olney's "Some Versions of Memory/Some Versions of *Bios* : The Ontology of Autobiography" (1980) to the chapter in Timothy Dow Adams's recent book, *Telling Lies in Modern American Autobiography* (1990), critics have attempted to articulate the relationship of Wright to the "black boy" persona whose status as a representative of and commentator on southern black culture has proved persistently controversial. What critics have come to agree on, however, since the early 1970s, is that *Black Boy* is a highly self-conscious and carefully crafted work that displays considerable attention to narrative technique. Moreover, critics of the last ten years have increasingly emphasized the centrality to *Black Boy* of the narrator's desire to become a writer and his identification with language as his ultimate means of transcending that which inhibits self-realization in and beyond the text.

While the 1970s saw the growth of an increasingly sophisticated critical literature devoted to some of the most famous texts of the black autobiographical tradition, the decade also gave its attention to books that did not easily conform to the male-centered tradition exemplified in *Black Boy* or *The Autobiography of Malcolm X*. feminist criticism in the late 1970s, particularly essays focusing on Maya Angelou's *I Know Why the Caged Bird Sings* (1970), forecast a major redirection of black autobiography criticism.

George Kent's 1975 article, "Maya Angelou's *I Know Why the Caged Bird Sings* and Black Autobiographical Tradition," while no more specifically feminist than the discussion of Angelou's first autobiography in the books by Butterfield and Smith, argues cogently for the importance of *I Know Why* as a kind of model in which two traditions—those of black religion and the blues—that seem to be at odds in texts like *Black Boy* find "a just balance." One can hardly imagine a better way for scholarship on black women's autobiography to be launched. Kent neither accommodated Angelou to a male-defined tradition nor suggested that her uniqueness and success as an autobiographer were to be evaluated apart from the cultural traditions of black America that she so intimately know. Instead, he prepared the ground for many subsequent studies of Angelou's work that probe the extent to which and /or the means by which Angelou achieves the sort of "balance" that Kent ascribes to her.

Although Angelou's work attracted most of the attention that black women's autobiography received in the 1970s, criticism and research on the first-person writings of Zora Neale Hurston, along with a revived interest in black women's narratives of the slavery era, especially Harriet Jacobs's *Incidents in the Life of a Slave Girl* (1861), demonstrated that there was no shortage of writing in this tradition to be revived and examined. Two useful essays from the end of the decade, Mary Burgher's "Images of Self and Race in the Autobiographies of Black Women" (1979) and Regina Blackburn's "In Search of the Black Female Self: African-American Women's Autobiographies and Ethnicity" (1980), outlined for the first time the thematic range of black women's autobiography from the antebellum era to the 1970s and thus offered the first tantalizing glimpses of the breadth and diversity of this hitherto unrecognized tradition.

At the end of the 1970s, the study of the slave narrative received major impetus from the publication of two books, Frances Smith Foster's *Witnessing Slavery: The Development of Ante-bellum Slave Narratives* (1979) and a collection of essays edited by Dexter Fisher and Robert B. Stepto entitled *Afro-American Literature: The*

Reconstruction of Instruction (1979). Foster's book represents the first literary history of the antebellum slave narrative in the United States. She divides this history into two eras—the first from 1760 to 1807, the second from 1831—1865—and argues that the principal difference between the two lies in the increased concentration on the outrages of slavery and the humanity of blacks in narratives of the second era. That Foster is correct in this overall view of the slave narrative's development is unquestionable. What is most important, indeed unprecedented, in her work is her fundamental contention, backed by cogent argumentation and extensive citation from the little-known as well as the better-known texts, that the slave narrative was not a monolithic entity, but rather a dynamic and ever-evolving genre of black self-expression. Persuasive arguments have been written to the contrary, but through her careful historizing of the slave narrative, Foster's case for its "development" has held its ground. One testimony to the importance of Foster's study is the publication, two years after her book, of Marion Wilson Starling's *The Slave Narrative: Its Place in American History*, her pioneering 1946 Ph. D. dissertation. Starling's research anticipates that of Foster, and the two critics, when read together, base the study of the slave narrative in the 1980s in impeccable traditional literary historical scholarship.

The major contribution of *Afro-American Literature: The Reconstruction of Instruction* to autobiography criticism stems from the collective import of three essays on Douglass's 1845 *Narrative* included in the volume. In the first, "Narration, Authentication, and Authorial Control in Frederick Douglass's *Narrative* of 1845," Robert B. Stepto suggests a dramatic new way of understanding the text of a narrative like Douglass's by calling attention to the interplay between the narrative proper and the authenticating documents that enclose it. Stepto goes on to examine the rhetoric of Douglass's narrative as an index to the narrator's attempt to gain control over the signifying potential of his text. This essay has had a considerable impact on subsequent criticism primarily by challenging assumptions about textual form in black autobiography and by offering a critical language in which to discuss the crucial problem of self-authorization in black autobiography. Following Stepto's essay, Robert O'Meally's "Frederick Douglass' 1845 *Narrative*: The Text Was Meant to Be Preached," treats the relationship of the written text to the oral tradition, particularly that of black preaching, to which Douglass's eloquence owes so much. Like Stepto, O'Meally emphasizes the formal art of Douglass's narration and attributes much of it to his black oral resources. Critics before O'Meally had emphasized the relationship of slave narratives like Douglass's to white literary models, but on one had made such an effective or suggestive argument for the formal and substantive influence of black oral culture on Douglass.

Finally, Henry Louis Gates's "Binary Oppositions in Chapter One of *Narrative of the Life of Frederick Douglass an American Slave Written by Himself*" proposes a third, and specifically structuralist method, of investigating the formal dynamics of this autobiography. Gates's analysis of the opening of the *Narrative* reveals that Douglass understood the slaveocratic worldview to be premised on a fundamental binary opposition between "the absolute and the eternal," with which the culture of slavery endowed itself, and the "mortal and the finite," which the culture of slavery assigned to the slave and to nature. Gates then shows how Douglass plays the trickster with these oppositions by reversing their application, thus exposing their purely arbitrary, "humanly-imposed not divinely ordained" status in southern discourse.

This essay is the first in black autobiography criticism to show the influence of continental critical models. It problematizes the dimension of meaning in the slave narrative by suggesting that reference in black autobiography is never "natural" but always culturally determined, that texts like the *Narrative* lure the critic into accepting and using uncritically the very oppositional discourse that Douglass actually aims to discredit. Gates's essay anticipates a central concern of the increasingly theoretical black autobiography criticism of the 1980s: the development of a critical vocabulary and analytic method that will allow scholars to recognize *how* black autobiography signifies, what it does with and to the structures of discourse that it inherits from both white and black culture, and what those linguistic operations say about once-privileged notions of the "blackness" of African-American autobiography as well as the very notion of racial or self-representation in the form of what is called today (with unprecedented lack of confidence in the term) *autobiography*.

At least two things are remarkable about African-American autobiography scholarship in the 1980s. First, the largest proportion of that scholarship was devoted to the antebellum slave narrative; second, some of the most thoughtful criticism on black autobiography seems to have gravitated toward the slave narrative because of its priority as the site of the African-American's first recorded confrontation with "the prison-house of language," to use Frederick Jameson's often-cited term. While a number of sensitive and productive readings of slave narratives have been published in essay collections and monographs of the 1980s, the most far-reaching work on this genre of black autobiography appears in a handful of books, notably Houston A. Baker's *Blues, Ideology, and Afro-American Literature* (1984), William L.

Andrews's *To Tell a Free Story* (1986), and Gates's *The Signifying Monkey* (1988). Different as the books obviously are, each one may be read as a response to a problem first explicitly posed by Baker in remarks on Douglass's *Narrative* published in *The Journey Back* (1980). After arguing that the *Narrative* demonstrates Douglass's adoption of "a public version of the self—one molded by the values of white America" (39), Baker goes on to wonder "where in Douglass's *Narrative* does a prototypical black American self reside?" (43). His answer is skeptical, in keeping with the posture of the unwritten self, once it is subjected to the linguistic codes, literary conventions, and audience expectations of a literate population, [p. 205] is perhaps never again the authentic voice of black American slavery. It is, rather, the voice of a self transformed by an autobiographical act into a sharer in the general public discourse about slavery" (43).

Baker's doubts about the "authentic voice" of the slave narrative, and by implication of any African-American autobiography that employs the language and discursive conventions of the Anglo-American literary tradition, have had a salutary effect on black autobiography criticism. While never denying the inevitable accommodations that black autobiography must make to its white discursive milieu, critics such as Andrews and Gates, and even Baker himself, have argued that, however one wishes to code the voice of black autobiography, that voice is not ultimately dominated by its discursive circumstances; it makes of its encounter with discursive, its narrated scenes of reading and writing, a metaphor of the autobiographer's determination, in the words of Andrews, not just to attain freedom but to "tell a free story" about that all-consuming aim. By viewing freedom as not just the theme but the *sign* of the best of the slave narratives as well as of black autobiography as a whole, criticism of the 1980s seems to have become sensitized anew to the formal, stylistic, and rhetorical richness of African-American autobiography as a narrative tradition.

In *Blues, Ideology, and Afro-American Literature*, Baker homes in on "blues moments" in African-American discourse when the "trained" voice translates into metaphorical and formal terms the "unrestrained mobility and unlimited freedom" of the railroad, the focal and aural symbol of black vernacular expression in this country. To read and hear the blues in this extended fashion is to suggest that freedom plays through African-American narratives in ways hitherto unimagined, despite and because of black autobiography's awareness of what Baker terms "the economics of slavery" and racial oppression. Thus when he takes up Douglass's *Narrative*, Baker posits a tension of voices in that text: one acculturated and inauthentic in the ways argued in *The Journey Back*, the other much more self-consciously aware of its economic conditions and conditioning. In the latter stages of the *Narrative*, the Douglass who takes "a fully commercial view of his situation" (48) repossesses himself through marriage, "*individual* wage earning," and eventually employment as a "*salaried* spokesman" for antislavery. The result is a "convergence of the voices" that emerge from the *Narrative* and a reconciliation of "literacy, Christianity, and revolutionary zeal in an individual and economically profitable job of work" (49). Baker goes on to explain how Harriet Jacobs's *Incidents in the Life a Slave Girl* articulates "a sense of *collective*, rather than individualistic, black identity" (55), in marked contrast to Douglass's autobiography and that of his male compatriots in the slave narrative. Jacobs also negotiates the economics of oppression, Baker concludes, on her way to attaining a voice that invokes "sisterly communion by imaging a quite remarkable community of black women" (56).

In *To Tell a Free Story*, Andrews echoes some of Baker's criticism of Douglass's *Narrative*, which he identifies as part of the tradition of the American jeremiad, so ably reconstructed by Sacvan Bercovitch. As an American Jeremiah, Douglass was free to excoriate his country for its failure to live up to its ideals, as stated in the Declaration of Independence. However, the rhetorical posture of the jeremiad also required Douglass to celebrate the American Dream, to affirm the middle-class consensus about how to achieve it, and thus to endorse the ideology of "true Americanism" even as he denounced those who threatened that ideal with their perverted or "false Americanism." Andrews then goes on to discuss how Douglass equates the Southern slaveocracy with false Americanism, only to whitewash the racism and economic oppression he experienced in the North by embodying in the *Narrative*'s charming images of New Bedford the "true Americanism" of capitalist-industrial prosperity. By comparing to the *Narrative* what Douglass had been saying in his speeches and writing in private about his life in the North, Andrews suggests that Douglass did not feel free to express fully his sense of alienation from the American ideals that he seems so fully to endorse in the *Narrative*. Like Baker, Andrews believes that Douglass eventually did find his way to greater expressive freedom, but Andrews argues that Douglass's second autobiography, *My Bondage and My Freedom* (1855) signals this movement. Also reminiscent of Baker's approach is Andres's comparison of *My Bondage and My Freedom* to *Incidents in the Life of a Slave Girl* as culminating texts of multiple autobiographical traditions whose evolution and import it is the burden of *To Tell a Free Story* to delineate.

In *The Signifying Monkey*, Gates calls signifyin(g) "the trope of tropes" in African-American oral culture and written literature. Gates goes on to show that the essence of this trope is to parody, destabilize, invert, or otherwise make free with sign, signified, and indeed, the person who plays the role of the signifier. The persistence of signifyin(g) throughout black American literary history testifies to the priority of what Gates call the "speakerly text" in African-American writing, as contrasted to Roland Barthes's notion of the "writerly text" in the dominant Western discourse since the Renaissance in Europe. Gates emphasizes that African-American writers signify on both the texts of Western discourse and the texts (both verbal and written) of their own tradition. In fact, Gates's very idea of African-American literary tradition is grounded in the image of black writers as revisionists of texts and participants in a vast, as yet largely uncharted, intertext of signification in which presumed absences assume verbal presence, imbalances of power are linguistically redressed, and rhetorical spaces are repeatedly being cleared out, occupied, and then displaced by the play of black voices. Where does this revisionist tradition begin? In a brilliant discussion of five black texts from the late eighteenth and early nineteenth centuries, Gates locates the literary wellspring of the entire signifyin(g) tradition in the autobiographical narrations of James Gronniosaw, John Marrant, Ottobah Cugoano, Olaudah Equiano, and John Jea. Citing the presence in all these texts of "the trope of the talking book," and then brilliantly analyzing the revisions of that trope in each successive text, Gates makes a strong case for the earliest black narrators in English as masters of signifyin(g), fully engaged in the international debates of their era concerning the relationship of racial identity, linguistic performance, and ontological status in the Great Chain of Being. *The Signifying Monkey* attests to the literary complexity of early black autobiography more convincingly than any work of criticism before it, while it also adds compelling evidence of the primacy of the autobiographical tradition to the evolution of both the verbal artistry and the thematic substance of all subsequent narrative forms in African-American literature.

Looking to the 1990s, it is hard to imagine that critics and scholars of black American autobiography will veer sharply away from the interests and concerns that preoccupied criticism of this genre in the 1980s. The idea of black autobiography as a site of formal revisionism and the free play of signification may, we might hope, lead to a fresh examination of texts and traditions in the genre's history that have up to now received little attention. For instance, although the antebellum slave narrative has enjoyed high visibility in attempts to reconstruct the history of black autobiography, only slight research has been done on the postbellum slave narrative, not to mention the proliferation of autobiographies in the late nineteenth and early twentieth centuries that espouse ideological points of view apparently at various with those of Douglass's *Narrative* or *The Autobiography of Malcolm X*. A large gap of knowledge about black American autobiography from 1865 to 1940 still exists in criticism, and one may hope that the 1990s will find us better informed about this complex period of African-American literary history.

Another undeniable need in black autobiography criticism is for increased research on black American women's autobiography. With the publication of scholarly editions of Hurston's *Dust Tracks on a Road* (1984) [p. 208] and Jacobs's *Incidents in the Life of a Slave Girl* (1987), along with *Sisters of the Spirit* (1986), Andrews's edition of three early spiritual autobiographies, and the sixteen first-person narratives in the Schomburg Library of Nineteenth-Century Black Women's Writing, under the general editorship of Henry Louis Gates, the texts of the black female tradition in autobiography are rapidly returning to currency in American literary scholarship. While Frederick Douglass and Richard Wright remained the most often-discussed African-American autobiographers in the 1980s, Jacobs and Hurston attracted unprecedented critical attention during that decade too, a fact all the more striking in the face of the largely dismissive attitude of earlier autobiography critics toward *Incidents* and *Dust Tracks*. In "Race, Gender, and Cultural Context in Zora Neale Hurston's *Dust Tracks on a Road*," Nellie Y. McKay explains how the marginal position of Hurston as autobiographer positioned between black and white cultures and readerships shaped the problematic status of *Dust Tracks* and helped turn it into a textual "statue" of selfhood (to use Hurston's own metaphor) rather than the flesh-and-blood self-representation that many readers have expected to find in the book. McKay goes on to show that previous evaluators of *Dust Tracks*, particularly those disturbed by its evidently accommodationist politics, have failed to apprehend the politics of its author's identification with southern black culture and the linguistic strategies by which black women writers have affirmed their literary autonomy even at the expense of literal authenticity. The idea that Hurston's own concept and interpretation of black folk culture is itself the best model of how *Dust Tracks* should be conceptualized and understood is further elaborated in Francoise Lionnet's study of Hurston's autobiography in *Autobiographical Voices*. What Lionnet terms "autoethnography," a process of defining one's subjectivity as inevitably mediated through language, history, and ethnographical analysis, provides a new lens through which critics in the 1990s can reconsider not only black women's autobiography but texts by any African-American whose autobiography aims at elucidating selfhood through an articulation of ethnic ties and cultural roots.

A third direction in which the study of black autobiography may profitably move is towards comparatist studies of the pan-African dimensions of this genre. As he has done so often in autobiography studies in general, James Olney has pointed this direction in particular in his essay, "The Value of Autobiography for Comparative Studies: African vs. Western Autobiography" (1979), in which *Black Boy* is compared to Camara Laye's *L'Enfant Noir* (1953) to suggest that African works in this genre tend to be "autophylographical," that is, concerned with the tribal [p.209] self, whereas African-American autobiographies tend to be predicated on the idea of individualized self-expression. Such a contrast, however, may be more typical of male than of female-authored black autobiographies on the international scene. In any event, criticism in the 1990s will be much enriched by extensions of this sort of cross-disciplinary inquiry into the fullest intertextual dimensions of what an African heritage and a sense of African identification has meant to black autobiography.

What is most needed, and what is most to be anticipated, in future African-American autobiography criticism, ultimately, are books that reconstruct the history of this genre and/or offer theories of analysis and criticism that bring into play the full panoply of cultural, social, and historical research that has been done in the last thirty years on African-Americans. While no one is likely to attempt a study on the scale of Butterfield's survey of the entire genre, a number of scholars are currently researching and writing books on important traditions within the larger tradition. The ongoing work by Sandra Pouchet Paquet, Alice Deck and Nellie Y. McKay, and William L. Andrews on West Indian autobiography, African-American women's autobiography, and the history of African-American autobiography from 1865 to 1940, respectively, will continue to open new vistas on black American literary, cultural, and intellectual history. The value of this kind of work is attested by the enthusiastic response generated by the publication (since this essay's composition) of Joanne M. Braxton's *Black Women Writing Autobiography*, the first history of African-American women's autobiography. One of Braxton's basic theses—summed up in the subtitle of her book, *A Tradition Within a Tradition* —is that there is no single tradition, myth, or representative voice in or for African-American autobiography. Even within the tradition Braxton chronicles, the "outraged mother" and the "visionary" engage in a creative dialogue, if not an outright dialectic, revealing in "the Afra-American experience" that "many streams converge, improvising, dancing and playing, together and with the rivers from which they emerge" (208). No more apt metaphor could be applied to African-American autobiography as a whole, or to the criticism that students of this genre may look forward to in the years ahead.

(1991)

27. The Ground on Which I Stand
我的立场

August Wilson

奥古斯特·威尔逊

奥古斯特·威尔逊(1945—2005),剧作家、诗人与随笔作者。威尔逊 1945 年出生于宾夕法尼亚州匹兹堡的一个黑白种族混居社区,是家中的第四个孩子,父亲是德裔面包师,母亲是非裔。父母离异后,母亲再嫁,他随母亲搬到白人郊区,越来越能感受到种族主义的影响。因不堪忍受抄袭的错误指控,他从格拉德斯通高中辍学;1963 年参军,一年后退役;1965 年 4 月 1 日,购买第一台打字机,立志成为作家,后来积极参加黑人权力运动,创作诗歌,1973 年开始创作剧本,尝试以传统黑人艺术形式书写非裔美国文化。他以 10 年为界,创作了 10 部反映 20 世纪非裔美国人生活、历史与文化的剧作,其中前五部作品都在百老汇上演。作为美国最受评论界关注与好评的剧作家,威尔逊获得诸多奖项,如普利策奖(2 次)、剧评人奖(2 项)、纽约戏剧节评论奖(5 项)、美国戏剧批评家协会奖和托尼奖等,成为美国戏剧发展史上的一个高峰。

作为成功的剧作家,威尔逊非常重视黑人剧院的建设,在"我的立场"这篇文章中,他指出美国社会在文化建设方面对黑人族群的区别对待,其中关于是否需要建立黑人剧院的论述就是个非常好的例子。另外,他对是否应该不分种族地选择演员与导演的论述也招致很多非议,但是他敢于坚持自己的立场,认为如果过去黑人的戏剧主要重视娱乐性与消费性,那么现在应该敢于坚持自己的文化传统,更多地发挥自我定义的作用。他的文化立场体现了很多非裔美国作家、艺术家和批评家的黑人美学主张,至今仍具有比较广泛的影响。

Thank you. Some time ago I had an occasion to speak to a group of international playwrights. They had come from all over the world. From Colombia and Chile, Papua New Guinea, Poland, China, Nigeria, Italy, France, Great Britain. I began my remarks by welcoming them to my country. I didn't always think of it as my country; but since my ancestors have been here since the early 17th century, I thought it an appropriate beginning as any. So if there are any foreigners here in the audience, "Welcome to my country."

I wish to make it clear from the outset that I do not have a mandate to speak for anyone. There are many intelligent blacks working in the American theater who speak in loud and articulate voices. It would be the greatest of presumptions to say I speak for them. I speak only for myself and those who may think as I do.

I have come here today to make a testimony, to talk about the ground on which I stand and all the many grounds on which I and my ancestors have toiled, and the ground of theatre on which my fellow artists and I have labored to bring forth its fruits, its dating and its sometimes lacerating, and often healing, truths.

The first and most obvious ground I am standing on is this platform I have so graciously been given at the 11th biennial conference of the Theater Communications Group. It is the Theater Communications Group to which we owe much of our organization and communication. I am grateful to them for entrusting me with the grave responsibility of sounding this keynote, and it is my hope to discharge my duties faithfully. I first attended the Conference in 1984, and I recall John Hirsh's eloquent address on "The Other" and mark it as a moment of enlightenment and import. I am proud and thankful to stand here tonight in my embrace of that moment and to find myself here on this platform. It is a moment I count well and mark with privilege.

In one guise, the ground I stand on has been pioneered by the Greek dramatists, by Euripides, Aeschylus and Sophocles, by William Shakespeare, by Shaw and Ibsen, and by the American dramatists Eugene O'Neill, Arthur Miller and Tennessee Williams. In another guise, the ground that I stand on has been pioneered by my grandfather, by Nat Turner, by Denmark Vesey, by Martin Delaney, Marcus Garvey and the Honorable Elijah Muhammad. That is the ground of the affirmation of the value of one being, an affirmation of his worth in the face of society's urgent and sometimes profound denial. It was this ground as a young man coming into manhood, searching for something to which to dedicate my life, that I discovered the Black Power movement of the 1960s. I felt it a duty and an honor to participate in that historic moment, as the people who had arrived in America chained and malnourished in the hold of a 350-foot Portuguese, Dutch or English sailing ship were now seeking ways to alter their relationship to the society in which they lived, and perhaps more important, searching for ways to alter the shared expectations of themselves as a community of people. The Black Power movement of the 1960s. I find it curious but no small accident that I seldom hear those words Black Power spoken, and when mention is made of that part of our history, that part of black history in America, whether in the press or in conversation, reference is made to the civil rights movement as though the Black Power movement, an important social movement by America's ex-slaves, had in fact never happened. But the Black Power movement of the 1960s was in fact a reality ... that is the kiln in which I was fired and has much to do with the person I am today and the ideas and attitudes that I carry as part of my consciousness.

I mention this because it is difficult to disassociate my concerns with theater from the concerns of my life as a black man, and it is difficult to disassociate one part of my life from another. I have strived to live it all seamless ... art and life together, inseparable and indistinguishable. The ideas I discovered and embraced in my youth when my idealism was full blown I have not abandoned in middle age when idealism is something less then blooming but wisdom is starting to bud. The ideas of self-determination, self-respect, and self-defense that governed my life in the 1960s I find just as valid and self-urging in 1996. The need to alter our relationship to the society and to alter the shared expectations of ourselves as a racial group I find of greater urgency now than it was then.

I am what is known, at least among the followers and supporters of the ideas of Marcus Garvey, as a race man. That is simply that I believe that race matters. That is the largest, most identifiable, and most important part of our personality. It is the largest category of identification because it is the one that most influences your perception of yourself, and it is the one to which others in the world of men most respond. Race is also an important part of the American landscape, as America is made up of an amalgamation of races from all parts of the globe. Race is also the product of a shared gene pool that allows for group identification, and it is an organizing principle around which cultures are formed. When I say culture, I am speaking about the behavior patterns, arts, beliefs, institutions, and all other products of human work and thought as expressed in a particular community of people.

There are some people who will say that black Americans do not have a culture. That cultures are reserved for other people, most notably Europeans of various ethnic groupings, and that black Americans make up a sub-group of American culture that is derived from the European origins of its majority population. But black Americans are Africans, and there are many histories and many cultures on the African continent.

Those who would deny black Americans their culture would also deny them their history and the inherent values that are a part of all human life.

Growing upin my mother's house at 1727 Bedford Avenue in Pittsburgh, Pennsylvania, I learned the language, the eating habits, the religious beliefs, the gestures, the notions of common sense, attitudes towards sex, concepts of beauty and justice, and the responses to pleasure and pain that my mother had learned from her mother and which you could trace back to the first African who set foot on the continent. It is this culture that stands solidly on these shores today as a testament to the resiliency of the African-American spirit.

The term black or African American not only denotes race; it denotes condition and carries with it the vestige of slavery and the social segregation and abuse of opportunity so vivid in our memory. That this abuse of opportunity and truncation of possibility is continuing and is so pervasive in our society in 1996 says much about who we are and much about the work that is necessary to alter our perceptions of each other and to effect meaningful prosperity for all.

The problematic nature of the relationship between white and black for too long led us astray from the fulfillment of our possibilities as a society. We stare at each other across a divide of economics and privilege that has become an encumbrance on black Americans' ability to prosper and on the collective will and spirit of our national purpose.

I speak about economics and privilege, and if you will look at one significant fact that affects us all in the American Theater ... it is that of the 66 LORT theaters there is only one that can be considered black. From this it could be falsely assumed that there aren't sufficient numbers of blacks working in the American theater to sustain and support more theaters.

If you do not know, I will tell you that Black Theater in America is alive ... it is vibrant ... it is vital ... it just isn't funded. Black Theater doesn't share in the economics that would allow it to support its artists and supply them with meaningful avenues to develop their talent and broadcast and disseminate ideas crucial to its growth. The economics are reserved as privilege to the overwhelming abundance of institutions that preserve, promote, and perpetuate white culture.

That is not a complaint. That is an advertisement. Since the funding sources, both public and private, do not publicly carry avowed missions of exclusion and segregated support, this is obviously either a glaring case of oversight ... or we the proponents of Black Theater have not made our presence or our needs known. I hope here tonight to correct that.

I do not have the time in this short talk to reiterate the long and distinguished history of Black Theater—often accomplished amid adverse and hostile conditions— but I would like to take the time to mark a few high points.

There are and have always been two distinct and parallel traditions in black art.

That is art that is conceived and designed to entertain white society and art that feeds the spirit and celebrates the life of Black America by designing its strategies for survival and prosperity.

An important part of Black Theater that is often ignored but is seminal to its tradition is its origins on the slave plantations of the South. Summoned to the big house to entertain the slaveowner and his guests, the slave began a tradition of theater as entertainment for whites that reached its pinnacle in the heyday of the Harlem Renaissance. This entertainment for whites consisted of whatever the slave imagined or knew that his master wanted to see and hear. This tradition has its present life counterpart in the crossover artists that slant their material for white consumption.

The second tradition occurred when the African in the confines of the slave quarters sought to invest his spirit with the strength of his ancestors by conceiving in his art, in his song and dance, a world in which he was the spiritual center and his existence was a manifest act of the creator from whom life flowed. He then could create art that was functional and furnished him with a spiritual temperament necessary for his survival as property and the dehumanizing status that was attendant to that.

I stand myself and my art squarely on the self-defining ground of the slave quarters and find the ground to be hallowed and made fertile by the blood and bones of the men and women who can be described as warriors on the cultural battlefield that affirmed their self-worth. As there is no idea that cannot be contained by black life, these men and women found themselves to be sufficient and secure in their art and their instructions.

It was this high ground of self-definition that the black playwrights of the 1960s marked out for themselves. Ron Milner, Ed Bullins, Philip Hayes Dean, Richard Wesley, Lonne Elder III, Sonia Sanchez, Barbara Ann Teer and Amiri Baraka were among those playwrights who were particularly vocal and whose talent confirmed their presence in the society and altered the American Theater, its meaning, its craft, and its history. The brilliant explosion of black arts and letters of the 1960s remains, for me, the hallmark and the signpost that points the way to our contemporary work on the same ground. Black playwrights everywhere remain indebted to them for their brave and courageous forays into an area that is marked with land mines and the shadows of snipers who would reserve the territory of arts and letters and the American Theater as their own special province and point blacks toward the ball fields and the bandstands.

That Black Theater today comes under such assaults should surprise no one as we are on the verge of reclaiming and reexamining the purpose and pillars of our art and laying out new directions for its expansion. As such we make a target for cultural imperialists who seek to empower and propagate their ideas about the world as the only valid ideas, and see blacks as woefully deficient, not only in arts and letters but in the abundant gifts of humanity.

In the 19th century, the lack of education, the lack of contact with different cultures, the expensive and slow methods of travel and communication fostered such ideas, and the breeding ground of ignorance and racial intolerance promoted them.

The King's English and the lexicon of a people given to such ignorance and intolerance did not do much to dispel such obvious misconceptions but provided them with a home: in *Webster's Third New International Dictionary*,

BLACK ... outrageously wicked, dishonorable, connected with the devil, menacing, sullen, hostile, unqualified, illicit, illegal violators of public regulations, affected by some undesirable condition, etc.

WHITE ... free from blemish, moral stain or impurity; outstandingly righteous, innocent, not marked by malignant influence, notably auspicious, fortunate, decent, a sterling man.

Such is the linguistic environment that informs the distance that separates blacks and whites in America and which the cultural imperialists, who cannot imagine a life existing and even flourishing outside their benevolent control, embrace.

Robert Brustein, writing in an article/review titled "Unity from Diversity," is apparently disturbed that "there is a tremendous outpouring of work by minority artists" which he attributes to cultural diversity. He writes that the practice of extending invitations to a national banquet from which a lot of hungry people have long been excluded is a practice that can lead to confused standards. He goes on to establish a presumption of inferiority of the work of minority artists, and I quote, "Funding agencies have started substituting sociological criteria for aesthetic criteria in their grant procedures, indicating that 'elitist' notions like quality and excellence are no longer functional." He goes on to say, "It's disarming in all senses of the word to say that we don't share common experiences that are measurable by common standards. But the growing number of truly talented artists with more universal interests suggests that we may soon be in a position to return to a single value system."

Brustein's surprisingly sophomoric assumption that this tremendous outpouring of work by minority artists leads to confusing standards and that funding agencies have started substituting sociological for aesthetic criteria, leaving aside notions like quality and excellence, shows him to be a victim of 19th-century thinking and the linguistic environment that posits blacks as unqualified. Quite possibly this tremendous outpouring of works by minority artists may lead to a raising of standards and a raising of the levels of excellence, but Mr. Brustein cannot allow that possibility.

To suggest that funding agencies are rewarding inferior work by pursuing sociological criteria only serves to call into question the tremendous outpouring of plays by white playwrights who benefit from funding given to the 66 LORT theaters.

Are those theaters funded on sociological or aesthetic criteria? Do we have 66 excellent theaters? Or do those theaters benefit from the sociological advantage that they are run by whites and cater to largely white audiences?

The truth is that often, where there are aesthetic criteria of excellence, it is sociological criteria that have traditionally excluded blacks. I say raise the standards and remove the sociological consideration of race as privilege ... and we will meet you at the crossroads ... in equal numbers ... prepared to do the work of extending and developing the common ground of American Theater.

We are capable of work of the highest order ... we can answer to the high standards of world-class art. Anyone who doubts our capabilities at this last stage is being intellectually dishonest.

We can meet on the common ground of theater as a field of work and endeavor. But we cannot meet on the common ground of experience.

Where is the common ground in the horrifics of lynching? Where is the common ground in the maim of a policeman's bullet? Where is the common ground in the hull of a slave ship and the deck of a slave ship with its refreshments of air and expanse?

We will not be denied our history.

We have voice, and we have temper. We are too long along this road from the loss of our political will, we are too far along the road of reassembling ourselves, too far along the road to regaining spiritual health than to allow such transgression of our history to go unchallenged.

The commonalties we share are the commonalities of culture. We decorate our houses. That is something we do in common. We do it differently because we value different things. We have different manners and different values of social intercourse. We have different ideas of what a party is. There are some commonalities to our different ideas. We both offer food and drink, but because we have different culinary values, different culinary histories ... we offer different food and drink to our guests.

In our culinary history we have learned to make do with the feet and ears and tails and intestines of the pig rather than the lion and the ham and the bacon. Because of our different histories with the same animal, we have different culinary ideas. But we share a common experience with the pig as opposed to say Muslims and Jews who do not share that experience.

We can meet on the common ground of the American Theater.

We cannot share a single value system if that value system is the values of white Americans based on their European ancestors. We reject that as Cultural Imperialism. We need a value system that includes our contributions as Africans in America. Our agendas are as valid as yours. We may disagree, we may forever be on opposites sides of aesthetics, but we can only share a value system that is inclusive of all Americans and recognizes their unique and valuable contributions. The ground together. We must develop the ground together. We reject the idea of equality among equals, but rather we say the equality of all men.

The common values of the American Theater that we can share are plot ... dialogue ... characterization ... design. How we both make use of them will be determined by who we are ... what ground we are standing on and what our cultural values are.

Theater is part of the art history in terms of its craft and dramaturgy but is part of the social history in terms of how it is financed and governed. By making money available to theaters willing to support colorblind casting, the financiers and governors have signaled not only their unwillingness to support Black Theater but their willingness to fund dangerous and divisive assaults against it. Colorblind casting is an aberrant idea that has never had any validity other than as a tool of the Cultural Imperialist who views their American Culture, rooted in the icons of European Culture, as beyond reproach in its perfection. It is inconceivable to them that life could be lived and even enriched without knowing Shakespeare or Mozart. Their gods, their manners, their being is the only true and correct representation of humankind. They refuse to recognize black conduct and manners as part of a system that is fueled by its own philosophy, mythology, history, creative motif, social organization and ethos. The idea that blacks have their own way of responding to the world, their own values, style, linguistics, their own religion, and aesthetics is unacceptable to them.

For a black actor to stand on the stage as part of a social milieu that has denied him his gods, his culture, his humanity, his mores, his ideas of himself and the world he lives in is to be in league with a thousand nay-sayers who wish to corrupt the vigor and spirit of his heart.

To cast us in the role of mimics is to deny us our own competence.

Our manners, our style, our approach to language, our gestures, and our bodies are not for rent. The history of our bodies, the maimings ... the lashings ... the lynchings ... the body that is capable of inspiring profound rage and pungent cruelty ... is not for rent. Nor is the meaning of the history of our bodies for rent.

To mount an all black production of *Death of a Salesman* or any other play conceived for white actors as an investigation of the human condition through the specific of white culture is to deny us our own humanity, our own history, and the need to make our own investigations from the cultural ground on which we stand as black Americans. It is an assault on our presence, our difficult but honorable history in America, and an insult to our intelligence, our playwrights, and our many and varied contributions to the society and the world at large. The idea of colorblind casting is the same idea of assimilation that black Americans have been rejecting for the past 380 years. For the record we reject it again. We reject any attempt to blot us out, to reinvent history and ignore our presence or to maim our spiritual product. We must not continue to meet on this path. We will not deny our history, and we will not allow it to be made to be of little consequence, to be ignored or misinterpreted.

In an effort to spare us the burden of being "affected by an undesirable condition" and as a gesture of benevolence, many whites, like the proponents of colorblind casting, say "Oh, I don't see color." We want you to see us. We are black and beautiful. We are not patrons of the linguist environment that has us as "unqualified, and violators of public regulations." We are not a menace to society. We are not ashamed. We have an honorable history in the world of men. We come from a long line of honorable people with complex codes of ethics and social discourse who devised myths and systems of cosmology and systems of economics, who were themselves part of a long social and political history. We are not ashamed and do not need you to be ashamed for us. Nor do we need the recognition of our blackness to be couched in abstract phrases like "artist of color." Who are you talking about? A Japanese artist? An Eskimo? A Filipino? A Mexican? A Cambodian? A Nigerian? An African American? Are we to suppose that if you put all of them on one side of the scale and one white person on the other side ... that it would balance out? That whites carry that much spiritual weight? That one white person balances out the rest of humanity lumped together as nondescript "People of Color"? We reject that. We are unique, and we are specific.

We do not need colorblind casting. We need some theaters to develop our playwrights. We need those misguided financial resources to be put to a better use. We cannot develop our playwrights with the meager resources at our disposal. Why is it difficult to imagine 9 black theaters but not 66 white ones? Without theaters we cannot develop our talents. If we cannot develop our talents, then everyone suffers. Our writers. The theater. The audience. Actors are deprived of material, our communities are deprived of the jobs in support of the art: the company manager, the press coordinator, the electricians, the carpenters, the concessionaires, the people that work in the wardrobe, the box office staff, the ushers and the janitors. We need some theaters. We cannot continue like this. We have only one life to develop our talent, to fulfill our potential as artists. One life and it is short, and the lack of the means to develop our talent is an encumbrance on that life.

We did not sit on the sidelines while the immigrants of Europe through hard work, skill, cunning, guile, and opportunity built America into an industrial giant of the 20th century. It was our labor that provided the capital. It was our labor in the shipyards and the stockyards and the coal mines and the steel mills. Our labor built the roads and the railroads. And when America was challenged, we strode on the battlefield, our boots strapped on and our blood left to soak into the soil of places whose names we could not pronounce, against an enemy whose only crime was ideology. We left our blood in France and Korea and the Philippines and Vietnam and our only reward has been the deprivation of possibility and the denial of our moral personality.

It cannot continue. The ground together. The American ground on which I stand and which my ancestors purchased with their perseverance, with their survival, with their manners, and with their faith.

It cannot continue ... as well other assaults upon our presence and our history cannot continue. When the *New York Times* published an article on Michael Bolton and lists as his influence the names of four white singers and then as an afterthought tosses in the phrase ... "and the great black rhythm and blues singer," it cannot be anything but purposeful with intent to maim. These great black rhythm and blues singers reduced to an afterthought are on the edge of oblivion. One stroke of the editor's pen and the history of American music is revised, and Otis Redding, Jerry Butler, and Rufus Thomas are consigned to the dust-bin of history while Joe Cocker, Mick Jagger, and Rod Stewart are elevated to the status of the originators and creators of a vital art that is a product of our spiritual travails, and the history of music becomes a fabrication, a blatant forgery which, under the hallowed auspices of the *New York Times*, is presented as the genuine article.

We cannot accept these assaults. We must defend and protect our spiritual fruits. To ignore these assaults would be to be derelict in our duties. We cannot accept them. Our political capital will not permit them.

So much of what makes this country rich in art and all manner of spiritual life is the contributions that we as African Americans have made. We cannot allow others to have authority over our cultural and spiritual products. We reject, without reservations, any attempts by anyone to rewrite our history so as to deny us the rewards of our spiritual labors and to become the cultural custodians of our art, our literature, and our lives. To give expression to the spirit that has been shaped and fashioned by our history is of necessity to give voice and vent to the history itself.

It must remain for us a history of triumph.

The time has come for black playwrights to confer with one another ... to come together to meet each other face to face, to address questions of aesthetics and ways to defend ourselves from the nay-sayers who would trumpet our talents as insufficient to warrant the same manners of investigation and exploration as the majority. We need to develop guidelines for the protection of our cultural property, our contribution, and the influence they accrue. It is time we took the responsibility for our talents in our own hands. We cannot depend on others. We cannot depend on the directors, the managers, or the actors to do the work we should be doing for ourselves. It is our lives and the pursuit of our fulfillment that are being encumbered by false ideas and perceptions of ourselves.

It is time to embrace the political dictates of our history and answer the challenge to our duties. I further think we should confer in a city in our ancestral homeland in the Southern part of the United States in 1998, so that we may enter the millennium united and prepared for a long future of prosperity.

From the hull of a ship to self-determining, self-respecting people. That is the journey we are making.

We are robust in spirit, we are bright with laughter, and we are bold in imagination. Our blood is soaked into the soil, and our bones lie scattered the whole way across the Atlantic ocean, as Hansel crumbs, to mark the way back home.

We are no longer in the House of Bondage, and soon we will no longer be victims of the counting houses who hold from us ways to develop and support our talents and our expressions of life and its varied meanings. Assaults upon that body politic that demean and ridicule and depress the value and worth of our existence, that seek to render it immobile and to extinguish the flame of freedom lit eons ago by our ancestors upon another continent—these assaults must be met with a fierce and uncompromising defense.

If you are willing to accept it ... it is your duty to affirm and urge that defense, that respect, and that determination.

I must mention here with all due respect to W. E. B. Du Bois that the concept of a Talented Tenth creates an artificial superiority. It is a fallacy and a dangerous idea that only serves to divide us further. I am not willing to throw away as untalented 90% ofmy blood; I am not willing to dismiss the sons and daughters of those people who gave more than lip service to the will to live and made it a duty to prosper in spirit if not in provision. I am not willing to dismiss them as untalented cannon fodder and unwitting sheep to the Talented Tenth's shepherd. All God's children got talent. It is a dangerous idea to set one part of the populace above and aside from the other. We do a grave disservice to ourselves not to seek out and embrace and enable all of our human resources as a people. All blacks in America—with very few exceptions—all blacks, no matter what our status, no matter the size of our bank accounts, no matter how many and what kind of academic degrees we can place beside our names, no matter the furnishings and square footage of our homes, the length of our closets and the quality of the wool and cotton that hangs there—we all in America originated from the same place—the slave plantations of the South. We all share a common past and despite how some us might think and how it might look—we all share a common present and will share a common future.

We can make a difference. Artists, playwrights, actors—we can be the spearhead of a movement to reignite and reunite our people's positive energy for a political and social change that is reflective of our spiritual truths rather than economic fallacies. Our talents, our truth, our belief in ourselves is all in our hands. What we make of it will emerge from the self a baptismal spray that names and defines. What we do now becomes history by which our grandchildren will judge us.

We are not off on a tangent. The foundation of the American Theater is the foundation of European Theater that begins with the great Greek dramatist. It is based on the proscenium stage and the poetics of Aristotle. This is the theater that we have chosen to work in. We embrace the values of that theater but reserve the right to amend, to explore, to add our African consciousness and our African aesthetic to the art we produce.

To pursue our cultural expression does not separate us. We are not separatists as Mr. Brustein asserts. We are Americans trying to fulfill our talents. We are not the servants at the party. We are not apprentices to the kitchens. We are not the stableboys to the King's huntsmen. We are Africans. We are Americans. The irreversible sweep of history has decreed that. We are artists who seek to develop our talents and give expression to our personalities. We bring advantage to the common ground that is the American Theater.

All theaters depend on an audience for its dialogue. To the American Theater, subscription audiences are its life blood. But the subscription audience holds the seats of our theaters hostage to the mediocrity of its tastes and serves to impede the further development of an audience for the work that we do. While intentional or not, it serves to keep blacks out of the theater where they suffer no illusion of welcome anyway. A subscription thus becomes not a support system but makes the patrons members of a club to which the theater serves as a clubhouse. It is an irony that the people who can most afford a full price ticket get discounts for subscribing while the single ticket buyer who cannot afford a subscription is charged the additional burden of support to offset the subscription buyer's discount. It is a system that is in need of overhaul to provide not only a more equitable access to tickets but access to influence as well.

I look for and challenge students of art's management to be bold in their exploration of new systems of funding theaters, including profit-making institutions and ventures, and I challenge black artists and audiences to scale the walls erected by theater subscriptions to gain access to this vital area of spiritual enlightenment and enrichment that is the theater.

All theater goers have opinions about the work they witness. Critics have an informed opinion. Sometimes it may be necessary for them to gather more information to become more informed. As playwrights grow and develop as the theater changes, the critic has an important responsibility to guide and encourage that growth. However, in the discharge of their duties, it may be necessary for them to also grow and develop. A stagnant body of critics, operating from the critical criteria of forty years ago, makes for a stagnant theater without the fresh and abiding influence of contemporary ideas. It is the critics who should be in the forefront of developing new tools for analysis necessary to understand new influences.

The critic who can recognize a German neo-romanticism influence should also be able to recognize an American influence from blues or black church rituals, or any other contemporary American influence.

The true critic does not sit in judgement. Rather he seeks to inform his reader instead of adopting a posture of self-conscious importance in which he sees himself a judge and final arbiter of a work's importance or value.

We stand on the verge of an explosion of playwriting talent that will challenge our critics. As American playwrights absorb the influence of television and use new avenues of approach to the practice of their craft, they will prove to be wildly inventive and imaginative in creating dramas that will guide and influence contemporary life for years to come.

Theater can do that. It can disseminate ideas, it can educate even the miseducated ...because it is art, and all art reaches across that divide that makes order out of chaos and embraces the truth that overwhelms with its presence and that connects man to something larger than himself and his imagination.

Theater asserts that all of human life is universal. Love, Honor, Duty, Betrayal belong and pertain to every culture or race. The way they are acted out on the playing field may be different, but betrayal is betrayal whether you are a South Sea Islander, Mississippi farmer, or an English Baron. All of human life is universal, and it is theater that illuminates and confers upon the universal the ability to speak for all men.

The ground together. We have to do it together. We cannot permit our lives to waste away, our talents unchallenged. We cannot permit a failure to our duty. We are brave and we are boisterous, our mettle is proven, and we are dedicated. The ground together. The ground of the American theater on which I am proud to stand ... the ground which our artistic ancestors purchased with their endeavors ... with their pursuit of the American spirit and its ideals.

I believe in the American Theater. I believe in its power to inform about the human condition. I believe in its power to heal. To hold the mirror as it were up to nature. To the truths we uncover to the truths we wrestle from uncertain and sometimes unyielding realities. All of art is a search for ways of being, of living life more fully. We who are capable of those noble pursuits should challenge the melancholy and barbaric, to bring the light of angelic grace, peace, prosperity, and the unencumbered pursuit of happiness to the ground on which we stand.

(1997)

28. The End of the Black American Narrative
美国黑人叙事的终结

Charles Johnson
查尔斯·约翰逊

查尔斯·约翰逊(1948),小说家、哲学家、批评家。约翰逊出生于伊利诺伊的埃文斯顿,青少年时期就对视觉艺术感兴趣。他1971年毕业于南伊利诺伊大学,获学士学位,本科期间,发行了两本漫画。读研期间,他创作了7部小说,深受鲍德温、艾里森与加德纳(John Gardner)的影响,特别是后者的"道德小说"范式。1976年以来,约翰逊受聘位于西雅图的华盛顿大学,教授创意写作课程,1988年,在纽约州立大学石溪分校完成关于现象学与文艺美学的博士学位论文,出版多部小说,代表作有《牧牛传说》(*Oxherding Tale*,1982)和《中间航道》(*Middle Passage*,1990)等,后者获得美国国家图书奖。此外,他于1998年获得麦克阿瑟天才奖,2002年获得美国艺术与文学学院文学奖。

约翰逊的文章《美国黑人叙事的终结》(2008)追溯了从1619年到20世纪60年代中期民权运动达到高潮阶段美国黑人遭受的奴役、获得解放以后遭受的隔离与不平等待遇,以及美国黑人文学对种族问题的重视与再现。另外,他也明确表示,当代非裔美国文学应该超越传统的叙事主题,因为当代非裔美国族群与其他族群一样,面临更多基于阶级差异而非黑白种族矛盾的问题,过去聚焦黑白种族矛盾与争取民权的非裔美国文学,其局限性已经显而易见。当代美国黑人叙事不仅需要新的更好的故事,而且需要新的表达;更需要黑人个体而非群体的故事,真正实现马丁·路德·金曾经所梦想的,不是根据肤色,而是根据个体的行为与性格来判断一个人的目标。

有趣的是,围绕当代美国黑人文学主题与表达方式的讨论,在沃伦教授出版《何谓非裔美国文学?》(2011)之后变得更加尖锐,也使得进入所谓"后民权"与"后种族"时代的非裔美国文学的"政治性"特征更为明显地呈现在当代读者面前。

A New Century Calls for New Stories Grounded in the Present,
Leaving Behind the Painful History of Slavery and Its Consequences

It is ambition enough to be employed as an under-labourer in clearing the ground a little, and removing some of the rubbish that lies in the way of knowledge.

—John Locke, An Essay Concerning Human Understanding

Back to the things themselves!

—Edmund Husserl

As a writer, philosopher, artist, and black American, I've devoted more than 40 years of my life to trying to understand and express intellectually and artistically different aspects of the black American narrative. At times during my life, especially when I was young, it was a story that engaged me emotionally and consumed my imagination. I've produced novels, short stories, essays, critical articles, drawings, and PBS dramas based on what we call the black American story. To a certain degree, teaching the literature of black America has been my bread and butter as a college professor. It is a very old narrative, one we all know quite well, and it is a tool we use, consciously or unconsciously, to interpret or to make sense of everything that has happened to black people in this country since the arrival of the first 20 Africans at the Jamestown colony in 1619. A good story always has a meaning (and sometimes layers of meaning); it also has an epistemological mission: namely, to show us something. It is an effort to make the best sense we can of the human experience, and I believe that we base our lives, actions, and judgments as often on the stories we tell ourselves about ourselves (even when they are less than empirically sound or verifiable) as we do on the severe rigor of reason. This unique black American narrative, which emphasizes the experience of victimization, is quietly in the background of every conversation we have about black people, even when it is not fully articulated or expressed. It is our starting point, our agreed-upon premise, our most important presupposition for dialogues about black America. We teach it in our classes, and it is the foundation for both our scholarship and our popular entertainment as they relate to black Americans. Frequently it is the way we approach each other as individuals.

As a writer and a teacher of writing, I have to ask myself over and over again, just what is a story. How do we shape one? How many different forms can it take? What do stories tell us about our world? What details are necessary, and which ones are unimportant for telling it well? I constantly ask my creative writing students two questions: Does the story work, technically? And, if so, then, what does it *say*? I tell them that, like a work of philosophy (which is the sister discipline to storytelling among the interpretive arts), a narrative vision must have the qualities of coherence, consistency, and completeness. The plot of a modern story must be streamlined and efficient if it is to be easily understood. And, like Edgar Allan Poe in his 1842 essay "On the Aim and the Technique of the Short Story," I argue that a dramatic narrative should leave the listener with "a certain unique or single effect" that has emotional power. For the last 32 years, I've stressed to my students that a story must have a conflict that is clearly presented, one that we care about, a dilemma or disequilibrium for the protagonist that we, as readers, emotionally identify with. The black American story, as we tell it to ourselves, beautifully embodies all these narrative virtues.

The story begins with violence in the 17th-century slave forts sprinkled along the west coast of Africa, where debtors, thieves, war prisoners, and those who would not convert to Islam were separated from their families, branded, and sold to Europeans who packed them into the pestilential ships that cargoed 20 million human beings (a conservative estimate) to the New World. Only 20 percent of those slaves survived the harrowing voyage at sea (and only 20 percent of the sailors, too), and if they were among the lucky few to set foot on American soil, new horrors and heartbreak awaited them.

As has been documented time and again, the life of a slave—our not-so-distant ancestors—was one of thinghood. Former languages, religions, and cultures were erased, replaced by the Peculiar Institution, in which the person of African descent was property, and systematically—legally, physically, and culturally—denied all sense of self-worth. A slave owns nothing, least of all himself. He desires and dreams at the risk of his life, which is best described as relative to (white) others, a reaction to their deeds, judgements, and definitions of the world. And these definitions, applied in blacks, were not kind. For 244 years (from 1619 to 1863), America was a slave state with a guilty conscience: two and a half centuries scarred by slave revolts, heroic black (and abolitionist) resistance to oppression, and, more than anything else, physical, spiritual, and psychological suffering so staggering it silences the mind when we study the classic slave narratives of Equiano or Frederick Douglass. Legal bondage, the peculiar antebellum world, ended during the Civil War, but the Emancipation Proclamation did not bring liberation.

Legal freedom instead gradually brought segregation, America's version of apartheid. But "separate" clearly was not "equal." Black Americans were not simply segregated; they were methodically disenfranchised, stripped of their rights as citizens. From the 1890s through the 1950s, the law of black life was experienced as second-class citizenship. In the century after the Emancipation Proclamation, members of each generation of black Americans saw their lives disrupted by race riots, lynchings, and the destruction of towns and communities, such as the Greenwood district of black homes, businesses, and churches in Tulsa, Oklahoma, on May 31, 1921. The challenge for black America and the conflict for its story, then, was how to force a nation that excluded black people from its promise of "Life, liberty and the pursuit of happiness" after the Revolutionary War, and failed to redress this grievance after Reconstruction, to honor these principles enshrined in its most sacred documents.

What I have described defines the general shape of the black American group narrative before the beginning of the Civil Rights Movement, the most important and transformative domestic event in American history after the War Between the States. The conflict of this story is first slavery, then segregation and legal disenfranchisement. The meaning of the story is group victimization, and every black person is the story's protagonist. This specific story was not about ending racism, which would be a wonderful thing; but ending racism entirely is probably as impossible for human beings as ending crime, or as quixotic as President Bush's "war on terror." No, the black American story was not as vague as that. It had a clearly defined conflict. And our ancestors fought *daily* for generations, with courage and dignity, to change this narrative. That was the *point* of their lives, their sacrifices, each and every day they were on this earth. We cannot praise enough the miracle they achieved, the lifelong efforts of our leaders and the anonymous men and women who kept the faith, demonstrated, went to jail, registered black people to vote in the Deep South, changed unjust laws, and died in order that Americans of all backgrounds might be free. I have always seen their fight for us as noble.

Among those I pay special tribute to is W. E. B. Du Bois, one of the founders of the NAACP, who deeply understood the logic and structure of this narrative as it unfolded from Reconstruction through the 1950s. It was a sign of his prescience that he also could see *beyond* this ancient story while still in the midst of it and fighting mightily to change it.

In 1926, Du Bois delivered an address titled, "Criteria of Negro Art" at the Chicago Conference for the NAACP. His lecture, which was later published in *The Crisis*, the official publication of the NAACP, which Du Bois himself edited, took place during the most entrenched period of segregation, when the opportunities for black people were so painfully circumscribed. "What do we want?" he asked his audience. "What is the thing we are after?" Listen to Du Bois 82 years ago:

> What do we want? What is the thing we are after? As it was phrased last night it had a certain truth: We want to be Americans, full-fledged Americans, with all the rights of American citizens. But is that all? Do we want simply to be Americans? Once in a while through all of us there flashes some clairvoyance, some clear idea, of what America really is. We who are dark can see America in a way that white Americans cannot. And seeing our country thus, are we satisfied with its present goals and ideals? ...

> If you tonight suddenly should become full-fledged Americans; if your color faded, or the color line here in Chicago was miraculously forgotten; suppose, too, you became at the same time rich and powerful—what is it that you would want? What would you immediately seek? Would you buy the most powerful of motor cars and outrace Cook County? Would you buy the most elaborate estate on the North Shore? Would you be a Rotarian or a Lion or a What-not of the very last degree? Would you wear the most striking clothes, give the richest dinners and buy the longest press notices?

> Even as you visualize such ideals you know in your hearts that these are not the things you really want. You realize this sooner than the average white American because, pushed aside as we have been in America, there has come to us not only a certain distaste for the tawdry and flamboyant but a vision of what the world could be if it were really a beautiful world; if we had the true spirit; if we had the Seeing Eye, the Cunning Hand, the Feeling Heart; if we had, to be sure, not perfect happiness, but plenty of good hard work, the inevitable suffering that always comes with life; sacrifice and waiting, all that—but, nevertheless, lived in a world where men know, where men create, where they realize themselves and where they enjoy life. It is that sort of a world we want to create for ourselves and for all America.

This provocative passage is, in part, the foundation for my questioning the truth and usefulness of the traditional black American narrative of victimization. When compared with black lives at the dawn of the 21st century, and 40 years after the watershed events of the Civil Rights Movement, many of Du Bois' remarks now sound ironic, for all the impossible things he spoke of in 1926 are realities today. We are "full-fledged Americans, with the rights of American citizens." We *do* have "plenty of good hard work" and live in a society where "men create, where they realize themselves and where they enjoy life." Even more ironic is the fact that some of our famous rappers and athletes who like "living large," as they say, seem obsessed with what Du Bois derisively called "the tawdry and flamboyant" (they call it "bling"). Furthermore, some of us *do* use the freedom paid for with the blood of our ancestors to pursue conspicuous consumption in the form of "powerful motor cars," "elaborate estates," "striking clothes," and "the richest dinners."

To put this another way, we can say that 40 years after the epic battles for specific civil rights in Montgomery, Birmingham, and Selma, after two monumental and historic legislative triumphs—the Civil Rights Act of 1964 and the Voting Rights Act of 1965—and after three decades of affirmative action that led to the creation of a true black middle class (and not the false one E. Franklin Frazier described in his classic 1957 study, *Black Bourgeoisie*), a people oppressed for so long have finally become, as writer Reginald McKnight once put it, "as polymorphous as the dance of Shiva." Black Americans have been CEOs at AOL Time Warner, American Express, and Merrill Lynch; we have served as secretary of state and White House national security adviser. Well over 10,000 black Americans have been elected to offices around the country, and at this moment Senator Barack Obama holds us in suspense with the possibility that he may be selected as the Democratic Party's first biracial, black American candidate for president. We have been mayors, police chiefs, bestselling authors, MacArthur fellows, Nobel laureates, Ivy League professors, billionaires, scientists, stockbrokers, engineers, theoretical physicists, toy makers, inventors, astronauts, chess grandmasters, dot-com millionaires, actors, Hollywood film directors, and talk show hosts (the most prominent among them being Oprah Winfrey, who recently signed a deal to acquire her own network); we are Protestants, Catholics, Muslims, Jews, and Buddhists (as I am). And we are not culturally homogeneous. When I last looked, West Indians constituted 48 percent of the "black" population in Miami. In America's major cities, 15 percent of the black American population is foreign born—Haitian, Jamaican, Senegalese, Nigerian, Cape Verdean, Ethiopian, Eritrean, and Somali—a rich tapestry of brown-skinned people as culturally complex in their differences, backgrounds, and outlooks as those people lumped together under the all too convenient labels of "Asian" or "European." Many of them are doing better—in school and business—than native-born black Americans. I think often of something said by Mary Andom, an Eritrean student at Western Washington University, and quoted in an article published in 2003 in *The Seattle Times* : "I don't know about 'chitlings' or 'grits.' I don't listen to soul music artists such as Marvin Gaye or Aretha Franklin. ... I grew up eating *injera* and listening to

Tigrinya music. ... After school, I cook the traditional coffee, called boun, by hand for my mother. It is a tradition shared amongst mother and daughter."

No matter which angle we use to view black people in America today, we find them to be a complex and multifaceted people who defy easy categorization. We challenge, culturally and politically, an old group narrative that fails at the beginning of this new century to capture even a fraction of our rich diversity and heterogeneity. My point is not that black Americans don't have social and cultural problems in 2008. We have several nagging problems, among them poor schools and far too many black men in prison and too few in college. But these are problems based more on the inequities of class, and they appear in other groups as well. It simply is no longer the case that the essence of black American life is racial victimization and disenfranchisement, a curse and a condemnation, a destiny based on color in which the meaning of one's life is thinghood, created even before one is born. This is not something we can assume. The specific conflict of this narrative reached its dramatic climax in 1963 in Birmingham, Alabama, and at the breathtaking March on Washington; its resolution arrived in 1965, the year before I graduated from high school, with the Voting Rights Act. Everything since then has been a coda for almost haft a century. We call this long-extended and still ongoing anticlimax the post-civil-rights period. If the NAACP is struggling these days to recruit members of the younger generation and to redefine its mission in the 21st century—and it is struggling to do that—I think it is a good sign that the organization Du Bois led for so long is now a casualty of its own successes in the 1960s.

Yet, despite being an antique, the old black American narrative of pervasive victimization persists, denying the overwhelming evidence of change since the time of my parents and grandparents, refusing to die as doggedly as the Ptolemaic vision before Copernicus or the notion of phlogiston in the 19th century, or the deductive reasoning of the medieval schoolmen. It has become ahistorical. For atime it served us well and powerfully, yes, reminding each generation of black Americans of the historic obligations and duties and dangers they inherited and faced, but the problem with any story or idea or interpretation is that it can soon fail to fit the facts and becomes an ideology, even kitsch.

This point is expressed eloquently by Susan Griffin in her 1982 essay "The Way of all Ideology," where she says, "When a theory is transformed into an ideology, it begins to destroy the self and self-knowledge. ... No one can tell it anything new. It is annoyed by any detail which does not fit its worldview. ... Begun as a way to restore one's sense of reality, now it attempts to discipline real people, to remake natural beings after its own image."

In his superb book *In My Father's House*, philosopher Kwame Anthony Appiah writes, "There is nothing in the world that can do all we ask race to do for us." We can easily amend or revise this insight and apply it to the pre-21st-century black American narrative, which can do very little of the things we need for it to do today.

But this is an enduring human problem, isn't it? As phenomenologist Edmund Husserl revealed a hundred years ago, we almost always perceive and understand the new in terms of the old—or, more precisely, we experience events through our ideas, and frequently those are ideas that bring us comfort, ideas *received* from our parents, teachers, the schools we attend, and the enveloping culture, rather than original ones of our own. While a story or model may disclose a particular meaning for an experience, it also forces into the background or conceals other possible meanings. Think of this in light of novelist Ralph Ellison's brilliant notion of "invisibility," where—in his classic *Invisible Man*—the characters encountered by his nameless protagonist all impose their ideologies (explanations and ideas) on the chaos of experience, on the mysterious, untamed life that forever churns beneath widely accepted interpretations and explanations of "history" and "culture," which in our social world, for Ellison, are the *seen*. I know, personally, there is value in this Ellisonian idea because in the historical fictions I've been privileged to publish, like "Martha's Dilemma" in my second collection, *Soulcatcher and Other Stories*, I discovered that the most intriguing, ambiguous, and revealing material for stories can often be found in the margins of the codified and often repeated narrative about slavery. In this case, I dramatized a delicious anecdote about what happened to Martha and her slaves right after the death of George.

What I am saying is that "official" stories and explanations and endlessly repeated interpretations of black American life over decades can short-circuit direct perception of the specific phenomenon before us. The idea of something—an intellectual construct—is often more appealing and perfect (in a Platonic sense) than the thing itself, which always remains mysterious and ambiguous and messy, by which I mean that its senseis open-ended, never fixed. It is always wise, I believe, to see all our propositions (and stories) as provisional, partial, incomplete, and subject to revision on the basis of new evidence, which we can be sure is just around the corner.

Nevertheless, we have heavily and often uncritically invested for most of our lives in the pre-21st-century black American narrative. In fact, some of us depend upon it for our livelihood, so it is *not* easy to let go, or to revise this story. Last October, Nation of Islam minister Louis Farrakhan spoke for two and a half hours at the Atlanta Civic Center. He and his mentor, black separatist Elijah Muhammad, provided black Americans with what is probably the most extreme, Manichean, and mythological version of the black American narrative, one that was anti-integrationist. In this incomplete and misleading rendition of the black American story, the races are locked in eternal struggle. As a story, this narrative fails because it is conceived as melodrama, a form of storytelling in which the characters are flat, lack complexity, are either all good or all bad, and the plot involves malicious villains and violent actions. Back in the 1930s when Elijah Muhammad shaped his myth of Yacub, which explained the origins of the white race as "devils," he sacrificed the credibility of both character and plot for the most simplistic kind of dramatic narrative. Farrakhan covered many subjects that day last October, but what I found most interesting is that he said successful black people like Oprah Winfrey, Senator Obama, Colin Powell, and Condoleeza Rice give black Americans a false impression of progress. In other words, their highly visible successes do not change the old narrative of group victimization. Minister Farrakhan seems unwilling to accept their success as evidence that the lives of black Americans have improved. He seems unwilling to accept the inevitability of change. He was quoted in the press as saying, "A life of ease sometimes makes you forget the struggle." And despite the battles for affirmative action that created a new middle class, he added, "It's becoming a plantation again, but you can't fight that because you want to keep your little job."

I beg to differ with Farrakhan, with his misuse of language, his loose, imprecise diction, because we obviously do *not* live on plantations. And wasn't job opportunity one of the explicit goals of the black American narrative? Farrakhan's entire life has been an investment in a story that changed as he was chasing it. So we can understand his fierce, personal, and even tragic attachment to dusty, antebellum concepts when looking at the uncharted phenomena in the early 21st century that outstrip his concepts and language.

However, it is precisely because Farrakhan cannot progress beyond an oversimplified caricature of a story line for racial phenomena that the suddenly notorious Rev. Jeremiah Wright praises him, saying "His depth of analysis ... when it comes to the racial ills of this nation is astounding and eye-opening," and, "He brings a perspective that is helpful and honest." Recently Wright called the Nation of Islam leader, "one of the most important voices in the 20th and 21st centur[ies]." I do not doubt that Wright and Farrakhan are men who have experienced the evil of racism and want to see the conditions of our people improve, or that both have records of community service. But it is the emotional attachment to a dated narrative, one leavened with the 1960s era liberation theology of James Cone, that predictably leads Wright to proclaim that the U.S. government created the AIDS virus to destroy blacks (he invokes the old and proven, the ghastly Tuskegee syphilis experiment, in an effort to understand a new affliction devastating black people, and thus commits the logical fallacy, known as misuse of analogy); that Jesus was "a black man"; and that the brains of blacks and whites operate differently. The former pastor of Trinity United Church of Christ in Chicago has made these paranoid and irresponsible statements publicly again and again without offering the slightest shred of evidence for these claims. "A bunch of rants that aren't grounded in truth" was how Barack Obama described his former minister's incendiary oratory, which is clearly antithetical not only to the postracial spirit of the Illinois senator's own speeches but also to his very racially and geographically mixed background. For in the realm of ideological thinking, especially from the pulpit, feeling and faith trump fact, and passion (as well as beliefs based on scripture) replaces fidelity to the empirical and painstaking logical demonstration.

Furthermore, such obsolete stories can also lead to serious mistakes in scholarship. I'm thinking now of Henry Louis Gates Jr., who in 1988 directed the publication of Oxford University Press's 40-volume Schomburg Library of Nineteenth-Century Black Women Writers. In his foreword, Gates praised the lost works of these black women writers as being the literary ancestors of Zora Neale Hurston, Toni Morrison, and Alice Walker. Furthermore, he said it was the discovery of a particular lost black novel, called *Four Girls at Cottage City*, published in 1895 by Emma Dunham Kelley-Hawkins, that inspired him to direct this Schomburg series in the first place so, he said, "I can read them myself." Okay, so far so good. But in 2005, Holly Jackson, then a doctoral student of English at Brandeis University, was given the academically pedestrian, grunt-work assignment of writing an entry about Kelley-Hawkins for the African American National Biography. At the time very little was known about Kelley-Hawkins. After checking birth records in the Massachusetts Vital Records, and other documents, Jackson realized that Kelley-Hawkins was not black—as five decades of scholars had assumed—but white. Yet all the evidence to suggest her whiteness was clearly present in the books she wrote. Something that had always puzzled scholars, Jackson said, was "the apparent whiteness of her characters, who are repeatedly described with blue eyes and skin as white as 'pure' or 'driven' snow." Even more fantastic are the theories that literary scholars came up with to explain why Kelley-Hawkins, supposedly a black woman, made no references to race or blackness in her two novels written in the 1890s. Jackson says, "Scholars have explained this away by arguing that the abundance of white signifiers is actually politically radical, with some even going so far as to argue that this extremely white world depicts a kind of post-racial utopia," a modem world where, according to critic Carla L. Peterson, "racial difference no longer existed."

Obviously, all these explanations are hogwash. Fifty years of scholarship based on these mistakes—articles, dissertations, courses in African American women's writing that include the work of Kelley-Hawkins—turns out to be an illusion created by the blinding intentionality of those who wrote about this white author based on a tangled knot of beliefs and prejudices, their concept of her completely distorting the facts. Once Gates learned of this research by Jackson and also investigations by Katherine Flynn, a genealogist, he immediately went into the mode of damage control. He told a reporter that the work of Kelley-Hawkins would at least be removed from future editions of the Schomburg series, and he downplayed the significance of these discoveries by Jackson and Flynn. But Jackson, being a true scholar, would not allow this intellectual scandal to be swept under the rug. Of this "enormous historical misconception," she said, "there is so much at stake here, because of all the writing that has been done based on a false assumption about race." She asks us to wonder, "How have her [Kelley-Hawkins's] overwhelmingly 'white' texts successfully passed as black for so long in the absence of any corroborating historical data? How does this discovery change our understanding of African American literary history?" Finally, she said, "We have stretched our understanding of how black women have written in America to incorporate texts that do not fit."

I've gone into great detail about the Kelley-Hawkins story because it is a cautionary tale for scholars and an example of how our theories, our explanatory models, and the stories we tell ourselves can blind us to the obvious, leading us to see in matters of race only what we want to see based on our desires and political agendas. When we confront phenomena of any kind, we are wise if we assume the position phenomenologist Herbert Spiegelberg called epistemological humility, which is ahealthy skepticism about what we think we already know. When constructing our narratives, it would also help if we remember a famous and often-quoted statement by C. S. Lewis on the characteristics of the human mind: "Five senses; an incurably abstract intellect; a haphazardly selective memory; a set of preconceptions and assumptions so numerous that I can never examine more than a minority of them—never become conscious of them all. How much of total reality can such an apparatus let through?" How much, indeed.

But if the old black American narrative has outlived its usefulness as a tool of interpretation, then what should we do? The answer, I think, is obvious. In the 21st century, we need new and better stories, new concepts, and new vocabularies and grammar based not on the past but on the dangerous, exciting, and unexplored present, with the understanding that each is, at best, a provisional reading of reality, a single phenomenological profile that one day is likely to be revised, if not completely overturned. These will be narratives that do not claim to be absolute truth, but instead more humbly present themselves as a very tentative thesis that must be tested every day in the depths of our own experience and by all the reliable evidence we have available, as limited as that might be. For as Bertrand Russell told us, what we know is always "vanishingly small." These will be narratives of individuals, not groups. And is this not exactly what Martin Luther King Jr. dreamed of when he hoped a day would come when men and women were judged not by the color of their skin, but instead by their individual deeds and actions, and the content of their character?

I believe this *was* what King dreamed and, whether we like it or not, that moment is now.

(2008)

参 考 书 目

1. Andrews, William L. and Frances Smith Foster, and Trudier Harris (eds.). *The Concise Oxford Companion to African American Literature*. New York: Oxford University Press, 2001.

2. Arnett, Ervin Hazel (ed.). *African American Literary Criticism*, 1773—2000. New York: Twayne Publishers, 1999.

3. Gates, Henry Louis and Nellie Y. McKay (eds.). *The Norton Anthology of African American Literature* (second edition). New York: W. W. Norton & Company, 2004.

4. Graham, Maryemma and Jerry Ward (eds.). *The Cambridge History of African American Literature*. New York: Cambridge University Press, 2011.

5. Jarrett, Gene Andrew (ed.). *The Wiley Blackwell Anthology of African American Literature*, *Volume 2 1920 to the Present*. Malden: John Wiley & Sons, Ltd, 2014.

6. Jarrett, Gene Andrew (ed.). *The Wiley Blackwell Anthology of African American Literature*, *Volume 1. 1746-1920*. Malden: John Wiley & Sons, Ltd, 2014.

7. Leitch, Vincent B. *The Norton Anthology of Theory and Criticism*. New York: W. W. Norton & Company, Inc., 2001.

8. Mitchell, Angelyn (ed.). *Within the Circle*: *An Anthology of African American Literary Criticism from the Harlem Renaissance to the Present*. Durham: Duke University Press, 1994.

9. Napier, Winston (ed.). *African American Literary Theory*: *A Reader*. New York: New York University Press, 2000.

10. Nelson, Emmanuel S. (ed.). *Ethnic American Literature*: *An Encyclopedia for Students*. Santa Barbara: Greenwood, 2015.